PARANORMAL
Dating
AGENCY

NEW YORK TIMES & USA TODAY BESTSELLING AUTHOR
MILLY TAIDEN

This book is a work of fiction. The names, characters, places, and incidents are fictitious or have been used fictitiously, and are not to be construed as real in any way. Any resemblance to persons, living or dead, actual events, locales, or organizations is entirely coincidental.

Published By
Latin Goddess Press
New York, NY 10456
http://millytaiden.com
Twice The Growl
Geek Bearing Gifts
Her Purrfect Match
Curves 'em Right
Copyright © 2014 by Milly Taiden
Edited by Melinda Fulton
Cover by Willsin Rowe
Formatting by Inkstain Interior Book Designing

All Rights Are Reserved. No part of this book may be used or reproduced in any manner whatsoever without written permission, except in the case of brief quotations embodied in critical articles and reviews.
Property of Milly Taiden 2014

ACCLAIM FOR MILLY TAIDEN
FOR *TWICE THE GROWL & GEEK BEARING GIFTS*

Twice the Growl: "There is comedy, idiotic ex's, hot new lovers, and an elderly matchmaker. It was great and I enjoyed it and am even looking forward to the next one!"

Geek Bearing Gifts: "Wow! It is okay getting hotter, sexier, and more intriguing! The second book in the PDA series is even better than the first! Milly has done it again. You will laugh, get irritated, aggravated, and excited!"

—Theresa Esterline, I Heart Books

Twice the Growl: "Milly Taiden gives every woman their dream! To hunks that are solely focused on one woman in every aspect, especially sexual satisfaction. It's a sweet, lusty tale that delivers a hot, erotic story and with characters that you would really like to know up close and personal."

Geek Bearing Gifts: "Would I recommend this book: Yes! Milly Taiden successfully spins an erotic tale of passion, need, and symbiotic introspection in her Novella, "Geek bearing gifts". Milly aptly takes the dream of having a relationship not based on sex and complements it with erotica.

—Fran, Twin Sisters Rockin' Book Review

"One shifter is good but two is panty changing reading. Forget that just leave them off as you read Twice The Growl."

—Barb Hicks, Bad Barb's Reviews

"I can always rely on Milly Taiden to write a fun, quick, sweet and sexy romance. Sometimes we need a nice short sweet romance, with fun characters, before diving back into a big read."

—Angela Caldwell, Angela's Guilty Pleasures

—For My Readers

You love my big beautiful female main characters. You like my growly alpha males. You enjoy snark and humor. You adore sexy,
sinful, dirty tales. And I love you all for it!
To my wonderfully supportive Street Team (Sexy Biter Book Pimps)... You rock!
To my sister and husband. I love you both.

TWICE THE Growl

book 1

ONE

Talia Barca stared gloomily at her drink. How would she ever survive the next time she saw her ex-husband? The rat bastard.

"So what are you going to do?" her cousin, Nita Islas asked. The soft question broke through Tally's misery.

"I don't know," she muttered and lifted her amaretto sour to her lips. She gripped the cold glass tightly so the shaking of her hand wouldn't cause her to let it drop. Stupid nerves. There was no real reason to be nervous and yet she was. So what that she hadn't seen her ex in years. Her entire family had been invited to her cousin's upcoming wedding, a wedding he'd also attend. That meant nothing. Okay, it did mean she had to see his dumbass again. To make matters worse, if she didn't attend she'd look like she hadn't gotten over him. How stupid was that when she'd been the one to put in for the divorce in the first place.

"Stop thinking so hard, babe." Nita shrugged her shoulders. Her black, wide-neck top dove to the side and showed off a sparkly bra strap over golden brown skin. "I mean our entire family should know at this point that he was a jerk to you."

"You already know they think it was miscommunication. Makes shit worse that he's been great to most of them. That's why they never really pushed him out of their circle." She swallowed a gulp of her drink, draining what was left in the glass.

"If my parents weren't traveling most of the year they'd support you too. This isn't fair if you ask me. I mean the guy was a dick to you."

A dick with a small dick. That's what she'd called him once she'd given up on trying to make shit work. She sighed. An entire week near Paul of wedding festivities was not what she was looking forward to. He had a god-complex the size of Texas. It made no sense since he didn't have the body or equipment to back that up. Not even something a person should be proud of. He was an all-star asshole.

"I'll think of something." Tally sighed. She'd better think of something ASAP or she'd have to decline attending and that would look even worse. She didn't hide from shit, but Paul was one of those people that the mere thought of him gave her a headache.

Nita slapped her drink on the table with a thump. "What about Mrs. Wilder?"

"Gerri? My neighbor?"

"Yes!" Nita leaned forward. "Didn't she tell you as we were walking out tonight that she's running her business from her apartment in your building?" Nita's brown eyes widened with excitement. "If I recall, she said it's a matchmaking or dating service or something like that."

Tally frowned and swept a long black curl behind her ear, trying to remember the conversation. Mrs. Wilder was her older neighbor from across the hall and a lot of fun. They were the only two on her floor and so Tally visited the older woman quite often. The reason was more so she wouldn't feel alone than Mrs. Wilder being old. Tally didn't really get along with her family thanks to asshole Paul. Now her days were either spent with Nita or Mrs. Wilder. The older neighbor always had a ton of male visitors. She came from a huge family and she'd mentioned some of her grandsons would be moving in to the building in the next few weeks.

"She did say something like that," Tally mused.

"Well, there you go!" Nita passed her empty glass to the waitress, grabbed a fresh one and lifted it to her lips. "Problem solved."

Maybe. Or maybe she'd be in deeper shit if she allowed the elderly woman to mess with her personal life. When it came to men, Tally had some seriously sucky luck. She glanced around the bar that was located a few blocks from her building. The crowd was younger than she cared to be surrounded with, but in a college town, it was bound to happen. At thirty-two, she'd started to feel like a miserable old lady surrounded by hot young men. She didn't see how her personal life could get any better.

"You need to talk to more men," Nita said as if reading her mind.

"I'm too old for dating," she grumbled but smiled at the waitress who'd given her a new drink. "I'm about to get my cat lady starter kit any day now. Men are too much work."

Nita laughed. "You're insane. You're gorgeous! What the heck would possess you to say you're too old? Thirty is young!"

"Thirty-two."

Nita rolled her eyes. "It isn't like you're ninety."

"Sure feels like it," she whispered with the drink by her lips. She winced at how strong it was. Apparently the waitress felt she needed more than her usual dose of liquor. Tally had to agree. She needed a damn miracle.

"All you have to do is stop dating the wrong men," Nita stated matter-of-factly.

She pinned Nita with a glare. "I thought that's what I was already doing. I mean I work at a damn lawyer's office. I don't date any of those assholes. But why is it that when I meet what seems to be a nice, decent man, he turns out to be some kind of double bastard with a side of dickhead?"

Nita's brows curved up. "Wearing a suit to work doesn't mean you should live in one. Cut loose, woman!" She exhaled loudly and pointed a red-tipped fingernail at Tally. "You need to get laid properly."

"Shush!" She glanced around the bar. A couple of the younger guys threw winks in their direction. Flames of embarrassment heated her cheeks. "You're going to get us kicked out of here."

Nita giggled. "What I'd like is to get you hooked up."

"I'd settle for a date."

Nita shook her head. "No. We need drastic measures here. You need to get laid."

"Nita!" She gasped, covering the side of her face with her hand. "Shut up! You make me sound like a desperate cougar."

"Aw come on, Tally. I hate that you have to worry about a date for a family function. You're such a wonderful woman. This isn't something you should be stressing. You should be kicking men out of your door every night."

Right. Because she was such a wild one. Not. With her black-framed glasses, unruly, curly hair, larger than most women curves, and somewhat bitchy personality, she didn't really see herself as a femme fatale.

"I think you've had too many of those drinks." Tally smiled and patted Nita's hand. "I'll figure something out. I might ask Mrs. Wilder for some help. Who knows? Maybe she can succeed where I haven't."

"I like Mrs. Wilder. I don't care that she can probably chew me into little pieces even at her old age." Nita scrunched her nose. She twirled the small straw in her glass in circles. "It's a good thing she likes you, and therefore me by default, because I have heard some crazy stuff about those shifters."

Tally knew Mrs. Wilder wasn't your regular granny, but she was such a sweetheart. And she was someone she could share her cake addiction with. They took turns baking different things and sharing with each other. It's what fed Tally's chocolate urges and kept her with way too many curves to count.

"Yeah." Tally sucked down a gulp from her new drink. "Who would've thought that I'd become such good friends with a shifter granny."

Nita grinned. "Why wouldn't you? She's sorta bitchy, like you."

"Gee, thanks," she said drily.

"It's a compliment. I'm so tired of these bubbly women that are fake about how they feel. Feel bitchy? Be bitchy." Nita picked up her glass and pointed to Tally. "This world is filled with too many fake people. You're not trying to be a copy of anyone, Tally. That's why I love you. You're always going to be an original."

Tally grinned. Clinked glasses with Nita and sipped her drink. "Thanks. So far that hasn't really brought anything good into my life."

"It will," Nita assured her. "Go visit Mrs. Wilder and for once tell her you need help. It's not the end of the world to admit to needing a man."

Tally chuckled. "I don't need a man. Not really. I need someone to be my date for the week from hell."

Nita shrugged and motioned the waitress for the check. "Maybe Mrs. Wilder will hook you up." She gasped. "Oh, my gosh! What if she hooks you up with one of those scorching shifters she has visiting her all the time?"

"Now that would be something to celebrate." Tally giggled. "They are so sexy. She told me she has anything from bears, to wolves, to big cats."

"Wow." Nita sighed. "Bears and big cats. I used to have a best friend who was a bear."

"Really? When?"

Nita pursed her lips. "When we lived near the mountains for dad's job with the fish and wildlife department."

"Was this before you all came back here?"

Nita nodded. "Yeah. We were sophomores in high school. He was so cute with his glasses and almost too innocent face. I told him everything."

"What happened?"

"My family came back here. I loved coming back here after all the years on the road, but that meant my bear friend was left behind. He and I lost touch," Nita said softly.

Tally pulled out one of the many cards Mrs. Wilder had shoved in her hand every time she went over to visit. "Here you go. Why don't you sign up and see what she can get you?"

Nita stared at the clear business card in awe. "Do you really think she can set me up with one of her shifters?"

"Check out the fine print. She's made me read it more than once. She will set you up with whoever she deems to be the right man for you." She read the tiny words on the back of the card and adjusted her glasses. "So, you're pretty much guaranteed a man. I haven't seen a single bad looking one yet."

"You have to do it, Tally." Nita blinked wide excited eyes at her. "I need to know what she does. You're in need of a date. This really is the perfect solution."

Tally sighed. "At least you're not suggesting those other websites that find your 'perfect' someone."

Nita blinked once. Twice. Then burst into giggles. "I'm sorry. It's not funny after your last episode."

Tally clenched her teeth. She hated that her mother, of all people, had bought her a membership to a dating site that promised to find her soul mate. She swore that every man they sent her way had to have been rejected by every other woman. There was no way that her soul mate was really a forty-five year old man with seven kids, who lived with his mother, had no teeth and worked a maximum of ten hours a week. No way.

TALLY STROLLED TO her apartment building. Her mind never deviated from thoughts of her dilemma. A date to a family wedding so she wouldn't look like a complete loser in front of her ex. That's what she'd come to. Why did she care so much this time? She didn't know. It might be because she'd been the one rejected by everyone other than her grandmother and Nita. She'd been the one snuffed at functions while Paul, the asshole, had been embraced. She wanted a way to show them that she was doing well. No—she wanted to show she was doing great. Childish? Absolutely, but she didn't care.

Her building in the center of the city was very old. It had the look of something out of the twenties. However, it was well-maintained, with a doorman that had a very slick smile and way too many teeth.

"Good evening, Ms. Barca," Tom, the door man, said. She forced a smile to greet him, her mind still going over her frustrating family.

He sniffed. It was a common thing with a shifter, the sniffing. She wasn't bothered by it. Too many times he'd been the one to give her a heads up of a new perfume that didn't agree with her. So she was more than happy to ignore it.

"Hi, Tom. Have a good night." She dug into her handbag for her keys. The elevator doors opened up ahead. She hated waiting, so she dashed forward to catch it before it closed.

Once she'd gotten inside, she pressed the button for the top floor where she and Mrs. Wilder lived. The doors were about to close when a hand shot out of nowhere and stopped it.

"We almost missed it," a deep, rumbling voice said. The voice belonged to a big, bulky, tree of a man with shoulder length hair, wearing a black tee, torn jeans and a biker jacket. Hot damn!

"Sorry about that," said the man behind him. Holy wet panties. If the first guy, with his big body and rough, rugged looks made her stare, this one made her mute. Almost as tall as the first guy, which meant they were both over a foot taller than her five feet four inches, this man appeared fresh out of a *GQ* magazine. He wore a white collared shirt with folded sleeves to show his forearms, black slacks and a dimpled smile that made his blue eyes sparkle.

"That's...okay," she mumbled.

She forgot all about the elevator and tried to focus on her breathing. The cab was big enough when she was alone, but with those two mountain of men, it felt tiny. Hell, she could feel their body heat closing in on her. And it felt oh so good.

The doors closed. Neither of the men pressed a button. She tried not to gawk, but that was damn hard when the inside of the elevator was mirrors and all she saw was the two gorgeous men wherever she glanced.

She peeked up the biker's body, from his torn jeans, to the bulge in his pants. Crap. That was a big bulge. She slid her gaze up his chest, to the tattoos crawling around his neck, up to his lips. Lips that were currently curled in a sexy grin. When she reached his eyes, she almost melted to the floor. A bright golden color had taken over them.

"Hi, I'm Theron."

I must be dreaming. She gulped. "I'm Tally."

Her attention shifted to tall, blond and sexy. A soft growl sounded from him. She blinked her eyes behind her glasses. Wow. Then it hit her. They were shifters. Both of the men in the elevator with her were also super dangerous. She cleared her throat, her vision not once wavering from blue eyes.

"I'm Connor."

I'm definitely in trouble. She inhaled sharply. "Hi."

She hated that she squeaked the word out, but being that close to those two made her feel all kinds of tiny. Even with her big hips and ass, she did not feel like a very curvy woman. Instead, she felt sort of...small, delicate and... What the fuck was wrong with her?

The elevator dinged on her floor. She scurried out. Not once did she take a look back. Ribbons of fire crept over her cheeks. If those guys had any idea that she'd been fantasizing some very indecent stuff with both of them they would probably stop those sexy smiles. What was her life coming to? She hadn't considered two men sexually at once in...ever! Now she was ready to jump into the arms of a biker and a businessman and beg them to do her every way possible. She opened the door to her apartment and locked herself in. Safety. Her hasty retreat probably made her look like a scared fool, but she really didn't care. If she spent any more time with those two, she might let something inappropriate come out of her mouth. Nita was right. She definitely needed to get laid. Pronto.

TWO

THERON GRINNED AT Connor. They watched the petite and very curvy woman almost trip on her heels trying to get away to the other end of the floor his aunt Geraldine lived at. The scent of her arousal drifted down the hall with the woman. She was flustered but damn was she cute. With her pretty brown eyes, wide behind the black-framed glasses, her long hair in a mass of wild curls and those luscious, pouty lips calling attention, she was way beyond beautiful.

Then there were the curves. In that prim black dress, she'd hidden what he could clearly tell was a gorgeous body. Wide at the hips and narrow at the waist, she was attention-grabbing. Her large breasts and round ass made his cock stand to attention. He licked his lips, savoring the lingering taste of her need.

"I want her," Connor growled softly.

Theron nodded, feeling the same need for the tiny sexy woman. "Me too. We can wish."

Theron didn't bother knocking. He listened to the steps of his aunt closing in on them. A few moments later and the door opened to his favorite person. Four feet eleven, and an absolute firecracker, Geraldine "Gerri" Wilder knew exactly how to make any man, no matter how old or tall, feel like a misbehaving kid.

"Get your ass down here and give me a kiss." Gerri slapped his arm. The move didn't sting or hurt, but was her way of getting him to remember she was the adult as far as she was concerned. "You know I can't reach your cheek unless I have the stepstool out."

"Sorry, Aunt Gerri." He chuckled and bent down to kiss his aunt.

Gerri tossed the white chunk of long hair she usually had falling at the side of her face back. The white strands contrasted with the rest of her black hair and gave the older woman an exotic flair.

Gerri harrumphed. "Get your asses inside or I'll have to find that stepstool."

Theron and Connor entered Gerri's apartment and grinned. The scent of fresh baked bread, cake and cookies hit them. They loved when she baked, which was all the time.

"You know I love you, Gerri," Theron began.

"Oh no you don't." She shoved them away from the kitchen toward the dining area. "You'll have to eat dinner before I bring out the sweets. You know the rules."

Gerri didn't care that they were both in their thirties or ready to be the Alpha triad for the Wildwoods Pack. Nope. She only cared that they behaved how she wanted. So they humored her. Besides, both of them loved her to bits.

"How's the mate hunting going?" Gerri asked as they sat down to dinner. The table had been set with large platters of food for the three of them. Being shifters meant large appetites and Gerri accommodated and indulged her nephew and his friend.

The mate hunting was going poorly. With Theron, the Alpha, and Connor, the Omega, being the leaders of the Wildwoods Pack, it made it difficult to find a mate that could be shared between them. Either Theron couldn't find a woman he wanted to help them lead due to her lack of personality, or Connor didn't feel a woman's emotions were in the right place to be their mate.

"It's not going anywhere," Connor replied.

Theron watched his best friend, the one person he shared everything with, including women, sigh in defeat. Their link as Alpha and Omega made them closer than twins, but it also made it difficult to find a woman right for them. Women in the Wildwoods Pack were petty, jealous, and not the kind either would choose to be the third puzzle piece of their Alpha triad. The woman they needed had to be...right. She needed to be open to, not just their relationship, but the link that would ensue between the three. She would be just as Alpha as Theron and just as emotionally empathic as Connor once their bond sealed.

"If you two boys would stop being so hardheaded," Gerri grumbled, passing the mountain of mashed potatoes to Connor. "Then it would be easier for this to happen."

Connor shook his head, his blond hair mussed from running his fingers through it. "She has to be right. A woman on her own. With a personality to match. Someone who won't let the fact that we're who we are intimidate her."

Theron grinned. "And she better be a stunner."

Gerri glared and curled her lip. "Of course, how could we forget that important bit?"

"Hey." Theron chuckled. "She has to agree with both our human and animal sides. That's four degrees of approval."

Gerri's dark brow lifted slowly. "Because you are such a discerning Alpha." Then she turned to Connor. "I know you need to emotionally connect. But him?" She motioned a finger at Theron. "He's a whore."

No. He wasn't. Theron loved women. All shapes and sizes. Although he preferred the short, curvy kind with more than a little to hold on to. He really liked the glasses and long curly hair of Gerri's neighbor. She reminded him of a sexy librarian or schoolteacher. There were also her lips. Christ those pouty lips had given him instant visuals of her mouth on his cock.

"Anyway, we give up," Connor said. "We want you to help us."

Gerri perked up in her seat. She glanced back and forth between them before speaking. "You're both in agreement with this?"

Not if Theron had his way. But if she could get them someone as sexy as her neighbor, they were all for it.

"Yes, we are," Theron agreed half-heartedly.

Gerri's gaze focused on him. "You will do whatever I say to get you the mate that's right for you?"

He hated having to revert to a dating service, even if it was a paranormal one.

"Yes. I know all about the success of your dating service Aunt Gerri. I don't like having to go through this to get the person that should come to us naturally."

Gerri shrugged, cut her steak and then grinned. "Sometimes you need an extra set of hands." She giggled. "Well, in your case a third set."

His aunt was too much. Connor grinned. Then they were all chuckling.

"Do you need like a list of things from us?" Theron asked. He already knew who he would suggest to her. Even if she wasn't good mate material he'd love to get his hands on his aunt's neighbor. Her scent had driven his wolf to wake and want to play.

Gerri frowned. "Do I look like an amateur?"

Connor's blue eyes widened. "No, but..."

"You will take what I suggest and you won't question me. I know who you two need."

And that's why Gerri was the one handling the Paranormal Dating Agency and they handled the pack.

"If you're sure you don't need anything from us, then we're open to whoever you have in mind," Theron stated for them.

They'd discussed it. Sharing a woman wasn't uncomfortable for them. Due to their connection, it was easier to bond with a third. Though they were not blood related, the animal spirit link between them was so strong, it was almost like they were one entity. Theron was the Alpha that fought and kept people in line. Connor was the emotional rope that united the pack. He took the brunt of the pain, frustrations and turned it all into soothing peace. Together they made the Alpha pair. Once they had their mate they'd be the Alpha triad.

With the meal over, they moved to the living room. That's when Gerri finally let them have cake. Theron didn't even attempt to hide his love for his aunt's baked goods. Gerri was amazing when she baked.

"We should take you to live with us, Aunt Gerri," Theron mumbled between cake bites.

"I don't think so. I have a business to run." She grinned and sat back on her comfy sofa with a smile. "But you are both welcome to visit me whenever you want."

"So..." Connor glanced at him. His worried look told Theron he needed reassurance regarding the mate business. They both knew women in the pack would make life difficult for whatever female they chose if she wasn't part of the Wildwoods Pack.

"Connor, darling." Gerri leaned forward and patted his knee. "Stop stressing so much. The right woman will come for you." She turned to Theron. "I do need to make sure you both will do what I say. It won't be as simple as you might expect. It's not like I'll find your mate in the blink of an eye."

Theron's animal went on alert. He worried that putting their faith on a dating service would be another failure in their search for a mate.

"We understand."

"Alright." Gerri nodded sharply. "Be ready for a possible date soon. It might be a little out of the ordinary, but I think it will work out for you boys."

Theron glanced down at the delicious cake, no longer hungry. Figured that anything to do with a mate would be a new challenge. They hadn't realized how much of a challenge it would be.

When Theron's parents and their third passed in a forest fire, he hadn't fully understood the difficulty of being part of the Alpha triad. He only knew that his parents expected it of him and he would do whatever was necessary to keep the reins on his pack. Even if it meant going outside the pack to find their third.

TALLY HAD ALREADY changed into her pajamas when Mrs. Wilder sent her a text to come for some cake. The scent of the woman's baking had filled Tally's apartment and made her crave sweets like she was looking for a high.

She didn't have to knock, Gerri opened the door before she even got to it. "Hi, Mrs. Wilder."

Gerri rolled her eyes and motioned her into her apartment. "I've told you that Mrs. Wilder makes me feel old. And I am *not* that old."

Tally grinned at the older woman's pout. She sat down on one of Gerri's pretty beige sofas. The cake was already served and sitting on the coffee table, along with some tea.

"Thank you so much, Gerri." Tally didn't worry about eating sweets late at night. She was too stressed to think about her body. Besides, she was comfortable in her skin, for the most part. Unless really sexy men stared at her the way the two in the elevator had. Like she was a feast and they were starving. That definitely made her wonder if she was missing something when it came to her body. Some kind of image she wasn't aware of. Men didn't usually go out of their way to smile at her like the two had that day.

"You're very welcome." Gerri sat across from her and picked up the notepad next to the cake at her side. "So, I've been thinking about your message."

Tally knew she should have worded it better, but she couldn't. The truth was, she needed help. "The 'I need your help before I look like a loser in front of my family' one?"

Gerri's lips twitched and curved into a full blown smile. "You won't look like a loser." She waved a blue pen in Tally's direction. "You have me now. I would never allow it."

Tally thought of her ex and her family members. They were all so close. She'd always felt like the outsider in her own family because of Paul. Nita was the only one who knew her side and believed her. Everyone else had been taken in with Paul's slick game. He knew how to work people into believing whatever he wanted. For a while, she'd been one of the people fully invested in him. Then one day, the blinders came off.

"Did you come up with anything?" Tally asked. A sliver of nerves made her hand shake. She hated being so up in the air. She couldn't not go to the damn wedding. Paul had broken her off from the group and made it seem she was the one who had destroyed the relationship with Paul instead of him with his lies.

She had nothing to hide. So why should she be the one not attending. Fuck Paul. And the rest of the family if they felt she was at fault over a relationship too fucked up to work. She'd be damned if she let them push her away. If she didn't go it would be her choice. Not their opinions that would do it.

"I did." Gerri considered her for a long moment.

"Okay..."

"I have some questions for you first." Gerri glanced down at her notebook.

Tally picked up her tea and took a gulp.

"Have you ever had a ménage?"

She choked on the tea she had in her mouth. Gerri passed her a napkin without batting an eye, as if used to that kind of reaction.

"Excuse me?" She coughed.

"Honey, you do know what a ménage is, right?" Gerri's features crinkled in concern.

"Yes, I do. And no, I have never had a ménage."

What the hell did that have to do with getting her a date for a wedding from hell?

"Would you be averse to one?" Gerri shook her head. "Wait, that's wrong."

Thank goodness she'd realized it was wrong to be asking her things like that.

"I mean, would you ever allow yourself to be involved with two men at once?"

She blinked. Her mouth hung open with surprise. She couldn't even find a way to tell her that it wasn't any of her business. Obviously asking the older woman for help had been a bad idea.

"Gerri." She put the cup down, ready to stand. "I really don't think—"

Gerri gave her a look that shut her up. "If there were two men that could give you the most amazing sex of your life, would you do it?"

Well, when she put it like that.

"Um." She bit her lip. "Together?"

"Yes, together."

"Are they going to do stuff to each other or only to me?"

Gerri gave a tired sigh. "No, darling. It's all about you."

"Hey, I don't know much about this stuff or how it works," she said, a little irritated that Gerri looked at her like she was a woman having sex for the first time. She'd had sex, dammit. She hadn't had any amazing sex. She'd had lots of crappy sex for sure.

"I'm sorry, Tally. I don't mean to put you on the defensive. There are ménages that involve men and women all getting involved with each other. I want to know your preferences."

"I wouldn't be averse to trying. I mean, I'm not a damn virgin but I'm not stuck in the old ages either. I'm not the most adventurous woman out there," she admitted. "Two good-looking men? Giving me great sex? That is kind of a no-brainer."

Gerri chuckled. "Smart woman."

She leaned forward, trying to see what the hell was on the notepad. "What does this have to do with my date?"

"Nothing. Merely curious." She shrugged. "We have so many handsome men in my system. Care to describe how you like yours? Are you more into businessmen with kind eyes and wicked smiles or do you prefer hot bikers with tattoos and ass-hugging jeans?"

"Shit. If I could get those two rolled into one, I would be the happiest woman in the world." She sighed.

Gerri had described the two men from earlier. The image of the two men pleasing her in all kinds of ways sent her temperature skyrocketing.

"Got someone in mind already?" Gerri's eyes went wide for the first time. "You do!"

She shook her head in denial, heat crowding her cheeks. "I remembered your guests from earlier. Those guys were sinfully sexy."

A slow, predatory grin slid over Gerri's lips. "My nephew and his friend. Yes, they are very handsome boys."

More like hot as hell with a side of scorching, but handsome worked too.

"How's your luck been with men?" Gerri asked.

She didn't bother lying. "The pits. All I meet are jerks or rejects from the weirdest date club."

"Really? But you're such a pretty girl," Gerri mused.

"Come on, Gerri." She twisted her lips into an unhappy smile. "I know I'm not bad looking, but my hair is too curly, I have too many curves and my attitude apparently needs some sweetening was what my last two dates told me." She clenched her teeth hard. "They also said I shouldn't have such high expectations because looks aren't everything," she grumbled, folding her arms over her chest. "This because I mentioned to one guy that his profile photo was not him."

"Oh?" Interest sounded in Gerri's voice.

"He used a photo of a very good-looking man. A man he looked nothing like." She frowned, growing angry all over again over that episode. "Apparently the photo was of a British actor. My date said he was always told he looked like that actor so he didn't see the need to post his own photo when that would do."

"But he doesn't look like the actor?"

She bit her lip to keep from growling. "No. The actor had hair. My date didn't. The actor was fit. My date looked like a slob. His sweats had stains on them. And..." She scrunched her nose. "He had really yellow teeth."

"Wow," Gerri said. "That sounds like a terrible date."

"It gets worse." She glanced down at her plate covered with smudges of icing. "He took me to have coffee and I ended up having to pay for him because he 'forgot' his wallet."

"Oh, you poor girl." Gerri gasped, horror visible over her features.

"I have at least one hundred other stories like that. Dating sucks and I won't do it anymore. But I need someone to come to my family wedding and I want the man to be the hottest you can find. Even if I never see him again," she said hopefully. "I want everyone to shut their mouths about my dating life already. So, can you help?"

Gerri nodded. "Yes, I believe I can."

"The hotter the man, the better. I want tongues to wag."

Gerri's giggles filled the apartment. "My dear, you are most definitely my kind of client. I have exactly what you need."

"Good." She stood. "I'll need him for my first event, the bridal shower, in a week. Have him show up at the restaurant. I don't have time to come home. I have a long day and we'll have to meet there." She headed for the door with Gerri by her side. "I trust your instinct. So whoever you pick for this I'm okay with."

Gerri grinned. "I'm glad. You'll have an open mind though, right?"

She had the biggest open mind. Shit. She was letting an elderly friend find her a man for a wedding. If that wasn't crazy she didn't know what was.

"Yes, I'll have an open mind." She stopped at the door. "Make sure he has hair, nice teeth and clean clothes. Other than that, I can probably let everything else slide."

"Can do," Gerri promised. "Don't worry. Your dream date will come true."

She laughed. "I'll settle for a nice guy. One who won't expect me to put up with body odor."

"Trust me, nothing like that here."

She nodded and waved as she headed for her side of the floor. "Good night, Gerri."

"Good night, Tally. Have faith. It will all work out."

Easier said than done.

THREE

TALLY GROWLED AND honked. Again. She was so late. Her date had probably left already. Not that there was any way she could have known her asshole boss would hand her a stack of calls to make right when she headed for the door.

"Bastard." Lawyers sucked hairy balls.

Rush hour traffic only added to her frustration, but she pushed it away. Gerri had called her and said that she would be pleasantly surprised by her date. Tally's excitement grew once again. Though a bridal shower was far from her idea of a perfect date, she wanted to make a certain 'I could give two fucks what you think' impression with her family. Hopefully whatever hot man Gerri had chosen would help her do the job.

She swiped clammy hands over the skirt of her strapless blue maxi dress. She wasn't usually into strapless, but it was pretty and she really liked how the dress fit.

Nita had instigated her into buying it. Telling her that it made her look sensual and sexy. She'd spent years ignoring her own sex appeal and hiding her curves because she was, according to her family, fat. She wouldn't do that anymore. Her body was hers and if she wanted to strip to nothing and wiggle her ass for her new date, then she'd do exactly that. Right after she had a few drinks. Liquid courage was her best friend.

The restaurant the family had chosen for the bridal shower was an expensive one. That meant that everyone had to look the part. Air tripped in her chest. She'd forgotten to tell Gerri to make sure the man was dressed appropriately. She would not freak. Would not freak.

Dammit, she was freaking. What if the guy showed up in shorts and a tank top?

"Oh, lord." She slammed her hand on the steering wheel as she turned the corner to enter the parking lot of the restaurant.

Her brain had decided that was what would happen. Her date would be inappropriately dressed and she'd still end up looking like a fool. Not what she needed.

She hopped out of the car. Forget demure and composed, she rushed into the entrance of the hotel and ran down to the private party room. She stepped on a wet spot on the floor and skidded down the hall.

Bam!

She slammed into a huge body that appeared out of nowhere. Massive hands curled around her arms to hold her steady. She glanced up and lost her breath.

"Hello, beautiful Tally," said the blond guy she'd met at the elevator in her building.

Before she got a chance to find her voice, hot guy number two from the elevator made an appearance. She'd walked into the Twilight Zone.

"Oh, god," she mumbled.

"She's got a great voice," biker guy said. Wait. She remembered his name. Theron. And blondie was Connor.

"What are...what are you two doing here?" she asked. There was no stopping the awe in her voice over how amazing the two men looked in a suit. Her mouth watered. In regular clothes the men were scorching enough to melt panties, but in suits, they gave new meaning to panty-dropping sexy.

"We," said Theron as he moved around to her side. "Are your dates for the next few days."

She gasped. No way. Gerri couldn't be that evil. "I think you must be mistaken."

Connor smiled, the grin turned his movie star good looks to orgasm-inducing sinful. "We are your dates, Tally. Would you reject us?"

"I don't need two dates," she stated more to herself than them. She really didn't need two sexy men eyeing her like she was the hottest woman in the world. Did she?

Theron lowered his head. "We're a pair," he whispered by her ear, his breath tickling the side of her face.

She bit back a moan and squeezed the clutch in her left hand in a death grip.

Someone turned the corner at that moment. It was Paul with his new girlfriend. She really did have the worst luck.

"Talia?" Paul said, glancing back and forth between Tally and her escorts. "I'm surprised to see you here."

His tone said he expected her to bow out because he was there. Not in this lifetime jerk-wad.

"Oh? Why's that? I did tell Roland and Susan I was coming." She forced herself to smile. Anger heated her blood. She wanted to lash out and punch the high and mighty smirk off his face.

"Who are your companions?" Paul asked, shoving the slim blonde woman forward. "This is Candy."

"Nice to meet you." The blonde smiled. She was friendly where Paul gave them a snobby smirk.

Tally glanced up at the two men on either side of her. What could she say?

"I'm Theron and this is Connor," Theron introduced them for her.

"Are you co-workers of Tally?" Paul asked, much too interested.

"No," Theron answered before Tally got a chance to. "We want a lot more than professional things out of her. She's ours."

"Excuse me?" Paul lost the smile. It was almost worth it that Theron made her sound like a hooker who they'd bought, if only to see the surprise on Paul's face. "Are you saying you're sleeping with her?"

"Paul!" the blonde admonished.

"I really don't see how that's any of your business," Tally spit out.

Theron grinned down at Tally, curling his hand around her wrist. She bit her lip, holding back the urge to shudder. Then, to make things worse, he drew circles with his thumb over her skittering pulse. Meanwhile, Connor slid his fingers over the back of her neck.

For a moment she forgot all about Paul and focused on the sensation of the two men caressing her.

"Tally is much too special just for sex," Connor said, pinning her with his gaze.

Theron lifted her hand up to his lips and kissed over her erratic pulse. "That's right. We're interested in the long-term of having her. She's the only woman who can make us whole."

Lust pooled at her core. Fire shot from her nipples down to her clit. If she could get the two guys alone at that moment, all bets were off. To say things that perfect to her ex without her even asking them to meant Theron and Connor were ideal for what she needed.

"Aw," said Candy, breaking the intimate moment between Tally, Connor and Theron. "You guys are so cute. Why don't you say things like that to me, Paul?"

Tally cleared her throat. Her mind was a whirlwind of erotic images where Theron and Connor were doing some pretty dirty things to her. And she was begging for more.

"Well," Paul said in a clipped voice. "We'll see you inside."

He entered the private party room and left them behind without another word.

"Jesus, you guys are good." Tally's mind reeled. They were both still caressing her and they were now alone. The sensual smiles did some things to her lungs she couldn't explain. It was like she'd lost the ability to breathe normally. "You can stop now."

Theron chuckled. The sound made the hairs on her arms stand on end. It was deep, rich and so sexy her girl bits quivered with need.

"Why would we want to do that?" Connor asked, voice low and rough. His light touch drove her closer to forgetting what she was there for and focusing more on what she wanted to go do.

"Um..." What was the question? "Didn't Gerri explain to you guys I only need to pretend to be dating to get my family to see I am not a total loser and they can kiss my ass?"

"I'd prefer it if you allowed me the privilege instead," Theron said softly.

She blinked and met his gaze. "What privilege?"

"The one of kissing your delectable ass."

Wow.

She moved away from them, her mind a total mess of wants and needs. "Hang on a second. I didn't really expect two escorts tonight. I don't really know what to do with two of you. And you don't have to act like I'm the hottest woman in the world when nobody's around."

"But you are the hottest woman to us," Theron stated and Connor nodded.

They closed the distance around her. She didn't want to want them, but she did. Both men pulled at some deep primal urge inside her. It was like a whole new part of her was being exposed and she wasn't sure what to do with it.

"We'll make it good for you," Connor said as if reading her mind.

Oh, she had no doubt about that.

Theron cupped her cheek. "No, we'll make it fucking amazing for you."

Jesus H. Christ!

"All you have to do is give us a chance." Connor smoothed his hands around the curve of her ass.

Her pussy ached with how turned on she was. "A chance at what?"

"Being ours."

"We need to go inside," she murmured. Only half her brain reminded her that they were one door away from chaos and she needed to control her hormones.

CONNOR WATCHED TALLY from across the room. Theron handed him a glass of champagne.

"What do you think?" Theron asked.

Connor knew what Theron wanted to know. Was she emotionally stable and strong enough to be part of their Alpha triad? She was. Though there was a lot of sadness and one very fiery attitude in her, Tally was perfect for them. He knew it from the warmth that hit him to the bone when he touched her. Theron had the same feeling. It was one of the things he could sense from their connection.

"She's perfect. In every way." He didn't bother to hide how much he wanted her himself. "If she can accept us, our triad would be complete."

Unlike a lot of packs. Wildwoods Alphas came connected to an Omega. Theron and Connor had known from birth they'd be a triad. It was normal. For years they'd shared women, but never a mate. This was new ground. Choosing a human mate made things even more difficult. There was the question of what if her body didn't take the change? What if she was challenged for her position?

"The females could be trouble. Especially Keya. She's been angry about our rejection for a while now," Theron said. They glanced at each other and then back at Tally. She appeared deep in conversation with an old woman. Every few moments she'd laugh or smile. That was their sign she didn't need any intervening.

"Yes, but we'd have to treat her like one of our own and let her handle it how she sees fit."

Theron handed a passing waiter his empty champagne flute then folded his arms over his chest. "Up to a point. No way I'd let anyone hurt her. She's so tiny. And Keya comes from a former Alpha family. She might not be Alpha in our group, but it's in her blood. She wants to lead. I won't let anything happen to Tally."

"She's a lot stronger than she seems, Theron. Very fierce." Connor homed in on the tripping heartbeat that belonged to Tally. She was aroused. A second later, she glanced up and met his gaze. Oh, yeah. She wanted a taste. She might not know how deep things truly were, but for now, they'd take her sexual attraction to them and use it to encourage her to be with them.

"Could take a while to get her on board with our needs," Theron grumbled.

"Then we need to use whatever means necessary to make her see our side of things." Connor grinned at Tally. She licked her lips and skittered her gaze away from them.

"I think I like where this is going." Theron chuckled. "This will be fun."

"I'll start it off," Connor offered and readied to march to Tally.

"Keep your eyes on the prize," Theron growled low.

Their prize was sweet Tally and her sexy body all for them. For a mate. Connor strode to Tally to do whatever necessary to break down her walls. A handful of steps and he was there.

Connor tapped her on the shoulder. Her skin was so smooth, softer than anything he'd ever touched. And the color was driving him to distraction. A smooth caramel that put his paleness to shame.

She glanced at him, her eyes wide behind her glasses. He loved how innocent she appeared before lust filled her dark brown eyes.

"Would you like to dance?" He offered his hand and watched her stare at it for a mute moment.

"Go on, girlie," the older woman said. "He's handsome and you look amazing in that dress. Ignore all the idiots and have a good time."

"Thanks, Grandma Kate."

"Don't worry, if I see Nita I will tell her you are looking for her." The old lady grinned.

Connor pulled her into his arms on the dance floor, already packed with a bunch of couples. The music was soft, so there was no need for outrageous dance moves that might get someone hurt.

Tally glanced everywhere but him. He sensed the tension in her muscles. Her arousal was what brought a smile to his lips.

He leaned down, pressing their bodies tight together and murmured by her ear, "You need to relax, Tally."

She inhaled sharply. Her ragged breaths and almost inaudible moan made his cock jerk. He slid a hand down her back to the curve of her and pressed her into him. He wanted her body cradling his cock.

"Oh, my..." she whispered.

"That's all you, beautiful." He brushed his lips over her shoulder. "I'm so hard I can't think straight."

She reeled back, staring at him wide-eyed. "But—but I haven't done anything."

He smiled at her shocked expression. "You're doing enough by smelling so delicious and looking so appetizing."

He guided her to a darkened corner where he could press her closer to him and torture himself with her softness.

"Connor, you're both really handsome men, but I have never..." She glanced around. "This isn't the same room."

He'd pushed her through an open curtain to an empty side room. "I wanted to be alone with you."

She blinked and licked her lips.

"Christ, Tally. If you keep doing that I won't be responsible for my actions."

Her wet pink tongue swooped over her bottom lip again. "Doing what?"

He pressed her back against a wall. "That. Licking your lips and reeling me in to do the same. I have to taste you."

Her mouth opened on a gasp and he used it as his first opportunity to kiss her. Their lips touched and instant fire spread through his veins. She moaned in the back of her throat. The sound was soft and so damn sexy he gripped her waist harder than he intended. He ached to be inside her, feeling her pussy stretch around his cock. The moment she curled her tongue over his, all reality ceased to exist. She was the only thing his wolf and Connor focused on.

She raked her nails up his arms. She squeezed him hard over the material of his jacket. With each grasp, she added a husky little moan that drove him wild. She wiggled her hips closer. She was wet. So wet. He could tell from the thick perfume drifting from her.

He pulled away from the heaven of her lips to kiss down her jaw.

"Tell me you want this." He bit down on her bare shoulder.

"Oh, god," she moaned.

"Tell me you want us both. Tell me you'll try." He pressed kisses down to her breasts. He wanted so badly to push the material down and suck on her nipples. To lick and lave and bite her into coming.

"I..."

He rocked his cock into her. His hard and throbbing length got no relief. Desire twined knots in his spine, down to his balls.

He cupped her breasts over her dress, squeezing her tits and licking at her exposed flesh. Her moans dug deep into him. They pushed him to continue the dangerous seduction. She gripped his jacket and pulled, until their lips were once again feasting on each other.

Her boldness only made the animal inside him hungry. She slid a hand down and cupped his cock. Her small grip tightened fast. He groaned, loving the feel of her on him even if over his pants. She might be pressed between him and the wall, but she was the one controlling things.

Then, the sound of footsteps closing the distance jerked him out of his sexual haze. He blinked and curled an arm around her, darting straight for the door to the outdoor section of the restaurant.

The moment might be gone, but he knew her fire only needed some fanning. She was definitely the one for them. It was time to wear down her defenses and get her to come to them willingly.

FOUR

TALLY BLINKED PAST the sexual haze and tried to remember what the hell had happened but she couldn't. She'd been at a bridal shower for her family. Then she'd been making out with Connor. After that they'd driven her home and now she was sitting in their car wondering what the hell was going on.

She climbed out of the vehicle on unsteady legs. As if he read her mind, Theron was there. He gave her an arm to lean on and she bet, if necessary, he'd have carried her to her door. How she knew that? She had no idea. But her instinct when it came to Theron and Connor was like a radar pointing straight to heaven.

When they got to her apartment, she couldn't think of anything to say. She ached and her body throbbed with unfulfilled need.

She met Theron's sexy dark gaze. "I—"

"We won't push if you aren't ready," he said.

Connor stood just a step to her right.

Theron bent down and cupped her face. Their lips were mere inches from each other and by god did she want to get a taste of him too. "We don't have to go if you ask us to stay."

She gulped. Her legs shook at the implication. Both of them. Pleasuring her. Solely focused on whatever it was she wanted and making it a reality. She wasn't sure if she was nervous, excited or scared over the prospect. No man had ever given her great sex. Despite their amazing good looks and sexy talk, she didn't know how they'd rate in bed.

"Try it," Theron encouraged. "I'll lick your pussy until you can't move."

She leaned back against her half-open door, her grip tight on the handle. Theron caressed her face, down her neck to her breast. He didn't touch her aching nipple. Not even to taunt her. He bypassed it and she almost growled in anger. She was so turned on that minimal touches could get her to explode.

Connor took that moment to move in on her. He pushed forward, caging her between the two. "If you allow us, you'll get enough pleasure tonight to last you a lifetime."

She groaned. Christ why did he have to say shit like that?

"But if you give more time with us a chance, you'll get a lot more than you ever imagined."

Dear God. How could he say things like that and expect her to run inside and say good-bye? Screw wondering. Nita was right. She needed to get laid.

She glanced from one to the other and nodded. "Come inside."

The moment the words left her lips, both men took over so fast she wasn't sure what happened. One second she was at the door, the next she was in the middle of her living room with Theron kissing her, his hands cupping her face and Connor pressing his cock against her back, his hands squeezing her breasts.

Clothes flew off. Theron growled against her lips. His tongue darted between her lips and dominated hers. It was like a battle of wills. She didn't know how long she could last, giving him back suck for suck, lick for lick. Not when all she knew was need. Desire. The urge to beg him to make her come.

Connor tugged her dress down her body along with her panties. Air puckered her nipples tight. Then his hands were there. On her skin. Tweaking her nipples and sliding down to cup her pussy.

"Fuck, Tally," Connor groaned. "You're wet. So wet."

He spread her pussy open, one finger pressed right at the heart of her pleasure.

She moaned, her body rushing to the peak she wasn't ready for. Theron continued to make love to her mouth. His tongue swiped in and out, thrusting and retreating with the same rhythm of a man fucking a woman.

Theron kissed down her jaw. He fluttered kisses down to her breast. She gasped as a roll of heat shot down her body. He sucked her nipple into his hot mouth and grazed his teeth over her flesh. She bit her lip, her mind lost in the sensation of pleasure from his tweaking one nipple and sucking the other, to Connor moving his hands to mold her ass.

"You're so beautiful," Connor whispered by her ear. His words were low, rough, with a bite of growl that only made her wetter.

Theron pushed her tits together, moving back and forth from one to the other. He licked, he sucked, he bit and she gasped for air. Her leg muscles gave out on her, but Connor was there. He held her by the waist and pressed his lips down her spine.

"I got you. You like having us touching you, Tally?" he asked.

She blinked, trying to get a good view in the dimly lit room. Her brain had stopped working and all thoughts focused on how quickly she was readying to burn from the inside.

"I do. I like it...a lot," she admitted.

She'd never have thought herself this adventurous. Somehow, the boring administrative assistant had taken a leap into the pool of the daring. With one man caressing her from behind and the other licking his way down her front, she'd turned into a risk taker and she was damned if ever she went back.

"Tell me what else you like," Connor asked, his breath stroked her lower back.

"I want to be touched," she stated, digging her nails into Theron's arms for support. Breaths rushed in and out of her lungs. Each lick from Theron's lips on her nipples seared a desire to be possessed by the two men.

"How?" Connor tapped her to spread her legs wide. Then he spread her ass cheeks and slid his tongue down her crack. Her breath hitched with each swipe of his tongue around her hole. An instant trembling took hold of her legs, but Theron held her up with his strong hands.

She slid her hands into Theron's long hair and raked her nails over his scalp.

"Oh, my God!"

Theron's mouth left her achy nipple with a wet pop. She glanced down to meet his bright golden gaze.

"You smell fucking delicious." His voice, pure churned gravel, turned her already tight nipples into hard little points.

She yanked him up by his hair. The brightness in his eyes increased and a low rumble sounded from his throat.

"Take your clothes off," she ordered.

He grinned. It was a sensual delight for her to watch him slowly remove his jacket and the rest of his clothes. Connor had moved down, to lick up and down the back of her thighs to her pussy and back to her ass.

She lifted her hands to her breasts. Theron's nostrils flared. She pulled and pinched at her nipples.

His pants dropped to the floor. He had to be one of the most beautiful men she'd ever seen. Body covered in tattoos, nipples pierced and an erection so impressive she wanted to drop to her knees and suck him.

"You like what you see?" His words were flirtatious, sexy.

"I do. Do you?" She squeezed her breasts, cupped them and silently offered the large mounds to him for his pleasure.

"Baby, I more than like what I see. You've got me so hard." He gripped his shaft in his hand and stroked up and down in a bold move. "I can't wait to fuck you."

He leaned forward, took one of her nipples into his mouth and bit down. She gasped. The combination of him biting her and Connor now shoving his tongue up and down between her pussy lips turned her legs to jelly.

She blinked and Theron was gone. His move took place so fast she didn't realize for a few seconds his lips weren't on her. The scuffling of moving furniture sounded. He grabbed her from behind and tugged. She fell on one of the sofa chairs, with Connor still between her legs. Theron came around the chair, his cock level with her face.

She glanced up and licked her lips. "Come closer. You want me to taste you?"

"I want to see your pretty lips wrapped around my dick," Theron said, his voice rougher than before.

Connor turned, he pushed her legs over the armrests of the sofa and rubbed his face on her pussy.

"You taste like the sweetest dessert," he groaned between her legs.

She leaned back, pushed her ass closer to the chair's edge and turned her head to face Theron. She gripped her hand around his cock, stroking him from root to tip.

She met his gaze as she touched him. His jaw clenched. Heat emanated from his body in powerful waves. "Is it hard for you to let me touch you?"

"Yes," he groaned.

She opened her lips, licked a slow circle around the head of his cock and glanced at him again. "Why?"

"Because..." He moaned as she took a lick from his balls up to the crown of his shaft and flicked her tongue in circles. "I want to be deep inside you. Feeling your wet hot pussy gripping my dick in a tight hold."

She spread saliva with her tongue over his cock. Theron slid his fingers into her hair, grabbed chunks of it and pushed his dick into her mouth.

"Suck it."

FIVE

Connor shoved a finger into her pussy, the dual intrusion pushed at the arousal coursing through her body. She moaned, took more of Theron's large cock into her mouth and wiggled over Connor's mouth.

Connor licked and laved her pussy. She was already soaked with her own cream. He pressed his tongue over her clit. He retreated and drove back in. Passion burned bright at her core.

Theron thrust in and out of her mouth. Slowly at first, but then with more power and speed. She rubbed the underside of his cock with her tongue. Every plunge into her mouth sent fireworks to her clit. Her jaw burned from how wide she had to hold her mouth open, but Connor's continued sucking of her pussy took her mind off any discomfort.

"Fuck, baby," Theron growled. "You have such a wet little mouth."

She jerked him with one hand in conjunction with her sucks. He was hard and smooth as silk. She slid her other hand down to grip Connor's blond hair and pressed him closer to her pussy.

"That's right, princess," Theron groaned, moving in and out of her mouth. "Show him how you like to get fucked."

Her belly quivered. Theron gripped her hair tighter with one hand and fondled one of her breasts with the other. Connor moved his fingers out of her pussy. They were replaced with his tongue. He fucked her, lapped at her juices and growled. At first it was soft, but each little growl built the anticipation twisting knots in her core.

Then his licks turned faster. Harder. Rougher.

He turned relentlessly with speed and agility. She gasped. It was hard to keep up with sucking on Theron's cock when she was ready to come. Her muscles tightened.

Theron pulled his cock out of her mouth and leaned down to kiss her. He drove his tongue into her mouth and rubbed it over hers. This time she was there with him. Desire unlocked something inside her she didn't know existed. A thirst for more. A need for a deeper sexual enjoyment. Something she'd never had with any other man.

The tension at her core reached a limit. Connor sucked her clit into his mouth. And growled. Pleasure blasted through her body in a wave that caught her off guard.

She choked out a scream, digging her nails into Connor's scalp, holding him between her legs. Her body shook as the wave crested. She barely breathed. He continued to lick and suck her through multiple mini-orgasms. It was unlike anything she'd ever experienced before.

Gasps and quick breaths were the only sounds in the room. That and a low rumble from Theron.

He cupped her face in his hands and brought his own mere inches from hers. "I want to fuck you so bad I can't think straight."

She glanced down at Connor, who licked her scent off his lips. "What about you?"

Connor grinned. "Don't worry, beautiful. I know how to wait my turn."

She didn't get a chance to say more. Theron lifted her in his arms, then sat on the sofa she'd been sitting on and slowly lowered her body on to his. She pushed forward, biting her lip as the head of his cock speared her pussy.

"Oh, fuck!" Theron growled. "You're a tight little thing."

Little? There wasn't a little thing about her. She moaned at the almost burning sensation of his cock pressing into her pussy walls. He was big and long and thick. All wonderful things except that she hadn't had sex for a while and most of the men she'd been with didn't have his length or girth.

She met Connor's gaze, watched him strip and then sit on a chair from the dining room, directly in front of them. He was fully erect and ready.

Theron pressed her down on his dick, hard. She groaned at how filled she felt. He was in her fully, so deep she could barely breathe.

"That's fucking perfect," he groaned. He lifted and dropped her on his cock. She didn't need further urging. She rocked on his lap, not really lifting but rubbing her insides with his dick in an incredible way.

"Oh, my..."

Theron grabbed chunks of her hair and pulled her back. He licked the back of her neck and cupped her breast with his free hand. "I like how wet you are. So slick and tight."

She gulped, her gaze still locked on Connor. Connor jerked his cock. A bead of liquid dripped from the slit of his dick. He spread his palm over it and continued to stroke. A new ball of tension started to twine inside Tally.

Theron rocked his hips under her, urging her to move faster. "Ride me, baby."

His words, so rough and low with that hint of need, pushed her arousal higher.

Connor continued to touch himself, his beautiful tanned ab muscles contracted with every up and down motion he did. His breath sounded ragged. Or maybe that was hers. She couldn't be sure what she was hearing anymore. Her own heartbeats sounded louder than anything else.

Theron grabbed her hips. He lifted and rammed her hard on his cock. Each slide down woke nerve endings she didn't even know existed. Her body was a giant time bomb waiting to explode.

Connor licked his lips, his eyes glowing with his animal power. "You are so fucking sexy," he groaned. "I love watching your tits bounce while he fucks you."

Her pussy clenched around Theron's cock. It was so erotic to hear him say that.

"I can see your clit peeking between your pussy lips," Connor said. "Want me to lick it?"

He really loved oral, but it made her want to do something for him instead. "Why don't you come over here so I can help you out with that?"

He stood, stalking his way to her. She was still bouncing on Theron's cock when he stopped in front of her. Connor roped her hair around his hand and she leaned forward to take his cock into her mouth.

Connor groaned. She suctioned her cheeks tight, allowing him deep into the back of her throat with ease. His size wasn't as imposing as Theron's so it was easier to suck him off.

"God, you have such perfect lips," Connor groaned.

"She's got a perfect pussy too," Theron rumbled from behind her.

Somehow, she was able to ride Theron and suck Connor without losing her rhythm. She jerked Connor with one hand while she sucked. His cock was smooth. Almost like hot velvet in her mouth. Meanwhile Theron's bigger dick rubbed her insides like no other man's ever had.

Connor started to thrust in and out of her mouth with more speed. Theron's body turned tight under her. He sat up, curled a hand around her clit and fingered her hard little nerve bundle.

"I want you to come with me," Theron growled. "I want to feel your pussy sucking my dick and drinking my cum."

Her nipples ached with how badly she wanted to come. The things he said were more images to add to the erotic arsenal assaulting her brain. Connor's body tensed as well.

Theron rammed her down hard. Once. Twice. He pinched her pussy and she pulled Connor's cock out of her mouth to scream.

A new, much more intense orgasm rocked her. Her pussy gripped tight on Theron's cock. He did one more deep painful thrust and roared. His cock grew, pulsed and filled her with his cum. She was knocked into a second powerful orgasm from the feel of his cock almost vibrating inside her.

She jerked Connor, he clenched his jaw and threw his head back. Her instinct took over. She leaned forward as his semen spurted out of his cock. Loud growls sounded from Connor. His cum landed on her breasts and slowly slid down her chest and nipples.

He groaned with each continued jerk until his cock was semi-hard but spent. She leaned back into Theron's body. He was still deep inside her. She lifted her hands to rub her breasts and massage the cum over her tits.

Connor groaned while watching her. "You have no idea how much I like that."

She licked her lips. "I liked you coming on me more."

Her night of a seemingly simple bridal shower date had turned into unbelievable sex. She didn't want to think too much or she'd start finding all kinds of flaws with the past few hours.

Connor helped her off Theron and lifted her in his arms. She allowed him to at that point. Her legs were still shaking and she didn't want to fall on her face.

"Which way is the bedroom?" Connor asked, the sexy grin back on his lips.

She directed him and glanced over her shoulder as Theron followed close behind.

TALLY WOKE TO the smell of food. Her stomach grumbled. She turned on her side and blinked her eyes open when memories of the previous night rushed through her brain.

Oh. God. She'd had sex with two men. Two incredible hot and very skilled men. She sat up in a rush. Her bedroom was a mess from when she'd jumped in the shower with Connor, only to have Theron state she had to have a shower with him too. Towels littered the floor and clothes were thrown all over.

"What did I do?" She gasped.

She jumped out of bed and tossed clothes out of her way to find her purple fuzzy robe. Spotting a hair tie, she twisted the long, curly and very messy mass into a bun on top of her head. Then she rushed to the bathroom and washed her face and brushed her teeth. Finally, she found her glasses on the dresser and put them on.

Nope. She was not going to look at her reflection or she would surely have a mild panic attack.

Loud laughter and the smell of coffee urged her to the kitchen. Theron sat in a pair of sweats and no shirt at her kitchen table with a plate of food. Connor sat next to him in boxers and a tank top with a cup of coffee in front of him.

To make it all even better, Gerri sat there with them. Smiling.

"Hi?"

"Come over here, darling." Theron slapped his lap and motioned her forward.

Blood heated in her face. She'd never been overtly sexual with men like she had the previous night, so this was new territory.

"Sweetheart, you need a better robe," Gerri said, her gaze taking a deep dive down to the material that dragged behind Tally.

"Thanks, but I like this one." She strolled forward, almost tripping.

"Well, it clearly doesn't like you." Gerri shrugged. "Come eat. I made enough food for everyone."

Tally's dining room table, which was seldom used, was covered with plates of food. From scrambled eggs, bacon, sausage, pancakes, to fruit and pastries. It was like a restaurant had moved into her apartment.

She bypassed Theron's lap and sat on the fourth and empty seat at the table. She opened her mouth but no words came out. Really, what could she say to Gerri? That she was angry at her for sending her two of the hottest men she'd ever met? Men that had given her more orgasms in one night than those she'd given herself throughout her thirty-two years? Instead, she went for the coffee and prepared herself a mug.

"Are you okay?" Connor asked. His worried frown appeased her fears somewhat.

"Yes, I'm fine," she lied.

Connor, Theron and Gerri glanced back and forth at each other.

"You are most definitely not fine," Gerri stated. "You are clearly having an emotional dilemma."

She would not, could not, talk about that with them. No way in hell.

"Connor," Theron said, taking the attention off her. "Maybe if we explain our way a little, Tally would understand some."

Gerri stood. "I'll go back and do dishes. You all talk."

She wanted to listen to them, but she also felt she had to address Gerri. Didn't look like she'd get the chance now.

"Do you prefer to speak to us together or one on one?" Connor asked, reading the turmoil inside her. He was clearly perceptive and she had a difficult time as it was talking to them at the same time.

The men glanced back and forth at each other and Theron stood. "I'm going to take a shower." He leaned over the table and kissed her. "I'll be back shortly, beautiful."

CONNOR WATCHED INDECISION flash through Tally's eyes. He smelled her confusion over the new situation between them. As Omega, his first instinct was to calm her down. As a man who wanted her for a mate, he needed to make sure she was comfortable with how things worked for their pack.

"I need to understand what it is you two want," she said, voice low. There was a slight tremble to it that kicked him hard in the gut.

"You know we are shifters," he stated, more to verify what she already knew.

She sipped the cup of coffee and glanced at him, her gaze direct. "Yes, but I didn't realize you all shared women."

"Not all packs do. Things vary from one to the next. For Wildwoods, sharing a mate is custom and part of the norm. It's a way of life." He grasped her hand on the table. "Other packs share a single mate among multiple pack members. We've come across the single couple packs. Nothing is taboo in the shifter world."

Questions lit in the depth of her gaze. "What do you mean nothing is taboo?"

He shrugged. "When the heat strikes, couples could have sex anywhere. People shift and don't have clothes, it's natural to walk around naked."

Her eyes widened and her mouth turned into a perfect pouty O. "Walk around naked?"

He grinned. She probably didn't realize it, but when he'd said people have sex anywhere, her cheeks had turned a dark crimson and she'd licked her lips.

"Yes. Sex is natural. So is nudity. We're very sexual creatures." If she was going to be part of the pack, she needed to know what she would be getting into.

"So you..." She cleared her throat. "You and Theron, you want me?"

"Yes." God, how they wanted her.

For the first time ever, the men and the animals were in sync. She'd been the answer they needed. They wanted her for a mate. And there would be no turning back.

"For how long?" She scrunched her nose. "You want me as a lover, shared between the two of you for a while?" She pushed her cup to the side and pursed her lips. "So if one of you gets tired of me, does the other one get me? Or do you both pretty much just go with mutual votes?"

SIX

"Don't do that." He shook his head. "That's not how we are."

She leaned forward on the table, the scent of her distress mingled with anger. A new light of hostility sparked in her eyes. "I'm sorry but I just don't see how a relationship of being lovers could work long-term."

That was the main problem with non-shifter mates. They didn't get the different way of life. "We are born and raised this way."

He knew he wasn't getting through to her, so he stood and marched around the table. He offered her his hand and watched her stare at it for a second. She took it. He moved to her long sofa and pulled her on his lap. She struggled for a moment, but once she saw he wasn't letting her go, she stopped and sighed in defeat. He shifted her so her back was leaning on the armrest and he could look at her face.

"What is the one thing you've always wanted in a mate?"

"A partner? I guess someone who is honest and can love me for me and not for who he feels I should be."

"Think of us as the first men that will give you that." He pushed a stray curl behind her ear. She blinked with curiosity behind her glasses.

"What do you mean give me that?" She glanced down at his mouth.

He wanted so bad to stop the conversation and kiss her. She had the most beautiful pouty lips and he'd never tire of watching her slide her tiny pink tongue over them.

"When we search for a mate, it has to be someone who is perfect for us on multiple levels. Mainly we have to be attracted to her in our human bodies. Your scent has to attract the animal inside."

She raised her brows in obvious shock. "Wait, you and Theron had to want me and so did your...eh, wolves?"

He nodded. "We hadn't had luck until you. We love a woman with curves. That is just our preference. You're gorgeous. I wouldn't dare compare you to anyone else because nobody else has made me want her as much as you. No other female has made Theron and I agree she is the one meant to fit as our third and make us whole."

"I...I don't know what to say," she mumbled. "There's so many women out there that have a lot more experience with two men."

"Oh, darling." He brushed his lips over hers, not able to contain himself any longer. "You are the one. No matter what any other woman has, you have given our connection the emotional boost it needs for Theron to lead and for me to engage the pack. You're who we need. Something about you is perfect for us."

"Connor, this all sounds so nice, but what happens when you tire of me?" She sounded sad.

"That won't happen."

"What do you mean? It happened with my ex-husband and a host of ex-boyfriends. I have bad luck with men."

"A mate is for life. There are no others once one is found. Only one mate for our pair."

"You mean to tell me that without knowing me at all, but based purely on instinct and scent, you two feel I'm right to spend the rest of your lives with?" The disbelief was obvious in her tone.

"Yes." He didn't bother denying it.

"Connor, come on. I'm a pretty modern person, but taking on a relationship with two men, something I've never done, is scary enough. Added to that you want this to be something committed? I don't know if you know this, but we just met. This is crazy."

"Give us a chance, Tally." He glanced deep into the fear he saw in her eyes and tried to soothe the tumultuous emotions in her heart. She was a strong woman, but fear could make her choose the path they didn't want for her.

"I have to think."

"I have an idea," Theron said, entering the room as she finished her sentence. He was freshly dressed and appeared unperturbed by her words. He gave Connor an open mental link to allow him to see his thoughts.

Connor's fears for Tally dissipated somewhat. Theron's idea was sound. If they could pull it off, then she wouldn't have the worries in her mind.

"What's your idea?" Tally turned to Theron.

"We date." He grinned. "It's what humans do, right? Date to get to know if someone is mate material?"

She nodded. "They do, but wait, so this means the whole mate thing is off the table?"

"No!" he and Theron said at once.

"It means you need to be reassured and we are happy to do whatever is necessary for you. You're our priority now. We want you to be happy and comfortable or we won't be," Theron replied.

"Well." She frowned. "I still have this wedding to go to. I guess that's as good a place to start as any. But that's not until next weekend."

"How about we start with something simple," Theron suggested. "Come with me for a walk."

Connor nodded when she glanced at him. "Go for it. I think spending time one on one first and then as a group could really help you see how much this can work."

"Are you sure? Won't that mess with the idea of being a..."She gulped. "A triad?"

Theron grinned. "Not even a little. Connor and I know each other well enough to know neither would ever try to push the other one out of the way. What we want is unity."

"I'll shower and change in your guest room," Connor offered. He sensed she needed the time to be alone, to think about what they offered and to decide what she wanted. "We'll go and give you some time to yourself. Tomorrow, Theron can come and take you for that walk if you're in agreement."

The last thing they needed was for her to feel like she was being pushed into anything. They wanted her ready, willing and able to be the woman for them. Though they already knew she was the one, she still had to come to that conclusion. No amount of pushing or pressure on their part would encourage her trust. That would come with time.

THERON GLANCED AT Tally. She wore a long, sexy dress that hugged her curves like a second skin. It wasn't tight, it draped perfectly over her large breasts, small waist and abundant hips. His mouth watered the moment he saw her.

She'd worn her hair in a ponytail that drove him crazy. He loved her curls and wanted to see them hanging loose down her back. She pushed a long strand behind her ear and adjusted her glasses. The prim, schoolteacher look had never been such a turn-on.

How was it possible that she did that to him? She was so unaware of her beauty. It would probably kill him if she continued to bite and lick her bottom lip for much longer. She hadn't said anything of his holding her hand the entire time they'd been walking through the massive park. He'd deliberately brought her to one that bordered his land. It was silly, but thinking of her that close to his home brought a smile to his lips. If only he could do something to alleviate the confusion he sensed in her.

"What is it that concerns you about a relationship with us?" he asked.

She sighed loudly. They went a few steps more before she finally answered. "I've been married to the jerk you met a few days ago. I've dated so many men that only wanted to sleep with me or to find a woman to take care of them." She stopped and turned to him. "Frankly, I'm sick of it. I'm not doing it anymore."

"You shouldn't have to. A partner should be someone who takes what you already have and makes it better. Someone who makes you happy to have them in your life."

Her sad smile broke his heart. "That's what we'd like to think. And that's what men always advertise. I'm not sure I'm the right woman for you two. I'm too bitter."

"You're not bitter. You have just had some very bad experiences and I understand your hesitation." He cupped her cheek and stared deep into her troubled eyes. "All I can ask is for you to give us a chance. No pressure. If at any point you feel the need to go or that this isn't working, we understand," he lied. They'd probably die without their third, but he wouldn't tell her that. She didn't need to be pushed. She needed coaxing.

She pursed her lips and turned back to strolling. "When I was a kid, I swore my parents had the most amazing marriage ever. I mean really awesome. They were always hugging and smiling and laughing. I wanted that for me." She chuckled. The sound came out a pained laugh. "Then I grew up. I heard the yelling behind closed doors. I saw the bruises she tried to hide. I questioned her and do you know what she said to me?"

Waves of her pain surrounded them. He had a hard time yanking back the animal who wanted to offer her comfort. He bit back the growl threatening to escape and pulled her closer to his side. "What did she say?"

"She said that cheating comes natural to everyone. That it was my responsibility to accept it and let it go. That if I wanted a marriage to work I would have to understand my place as a woman." She shook her head. "I don't buy that for a second. I refuse to believe it and I won't settle for it."

"So she feels it's okay to have a relationship with a partner that isn't committed to being with only one person?"

She nodded. "It gets better. She said the only way she's stayed married this long is by having affairs herself. All her time away with family and friends allowed her the ability to meet up with men and do her own thing."

His chest ached with the bitterness spilling from her lips. She hurt badly and he didn't know how to stop it. "You have to understand not everyone thinks that way."

She shrugged. "I know. I've met other couples who don't have that as part of their lives. But the truth is, I have bad luck with men." She veered off the main park path and crossed to a desolate hill with a thick grassy patch. She stopped, glanced down at the view of the forest and sat down. "I have awful luck with men. Hell, I have terrible luck in general. You both don't need my bad luck in your lives."

"Let us be the judge of what we need. All we want from you is a chance."

She gazed out in the distance. "I have no experience with shifters other than Gerri. And she's a handful."

He grinned at the sound of her soft laugh. "That she is. She has been like a mother to me and Connor."

Tally folded her legs under her and turned to him. "How do you do it?"

He saw interest and curiosity spark in her eyes. "Do what?"

"How do you share a woman and not worry that she will fall in love with one over the other or more than the other?"

That was tough. "In an ideal world, you'd fall in love with both of us. We want you to have the emotional link with both of us to create a strong bond."

She nodded slowly but said nothing.

The breeze swirled strands of her hair forward. He leaned close and placed the strand sticking to her lips behind her ear. Her eyes widened behind her glasses. Then, to tantalize and drive him completely crazy, the scent of her arousal drifted into his lungs. Her heartbeat accelerated under his touch. Her skin heated and she licked her lips.

"I hope you understand." He moved closer, pushing her to lean back on the grass, until her back hit the ground.

"Understand?" Her voice quivered.

"I can't stop myself." He stared at her mouth and allowed the hunger he felt inside to show itself a bit in his features.

Her eyes widened and she gasped.

"I can't control my need to feel your body under me," he said and leaned over her. He groaned as he lay between her legs, his cock nestled over her pussy. "You are so soft, Tally."

She gulped. "Theron, I don't think—"

"That's right, darling. Don't think. Just go with your instinct." He leaned down and crushed their mouths together. She tasted divine. Like the sweetest honey and ripest fruit. Her body cradled him with her softness. He almost came on the spot at the first swipe of her tongue over his. No longer tentative with her touches, she thrust into his mouth and moaned. The sound was sexy as hell. For every groan, she moaned. For every thrust, she curled her tongue over his. He pulled at the hem of her skirt, pushing it up her thigh. He needed to feel her smooth skin under his palms.

She yanked her face sideways, whimpering, "Oh, Theron. Christ that feels good."

His cock jerked in his jeans. There was little he could do to stop the thrusting between her legs. She spread her legs wider and glanced into his eyes. "Do it. Now. Here."

Normally he wouldn't let himself get carried away this way. But her eyes, dark with desire, and her lips, swollen with his kisses, had his wolf pushing at the skin. Everything inside him shifted into pleasure mode. It was all about getting her off right now.

He kissed a path down her neck, to the neckline of her dress. With a single tug, her bra popped above the dress. The sheer lace holding her breasts showed off her puckered brown nipples.

She wiggled under him, the heat of her core driving his cock to painful hardness.

"Please..." she moaned a husky little plea that sent shudders down his back. She probably didn't realize how much she affected them. At that moment, all he wanted was to please her. To see her smile and watch her body unravel when pleasure hit.

He sucked a nipple into his mouth over the lacy bra, using the material to add a new dimension of torture to his woman.

"Oh, God!" She slapped her hands on his biceps. Her hips rocked into him. The sensation drew a groan from his dry throat. She was so responsive. To even the smallest touch. She'd gasp or mewl or moan. So softly. So desperately that he could think of nothing but shoving his cock so deep into her he'd watch her eyes roll to the back of her head and scream as she came.

He bit down on her nipple at the same time she scored her nails hard on his arms. Her eyes were closed and her mouth puffed air in and out of her pink lips.

They'd wanted a mate for so long. One who would please them physically and emotionally. Though she was emotionally scared, she was so fucking perfect in every way for them. Her body turned him on like no other woman had before. It might be her hidden sex appeal. She didn't need to flaunt it. Her inner light shone through the fear.

He peeled back the bra and sucked her tit into his mouth. Her gasp and immediate shudder pushed the animal forward. He had a hard time controlling the beast. He liked her scent. Liked her taste.

He licked back and forth between her breasts, sucking, nipping and repeating.

"Theron...I don't think I can take much more of this." She met his gaze. Her passion-dazed eyes broke the limit on his control.

He slipped his hand between her legs and found her wet center. Christ, she was soaked and dripping heat. He ached to be inside her, to feel her pussy clutching at his cock with every slide into her velvety walls. Spreading her lips open, he slid a finger around her clit. She curved her back, pushed her pussy into his hand and groaned.

"More. Give me more, please."

He loved the sound of desperation in her voice. Her muscles shook with how tense she was. He slowly fingered around her clit, tapping the tiny hard bundle lightly before moving away. He knew she was close and wanted to make it really good for her.

"Oh, baby you are so fucking wet. Do you know how badly I want to be inside you?"

She raked her nails up his arms and into his hair to tug his mouth back on her nipple.

"Suck me. Make me come," she ordered.

God, she was so sexy when she got all dominant and aggressive. He knew that wasn't something she did often. He sensed her normal hesitation deserting her. He sucked her plump breast and bit down on her nipple. At the same time, he slid two fingers into her slick pussy and fucked her so slow he knew she'd probably yell at him soon.

"You...are...evil," she moaned. "I am going to shatter if you don't hurry."

"Oh, no. You're exactly where I want you, beautiful." He licked the valley of her breasts and nibbled on the other nipple. "I want you so desperate that when you come, your juices flow over my hand."

Her chest quaked with how hard she breathed. He blew air over her nipples. They scrunched up into tighter little points.

He quickened his moves, thrusting in and out of her pussy with first two, then three fingers. He prayed that his erection wouldn't turn into blue balls because this was not going to be one of those times where he'd get to slide up into her sleek wet pussy and get to feel her contract around him like a velvet glove.

Her breaths panted out of her in low moans. He watched her face, her features concentrated fully on reaching the peak. He bit down on her nipple and tapped her clit hard. She choked out a moan. Her grip on his hair loosened as did her body under him. She went soft and a low gasp sounded from her.

She glanced at him and smiled. Not a half smile, either. It was a smile of someone having been pleasured to the point she couldn't stop the grin.

"I have never done anything like that in a public park," she said, blinking the sexual clouds out of her eyes.

"It doesn't matter where we are, Tally." He swiped his tongue over her nipple one more time before fixing her dress. "Your pleasure is my priority."

He stood, ignoring his aching hard-on and helped her to her feet. "Are you good to walk?"

She nodded but glanced down at his cock. "Are you good to stay that way?"

He grinned. "This wouldn't be my first time going home with no relief. I can handle it." He cupped her face and kissed her softly. "I wanted this to be for you. I'm perfectly fine as I am."

He wasn't really fine, but fuck, he wouldn't make her feel like she had to suck his cock in the middle of a public park either. He wanted her to have this moment. It wasn't about him needing her to return the favor.

"Are you sure?" she asked and glanced around as if trying to decide what to do next.

"Baby, this was all about you. I am happy to wait." He met her gaze. "For you, I'll wait as long as I have to."

SEVEN

TALLY TOOK CONNOR'S hand. He leaned down into the vehicle to help her out. The front of the banquet hall was filled with expensive cars. Her cousin's wedding had finally arrived. They'd gotten to the church in time to sit in the back row and watch quietly. No one had noticed them or paid them any mind. Exactly how Tally liked it. The reception would be another story. She'd been dating Connor and Theron for a week now and things were a lot better than even she anticipated.

"You're going to have to come out of the car, darling," Connor taunted. She'd voiced her opinion on how unexcited she was about the entire event, but her call with Nita and then her grandmother had sealed the deal. She'd go and show her face. Show everyone she was alive and well with two hot men by her side.

"I'm coming," she grumbled. The wind whipped her curls all over her face. She'd forgone the glasses for a set of contacts.

"I really hate that you didn't wear the glasses today," Theron said, coming around the car to her side. "I have a thing for the prim schoolteacher look."

She had no idea what he was talking about. Tally might not be overtly sexual with displaying herself, but she didn't try to hide her body either. She wore what she liked. That was usually long, soft dresses. For the wedding, she'd decided to wear a shorter dress that hugged her curves. Connor had complimented her on it at least five times in the past hour.

"Have I told you how beautiful you look in that dress?" He winked.

Make that six times in the past hour.

"I don't think so, no." She grinned. "I may never get out of this dress if you keep it up."

She allowed them to lead her into the reception hall. They'd deliberately taken their time so that things were busy by the time they arrived. The reception was being held locally in a large banquet hall. A massive party location known for hosting top-notch events.

She found their names and seating assignments on a table at the entrance to the main hall. Inside, music pumped over large speakers. Disco lights blinked in different colors and a DJ urged the crowd to do the electric slide.

"I'll go get us some drinks," Theron offered when they reached their table.

The crowd cheered as the music ended. A new slow song started and the DJ called couples to the floor.

Connor squeezed her hand. "Come on, let's dance."

"I don't know..." She stumbled to her feet and followed behind him.

"You want to dance. Stop worrying over what others will think."

He was right. She did want to dance. That was one of her favorite songs the DJ was playing. Connor held her close, staring deep into her eyes.

He lowered his face close, until his lips were by her ear. "Ignore the people."

She laughed. She was the one that usually said that. When had things changed? And more importantly, did she really care what anyone thought? Not really. She smiled and let her muscles relax. Until that moment, she hadn't noticed how stiffly she held herself.

"That's my girl."

Their dance and fun time was short-lived. Someone bumped into them from the right. She opened her mouth to apologize but stopped at the sight of Paul and Candy.

"You came?" Paul asked, his face a mask of disgust.

"Of course I came. This is my family." She stopped dancing to face him.

"Have you even bothered to think of what it's doing to them for their friends to see you waltzing around with two men like—"

"I'd be very careful of the words that come out of your mouth," Connor whispered, his voice hard.

Paul glared at him and then back at her. "You have no shame at all, do you?"

"I don't see why you're worried over my personal life. You're not part of my family." She curled her hands into fists. Connor stood behind her, he'd tried to gently get her to move to his side, but she didn't budge. This was her fight and she was going to handle it all by herself.

She saw Theron from the corner of her eye, ready to move forward. She met his gaze for a second and shook her head.

Grandma Kate stopped dancing with her uncle and joined them.

"What is going on? Why aren't you all dancing?"

Nita moved to Tally's side. She had waved at her cousin when she'd walked in, but hadn't spoken to her yet.

"What's the problem here?" Nita asked, her voice held more than a little aggravation. "Why did you stop them from dancing, Paul?"

Paul gave Nita a murderous look. "I'm genuinely disturbed for the family."

Nita and Tally's gazes met. Nita rolled her eyes and Tally sighed.

"Why are you disturbed, Paul? I see no reason to be worried," Grandma Kate said.

"With all due respect, Kate, your granddaughter is making a spectacle of herself with these two men she's brought to the wedding." He huffed.

Connor let loose a soft growl and Paul took a step back.

"Why are her dates any of your concern?"

"I'm worried for you, madam," he stated. "I would not like to see your good name and that of your family spoken of poorly due to Tally's sexual deviance."

"My what!" Tally screeched. She'd kill him. The jerk had actually had the guts to talk shit about her in the middle of a packed dance floor.

"You heard me!" Paul threw back loudly. The music stopped and everyone listened to the argument. "You're sleeping around from one guy to another but that's not enough for you, is it? You have to bring them to a family event. To show the rest of polite society what kind of life you lead."

Tally lifted a hand to slap him, but Connor was quicker. He grabbed her arms and pulled her back. "He's not worth it."

"Let her hit me," Paul instigated. "I'll have her arrested for assault."

"You asshole!" Nita hissed. "You think we'd take you over Tally?"

Paul turned to Grandma Kate. "I'm sorry to say this, but your granddaughter is a whore!"

The crowd gasped. Grandma Kate took a step closer to Paul, raised her sixty-five year old hand and slapped him so hard it resonated around the hall.

"You listen and you listen to me well," Kate said softly. "This is my family. Talia is my granddaughter. You're nothing. Get out of here before I find my cane and shove it up your uptight ass."

Paul's wide eyes and shocked face was one look Tally would never forget.

"I—"

"Get out!" Kate yelled. "I'm too old to put up with crap. Others might have let your assholery slide, but I won't. I don't want to see your face at any other family functions, or believe me, my cane will find a new home up your ass." She turned to Tally's uncle. "Get him out of here."

Tally's uncle nodded. "Whatever you say, mom."

Connor released Tally. She started to move away from the dance floor when her grandmother stopped her.

"Talia, come here, please."

Tally turned back to Grandma Kate and stopped next to her. Kate grabbed Tally's hand in her own and glanced around the hall. "This is my granddaughter. She'd had a poor excuse for parents, but she's got me."

"She's got us too," Theron yelled.

"And me," Nita added.

Kate nodded. "So if anyone here says anything about my Tally, they'll be seeing a side of me anyone rarely sees. She's not alone."

Tally's eyes filled with tears. She never needed anyone to protect her or stand up for her. But there she was, surrounded by her grandmother, Connor and Theron and Nita, all showing her how truly special she was.

"Put the music back," Kate said to the DJ. "We're not done dancing over here."

TALLY GIGGLED AGAIN. "Theron if you keep pressing that same spot I'm not going to stop squirming."

He lifted her foot to his face. "What spot? These feet are so tiny."

She giggled again. His attempt at a foot massage had started well, but had turned into a tickle Tally session. She laid on the sofa, her torso on Connor's lap and her feet on Theron.

"My feet are not tiny. You better stop saying that."

"They really are," Connor agreed, brushing curls away from her face.

"Are you two blind? Didn't you see how swollen they are?" She glanced into Connor's laughing eyes.

"You decided to dance the night away."

She groaned. "I know, but how could I dance so much with you and then not with Theron?"

Theron snorted. "I was more than happy to watch you dance. I told you that."

She shook her head, watching him rub circles over her ankles. "I felt guilty. I want you both to feel my time is spread evenly with you."

"Tally, we don't suffer from insecurities. We're united, not competing," Theron replied.

If only she could remember that. Most of the time she was too worried about not making one feel less wanted than the other that she sometimes overdid it.

"I had fun tonight," she said. Thinking back to all the family events of the past, none came close to her cousin's wedding.

"Your grandmother sure laid it out there for Paul," Connor snickered.

"Oh my god, did you hear her tell him she'd shove her cane up his ass? If I hadn't been so angry I would've burst into giggles."

"You know, she was right," Theron said, meeting her gaze with a smile. "You're not alone. You've got us, too."

She wanted to open up and say something emotional, but held back. She'd been analyzing her feeling and had come to the conclusion there was something deeper there between the three of them. Something she couldn't name yet, but that she was willing to spend more time developing.

"Thank you, I appreciate that."

EIGHT

"So remind me again, why having two men any woman would kill for that want you is a bad thing?" Nita smiled at the waitress that brought their coffee and cake.

"I'm not saying it's a bad thing for them to want me," Tally grumbled.

Maybe. Okay, she didn't think it was bad they wanted her. Hell, it was like her deepest wet dream come true. Two super-hot guys who wanted her, spent time making sure she not only saw their interest, but felt wanted.

"So why the long face?" Nita put her usual too much sugar and cream and sipped her coffee.

"Because of my history, Nita. I have bad luck with men. And these guys are so..." Wonderful. She didn't want to say it, but for the past few weeks, she'd either gone to dinner, movies, walks and shows with one the other or both. And the sex? The best, porn had nothing on them. They were the best team out there. One focused on a particular part of her while the other worked another until she was begging one or both to fuck her. Heat crowded her cheeks. She'd lost every last scrap of inhibition and had let loose the sex drive she had no idea lived inside her.

"So what?" Nita asked, bringing her back to the present.

"So damn nice! They deserve a good woman who will make them a good mate. Not some insecure, bitter, fat girl that man-hates and wants to tie them in the closet so nobody else gets their claws on them," she said honestly.

"First of all, you are not a fat girl. You have curves. And so the fuck what if you are fat, I am too and let me tell you, we fucking rock."

"I know that. I am not saying we don't. Until I met these two, I never felt self-conscious of my body. I'm pretty happy with myself. I know I won't be a skinny woman. I know I can't fit into the sizes most women wear and that's okay. I am fine with that. What I am having a problem with is the fact that they bring out my insecurities."

She eyed the cake on her plate. If only it would solve all the problems in her life. There was no real answer to things other than taking chances. She didn't like the idea of making a decision she'd later regret. She was at a point in life where she felt she'd wasted all the time she was going to waste in a useless relationship.

"Let me ask you a few questions," Nita said. "How do you feel when you are with Connor?"

She smiled. "He's such a sweetheart. So worried about my feelings all the time. He has this...something that he knows when I'm feeling worried or sad and he'll hug me without saying a word."

Connor's actions had really broken through a lot of barriers in her. She tried, but it was useless to keep him at a distance. His constant care and concern for her proved to her that he was genuine in his feelings.

"I think one of the biggest parts of all this is that he is so scared about me meeting their pack." She bit down on a piece of heavenly chocolate cake.

Whenever they spoke of her meeting the pack, Connor would frown or hold her tighter as if hoping to protect her from the people she'd have to one day meet if she took them up on their offer.

"What about Theron?" Nita pressed. "How do you feel with him?"

Oh, lord of all naughty things. Theron had the sex drive of her dream man. He was rougher, tougher and wilder in bed. He wanted to do things to her she'd never even thought of. While Connor was the sweeter side of the man of her dreams, Theron was the rugged, panty-tearing biker that could fuck her raw and leave her shaking in the aftermath.

Together they made up the perfect man. Her perfect combo. But time was running out and she'd have to tell them soon if she was willing to be their mate or if they would need to continue their search for someone else.

"Tally?"

"Theron is amazing in bed. He has a fantastic sense of humor and if I could bottle the two of them up we'd have the recipe for the man every woman dreams of."

Nita slammed her cup down on the saucer. "I still don't understand what the hell your problem is!"

Tally watched her cousin glare at her for the first time in years. "What the heck, Nita?"

"No, you listen. You have two men you've described as every woman's dream, licking at your heels and ready to do your bidding. Men offering you protection, love, devotion and a relationship neither would ever do anything to damage and you still can't decide?"

She bit her lip and glanced away. Nita was right. What the hell was wrong with her? When would she ever meet two men as willing and ready to make her their life? Not anytime soon if ever.

"You're right. I'm such an idiot."

Nita grinned. "You're not an idiot. You're scared to try something new. But there's something you seem to have forgotten in your search for everything wrong with these two guys."

"What?"

"You're already in a relationship with them or they wouldn't be practically living in your house. You sleep with both of them. You have sex with both of them. Hell, you shower with one and then the other." She sniggered. "I bet you'd do both in the shower if your shower wasn't so damn small."

She flushed and glanced around. "Hey, just because I am ready to give the whole mate thing a chance doesn't mean I want the entire world in on my sex life."

"Fine, but you really need to give those men the mate they desperately need." Nita patted her hand. "They've been patient with you for almost two weeks. They need you to make a move already." Nita stared deep in her eyes. "You are not a punk, prima. You're a self-assured woman who knows what is good and what isn't. Is this good for you? Do these men make you happy? Only you know the answer to that."

She thought about Nita's questions for the rest of the day. She was right. Tally had become a good judge of what was good for her life. She knew that Connor and Theron had taken more than just an interest in all the things that made her happy. They'd turned the entire situation into a way for her to see that a relationship between the three could work.

Neither man pushed or pulled for more of her attention than she wanted to give.

They were so concerned with what she wanted that she was shocked at how much they paid attention. It caught her off guard one night when Connor showed up with a tub of her favorite ice cream. He said she'd been running low. It was her favorite when they watched TV at night. For him to notice that was beyond what she'd ever expected out of anyone.

Even Theron, the big sexual wolf had found ways to make her feel cared for when she wasn't aware of it. He'd given her hugs and kisses when they sat down doing simple things like talk. Whenever they walked anywhere, he always held her hand. It was all those little things that added to the bigger thing she'd tried to deny. Her obvious feelings for them.

Denying it wouldn't make it go away. They cared and dammit she did too. It was time to stop with the games and come out with what she knew they needed. Her answer on being their mate. They hadn't mentioned it again except the few times they spoke of her going to meet their pack. But she knew that they waited anxiously for her to make up her mind.

That evening, she got home and found dinner on the table, candles lit and wine chilling. Theron sat on the sofa watching a game while Connor read a newspaper.

She stopped at the sight of both men. Her stomach flipped when they smiled. Her heart filled with an emotion she didn't want to define just yet.

"We need to talk," she burst out.

Their smiles dimmed. They glanced at each other and back at her.

"Tally, if anything's wrong—" Connor started.

She raised a hand and cut him off. "Stop, please. I need to talk. You both need to listen."

They nodded but remained silent. She put her handbag on a chair and slipped off her heels. To help herself relax, she curled her toes into the soft beige carpet and sighed. If nothing else, the softness allowed her to take a mental breather and focus on what she wanted to say.

"Okay, so you both said you wanted to have this mating relationship with me, right?"

Dual nods again.

"And you both promised to be faithful and not look for another woman while we're together," she said, saying their words back to them. "I've made a decision. I don't know how or why you two decided I was the woman for you." She watched both, loving Theron's fierce concentration on dissecting everything she said and Connor's encouraging smile. "I'll be your mate." She cleared her throat. "That is, if you still want me."

Both men jumped to their feet.

"Of course we want you!" Theron growled.

"You are the only woman we want," Connor added.

She shifted from foot to foot, unsure what to do. Connor nodded at Theron, who marched toward her, the bright glow of his animal clear for her to see. He swept her into his arms and carried her to the bedroom.

"What are you doing?" She gasped, throwing her hands around his neck to hold on.

"We're about to make you our mate." He rubbed his face on her cheek.

"Now?" she squeaked. She hadn't expected it would happen right away. She thought there was some kind of...ritual or something that needed to happen. Like when one got married. Only shifter style. Went to show she really needed to ask more questions about their kind.

Connor followed directly behind them. He removed his clothes, dropping all articles on his walk to the bedroom. She bit her lip at the sight of his strong sexy body. He didn't have all the tattoos that Theron had. Instead, his body was pure muscled perfection. Hairless and smooth, she could lick him for hours and not need a break.

She glanced down at his fully erect cock. Her mouth watered. Damn she loved touching his body. Having him touch her. Hell, having both of them touch her was the highlight of her day. On days they both treated her like she was some kind of goddess, she went to sleep with a smile on her face. Most days, she woke up that way too.

Theron dropped her on the bed. She landed on the soft blankets with her legs spread open. Modesty had gone out the window. Connor searched through her nightstand drawer for something while Theron stripped. He was also fully aroused and so big and ready she bit her lip to keep from moaning.

"Come here," Theron ordered. His facial lines tightened but remained human. As though his animal wanted control.

She crawled toward him on the bed. When she reached the edge, he glanced at her lips, his eyes bright gold. "Are you very attached to this dress?"

She blinked. Christ that deep rough voice set her blood on fire. "Not really."

"Good." He caressed her cheek and slid his hand down her front so softly she was caught off guard by the low sound of tearing fabric.

She peeked down to see the front of her dress split open. Theron grabbed the material and slid it off her body so carefully, she almost didn't believe he'd been the one to tear it. Her bra and panties suffered the same fate. The articles of clothing were discarded and soon she was kneeling naked on the bed.

Connor came around the bed with a bottle of lube. She gulped, her hormones went into a frenzy. Theron slipped a hand into her hair and tugged her forward. He kissed her hard. Their lips and tongues melded and clashed. A struggle for dominance ensued. She no longer worried about being shy with either man. She'd allowed her inner demanding woman to come out. She took what she wanted from them. Her feelings for them had allowed her to open the door to trusting that they'd meet her needs both in and out of bed. And now she couldn't get enough of them.

Theron cupped her heavy breasts. He molded and squeezed her sensitive flesh in his calloused hands. She moaned into the kiss. He pinched her nipples, tweaking and fondling her. The hard tugs sent electrical shards straight to her clit. She was wet, throbbing. Her body burned for her two men.

He pushed her tits together and broke their kiss.

"You know I love sucking your nipples. You have beautiful tits and I love the faces you make when I suck them."

She inhaled sharply, her brain a complete mess. Her skin felt on fire. The urgent need to have them both inside her hit her so hard she lost her breath. That's what would make her whole. Both men taking her. Owning her. Making her theirs.

"Lie back, gorgeous." Theron crawled on the bed at the same time she leaned back on the pillows. She spread her legs fast. His look of pure hunger and possession only added gasoline to the raging fire inside her core.

He curled large arms around her big thighs and inhaled. "So fucking sweet. Every time I taste you it's like eating ripe berries."

Her mouth lost all moisture. Her tongue stuck to the roof of her mouth. Connor came around the bed, his eyes also glowed a bright gold.

She gasped. Theron's lips brushed her clit at the same moment Connor leaned down and kissed her. Their kiss started off light. A mere sweep of his lips over hers. Theron's tongue flicked hard from her ass up to her slit. She groaned into Connor's mouth. The sensation of Theron's thick tongue fucking her pussy sent a fresh wave of cream down her channel.

He rumbled. She slipped one hand into his hair and gripped a chunk, while she slid the other hand between Connor's legs and found his cock. She jerked him in her grasp. Her tight hold and jerk had him moaning in no time.

Theron growled while rubbing his tongue on her pussy. He licked up and down her slick folds. Up to her clit and down to her hole. Over and over. She sucked on Connor's tongue, wishing she was sucking his cock, but her brain couldn't think past the wonderful sensation of Theron's eating her pussy like he was starved and she was his final meal.

She jerked Connor, felt the wetness dripping over her hand and used his pre-cum to coat him and continue jerking. Connor pinched her nipples. She was oh so sensitive when it came to having her breasts squeezed, tweaked or fondled.

She pulled away from Connor's mouth to gasp. "Oh, my..."

Connor wouldn't be deterred. He consumed her lips once again in a hard kiss that drove his tongue deep into her mouth. He rubbed and twined his mouth over hers like a snake doing a mating dance.

Theron flicked his tongue over her clit in a quick rotation. He didn't stop. Not when she started shaking or taking hollow breaths in her kiss with Connor. Not when Connor pinched harder and she became lost in the sensations of both men playing her body like a musical instrument.

Connor licked a wet trail from her lips to her chest. He sucked one of her nipples deep into his mouth and bit down on her breast. She moaned as he did the same thing back and forth to both nipples.

Theron moved his tongue faster. His sucks turned rougher. Finally he sucked her clit into his mouth and grazed his teeth over the throbbing nerve bundle. She gasped. Choked. Both men bit down and she screamed. Tension snapped inside her as a wave of pleasure blasted from her pussy out to her limbs. She felt weightless. As if all her bones had liquefied and she couldn't even get her lungs to work.

Connor lifted her into his arms. She was still trying to take a breath when he sat down at the edge of the bed and put her in position to straddle him. She gripped his shoulders and placed a thigh to either side of him then slid down. He held his cock as she lowered to his lap. He slid his shaft back and forth, using her juices for lubrication. A breath later, he was pulling her hips down, urging her to take his dick into her slick sex.

"Oh!" She loved the feel of him stretching her pussy and rubbing her insides. She immediately started to ride him, her body ready and wet, looking for another release not too far away.

Connor leaned back, he pulled her down with him. Then Theron was there, his hand caressing the curve of her ass down to her hole.

"Do you know how we're going to claim you?" he asked.

She shook her head, a hot shudder shot down her spine.

Theron pressed his lips on the back of her right shoulder. "We're going to fuck you at the same time. Connor will be in your pussy." He groaned. "I do love your pussy. But today I get your sweet sexy backside." He grabbed handful of her large cheeks and squeezed hard. "I get to slide my cock into this tiny hole and feel you grip me tight." He licked down her spine. "Then I get to come in your ass at the same time he comes in your pussy." His voice turned deeper. Rough. "And do you know what happens after that?"

She moaned and swallowed hard. "No."

NINE

Connor continued to urge her to ride him. She loved his cock inside her. But to have them both. That was something they had yet to do. Something she'd been dying to try but hadn't suggested for fear they would reject the idea.

"After that, I get to fuck your pussy and he gets to fuck your ass and we get to do you all over again," Theron rumbled. "Until we've both had you and filled you with our seed. We'll both bite you and then you'll be ours. Nobody else could ever claim you because you will wear our scents. Our marks. You'll be ours fully."

She almost came listening to his words. Connor slid his hands up to cup her breasts and thumb her nipples.

"You are so sexy, Tally," he said softly. "Your body is gorgeous and I love being inside you."

She didn't get a chance to say anything, not that she could. Theron dropped a trail of lube down the crack of her ass. Then he worked the lube into her with one finger. She wiggled on Connor's hard cock, wanting to ride him but at the same time waited to see what else Theron would do. He added a second finger, the burning of her anal muscles increased.

"Don't tense, sweetheart," Theron whispered, pushing his fingers in and out of her. At first slow and then with increased speed and frequency. "That's right, let your muscles relax. Take my fingers."

He plunged them deep into her hole. In. Out. Then he added a third finger, the burning and stretching a lot more intense than before.

Connor attached his lips to her tit and he sucked hard. She jerked on his lap. Her pussy squeezed at his dick as she tried to pay attention to his pulsing cock and Theron's fingers. She pushed back, wanting Theron to continue the thrusting of his fingers once she got over the burning discomfort.

He pulled out and Connor moved to her other breast. He sucked her all over. Hard. Rough. So unlike him and it felt so good. She forgot all about Theron until he pushed the head of his greased up cock into her asshole. The burning started again, but not as much as before.

"Fuck," he groaned, his breath right by her ear. "You're so tight. I can hardly get in there. Relax those muscles and let me in, baby."

She pushed back. The move rocked Connor's dick in her pussy and she moaned at the sensation. Theron pressed into her ass. He slowly drove himself into her. Before she knew it, he was in her. Both men deep inside and pulsing hard.

"Jesus. Someone move or I'm going to die," she groaned.

Theron pulled back until he was almost fully out and then pushed all the way in. Not hard, but not as softly as before. She rocked on Connor's dick. Then both men took control. Connor held her up and lifted his hips to thrust into her at the same time Theron pulled back. When Theron drove into her, Connor pulled back. Both men worked with amazing speed and rhythm. She clawed at Connor's arms.

"Oh my God. Oh my God. Oh my God!" She couldn't seem to catch a breath.

Her ass and pussy clenched in tandem with both thrusts and retreats. She'd never felt anything like it. The sizzle in her womb turned into an electric spark that lit every cell in her body. She moaned. There were no words to describe how amazing it felt to be taken by both the men she wanted at the same time. A new emotion unlocked in her heart.

Theron licked the back of her right shoulder. He thrust deeper, harder. Every drive pulled a new moan out of her. Connor swept his tongue over the front of her right shoulder. Both men fucked and licked her at the same time. She could not for the life of her form a coherent sentence or thought.

Connor slipped a hand between her slick pussy lips. Right where her hard little clit peeked from its hood.

"Come on, Tally," Theron groaned on her back. "Let go, baby."

Connor thumbed the tiny bundle, slow at first and then harder. Rougher. Until she could do no more than feel the tension snap and her body shake from the almost painful orgasm that overtook her. Waves of bliss rocked her from head to toe. Theron and Connor both growled and bit down on her at the same time. She moaned. The painful bites sent her over the edge so fast she choked on the air rushing into her lungs.

Their movements turned jerky, until they stopped altogether and at first Theron growled into her back. Then Connor did the same, his teeth still biting into her front. Both men came in her then. Hot. Deep. For long moments their cocks pulsed and jetted warm semen into her ass and pussy. She couldn't have moved if she wanted to. She was held up by Theron's arm around her waist.

They fell on to their sides on the bed. Connor pulled out of her body first, then Theron slowly followed. His wet cock nestled right between her cheeks. She moaned as they both caressed her breasts, down to her waist and rained kisses all over her. From her neck to shoulders, they kissed everywhere they reached. Theron slid his hand down her side, to her breasts and fondled a nipple. Connor roamed a hand around her hip to grab a handful of her hips.

"You're ours now," Theron murmured. "There's no one else for you or us."

She sighed. She knew that already. She hadn't made the decision lightly. They might not be what she considered the traditional couple, but she'd never had luck with a traditional anything. This was a new step in her life and she had to do whatever made her happy.

Theron and Connor made her happy.

"I want inside your pussy." Theron kissed behind her ear. Goosebumps broke over her arms.

"You do?" She moaned and flipped over to face him.

He grinned, his bright golden eyes those of a predator. "Oh, baby. I always want inside your tight pussy."

"And it's my turn in your ass," Connor rumbled behind her. He slid a finger between her cheeks and into her hole. Her anal muscles sucked it right in. "Fuck that is awesome."

"I think a shower is in order first," she mumbled.

"No," they said in unison.

"Our mating process isn't over until we've both had you. Every way possible." Theron licked his lips. "Once we have, then you can have all the warm baths you want. Until then..." He pulled her head toward his and kissed her. "We fuck."

Though she wasn't used to the animalistic tones and the need for dirty sex, she definitely enjoyed having Theron and Connor inside her at the same time. That was something she'd easily grow used to.

"Fine. Fuck me. Both of you. But then you better feed me."

"Today we go visit our pack," Theron declared just two days after their mating.

"Are you sure? I mean, I thought you guys were all worried about me being around your pack women," she grumbled. She didn't like that they took turns going back and forth to deal with the Wildwoods Pack and she was often left without one of them. Though it gave her alone time with the other mate, she would like the time to be because they wanted it that way, not because they were afraid to bring her around their people.

"They'll get used to you. Or deal with me."

"What if they don't like me?" she muttered.

"Then I'll handle them."

She shook her head with a grin. "You can't fix everything for me, Theron. I have to be able to handle your pack too if they're going to be a part of my life."

"Yes, but that's what I'm there for. I'm the alpha. You're my mate. And I won't let anyone disrespect you."

"I'm more worried about you not letting me out of your sight until you've had your way with me again."

He gave her a hot look. "You have gotten to know me so well. You've gotten used to my kind of sex."

She had and boy did she love it.

"You mean the all day, every day kind?" She was still getting used to the aches from the longest night of sex ever. She'd enjoyed it, but damn had she been fucked raw. Of course, just thinking about it made her instantly wet.

"I like that smell," he said with devilish grin.

"Oh, cut it out. You do this to me every single time you look at me," she grumbled.

He sat down on the armrest of the sofa and pulled her between his legs. "I want you to always have that need for me. For us. I want you to get wet when we look at you. When anything reminds you of us. You are ours and that means we want you to want to be with us. All the time."

She sniffed. "That doesn't help me when I have to go to work, you know."

He chuckled and hugged her. She curled her arms around his neck and leaned into him.

"I know it doesn't, but you decided you wanted to continue working. We've given you the option to stop."

She shook her head. "No way am I depending on you two for money for the rest of my life. I'm an independent woman. I pay my own way in life."

He slid his hands down her back and pressed her ass forward until her pussy was flush with his erection.

"Oh, Theron, stop…"

"I won't. You are my mate and I want to fuck you every hour of every day. You have a body that makes me so hard I can't think straight."

She gave up. Heck who was she kidding? She wanted him to fuck her too. She walked back and tugged the dress over her head. He was so easy. He growled and she giggled. "Connor will be sad he missed this."

"He can have alone time with you later." Theron grinned.

That was the amazing thing about them. They both knew she needed to spend alone time with each so their individual relationships could deepen. It was what made the entire mating that much more special. She glanced down and before she knew it he threw her over his shoulder and ran for the bedroom.

"Theron!"

"You walk too slow, baby. I want to fuck now!"

She laughed as she landed on the sheets in a tangle. She didn't get a chance to fix herself when he was on her, his hands held either side of her head.

"I love you, Tally."

She gasped, her heart beat painfully loud in her ears. "Are you sure? It's so soon."

He nodded. "I don't want to hear you say the words if or until you ever feel the emotion. But I wanted you to know. You've seeped into my pores, sunk into my blood and made me an addict. I can't be without you. I don't want to be."

She blinked back tears. She didn't think Theron had those kinds of words in him. "I don't know what to say."

"Don't say anything, love." He pressed a kiss over her lips. "You're here. That's all I need."

She nodded and kissed him back. The relationship between them grew another string at that moment to make their link that much stronger. When he made love to her that day, she felt it in the deepest areas of her heart. Those areas she'd thought untouched until then.

TEN

TALLY BIT HER lip. Nerves sucked. But she didn't know how to stop herself from showing them. Theron led her into a community of houses in a forested area. It was growing late in the day. The sun's light had dimmed through the thick trees. She'd swear it was closer to nighttime than early evening.

"Theron…"

"Relax, darling. You shouldn't be afraid," he admonished.

"I'm not afraid." She truly wasn't. She was nervous. Meeting people had a bad effect on her. She tended to be sarcastic and a lot of times nerves made her babble. "I'm a little weirded out about meeting new people is all."

"Don't worry, love. We'll both be here for you."

Lovely. The fact both her men, which happened to be the leaders of this pack, were there as her babysitters didn't really give her any warm fuzzies.

"Where's Connor?" she asked just as they reached an open area where a large group gathered at the center. She stopped dead in her tracks.

There were a lot of glowing gold eyes staring at her. Instinct told her to move back. To get away from the danger, but something new and angry roared to life inside her. An emotion she'd never known she possessed spread wings and took hold of every one of her cells. Dominance.

She squared her shoulders and continued forward. No longer worried about what the people might think, now she worried about what Connor and Theron would think of her.

"Thank you all for coming tonight," Connor greeted the large group. His voice was low, so she didn't know how she could hear him so far away.

"We want to meet your new third," a woman said. She was tall. Much taller and slimmer than Tally. With beautiful porcelain skin and rich auburn hair. The woman didn't smile. She eyed Tally with open interest. "My name is Aura. What is yours?"

Tally opened her mouth but Theron answered for her.

"Her name is Talia or Tally," Theron said to Aura.

Another woman, circled by three others, moved forward. She had chocolate-brown skin and short curly hair. Almond-shaped eyes glared at Tally. "She doesn't look to be Alpha mate material."

Theron growled low. Tally almost got whiplash glancing to the side to see his partially shifted face and looming stance. "You have a problem with our choice of mate, Keya?"

The woman, Keya, continue to stare at Tally with hostility. Her eyes brightened with her animal. "Maybe. You know the rules, Theron." Keya took a step forward. The other women hovered behind her. "She can be challenged."

"Why would she be?" Theron growled. "She's our choice. It is not up for debate."

Tally's insides burned with anger. She'd never been a people person, but Keya's death-glares were making it hard for her to want to like her. Fury bubbled in her blood, growing heated and explosive with every word thrown back and forth between Theron and Keya. Her muscles burned. She blinked the group into focus, but it was hard. Her vision swam every few seconds. It was like having her pupils dilate and try to focus once again.

"She looks like a weakling," Keya spat. She took another handful of steps until she stood in the center of the clearing. People moved back to give her space. The crowd was quiet.

Tally glanced at the spot where Connor stood. She cocked her head to make out what his features tried to tell her. Then, she heard it. A distant calling to her in her mind.

"What exactly do you want, Keya? You were not a choice for us at any point." Theron's voice sounded like it was coming from under water.

"I demand a challenge for the Alpha third spot. Now," she said, her voice deep with her coming shift.

"Talia is not ready for a challenge," Theron argued.

"Too bad. You are Alpha. You know our rules. She accepts or she leaves and her position is mine," Keya said.

Theron growled next to Tally. She'd swear she could understand his growl which was absolute insanity.

Then she heard the calling in her brain again. She marched to the woman, ignoring Theron, and stopped in front of her.

"They don't want you. Don't you understand English?"

The shifter smirked and Tally's new and unusual anger flew off the handle. She slapped the other woman hard. So fast she almost wouldn't believe it had it not been for the shocked gasp that sounded around them.

"You are so dead." Keya growled and swiped a shifting claw across Tally's arm.

Fire spread across her shoulder and blood oozed down to her elbow.

"Enough!" Theron's voice thundered.

"Let them fight, Theron," Connor ordered. "You know our rules. We cannot break them for anyone. Especially our own mate. She will be fine."

Tally almost smiled at the amount of conviction in Connor's voice. She could hardly see one step ahead of her and her insides felt like they were going up in flames.

The burning in her limbs increased. Keya pushed her hard. She stumbled back and lost her footing. She twisted her body at the last second and landed on all fours.

"Look at her. How could you want her when she cannot even defend herself in her human body? Do you think she will survive my wolf?" Keya's voice grew so rough it was impossible to make out her words. "We shall see now."

Tally forgot all about Keya and her animal. She focused on the pain and spreading fire taking over her muscles.

"What is she doing?" someone asked.

"She's in pain," she heard Aura say. "She needs help. She is our new Alpha."

"No interfering," Connor commanded. "Tally will be fine."

Tally wanted to yell at him to shut the fuck up and help her. If only she could figure out what was wrong. She'd lost control of her body. Muscles shook and burned. The sound of something breaking came from so close she worried Keya had attacked her and she was too far gone to notice. Of all the people, the last person she'd think would allow her to be in pain was Connor. That big jerk.

She grabbed hold of her anger and let it grow. It expanded. Something tickled under her skin, pushing out. Then a large growl tore from her throat.

"She's—"

"Shifted," Theron said with pride.

The fact she was on all fours and in a wolf body would have to wait to be dissected at another time. Keya's large brown wolf charged to Tally. Keya was fast. She zoomed right for her, canines on full display. But Tally wouldn't let anyone, man or woman, abuse her in any form. Fuck that.

She waited until the last second, jumped to the right and turned, kicking Keya's wolf with her brand new hind legs. She kicked as hard as she could and it seemed to work. When she turned, she saw Keya's animal sliding on the dusty clearing.

"You think you can beat me?" Keya spoke through some kind of animal link.

"I am not trying to beat you. You're the one that doesn't know how to understand that Connor and Theron don't want you. Why don't you stop? It doesn't have to be this way." She tried to reason with the other woman.

"No." She growled and made a leap for Tally again. This time she managed to dig a claw right into Tally's side.

"*Fuck!*" Pain shot all down her side, igniting the fury that pushed for her change.

The wolf within wanted to be in control. There was no other way. Tally allowed the beast free rein.

It was like watching a movie. She was doing things but no longer in control. The wolf in Tally was angry, hurting and not willing to give Keya another chance to back down. She didn't try to push off the other wolf.

She went right for her. Keya appeared shocked and was caught off guard when Tally clawed at her muzzle and snatched up one of her paws in her mouth. She crunched down, breaking something in the process.

Keya scratched back. She kicked and fought to push Tally off. Her angry efforts served for Tally to release the paw and dig her claws into Keya's side. Tally bit down on Keya's tail and yanked her back.

Keya howled in pain. Another round of gasps went around the clearing. Tally's animal was bent on revenge. She eyed the other wolf as Keya tried to turn with a broken leg. Tally jumped on her back and bit down on the neck area her animal knew to go for. Keya was no longer in control. The tighter Tally squeezed her jaw on Keya's neck, the louder Keya howled.

Death and killing was not in her. She might be a bitch, bitter and angry, but she wasn't ready to take anyone's life.

"Let her go, Tally," Theron whispered softly in her mind.

"You don't have to do anything that you don't want to," Connor added.

Tally released the injured wolf and took steps back until she stood between both Theron and Connor. The wolf inside her retreated at that point and her body took control once again. Limbs shifted. Connor and Theron helped her stand in front of the crowd.

Connor wrapped a blanket over her shoulders. "Sorry about your clothes, love. But it happens when you shift. You tear through things."

She nodded. Her throat was dry and she needed a bath. A nice long hot one.

"This is our third," Theron said, his voice steely. "The next person who wants to challenge her will deal with me directly."

Aura stepped forward. "There is no need for any challenges. We have not seen a human take to the wolf so quickly and aggressively. Clearly she is the right one to help you lead."

Tally cleared her throat. Keya was dragged from the site, still in her wolf body. Tally hadn't thought someone would dislike her just because she hadn't shown enough aggression. In her human life, she'd always been told she was too aggressive and bossy. Her life had changed to something so different she didn't know if she would ever understand it fully.

The crowd glanced at her and her men. Then they tore through their clothes and shifted. The large number of wolves would have scared her at any other moment, but instead, made her curious.

"What are they doing?" she asked.

The wolves huddled close and one by one lowered their muzzles to her feet. When they were all done, they scampered into the woods.

"They were showing you their loyalty. For a wolf to lower its head, they have to feel you are the stronger party. You're their Alpha now."

It took her a moment to realize the extent of his words. She shook her head and decided she had way too much to adjust to before she thought about that.

"Show me to a shower." She wrinkled her nose. "I ache and stink."

"You got it, beautiful. After that performance you deserve anything you want." Connor winked.

"Look at you, all blood thirsty. Who would've thought you had it in you." She laughed.

TALLY SAT BACK on the picnic blanket and watched the sunset over the horizon. Theron lay to one side of her and Connor to the other. For the past few weeks, they'd given her exactly what she'd asked for and all they'd wanted was her. Nothing but her. It was time.

"I love you," she said, still glancing at the setting sun.

They sat up so fast she bit back a giggle.

"Who? Who do you love?" Theron asked.

"Tell us, please," Connor's plea tore at her heart. She shouldn't have made them wait so long. They had embraced her as their woman from the very first day and she'd been too afraid to give in and take what they offered freely.

"Both of you." She glanced at Theron and brushed her lips over his. "I love you, Theron. You and your quirky sense of humor and amazing oral skills."

"I love you, Tally." He kissed her.

She turned to face Connor. "I love you, Connor. Your ability to look deep into my heart and help me see a side of me I never knew existed is priceless. Your care and concern over my feelings is unmatched."

"I love you, beautiful Tally," Connor murmured and kissed her softly.

"You both have given me what I never realized I wanted. Two men to make me whole."

They leaned in, Theron cupping her face to kiss her mouth and Connor sliding his hands under her tank top. She'd always joked that a woman needed two men to make her happy. In her case, that was the absolute truth. Two amazing, growly, possessive men to bring out the Alpha wolf in her.

EPILOGUE

"I JUST WANTED to thank you again," Tally smiled.

Gerri couldn't have been more pleased. Something had told her that Tally would be perfect with Theron and Connor. Her instinct never guided her wrong.

"You're very welcome my dear. I only want to see you all happy," she said honestly.

Tally grinned at the men to either side of her. "We are. We're very happy. And I owe it all to you."

"Thanks Aunt Gerri," Theron said. "We'll see you next week for dinner."

She waved them away with a smile. A moment later her cell phone rang.

"Paranormal Dating Agency, how can I help you?" Gerri answered her business cell phone with a smile.

"Hi, is this Mrs. Wilder?" A woman asked hesitantly.

"Yes, it is. Who might you be?" She glanced at the open file on her desk. An unruly bear shifter who didn't want a mate but his sister was adamant he get one. The name his sister provided for the mate was a much more difficult task. A human. One she'd recently become familiar with through her neighbor.

"This is Nita, Tally's cousin. She gave me your card and said you could um...that I could use your services."

Gerri grinned. Would wonders never cease? It was perfect. A plan formed in her mind. "She told me about you, Nita. Said you were a no-nonsense type of woman."

Nita laughed softly. "Yeah, that's me. So, I am interested in seeing who you can match me up with."

"I think I can help you." Gerri picked up the address to her unsuspecting bear client. "Tell me something, do you like mountain getaways?"

"I do, but I was looking for a possible date."

Gerri picked up a pen and wrote down notes. "This definitely is a date. You'll have to travel a bit since my client is out of the city, but I know he'll just love meeting someone just as no-nonsense as him."

"Oh, wonderful! I'm more than happy to try."

"Excellent. Come by and see me. I have everything you need."

Gerri hung up with a smile. That bear had no idea what was coming. Then again, neither did the human. This would be fun.

THE END

GEEK Bearing GIFTS

book 2

PROLOGUE

"So tell me what you're looking for," Mrs. Wilder said. She placed a large tray of cookies, biscuits and coffee on the table in front of Nita Islas. Nita's hands shook a little and she swiped her sweaty palms on her pants. There was no reason to be nervous, but she couldn't stop the slight shake of her leg.

"Well..." She hesitated. How to explain? She'd had such a strange relationship with the opposite sex that there was not much there. What she looked for? More than she'd ever had. Probably ever would, but she'd try anyway.

"Come on, girl." Mrs. Wilder, clucked her tongue, motioning with a hand for her to get on with it.

This wasn't relationship analysis 101 and if that were the case, they'd need way more than a few hours, and way more than a tray of cookies. A full gallon-sized bottle of vodka would be a good start. It wasn't that she was emotionally scarred by a previous bad relationship or anything like that. That, at least, would have been a sound explanation for her problem. She was okay getting physically close, but emotions were another thing.

Mrs. Wilder took a seat across from her with a notepad, tucking her feet under her long eyelet peasant skirt. "I told you I had someone in mind for you, but I called you in to give me more details of what you're looking for."

Pulsing soreness started in the back of her head. Nice. She didn't need a migraine. All because she wanted to find a man now that her cousin Tally had fallen in love. Nita felt lonely most of the time that she spent with her cousin and the two men Tally shared her life with.

"It's not that simple." It really wasn't. She'd been shy for so much of her youth that when she finally started to accept the fact that she was never going to be a skinny girl, she'd already reached adulthood. By then she'd decided to hell with romance and just set on a path of learning about embracing her sexuality. That had been all great and good but she hadn't had any deep meaningful relationships with men other than her best friend in high school. And he didn't count.

"Let's get down to business. What are you looking for? A hookup? Two men? Marriage, babies and picket fence? Are you looking for a man to do some naughty things to you while you're tied up?"

"Mrs. Wilder!" She gasped. Damn, she hadn't expected that. All that internal brooding had made her forget Mrs. Wilder could ask some off-the-wall questions. Tally had told her that Mrs. Wilder was not the usual elderly woman, but geez.

"I don't have all day, you know. I need my beauty sleep," Mrs. Wilder said. With her new flipped bob and perfect makeup on her wrinkleless features, she was hot for whatever her age was. Mrs. Wilder followed up her words with a smile and picked up her coffee. "You strike me as a woman who knows what she wants."

Nita thought about that for a moment, panic rising in her chest. She did know what she wanted, usually. The best relationship she'd ever had with the opposite sex hadn't been sexual. It had been open. Honest. Trusting. Did that make her a freak?

"I want a man to want me for me." Hearing the words come out of her mouth made her wince. A troubled knot tightened around her heart, clasping her normal self-assurance in a vice grip. "I wasn't wanted by boys growing up. Most girls didn't want to be around the fat girl. When someone did take the time to talk to me, they wanted something, and that something was usually to make fun of me."

Except for Ky. He'd never done that. All right, she really needed therapy.

Mrs. Wilder's previous smile dropped. The color of her eyes turned a bright blue. Almost icy. Her features tightened and an animalistic noise sounded from her. "Tell me that someone stopped all that."

She nodded her head up and down like a bobblehead, worried about Mrs. Wilder getting so upset. "Yes, my mother was very active in my school. I also had some great teachers who were always watching out for me. Even an old friend that encouraged me daily."

"Okay." Mrs. Wilder breathed in deep, her face returning to her human side.

"So you see, I want a man that will be interested in me as a person. Not just for sex. Not for money, which I don't have. Not for whatever he might think he can get out of me. I want to be wanted for the woman inside. And I sure as hell want to be wanted sexually too."

Mrs. Wilder cocked her head to the side, staring at her with her soulful eyes. "Darling, there are many sides to you. Your beauty, your body, your wit, your abilities at work. What do you want to focus on if anything in particular?"

She leaned back on the sofa, the seat dipping under her butt. The leather squeaked with the weight of her body. "I want more than sex. Don't get me wrong, sex is great."

Mrs. Wilder snorted, her eyes turned bright with amusement. Her lips twisted in a smirk and a small dimple showed on her right cheek. She appeared even younger when she smiled. "Sex is amazing when done correctly. Especially if he can figure out how to be all alpha and make your legs shake."

Oh, damn! She choked on the cookie she'd taken a bite of, chocolate spewing from her lips with each cough. She picked up a napkin and tried to clear her throat. Mrs. Wilder was a freak.

"Right. Yes, I'm not saying I don't want hot sex. Hell, I'd love some hot sex. I haven't had good sex in a long time," she mumbled, feeling all kinds of uneasy after saying that to Mrs. Wilder.

Mrs. Wilder raised her brows high. Her blue eyes went into a dark sapphire color and there was a hint of confusion in them. "I thought you wanted more than sex?"

Great. Now she wasn't just confusing herself with all this, poor Mrs. Wilder looked like she was ready to pull her hair out. "I want to be able to connect with someone more than physically. I want to feel the comfort of having that…"

"That?" Mrs. Wilder asked, her gaze probing.

How to explain it? "That feeling like you're meant for each other. That there are no secrets between you. I want a relationship, I don't want a booty call."

"Okay!" Mrs. Wilder exclaimed and then wrote in a leather notebook. "Now we're getting somewhere. No booty calls for Nita." She glanced up from the notebook. "I do hope you will want sex once you establish this man is right for you?"

"Um, yes."

She thought back to her last boyfriend, if she could call him that. They'd met up whenever, had dinner or drinks and sex. The memory of their sex made her flinch. Nothing to write home about. Though he'd tried to breach the distance she'd always placed between them, eventually he gave up. That's how it always happened. She needed to be with someone who brought trust and comfort out in her so she didn't have her guard up.

"So why is it so hard for you to find the right man?" Mrs. Wilder tossed the question out of left field.

Boy, when she hit with a question, she hit hard. "I don't know."

Mrs. Wilder rolled her eyes. For an old lady, she had a very youthful and bitchy personality. She reminded her of her cousin Tally.

"Yes, you do," Mrs. Wilder declared, her voice more assertive than that of Nita's worst high school teacher.

Talk about bossy. If she weren't so hopeful that she would match her to a halfway decent guy, she wouldn't be there talking about sex with a woman as old as her mom. "All right, it's because I refuse to get too emotionally attached. Plus most of my past boyfriends said I'm kind of distant," she grumbled, breaking the cookie on her plate into tiny crumbs. "Whatever that means."

"It means you need to let shit go and open your heart to love," Mrs. Wilder said, point blank. "Are you willing to do that? Take a chance on a good guy. If you don't, you won't ever find what you're looking for."

Shit. The old woman was right. She knew it too. That smug smile on her lips said it all. Mrs. Wilder had just pointed out Nita's biggest issue and it was up to her now to fix it.

"I can do it." Even if it killed her. She didn't want to live in the meaningless sex realm any longer. She wanted love. Emotions. She wanted happiness. Ah, what the hell, she wanted marriage and babies too.

"Then I think my first choice for you is probably the right one." Mrs. Wilder grinned.

ONE

"So tell me again, where you're going?" Tally asked from her side of the phone line, her voice loud and clear bounced around the interior of the car through the Bluetooth connection.

Nita glanced at her rearview mirror for the millionth time and sighed. She grimaced, ready to lie to her cousin even though she didn't want to. She hated lies with a passion. In fact, just the thought of lying to Tally made her stomach burn with discomfort. She knew she was a sucky liar, so she preferred not to do it. Plus, lies always got people in trouble. Every single time.

It wasn't that Tally would judge. Not at all. But she already felt like an idiot because she was thinking of going out of her way to go on a date with one of the shifters from Mrs. Wilder's Paranormal Dating Agency.

She'd allowed herself to be roped into a multiple day date. Not that she'd ever heard of one of those before. Nor ever done it in her life. The acid in her stomach burned up to her throat. She should have eaten something before her drive, but excitement had made it impossible. Mrs. Wilder had been very particular about keeping details of who her date was concealed. When she finally gave her the details, Nita'd been ready to hit the road for the mountains.

"I don't want you to have any preconceived notions going in," she'd said. "This is something new and you're both going to have to trust my judgment."

Trusting her judgment had strangely been easier than she would've expected. Maybe it was her hope for Mrs. Wilder to be right. Her words had told her one thing. Unlike Tally, she'd be getting one date and not two. Which was okay with Nita. She didn't think she had the patience to deal with two growly Alpha males.

"I'm just going to have a mini vacation for a few days," she lied. If all went well, she'd have a few days with a guy that might be the man of her dreams. Or a match made in hell. Whatever the deal, she'd only brought a few days' worth of clothes so she had an excuse to leave should she need it. Besides, she had a full week of Shark Week and Naked and Afraid on her DVR that she'd yet to watch.

She winced. She'd have to remember to make sure not to mention that to her date. The last guy she'd gone out with had given her a laundry list of reasons why watching any reality show was going to destroy all her smart brain cells. She'd wanted to tell him that his rant had killed any semblance of sexual spark in her. Other than the amazing drinks the bartender kept bringing her way, the date had been more uncomfortable than a visit to a new GYN.

She had high hopes for this new guy though. Mrs. Wilder had been so excited to match her up it had given Nita a big ego boost.

Apparently there were men out there who liked really curvy Latinas with a chocolate addiction and a bit of a sarcasm problem. Who knew?

"You do not leave your doctor without an assistant. Ever. So this is just...not normal," Tally replied, her tone sharper than usual with what sounded like worry.

Nita could imagine her cousin frowning as she spoke on the other end of the line. Tally knew her better than anyone. Nita was happy to have a good time any time, but when it came to her job, she had a strict 'no fucking up rule'.

"I need a little break. Sometimes it's good to take a few days to just eat ice cream, watch bad TV and wear PJs all day." Nita laughed, hoping Tally would think she was being honest. Though all those things sounded damn good to her. Maybe she would go home and do them all if her date went to shit.

"Yeah, I guess." Tally didn't sound convinced.

A glance at her GPS told her she had another half hour drive. In the quiet frickin' lone stretch of road. Nighttime fast approached. She should've made it a daytime date. But she'd been so damn excited about going on a date with a shifter, she'd forgotten all about her fear of the dark.

Thankfully, she always carried around pepper spray in her bag. Not because she liked drama or fights, but because she didn't want to ever be caught unaware by anyone. She lived in a dangerous city. Anything could happen.

"Besides, you, Connor and Theron are busy getting to know each other. You don't need me hanging around like a fourth wheel."

Tally gasped. "Nita Islas! How could you even say something like that? You're not a fourth wheel!"

Yeah, right. She definitely felt like a fourth wheel whenever they met up at a restaurant or for some drinks. Connor and Theron were all over

Tally. She wasn't jealous of her cousin. Hell, she was so happy she could squeeze the two men to bits. It was the fact she didn't have anyone in her life worth a smile that made it so difficult. Goddammit! She wanted her own man all over her groping her ass like they were teenagers on a first date.

"Have you called Mrs. Wilder?" Tally suddenly asked.

"Um..."

Tally growled on the other end of the line. "Why won't you do it already? I really think it could be helpful for you."

Again, she wasn't keeping things from Tally. She loved Tally more than most of her family, other than her parents and her grandma Kate. It's just that with her past relationship having turned into something out of the Twilight Zone, Nita didn't want to talk about anything without knowing where it was going first.

"I'm going to trust her to find me a man. I promise." She was going to hell in a limo at this point. Where were the antacid pills when she needed them? Lying to her best friend was bad. But Tally loved her. That made things that much worse.

"Okay. As long as you try." Tally said something so softly Nita didn't make it out. "I'm going to have to go now. We're about to go out to dinner and a show."

That was another thing. How in the hell did Tally end up with the best of both worlds? Hot men who did everything she wanted and amazing sex. Nita had never had it that good. The closest she'd come was the bear best friend in high school. Ky. And even though she hadn't cared about his features, he'd been a good-looking guy. He'd been so shy she'd had to make sure their friendship never turned weird by telling him how much she liked him. Her extra limb is what Nita's mom had called him. Wherever she went, he went.

For her entire sophomore year of high school he'd been her rock. There had been things they didn't discuss, like guys or girls. He got a bit growly at her mention of him finding a girlfriend. Not that she wanted him to go out there and find anyone who would take too much of his attention. It's just that Nita had been a big girl since she was born.

It wasn't that she ate unhealthy foods, though she had a sweet tooth that would make any baker delighted. She ate normal and exercised regularly with her dad. She was just big. The last thing she expected was for anyone as cute as Ky to ever notice her. She'd had insecurity issues as a kid. Major ones with a side of shyness.

In order for her to finally accept that she needed to embrace her body because it was the only one she had, she'd ended up going to therapy. It didn't end there. There was a mass of dieticians with meal and exercise plans. Her mother also took her to various health professionals that worked alongside her to help grow Nita's self-esteem.

After a few years, she finally learned to love her body. Once she did, it was so much easier— and fun —to be sexy and sensual. It stopped being uncomfortable for her to wear the sparkly short skirts and some of the tops that plunged and showed off her abundant cleavage. She was a new person. All because she stopped hiding behind what others thought and allowed herself to be Nita Islas, curvy Latina.

By the time she had found herself, learned to love Nita and stop letting haters take her self-esteem, she'd moved away from Ky. Her heart ached for her old friend. She could only hope he found some way to outgrow his own shyness and embrace the handsome geeky guy inside.

It was already dark by the time she reached the cabin. She hoped her host hadn't waited too long. A peek at her dashboard clock said she was only half an hour late. Damn it. A stickler for time, she hated being late. Especially when she knew how much of an impact keeping correct times made in her life. She glanced down at her wrinkled ankle pants and pretty but not overtly sexual purple top. Then she lifted her arms and sniffed to make sure she didn't stink. Nope. All was good there. Since she knew how sensitive shifter senses were, she had decided to opt for a light perfume.

She pulled out a tube of cherry lip gloss out of her bag and popped two breath mints. It wasn't a shower and toothpaste, but that's as good as it was going to get. With a quick, deep breath, she hopped out of her Prius and hiked to the cabin. Fall fast approached and that meant the temperature was just perfect for being outside without sweating bullets. She hoped her date liked walks.

Her heart started to hammer hard in her chest the closer she got to the door. What if he wasn't right with her? What if Mrs. Wilder had made a mistake? Fuck it. She kicked the kernel of insecurity in the ass and knocked on the door. The knock pushed the door slightly open.

"Hello?" she called out into the homey interior. She wasn't trying to get into the guy's life, but he had a place built for comfort. Large brown leather sofas with pretty gold and yellow decorative pillows sat in the living room.

She pushed the front door open some more. Maybe he couldn't hear her. Did she really want to date a shifter that was hard of hearing? Tally had told her they were known for their wonderful sensitive hearing. Figured, she snorted. Her date would probably end up being an old, hard-of-hearing shifter who probably couldn't shift. Now Mrs. Wilder's words made sense about having preconceived ideas of him. Dear God! What if he couldn't get it up?

"Oh, hell no!" she said through gritted teeth. The guy wasn't home for their date. He probably forgot her. Her temperature rose with her anger. How could he not be home and leave his door open? Nobody in the city did that. Curiosity made her take another step inside and call out again, "Anybody home?"

She wasn't really breaking and entering since she'd been invited there. At least she hoped using that as an excuse when her date showed up worked.

She moved deeper into the large cabin. It smelled delicious. Like someone had been cooking all day. That calmed her some. The cabin was big. What if he couldn't hear her from wherever he was? Pitchers filled with fresh wild flowers sat at every table. Still no sign of her host. Maybe he'd gone out to run an errand. If that was the case, why was there a massive Jeep parked in front? It made no sense to her.

She strolled through the cabin with caution, but still managed to ogle every beautiful piece of carved furniture.

His dining room table was gigantic with enough chairs to sit her entire family and then some. She started making up a story in her head about her date. He had so many children and grandchildren that he had to have a big table. He had to be really old at this point. Like ancient. Nita tried not to giggle, considering her date had clearly forgotten she was coming. It was obvious between the two of them that she'd been the only one excited for their date.

"Hello?" she yelled louder. Nothing.

The scent of food drifted from the open kitchen. She strolled into the space and bit back a moan. Christ. If there had ever been a kitchen made with lots of cooking in mind, this was it. Whoever picked the cabinets had done an amazing job. They were made of a beautiful wood that blended the inside with the outdoors. It was the huge stove and two double ovens that made Nita's mouth water. She loved baking. It helped her relax. Not that she was as good as Tally or Mrs. Wilder, but she hadn't killed anyone so far. Seeing this kitchen was heaven. Her date had already earned brownie points in her book and he wasn't even there.

She stalked closer to the huge refrigerator and almost tripped on something. A pair of feet. She gasped. "What the hell?"

Rounding the corner in a flash, she lost her breath at the sight of the large man sprawled on the shiny wood floor of the kitchen. He was so big that she stood there for a second, unsure what to do. Something clicked in her head and she moved closer. Once she reached him, she kneeled beside the man's face, which was turned to the side. She tried not to gawk, but it was impossible.

He lay there, in nothing but a towel, his muscled body displayed for her to view. And touch...if she dared. That was so wrong. So very wrong. But he was passed out. One tiny feel of his six pack wouldn't really be so bad, would it?

"Bad Nita! This guy needs your help, not for you to drool over his passed out body." She gently turned his head to face her. Air caught at the back of her throat. He was frickin' gorgeous. The hair on his chest wasn't so thick that she could still make out the muscles underneath it. Her throat went dry. Her palms itched to touch him and see how smooth he'd feel. She imagined running her nails over him and grazing them down to his innie belly button. Even that was sexy. Her gaze shot down to where the towel hung precariously over his hips, the sides having slid over to reveal his muscular and slightly hairy thigh.

Dear God! Without a doubt she was going to hell. If not hell at least somewhere she would be punished for lusting after a passed out, possibly dead, mountain man. How long had it been since the last time she had had sex that she was now mentally licking this poor man while he lay there needing help.

She raised a trembling hand to his neck to feel for a pulse. He was alive. Thank you God! This was probably the first time she'd ever given a silent prayer that a first date wasn't really avoiding her.

"Hello?" calling softly to him, she cupped his face in her hands. There was a large gash on the other side of his head and blood matted his hair. She should call 9-1-1 and stop feeling on the guy. Darn it, but she couldn't help herself. She tried to tap his face, but ended up sliding her fingers over his scruffy jaw. Yep. She was a pervert. Taking advantage of a man down. That ticket to hell was now first-class on the fastest jet known to man.

A soft groan sounded from the big guy.

"Wake up, sleeping beauty." She couldn't help herself. Should she kiss him? That would probably only add to her list of infractions in the book 'What Not to Do with a Passed out Stranger'.

She was dying to see his eyes. She knew they'd be spectacular. Sure enough, a few blinks and his long thick lashes fluttered open to a piercing stare. He lifted a hand to the one she had on his cheek and covered it with his own.

Oxygen froze in her lungs. His eyes might be hazel, but there was something about him that told her she knew him. She couldn't know him. She'd never have forgotten someone this big. This sexy. This— Shit! This naked!

She swallowed hard at the nerves knotting in the back of her throat. "Hi."

Sexy man licked his lips and winced. Fuck. For someone who worked in the medical field she was acting like an amateur. His head probably hurt and there she was feeling on him like a sex-starved maniac. Probably breaking some laws in the process.

Ky Stone's bear rumbled for him to wake up. The soft, sexy scent of the mate he'd long ago given up filled his lungs. Another rumble from the bear and the fog slowly dissipated. The scent of his mate grew stronger still. The bear pushed for a shift, but even though he wasn't fully awake, Ky was in control. Another rumble and the bear made his muscles ache with the strength of his power. He wanted out. Now.

Hold on.

He'd let the bear roam soon. Right now he needed to open his eyes and deal with the world. Except, he couldn't find it in him to let go of the scent growing more powerful by the second. Nita.

So he lay in the half-aware state if only to hold on to her scent a little longer. Only problem was the bear's loud roar inside was hard to tamp down.

The animal was angry. So was Ky. His head hurt and he knew someone had come in and hit him from behind when he'd been arguing with his sister over her matchmaking ways. She'd called to tell him she'd set him up on a blind date. Without his knowledge. Knowing Jess, she must have thought he'd hung up on her, angry over what she'd done when the call had gotten cut off.

He didn't need or want any female. The one he'd known long ago belonged to him. Back then he'd been a gangly teen with braces. He'd also had a massive case of shyness around Nita. Her beautiful smile and sparkling brown eyes had made him tongue-tied more times than he could count.

"Wake up, Sleeping Beauty." He heard her voice now. Shit. He must have been hit hard enough that he was hallucinating.

Why would the world be so cruel as to do that to him? He hadn't seen or heard from her in almost seventeen years. Not that he hadn't had women in that time. He was no saint. But he knew as well as his bear that Nita was the one for them.

He took a deep breath and her scent, sexy and warm, along with some flowery perfume, filled his lungs. If this was a hallucination he needed serious help. Fuck help, he wanted to savor every second of it.

Then he felt the slight touch of her fingers over his jaw, caressing him so lightly he thought he might have imagined it too. Except the bear wouldn't imagine it. He roared under his skin. The animal pushed to get out and be near her.

Quiet!

His bear wouldn't listen, though. Another rumble sounded from the animal. If she wasn't a hallucination, she'd hear his bear soon.

TWO

Ky opened his eyes to an older, much more beautiful Nita. She leaned over him. Her hair, long ago, held in a curly ponytail, now fell straight in a long mass. He met her gaze and watched her pupils dilate. Arousal. A slow smile crept over her full lips. A stream of light from the kitchen lamp covered her head in a halo.

"Hi. I'm Nita Islas."

Jesus. He wasn't hallucinating. She was real flesh and blood. She was in his house touching him. What the fuck had he missed?

He tried to sit up, but she pushed him down.

"Don't move, there's a gash on the side of your head. You're Kyer Ash, right?"

Why was she using his full first name and half of his last name? Nobody called him Kyer, Ash-stone or Ash. He was Ky Stone since he was a ten year old that got sick of being picked on because of his slim weight and name. "Yes, that's me. Just call me Ky."

A pretty rose color swept over her cheeks. "Hi, Ky. I'm sorry I'll call 9-1-1. I just got distracted...trying to make sure you were alive."

"No. No need to call anyone." He couldn't figure out why she was lying about making sure he was alive, but when she bit her bottom lip he realized he didn't really care. It was his Nita. And she was there.

"What are you doing here?" he asked, dying to know.

Her brown eyes went wide. "Oh, my gosh! Maybe that hit to your head was worse than I thought. Did you forget our date?" She lifted a perfectly manicured hand and held two fingers up. "How many fingers am I holding up?"

"Two."

"Times what?" she asked, a worried pitch in her voice.

If she hadn't appeared so concerned, he'd have laughed at the ridiculous question. "One?"

She blinked in clear shock. "You don't know your times table or were you guessing?"

Jesus. She of all people knew that he knew his times table backward, forward and squared.

He pushed up to a sitting position but didn't push away her hand. In fact, he moved closer to her. The bear rumbled softly. He liked what Ky had done. Sly bear.

"We had a date." It wasn't a question. It was a statement. Now he knew why his sister had been so excited about his date. She'd found Nita.

Nita nodded. One thing bothered him. She wasn't looking at him like she knew him. In fact, why wasn't she saying anything about their past?

"Yes. But under the circumstances. I am more than happy to postpone." She grabbed his arm and helped him to his feet. He leaned closer to her, bringing his body flush against her soft curves and then faked a flinch.

She curled her arms around his abs in an effort to offer more support. He might feel like an ass tomorrow, but right now he'd take her touch and enjoy it.

"Don't go," he rumbled. The bear, so close to the surface, made his voice deeper.

She offered her physical support to help him to the breakfast table he usually ate his meals at unless someone from the clan showed up with a problem. Being chief of the Stone Clan meant he dealt with issues all the time. Mainly over other clans in the area wanting to feed at their lake.

"Don't worry, big guy. I'll stay until I'm sure you won't pass out again," she whispered the words, her breath caressing his neck. It was hard to think past the pain in his head. To make matters worse, she inhaled, brushing her nose over his jaw. His cock went rock-hard.

He sat down and drank in the vision of his mate. The sole woman to make his bear and the man he was, whole. The aching gape in his chest filled with hope. Then it occurred to him, she didn't remember the geeky teen with glasses, bad haircut and braces. The image of him as a super skinny kid with clothes that fell off his gangly body wasn't really going to get in his way. He could seduce Nita as the man he was now. Bigger. Stronger. Self-assured.

He was the Chief of the Stone Bear Clan. He knew his body had changed. He knew women wanted him. Hell, watching lust flare in Nita's eyes while he'd been on the floor had been unreal. He didn't have the self-esteem issues now that he did back when he wanted to ask her to the movies but ended up offering to tutor her instead. Though that had been one of the best mistakes he'd ever made.

The time they'd spent together had been better than any single date. Going to the movies wasn't going to tell him how much she loved watching TV with her feet curled under a blanket. It didn't matter what they saw, she'd always hide her feet. Nor would he have found out that she moaned when she ate her favorite brand of ice cream. Much to his discomfort.

He would have never seen the smile of happiness when she told him of the latest book she read and how much she loved it when the hero and heroine ended up together and happy. All those and dozens of other regular everyday things he'd learned from tutoring her and spending a lot of time as her friend.

She glanced around his kitchen then back at the right side of his face. "Let me get something to clean that with." She rushed to the sink and wet a dish towel before returning back to him to wipe blood off his head. He didn't bother telling her the wound was almost healed. Nor did he explain he wasn't so much in pain as he was angry over the hit. Whoever had done it would be found out. Then they'd regret it.

They'd knocked him out at the worst possible time. He'd been arguing with Jessica over setting him up. Now that he thought about it, his bear had been agitated right before he was hit. If he'd paid attention to his animal's anger, he'd have known something was going on. But instead he'd been angry over Jess's matchmaking. How could he ever find the words to thank her for bringing Nita into his life again?

He reeled back when her hand caressed under his ear.

"I'm sorry, did that hurt?"

Hell fuck no! It felt damn amazing and he wanted her to do it again. She thought he moved back from pain. It had been a pure jolt of pleasure that blasted him and caught him unaware.

"No. It's okay," he mumbled the words out.

Curling his hands into fists, he tried to stop the urge to pull her over his lap and kiss her. To finally touch her lips to his and see how it would feel. He'd been dreaming of that day for almost seventeen years. Knowing she was there now was a shock to his system.

She moved back and forth in his kitchen like she belonged there. Who was he kidding? She did belong there. With him as his mate. He was having a hard time keeping the tongue-tied teen out of his mind and figuring out how to talk to her like the man he'd become. A leader. A chief. Someone who knew his own sex appeal. This was Nita. His Nita. He didn't want to sweet talk her like any other female. He wanted what he'd always wanted from her. Her love.

"How's your head?" she asked, rinsing the towel for the third time, her hips swinging with her movements. She was so sexy. So sensual. That outfit, though proper, had fueled every dirty fantasy he had ever had and multiplied it. The tight pants molded to her curvy hips and showed off her ass beautifully. Her purple top was cut low up front for a mouth-watering display of her breasts.

"Um..."

She'd never dressed this way as a teen. All her clothes had been so large and covered her up, he'd never really had a chance to lust over her like he did now. All those curves. Wide at the hips and narrow at the waist with enough to grab on to when he drove deep into her. *Fuck fuck fuck!* He should not be thinking of sex now. Not now.

"Still hurting, huh?" She scrunched up her nose and gave him a sympathetic smile. "I'm sorry. So what happened? Did you slip and fall or something?"

"Something all right." He cleared his throat. He couldn't go into details with her. Not when he didn't know what the hell happened. He'd definitely be finding out soon though. Growling sounded from where she stood.

"Tell me you didn't hear that," she said, her cheeks tinged red with embarrassment.

"I did." He scrubbed a hand over the back of his neck. "Your stomach is trying to tell me what a horrible host I am."

She groaned and widened her eyes. "You're not! You were hurt."

"I'm sorry." He found his manners. "Are you hungry?" The sound her stomach made and the fact she kept eyeing the food his sister had come over and cooked earlier told him she needed something to eat soon. If Nita was anything like she'd been as a teen, she would get cranky when hungry.

"I guess I must be. The drive wasn't long, but I was so busy all day I didn't get a chance to eat anything." She grinned and handed him the clean towel.

"Let me grab some clothes really quick and we'll eat."

"But your head—"

"Is fine. I'll be back in a second," he said and stood. He marched to his bedroom and threw some clean clothes on only to rush back to the kitchen.

She shoved him back in his seat. "Here. You sit, hold this," she said, handing him the washcloth once again. "Tell me where everything is and I'll bring the food to you."

Nita had always been a nice person, caring and considerate of those she felt deserved it. She'd always covered that with a layer of insecurity that kept most people at bay. He'd never seen the self-assurance in her as a kid that he saw now.

He pointed to a cupboard. "Plates are in there. Utensils are in the drawer by your left hand."

In no time, the food was on the table and she was helping serve it. He would have felt bad if not for the fact he really loved watching her move around his kitchen. Okay, she could've stayed in one spot and he'd still have been staring at her like a love-sick fool.

"How's the head?" she asked before starting to eat.

He glanced down at his plate instead of staring at her lips for the billionth time. He should be over his geek boy ways. Well, most of them. He still wore glasses as a human when his contacts irritated him. As a bear, his vision was good enough that he didn't have to worry about his sight. Besides, he'd never live it down if his clansmen saw him in his bear with a pair of black framed glasses on.

"I'm fine. Really. It wasn't a big deal but thanks for your concern." He reached out a hand and placed it over hers.

Her gaze shot down to his large hand covering hers. "It looked pretty bad but maybe it was all the blood. You sure you don't need a doctor?"

He brushed his thumb over the top of her hand. "No doctor. I'd never live it down if my clan knew I went for a tiny scratch like that."

"You must be a bleeder." She stared at his mouth and his blood traveled south.

He gripped the spoon tight enough to bend it and attempted a smile. "No. I'm a bear. I heal faster than others."

"Of course!" She laughed, her top dropping a fraction lower to show more of her cleavage. He shouldn't be staring at her chest, but he was a geek, not an idiot.

"I should have known that's why you stopped bleeding and your wound appeared to have healed before my eyes."

He didn't tell her the wound had been bad at first, but his bear had been huffing and roaring him back to health. During the moments he'd been unconscious, the bear had quickly pushed for him to come to his senses. That link between man and animal had saved his life more than a few times.

"What did you think I was?" From what Jess told him, the site she'd used to set him up with was a Paranormal Dating Agency and so Nita should have known he was not human.

She shrugged. "I didn't stop to think about it, to be honest."

The right side of her top slid down her shoulder to reveal a purple polka dot studded bra strap. Fucking hell. Why did fate torture him with glimpses of her undergarments? What he wanted to do was tear all her clothes off. His cock ached and she'd been there for all of a few hours. By the end of the night he'd have blue balls.

"I guess I was so caught up in you being passed out and bleeding that I didn't focus on the fact you can probably heal faster than I can from a paper cut." She smiled, her eyes sparkling with mischief. "Don't tell me what really happened was that you fainted."

He roared a laugh. She was still just as funny as she'd been back in high school. "Do I look like a fainter?"

She lifted the iced tea to her lips and took a swallow. He watched her throat work. He knew he was in serious trouble when that turned him on. She lowered the glass slowly and he was put through the torture of watching her lick the remaining drops of her drink from her lips. Dammit he had to struggle the bear back. Ky wanted her. Now.

"No, you don't. But trust me when I tell you I have seen bigger men than you cry and scream at the sight of blood. Some have outright fainted when they saw a needle."

He frowned at her words. "Are you a doctor?"

She shook her head, laughed and pulled her hand out of his. "I'm going to need this to eat."

"You could always break a record for one-handed eating."

She grinned. "Not in this lifetime. This stew looks divine. No way in hell I'm going to struggle eating with one hand. You might be cute, Mr. Bear, but I am a hungry girl."

Did she call him cute? Never had Ky loved hearing those words from a woman more than he did at that moment. He didn't want for her to see what a big deal it was, so he laughed it off. "Hey, your loss. That is pretty big in some parts of the world. I bet the Guiness Book of World Records people would be marveled. Fastest time for one handed-eating of stew might be a popular one. You never know."

"Riiiight." She slipped her spoon into the stew, inhaled and groaned. "This smells better than it did when I walked in."

Thank god for Jess and her love of making the seafood stew. She knew that was his favorite. He'd thought that she'd come over to sweeten him up like she usually did when she wanted him to release some of the money from her trust. His younger sister was too rash to handle her own money and she knew it. That didn't mean she wouldn't have moments of weakness where she wanted to go on massive shopping sprees and begged him to loosen the purse strings.

"Yeah. It will taste amazing too," he said, digging his spoon into the delicious meal his sister had made. The scent of spices and fish made the bear inside him growl with hunger.

"Gotta love a man that is so confident in his cooking." She chuckled and slid the spoon between her lips.

He held his breath as he watched her close her eyes and do the adult version of the moans he'd seen her do while eating ice cream as a teen. "Oh...my...God! This is so good!"

Hot damn! His throat went dry all over again and he had a hard time remembering to breathe. "I told you it was amazing."

She blinked. Like she'd just remembered he was there. And slowly swiped her tongue over her bottom lip. "Yeah. I should've listened to you. You're a great cook."

His heartbeat pounded in his chest so hard he worried she could hear it. He wanted badly to take her compliment for himself, but he wasn't going to lie about it. "My sister did the cooking. She came over earlier to surprise me."

Nita's slow lift of her lips into a sassy smile made his heart trip. "What a great sister. Was she worried you'd scare me off with your cooking?"

He shook his head, noticing how easy their conversation was. Things between them felt like they'd never been apart. Even with her not remembering him. "No. She worried I'd feed you grilled fish and vegetables. According to her it's the only decent thing I can make."

Nita snorted, biting her lip. He saw her struggle to keep a straight face. "I don't believe you. A big guy like you has to eat more than that."

He loved the playful look in her eyes. That twinkle did what so many dates in the past never had: it made him smile. It was like old times but better. "I am also very adept at making peanut butter and jelly with bananas."

"Oooh! My favorite." She lowered the spoon and picked up a piece of bread. "A man after my heart."

He'd never forgotten her favorite snack. Nita and those sandwiches, along with the memories of his time with her, were the reason he'd make some. Just to think of her.

"What made you hire a dating agency?" she asked, chewing the piece of bread so slowly he became entranced in watching her jaw movement.

"Nothing. I didn't hire the dating agency." He licked his lips and glanced down at his bowl. His food had disappeared but he didn't remember consuming any of it.

"So how did we end up here?"

The temperature in the kitchen rose the longer he watched her eat. Her breath hitched every few bites like she couldn't stop herself from enjoying the meal.

"My sister set it up." Much to his frustration at first. Now, though, he couldn't be happier and planned to express his gratitude by hugging his sister to bits.

She met his gaze. There was a question in her eyes and a flash of insecurity. He decided to reassure her. "I'm happy she did, though."

Her smile warmed him from the inside. "I'm glad I used the agency too."

THREE

Nita had butterflies in her stomach. When was the last time that happened? Other than the few times Ky had brushed his hand over hers back in high school? Never. Men had come and gone and none had made her feel all kinds of sweaty and slightly dazed with just their conversation.

She couldn't believe how nice and funny her date was. The more she spoke to him and stared at his gorgeous face, the more she swore she'd seen him somewhere before. It was his eyes. Something about the hazel color going back and forth from green to gold was driving her to distraction.

She opened her mouth to ask him about his childhood when someone strolled into the kitchen.

"Hey, Chief. I smell food," a man said, stopping short at the sight of her and her date smiling over empty plates.

"Liam, what are you doing here?" Ky asked, his tone not so much brusque but surprised.

Liam was a big guy with short dark hair and a light scruffy beard similar to the one Ky had. The only difference was that Ky had golden spiky hair and hazel eyes that still had her knees jellified. Ky also had a thousand watt smile with perfect teeth. Then there were his lips. Lord almighty, she couldn't wait to kiss them.

Liam's surprise turned into a knowing smile after a moment. He folded his large arms over his plain black T-shirt and shrugged.

"Jess called. She asked me to come over and see you. She didn't elaborate. I took it to mean you were in the middle of piling up some firewood for your den and needed help."

"I'm fine. I don't need help," Ky said. He stood, taking the empty bowls and placing them in the sink. The clinking of spoons and glass the only sound in the kitchen for moment. "Liam, this is Nita. Nita, Liam."

"Nita?" Liam's eyes widened with surprise.

"Yes. Nice to meet you, Liam. But..." Nita grinned at Liam. "I think he needs to see a doctor to have that wound checked."

Liam's smile disappeared. "Wound?"

"I'm fine," Ky replied. "We'll discuss it later."

Liam's brows lowered in a fierce scowl. A low growl sounded from where he stood. "I understand."

"I'm really sorry, Ky. I just think you should seek a professional medical opinion. You could have done some damage we're not aware of. Head wounds are very dangerous."

Ky stopped piling plates in the sink and turned to her. She thought he might be angry over her words, but instead, he grinned at her as if she'd said something funny.

"Thank you for your concern. It is incredibly humbling."

Wow. His smile when he said that was so sexy and his eyes turned a dark forest green. Fire curled into a ball in her belly and air caught in her lungs. Hell. Her heart did little flips in her chest.

"I should go then," Liam offered.

"No!" What the hell was she doing? "Please, stay."

Yes. She needed Liam to stay or she might do something bad. At her age. She needed a chaperone. This was going too well and she didn't want to mess it up by getting naked too soon. Naked could be good though, real good. She continued to chastise herself for not tugging on the towel while he'd been passed out. At least lifting a corner or something. It's not like he would've known.

There was something about Ky that reminded her of someone. She snorted internally. If he weren't so big, she might have said he reminded her of the other Ky, her high school friend. As it was, this Ky was enormous. With that sexy as sin beard and, holy molasses, all those muscles. She needed Liam to stay or she might climb Ky like a tree. Probably hump him like a dog too.

"Are you sure?" Liam asked, glancing at Ky for a moment.

"Yes," she replied. She turned to glance out the kitchen window. "It's late and the cabin I'm staying at isn't far from here so I should go."

"You don't have to go," Ky was quick to reply. "I have a guest cabin."

She grinned, a sense of happiness expanding in her chest. He wanted her to stay. Not that she wanted to go, but seeing his instant offer made her feel they were going in the right direction. "I know. That's where I'm staying. Did you forget that part too?"

Liam's loud chuckle filled the kitchen. It amused her to see a flush of color cover Ky's pale cheeks. He was so damn cute. Cute with a body she could do some dirty things to. She wanted to strip him down to nothing and lick him from head to toe. Shit. Her thoughts had turned sexual. Not good. Pretty soon she'd start visualizing him naked. Big buff bear in all his growly glory. Dear god!

Too late. The image of Ky with nothing but that sexy smile on his face popped into her head. She almost slapped her forehead to tell her brain to cut it out. But it was useless. Another image of Ky took hold of her mind. In this one, he was prowling toward her, his large body looming over hers. Then in her head, he lowered and kissed her senseless.

"I really think I should go." Liam cleared his throat, taking a few steps back.

"Nonsense. I'm going to need some sleep soon. I'll just head over to that cabin Mrs. Wilder mentioned. She gave me directions—"

"I'll take you," Ky cut in. "Liam stay here. We'll talk when I return."

Nita stood from the kitchen table. Her body felt tight and flushed. If she got any more turned on by thinking of Ky, she'd end up ravishing him in the woods. When did she start using the word ravish, anyway? That was Tally rubbing off on her.

"I need to grab my overnight bag and we are good to go," she told Ky. Then she offered her hand to Liam. "It was nice meeting you."

"The pleasure was all mine," he said with a flirty wink that probably got him lots of women bowing at his feet. "Trust me."

She had the feeling he was trying to tell her something, but she couldn't figure out what. He could just be messing with her after the way she'd told on Ky for being hurt.

Once she'd gotten her bag from the car, Ky led her down a path by the side of his house. It was a pretty straight walk that took them by a creek not far from his cabin.

"That's gorgeous," she said, staring at the moon reflecting on the water. "You must love living here."

Leaves crunched under their feet as they walked, the sound almost overpowering the buzzing of the butterflies swarming her chest.

"I do love living here." He grabbed her hand to help her over some bumpy areas on the path.

She wore sandals, but knew all about living near the mountains and had a pair of trainers and hiking boots in her bag.

"What about you? How do you like living in the city?" he asked.

She shrugged. "I mostly grew up there. It's what I'm used to."

"You've never lived outside of the city?"

She nodded in the darkness, then realized he probably couldn't see that. "Yes. I lived not far from here when I was a teenager. It only lasted about two years. Then we moved back home."

"I guess you didn't enjoy it?"

She frowned at the almost sad way he said the words. "I liked it. I think nature is beautiful and with a cabin as gorgeous as the one you have— with no weird annoying neighbors close by and a view to die for, plus the basic necessities —you'd be stupid to move to the city. I certainly wouldn't."

"I do love living here. I can have peace and quiet. At the same time, my clan is not too far so if they need me, I'm nearby."

They neared the smaller cabin. It was obvious someone had been in there not long ago. The lights were turned on in a welcoming sight.

"Jess." He sighed, digging his hands in his back pocket.

"I'm sorry?"

"My sister came over and turned on the lights for you," he rushed to add.

At the door, she turned to him with a smile. "I had fun at dinner. Are you still up for a day of walking the woods tomorrow?"

He pushed the door to the miniature cabin open. It was the cutest thing ever. She'd seen tiny houses before on television, but had never actually stayed in one. The inside was decorated in earth tones that blended perfectly with their surroundings. Colors had been combined with furniture to give the small space country charm.

"This has to be the prettiest little cabin ever!" she squealed. She felt like a big kid in a dollhouse.

When she turned to glance at Ky, he was busy leaning on the front door, smiling at her. That smile. Oh mother of all dirty thoughts. He gave her so many naughty visuals she had to remember to breathe and keep her sexual depravity inside her head.

"I'm glad you like it." He chuckled and she watched his chest rise and fall with his laughs. "My mother was fond of this cabin."

"You have to love it!" She sat down on one of the dainty sofas. "It's like Alice in Wonderland."

Ky raised a brow. "And who would I be, the Mad Hatter or the crazy cat?"

She stood again and strolled toward him. "I think you and Liam would make a great pair of Tweedledee and Tweedledum."

She burst into giggles at his indignant expression. How could she talk to him like that? It was all him. Something about him allowed her to be herself. No pretending. She felt comfortable enough with him to joke around.

"Are you kidding me?"

"Yes! Of course I'm kidding." She laughed. "I don't think Alice is the right fairy tale for you Mr. Bear."

She stopped a foot away from him. Her muscles locked, fighting back the urge to get closer to him.

A spark of interest lit his eyes. "What fairy tale would you see me in?"

She wanted to say a naughty version of Goldie Locks, but she was definitely not the golden one of the two. With his blonde spiky hair, he kicked any other version of Goldie Locks in the ass. "I'll have to think about it."

He glanced away from her, as if to leave, but then turned and closed the distance between them. She inhaled sharply, holding her breath. He got closer, until her back hit the wall and his body pressed flush against hers.

Oh dear God. If he didn't kiss her soon, she might stoop to begging. On her knees, since her legs were about to give out.

She thought with the way he'd gone all serious on her, that he'd grab her hard and kiss her roughly. But no. Instead, he raised a hand slowly, sliding it up her arm. Goosebumps broke over her skin. Their gazes held in a hot distracting lock that she didn't want to break. He finally cupped her cheek so lightly she almost swore he wasn't touching her. Her breaths pounded hard in her ears. Shivers raced down her back. She swallowed back the tiny whimpers trying to escape her throat.

"Did you know..." he whispered, his head lowering with every breath she took. "That your eyes are the color of smooth milk chocolate and as bright as a thousand stars?"

She'd never been told that. Ever. She had brown eyes. Men had told her they were pretty but nobody had compared it to something as decadent as chocolate. No one had said they were bright like stars. He said the words so quietly she thought he was talking to himself.

"And your smile," he continued. "Is more beautiful than any blooming flower come spring."

She opened her mouth to speak, but no words came out. It was then that he finally slanted his lips over hers. The slow burn in her blood flared into an intense inferno. He swiped his tongue over her lips first. Tasting. Proving. Almost asking for permission before moving in on her. She didn't wait. She met his tongue with her own and rubbed hers over his in a bold stroke. A loud rumble vibrated from his chest. Then he pushed her harder against the wall, deepening the kiss.

It was intoxicating. Fire and desire turned her insides into a ticking bomb of arousal. She whimpered, her nipples growing tight with need. She ached for relief. Flames of passion licked at her veins, warming her core, adding to the intense feeling of urgency inside her. Her panties went damp from how slick her pussy had gotten. She slid her hands around his waist and raked her nails over his back. The material of his shirt kept her from the warm skin she knew lay beneath.

The heat of his body engulfed her. She became giddy with the idea of getting him naked. Naked sounded good. Shit, that sounded real good to her. If he continued to flick his tongue over her and curl it around hers like some kind of mating ritual she might end up coming on the spot. From a kiss.

Oxygen pounded its way into her lungs and still she felt breathless. Her mind ceased to think of anything but sex. All rational thought had been discarded. Pure instinct drove her. This bear had been the first she'd clicked with on so many levels she stopped counting. Being with him felt right. Like the most natural thing to do.

She ran her hands down to his waist, came around the front of his jeans and slid to grasp his erection over the denim.

A new, deeper rumble sounded from Ky. She was about to fumble with his belt when all of a sudden he broke their kiss. *Nooooo!*

"Nita..." he moaned her name.

It was empowering to see him breathing hard and knowing he was just as ready to forget everything as she was. He wanted her too. Mrs. Wilder had clearly made the perfect match with them when it came to chemistry. It was explosive. Her lust-muddled brain wanted sex now.

"I should go," he said, the words had the effect of a bucket of ice water. What was she doing? This poor guy had been hurt. Bear shifter or not, she shouldn't be throwing herself at him like he was the last chicken wing and she hadn't had dinner.

"I—"

"Don't." He placed a warm, calloused finger over her lips. "This is more than sex."

She gulped. Hell yeah. She already knew they weren't going to have every day type of sex. This was going toward the 'I'm gonna fuck you stupid sex'. The hunger in his eyes was there for her to see. His cock was still rubbing over her belly like he wanted to find his way inside her. She'd gladly show him if need be, but he'd stopped. She should be ecstatic that a man had finally taken it upon himself to look at her as more than a piece of ass. Then why wasn't she? Sexual frustration to the power of almost a year without sex.

"Good night, beautiful Nita," Ky said and took the step separating them from the darkness of the woods, the warmth of his body leaving her had her feeling chilled.

"Good night," she whispered.

God. She hadn't even brought her vibrator. She was going to sleep all kinds of uncomfortable.

His big body slipped into the darkness and was gone in the blink of an eye. She shut the door and took a breath.

"Well, shit!" Talk about something different. Nita had stopped having problems dating the moment she'd embraced her body. At the same time, she'd never really let anyone deep into her heart. All the men in her life had been more short-term flings than deep relationships. Not that she'd really worried about it before.

Her cell phone rang at that moment. She ran for the chair she'd placed it on.

"Hello?"

"So how was the date?" Tally exclaimed. "Nita Islas! How dare you go on a date with some hot bear and not tell me? What did you think I'd do, judge you or something?"

She sighed and sat down with a thump. Time to tell the truth. "It wasn't you. I was just worried this was going to be another dead-end in the relationship department. I didn't want you to get your hopes up."

"Nita..."

"Okay," she admitted with a groan, sliding her finger over her still tingling lips. "I didn't want to get *my* hopes up."

Tally sighed. "I understand. So how did it go?"

"Well..." She thought back to the kiss. That part had been damn amazing. "Dinner was great. He's a nice guy that's genuinely sweet."

"And?"

"He's handsome."

Tally snorted with a laugh. "Just handsome?"

Dammit! "Okay, he's hot as hell. Damn, Tally. He's so hot my eyes watered."

"Wow! He sounds like someone you should bring over for dinner or at very minimum tie to your bed." She sighed.

"Oh, that's not the best part." She thought back to what he'd said before he'd kissed her. "He's a romantic and he kisses like a sex god."

Tally gasped. "Did you already have sex?"

"I just met him like three hours ago," she exclaimed.

"Hey, it's been known to happen." Tally giggled.

Yeah. She was right. And it almost had happened. If Ky hadn't put an end to it, she probably would have gotten naked faster than on a hot summer day with no air conditioning.

"He has these gorgeous hazel eyes. They turn this deep green or this golden color when he's talking." Or aroused. She'd seen how dark the green had gotten when he'd kissed her. She wondered what color they would turn when he came.

"Oooh. Girl you've never sounded so interested in a man's eyes before."

They reminded her of her old friend's eyes. Ky. Except her high school friend's eyes had never gotten dark green like Kyer's eyes did when he'd been turned on. Probably because she'd never seen Ky turned on back when she'd been in school. She'd had a crush on the guy the size of Alaska. Too bad he'd been so shy and she'd been so insecure. The combination had not been good at the time. It had kept her from voicing her thoughts.

"He's a nice guy." He really was and that wasn't just her hormones talking him up so she could feel good about giving it up.

Tally laughed. "A nice hot guy. Just what the doctor ordered for you."

"More like what Mrs. Wilder got me." She smiled.

That old lady was like a matchmaking god. She'd worked her magic on Tally and now, if things went according to plan, she might have played her cards right where Nita was concerned.

"All right, well I know this is a series of dates, so you know I will be calling you back tomorrow to find out how that went," Tally said. "Don't you dare ignore my calls or I swear I'll come hunt you down."

Hopefully she'd have something good to share.

"Take care. We'll chat tomorrow."

She shut off the phone and plugged it in to charge. Then she opted for a nice long bath. Her apartment was too small to do baths. That and the kitchen were the main reasons she wanted to move. Seeing Ky's gorgeous home only reinforced her need for more space. He lived on so much land. He didn't have annoying neighbors playing loud music in the middle of the night. After a long day of patients screaming at her, the last thing she wanted was to get no sleep because of noise upstairs or next door.

That was the price she paid for living in a busy city. But did she need to stay there? It wasn't like she was broke. If she didn't buy a house in the middle of midtown, she could afford something further outside of town.

The idea flourished. A house with a backyard where she could finally get a dog or cat. Her parents didn't live on the same side of the world anymore. They'd visit wherever she decided to move. So why was she still putting up with the insanity of the city?

Sitting in the quiet bath, with nothing but the kisses Ky had given her on her mind, she lost track of time. For the first time in a long time, she didn't have to rush somewhere. It was nice. And the way Ky had treated her had been so different. He could have taken things to the next level right there in the living room with the door wide open. Hell not only would she have let him, she'd encouraged him to do it.

She sat there for a long time. Her thoughts floated over the possibilities that maybe, for once in her life, she could figure out how to have more than just sex with the hot bear. With Ky so nice and sweet, it was easy to talk to him. Easy to open up even when he was just barely awake with a possible concussion. She was a terrible nurse to the big mountain man. Good thing he was a shifter or he might have died while she drooled over his abs. She should learn to behave when it came to Ky. Maybe after she'd seen him fully naked.

She snickered as she got out of the bath and dried off. Yeah, right. Like that was gonna happen. She'd keep thinking and visualizing Ky naked until she saw him naked. Then she'd just adjust her visions and keep seeing the right version of him naked in her head.

She slipped on a pair of shorts and a tank top. Energy buzzed in her veins. She was still wound up from that kiss. A walk could help her relax and go to sleep. She slipped on her trainers and headed for the creek she'd seen earlier. The brightness from the full moon allowed her to see without the need for a flashlight or her cell phone.

A low rumble sounded by the water. She peeked around a tree and gasped. Holy shit. She scurried back behind the tree, hoping that she hadn't been heard or seen. Then she took another look. A giant black bear rubbed his back on a massive trunk. He kicked leaves around and then moved by the edge of the creek and finally, jumped in.

FOUR

"SHIT!" SHE GASPED. WHO the heck jumped in the creek? And more importantly, did he know how to swim? Considering she definitely didn't know how, she really hoped the big bear was okay.

Gripping the tree bark with her nails, she waited breathlessly until a man emerged from the water. There went her ability to relax for the rest of the night. Ky got out of the water. Ky naked as the day he'd been born. The moonlight reflected off his skin, showing every single wet muscle in high definition.

She bit her lip, swallowed hard and continued to stare.

He combed his fingers through his short spiky hair and stretched his arms above his head. His body gleamed with wetness. He marched away from the water, toward the house. Still naked and so sexy she could do nothing to stop her feet from following behind him.

Careful not to make noise, she took her time sauntering after him. He went around the house, to a side entrance that led to his bedroom. A big bed was visible through the glass sliding door. She saw it all clearly from the spot she stood at behind a giant old tree.

He didn't bother shutting the door. Her pussy throbbed from intense arousal. He threw some items she couldn't quite make out on his bed. Her curiosity was more than piqued. She wanted him to pick up whatever he'd thrown on the bed so she could see what it was. Then he sat down with some pillows propped behind his back. She watched him press buttons on a TV remote. Still naked and with a very erect cock, he flicked through channels. She wondered how he'd watch anything in that state.

Why was she still standing there, peeping on him like some demented pervert? Because damn it all to hell, he was hot. That and she liked watching his body. All those muscles and that slight mat of hair on his chest. He was the complete opposite of every man she'd ever been with. Combine that with the sexual chemistry they had and she was fascinated.

Her gaze zoomed in on his hand. He had squirted something in it. Shit. Was that lube? Sure enough, he wrapped his hand around his cock and leaned back into the pillows. Oh, no. Oh this was bad. This was really bad. She should go before he—too late. She watched, mesmerized, as he jerked his cock with his big hand. He'd stopped watching whatever was on the television. His gaze had strayed to the open door and stayed there. If it weren't so dark, she'd swear he could see her.

If she weren't so aroused and needing relief, she might feel bad that she'd intruded in such a private moment. As it was, she started to squirm while standing there. Her harsh breaths pounded loud in her ears. Her clit twitched, needing to be touched. She slid a hand down the inside of her shorts, still focused on Ky. He appeared fixated on her. She rubbed her hand between her legs and bit back a moan. She was wet. Wet and desperate to be touched by him.

It felt good to touch herself. She knew without a doubt that Ky touching her would feel better than this, but she couldn't ask for that right then. She slipped past her clit and plunged her fingers into her wet center.

His handling of his cock turned rougher. He jerked hard, every few strokes rubbing the tip with his thumb. She couldn't see the color of his eyes from where she stood, but she would bet her entire savings they were deep green. He groaned every few moments, the sound managed to make her wetter.

She wanted to run into his room and offer to do the job for him. Just the thought of his cock sliding into her mouth brought an electric tingle to her aching pussy. She pressed a finger into her clit, tweaking the tiny nerve spot hard, tugging the bit of flesh with almost painful speed. With her other hand, she held herself steady by the tree. Her legs started to shake with her fondling of herself.

You need to get laid!

She lost the battle with her shaky legs and slid down to her knees. Even with her inability to stay upright, she didn't stop. She stared at him, continuing to press at her clit, fingers sliding over her pleasure bundle in hard circles. His chest rose and fell, his breathing harsh and labored. She heard his moans and knew it was getting harder for him. The same as it was for her. Her hand rubbed against the material of her shorts, but she didn't care. She gasped, and for a second swore he'd heard her.

God! She was going to get into trouble. There was no stopping at that point. Her hand had a mind of its own. She swooped down, sinking her fingers into her wet heat, coating them with her arousal and then gliding them over her clit. Back and forth. Each slow wet slide and press tightened the burning in her sex. Meanwhile, Ky's neck veins popped out, showing how close he was getting to losing his control. He pleasured himself with his eyes locked on her. It added gasoline to the fire raging like a perfect storm in her core.

She tapped her clit hard. Once. Twice. On the third time she had to bite down on her lip to keep from screaming and swore she tasted blood. She inhaled sharply, struggling to stop the whimpers riding the back of her throat. Her entire body shook as almost painful pleasure blasted through her.

Ky's jerking slowed. He tensed, threw his head back and roared. The loud sound was coupled with semen spurting from his cock. She had to blink repeatedly to get her vision to refocus. It was moments before he stopped breathing harshly and milking his cock. Then he moved. He stood up and left to an attached bathroom.

She took that moment to stand and get the hell away from the house. There had been times in her life she'd done silly things, but never had she ever peeped on a man masturbating. And she sure as hell hadn't started doing it herself while watching him. Not that there was an ounce of remorse in her.

She got back to the tiny cabin and locked herself in. No more nighttime walks. Only god knew what else she'd see if she stayed out there. Not to mention she might beg to join in. That's all she needed. For her date to think she couldn't control her urges.

After a really cold shower, she went to bed. Tomorrow would be soon enough to see Ky and decide if things between them were worth pursuing.

KY'S MORNING STARTED out with him in a pissy mood and way too early for his own good. He'd been unable to sleep thinking about Nita. Jesus

Christ. He'd seen her out there, playing with herself at the same time she watched him masturbate. He didn't know what came over him, but he'd loved that he'd turned her on to the point she needed to make herself come.

Nita moaning and touching her own body had been better than the video on his TV. He'd been mentally fucking her all night and when he realized he'd get no sleep, he chose to self-pleasure. But he hadn't expected her, outside his door, moaning and whimpering with one hand between her legs and the other holding the tree next to her. She'd made the most amazing face as she came, her features lost in the pleasure of her orgasm.

After he came, he'd gone to the bathroom to clean up, only to return and find her gone. At that point he was filled with confusion when it came to her. There was one thing that he did know. She wanted him. He shouldn't be surprised that women found him sexually attractive, but seeing Nita's response to him was better than anything. She had been the only woman he'd always wished would be interested in him. From the moment he'd laid eyes on her.

He grumbled on his way to the kitchen.

Liam sat there, smiling, using his pocket knife to sharpen a piece of wood into a sharp point. "Good morning, Chief."

"What's so good about it?" he snapped. Guilt crept up his neck. "Sorry, I don't mean to be angry at you. I didn't get much sleep."

Liam's brows rose with interest. "I didn't think you would, but I don't think it's for the same reason I expected."

To tell Liam about what had happened the previous night was a big no-no in Ky's book. Nita was the woman he'd wanted for much longer than he cared to admit to even himself. He didn't talk about his sex life, or the lack thereof with anyone. He was private and he wouldn't go there.

"No. It's not what you're thinking." Definitely not because he'd been balls deep in the woman he'd wanted for more than half his life. No. It was because he *hadn't* been that he got no sleep.

"Look, I left last night because I thought you two might want to spend some time together." Liam picked up a piece of toast and took a bite. "But you need to tell me about this injury."

Ky fixed a cup of coffee and spoke. "Someone hit me. Hard enough to knock me out while I was distracted and on the phone."

Liam frowned. "Didn't you scent them?"

He shook his head. "That's the thing. I think they wore hunter's block. I definitely would have scented someone approaching. As it was, I can't figure out how I didn't even hear when they came in."

Liam's snort wasn't surprised. "How could you hear anyone when you leave your doors open so people can come and go as they please?"

True. He didn't bother shutting or locking doors during the day. Most of his clan had open access to his cabin.

His thoughts drifted back to the previous night. Dammit. Heat spread over his muscles and down to his cock. The image of Nita on her knees not more than twenty feet from his room pleasuring herself still did things to his system no woman ever had.

He wanted her. Bad. More than he was willing to admit to her just yet. She didn't realize how special she'd been to him back in high school. They'd been young. His shyness and her friendship had kept him from doing anything bold like kissing her.

Most of the time their interactions turned to fun friendly activities. It was those activities that allowed his feelings for her to grow, to blossom into an even deeper set of feelings he'd hidden so well she'd never known. Now there she was, just a few hundred yards away from his house and willing to spend time with him. To see if they could be a perfect match. He already knew they were.

"We need to go hunting then." Liam broke through his thoughts like a splash of cool water.

He was about to agree when Nita knocked at his door.

"Good morning." She waved at them.

He watched her, searching for any sign of embarrassment over the previous night, but she continued to smile. In fact, her smile widened as her gaze roamed down his body in a visual caress he loved.

"Good morning," Liam lifted his knife in mock salute. "You look great today. Doesn't she look great, Chief?"

He realized he'd been standing there, staring at her without speaking. What a frickin' idiot. What happened to his ability to speak to women? It disappeared the moment Nita came back into his life.

"You look great," he said once he remembered how to use his vocal cords.

"Thanks." She slid a long curl behind her ear and glanced at the cup in his hand. "I would have made coffee in the baby cabin, but I couldn't find any."

"Baby cabin?" Liam laughed.

She grinned, nodding. "It's so cute. It's like a baby cabin. By the way." She entered the kitchen and headed for the table Liam sat at. "I appreciate the extra bathroom space and large tub. I worried about getting stuck in a little tub, but you had comfort in mind when you made that. It is probably the biggest part of that cabin." She met his gaze. "Aside from the bed."

Well, shit. Going back to check out the size of the bed sounded mighty good to him. He knew they'd both fit in it.

"Come in and have some coffee," Ky invited. "Do you mind if we do a walk down by the river with Liam this morning?"

She shook her head. "Nope. That sounds fun."

Guilt burned in his chest. "I know that isn't part of the date, but we have to go check on a few or our clan members and they're likely to be down by our meeting house."

"Yes, it's fine."

But something about the way she said the words worried him. It was her dismissive attitude. What changed between the previous night and now?

After breakfast, they hiked through the woods toward the river.

"How far…is this river?" she panted, her cheeks red from the sun and her hair clinging to the sides of her face with perspiration.

"If you're tired, we can take a break," he offered, his guilt growing at the sheen of sweat over her mouth and the tired sigh she gave.

"It's just that I'm not used to walking this much." She scrunched her nose. "Okay, I'm not used to walking at all, but I am happy to continue if you guys slow it down a little."

Fuck. What kind of bastard was he that he'd forgotten she was a city girl. He motioned for Liam to keep going ahead of them and handed her the water bottle he had in his pack. He'd packed it just for her, in case she got thirsty.

"Thank you," she mumbled, before gulping the water down.

"I'm sorry for the long walk. We're so used to walking and hiking these woods we forget the trails can be long and difficult for someone that's not from around here."

She groaned and sat down on a patch of grass. "It's okay. I'm so out of shape it's not even funny. I used to work out a long time ago, but I slacked like a good lazy girl the past few years. My last workout session consisted of me telling my trainer I needed a vacation from exercise."

He laughed at the face of pain she made and sat down next to her. "That must have gone over well."

She shook her head. "He didn't think it was funny in the least. He said to call him when I was ready to get sweaty."

"Have you called him?" he asked, now fully curious.

She raised a brow high. "It takes me almost four hours to get my hair to not look like a dry straw broom. I'm no longer interested in getting sweaty with him." Her lips curled in a sexy grin. "There's better ways to mess up my hair and get a workout."

"There most certainly are." He could count at least four that they could try and probably not mess up her hair much. He especially liked the one workout where she would get on her knees again.

She glanced around the quiet forest. "This is so beautiful. So tell me about you. How do you like being a bear-shifter chief? I bet that's got to be exciting."

He shrugged. He hated talking about himself. He preferred to learn about her and how her life had changed in the past years.

"It has its moments," he said, watching the sunlight shine off her gorgeous brown skin.

"You know..." She squinted out at the distance, leaning slightly into him. "You remind me a lot of someone."

His heartbeat tripped in his chest. "Someone you liked, I hope."

She smiled and turned to face him, the sparkle in her eyes filled with mischief. "Maybe. Okay, he was a great friend. I actually miss him. Your eyes and your name remind me of him. But you're not like him."

"How am I different?"

"Ky used to have a hard time looking me in the eyes. He also stuttered when we spoke." She sighed. "He was shy. Not that I was much better."

He shook his head, remembering the beautiful girl she used to be. Now he was faced with a sexy adult that still managed to make him tongue-tied. "I find that hard to believe."

She winked. "I was shy. Thankfully poor Ky never knew the kind of stuff running around my head or he probably would have killed our friendship." With another of those heart-melting smiles, she leaned toward him some more. "How did we end up back on me? Tell me about your family. Do they live nearby?"

He nodded and jumped back to his feet, offering her his hand and helping her stand. "They do. Only my mother and sister are around now." He continued to hold her hand as they made their way closer to the river. "My father passed some years back."

"I'm so sorry!"

"It's okay. It was a big fight against some hunters. We had some in our clan giving away private information on our river and winter food stock to a rival clan. They hired hunters and there was a very big war."

"That's awful," she said and patted his arm. "Losing family sucks big time."

Why did he tell her about his dad? He hated talking about it. His father hadn't been the best father or even the best husband, but he'd been a damned good leader. He'd held the clan together and devoted himself to ensuring the group prospered. But it was Ky and his financial savvy that had increased their combined portfolios. He'd gotten their land ownership to be twice what it was and had doubled the savings of every clan member.

Still, telling her about his father was big even for him. He'd held his father's death locked away, never talking about it. The pain from the loss of his father and the difficult relationship they'd had continued to burn bright in his chest. Anger and hurt had raged deep inside him for so long he'd forgotten how to live without them. If only the old bear hadn't been so insistent on going to face the enemy alone. If only he'd listened to Ky and waited for some enforcers. But no, he'd taken it upon himself to face the hunters and the rival clan. He'd ended up dead.

With every step they took closer to the river, he pulled her closer to his side. Until she was held by him in a one arm hug.

"So why did your sister decide to find you a date?" her voice broke the quiet walk.

He'd known it was coming. How to explain that Jess was tired of hearing about what was wrong with every female that wanted to have a relationship with him? He'd been okay with dinner and sex in most cases, but long-lasting? Not even as a joke. She'd given him grief over his lack of trying to find a woman to bear his cubs and help with the clan.

"She feels it's time I made a commitment to someone and stuck with her."

She stopped in her tracks.

He glanced at her, noticing the frown lines and curious stare. "What do you think? I mean, what she feels is great and all, but she's not the one that's going to be in a relationship, you are."

He took a step toward her, stopping right in front of her. She glanced up, not breaking their gaze. "What does Ky want?"

Ky. He wanted Nita. Had wanted her for so long he'd refused to give it too much thought for fear of how it would look that a grown man had been wanting the same woman for almost seventeen years. He'd pretty much erased the word relationship out of his brain because there was no Nita in his life.

"I agree with her." He lifted a hand and caressed her smooth cheek. "I want someone who wants to be in a relationship. I want to create something long-lasting with a woman who wants more than just sex."

She visibly gulped. "Sex is good, though."

He leaned closer, her scent digging deep, waking the raging lust he couldn't seem to stop for her. Even the bear roared for a taste. "Sex is real good."

Her pupils dilated as she glanced at his mouth. "Sex with a person you're attracted to is probably better."

"True. Someone who can make your blood run hot and give you all sorts of dirty thoughts."

She inhaled sharply and met his gaze. "How dirty is dirty?"

He moved closer still, until he was but a few millimeters away from her lips. "Oh, dirty. So dirty you'll never be clean again."

She gasped. "I think I want to meet that someone."

"You already have, beautiful." He pulled her into his arms and meshed their lips in a kiss so hot he couldn't stop the roar at the back of his throat. The bear wanted in on the action too.

She wrapped her hands around his neck and clung tight to him. He pushed her back against a large tree. Her soft body rubbed over his in mind-blowing caresses. He slid his hands up from her waist, to cup her breasts. Fuck, he'd been dying to touch them. Those tops she wore that played peekaboo and drove him insane for the past hours were killers.

Grabbing handfuls of her large tits, he cupped her and squeezed. Jesus-fucking-hell she was hot. Those sexy moaning sounds she made as he slid his thumbs over her hard little nipples turned his cock steel hard.

If that weren't painful enough, she raked her nails on the back of his neck, digging them deep. The stinging added another dimension to the arousal raging in his blood. Rational thought fled his brain. His sole focus became those moans, those whimpers in their kiss. The way she curled her tongue over his in a way no woman ever had before. He rocked his pelvis into her belly. How he wanted inside her. Fucking her. Feeling her pussy clench around him.

"Chief? You guys okay?" Liam called from down the path.

"Fucking hell!" He huffed. "Yes, we're fine. We'll be there in a sec." He glanced into Nita's smiling eyes.

"Looks like we need to find a better time for the chemistry quiz portion of our date."

"There is no quiz. We both know where this is going." He knew he pushed it laying it out right like that, but fuck it all, he was hard and he wouldn't be getting any relief anytime soon.

"You're right." She slid her hands from around his neck, slowly down his chest, stopping at his abs. "We both know where this is going. The question is, your bed or mine?"

Hell yes!

He grinned. "Who says we'll make it to the bed?"

FIVE

Nita had to count to ten backward and forward before she did something she'd never done and attacked a man. It didn't matter that he was taller, bigger and tougher. That scruffy beard, those sexy hazel eyes and that gorgeous smile was going to push her to a new level of desperate. She'd claimed that her cousin Tally was the one who needed to get laid, but clearly she was past due in the sex department. The last time she'd had sex had been so long ago her vagina probably had a vacancy sign with full blown neon lights down there.

She'd slowed down on the dating in search of something...different. A man who would be more than just sex. She hated lies. Somehow most of the relationships she'd been in involved her boyfriend's keeping things from her and her finding out later on. She was tired of it. She wanted honesty. She wanted everything out in the open. So far Ky had shown her he was the real deal. More than just sex.

So why then, did this man that made her want more than sex also make her think of the naughtiest things? It wasn't fair. She'd never been so ready to drop her panties and spread 'em like she was at that moment.

Sadly, she didn't even feel an ounce of shame over it. What she did feel was anger that Liam had interrupted their kiss.

The rest of the walk to the river was quiet with Ky holding her hand the entire way. It was new and different. Men she'd dated in the past hadn't done things like help her walk so she wouldn't fall. They hadn't held her hand just because they wanted to. And they certainly hadn't waited to push their way into her bed. Those men had been takers. Clearly Ky was a giver. Now if she could only get him to give her all the orgasms that wicked smile of his promised.

The river bend was beautiful. There was a waterfall and some large rocks that allowed for prime viewing of the lower valley. She'd bet watching the sunset from there would be unforgettable. The lush greenery and giant trees only reminded her of how little she had in way of a view back home. This openness called to her. She'd give up the city so fast if she found a house in the woods. Not that she was a fan of living alone, but maybe in time she'd find the man for her.

Someone like the bear.

She really liked where this was going with him. Her mind told her to take her time with him. But her body, that desperate bitch, told her to get him naked as soon as possible. Jesus. The bear naked. Those heavy muscles she'd felt under that plaid shirt might kill her from pleasure. If she could just lick her way up his jaw she might come without any actual sex. The way he kissed her alone disabled her ability to think.

"This is where we do most of our fishing," Liam said, pointing to the large river.

Oops. She'd blacked out the conversation while visualizing him and her doing naughty stuff. The big fall that scurried down to the giant river below showed her a clear view of the fish as they traveled down and up the current.

"Wow. I've never been fishing, but I am getting the urge to. Look at all those fish!" she exclaimed.

Ky nodded. "We have prime location here. It's been a big problem with nearby clans that want to fish without permission."

"So you won't let anyone else fish here?" She allowed him to help her further down the side of the river, toward the group of cabins below.

"We do if they ask permission. We don't want to overfish, so we have seasons. The problem is some of the other clans don't want to fish at the other rivers that are further away. They want to claim this one for themselves. It becomes a big problem when they start trouble with my people."

"Does that happen often?" She trailed next to him, following behind Liam.

Liam stopped some yards ahead of them. "We have a problem, Chief."

They reached the spot where Liam stopped. There was a pile of empty beer bottles and trash.

"It has to be the Greenfield Clan," Ky growled. "Heck. It could even be one of the clans from further away."

"Who are the Greenfields?" she asked, glancing at the large mess they'd left behind.

Liam pulled out a cell phone and sent a text. "They're our closest neighbors. I've asked Oliver and Caleb to help clean this up."

"And they are?" she asked again, feeling all kinds of lost from lack of information.

"Two of our guards," Ky replied. "They'll come take care of making sure this place is cleaned up."

At that moment, the sound of breaking leaves and someone approaching from the right side of the forest stopped the conversation. A man almost as tall as Ky with curly brown hair and a beard long enough to nest a family of pigeons approached them. "Hey there, Chief."

"Hi, David," Liam and Ky greeted at the same time.

"Ma'am." He nodded toward Nita.

"Hi." She waved.

"David, this is Nita. She's staying with me." Ky introduced them. "Nita, this is David Marsh. He's one of the guards in the clan."

She hadn't been called a ma'am before. It was official. She was old. She wasn't bothered though. David probably called every woman ma'am. His beard was bigger than his face. It was thick and full and there was a leaf or two stuck to it. She'd never been so tempted to check a man for small animals in his facial hair. She bet her car keys could hide in there and never be found.

"There's no dead animals in there," David said as though reading her mind.

"Sorry." She'd been caught staring. A flush of guilt crept up her neck.

David smiled. Though most of his face was covered in hair, she just knew there was a handsome guy under there. "It's okay. I do shave when the occasion calls for it, but with winter coming it's easier to leave it as is."

Hmmm, probably not smart to tell him it was only the end of summer and fall still hadn't come. If he kept his beard growing he'd end up with a blanket for winter.

"David, can you see if you can find out from some of the others what happened here?"

David gave a sharp nod. "You got it, Chief."

She held on to Ky and watched David turn to leave.

"Was nice meeting you, ma'am." She could almost tell he was smiling that time.

She waved at David. "Nice meeting you too."

"What will you do about the neighbors?" she asked, turning to face the hill again.

"Liam will go chat with them." He frowned, holding on tighter when she slipped on a rock. "Let's go back. It's lunch time."

She glanced over her shoulder when he said that. She'd thought Liam was at their back. He was already several yards away from them.

"Nice seeing you Liam!" she yelled.

Liam smiled, waved and turned back to the trail. Going up the hill wasn't as easy as going down. She ended up depending on Ky and allowed him to help her most of the way up.

When they reached his cabin, the smell of food overpowered her. She didn't realize how long their walk had been until her stomach growled. Ky smiled at her.

"We'll feed you now."

She would have been embarrassed except that whatever was being cooked smelled divine. Rays of sunlight highlighted the cabin in the woods giving it an almost fairytale look. It was like looking at a painting. Even the birds decided to chirp at that moment.

Seemed like nature was trying to tell her to move her ass out of the city. She'd not had a single allergic reaction or need for any of the meds she'd brought in case of poison ivy, poison oak, allergies, mosquitos or any other kind of bug bite. She rocked!

A short curvy blonde woman with her hair in a long braid down her back and a cropped top and shorts moved around the kitchen with ease. She stopped suddenly and turned to them, a wide smile covering her lips.

"Hi! I'm Jess." She rushed forward and enveloped Nita in a tight hug. "You're Nita. I feel like I've known you forever."

"Thanks, that's...so nice." Weird but nice. She glanced at the bear but he was busy frowning at Jess.

"Do you mind if I leave you both alone for a few minutes?" he asked. "I need to make a few calls to make sure Liam's all right and doesn't encounter any resistance at the Greenfield place."

"Go!" Jess urged. "I'll keep Nita company."

"Jess..."

"I'll behave." She grinned.

Some sort of non-verbal communication seemed to go on because after a few silent moments he sighed and left the room.

"Won't you please sit, Nita? Tell me how do you like it up here?"

Nita had to smile. The other woman's grin and energy was infectious. "I think it's beautiful. I'm actually tired of living in the city. My place is too small. I'm wanting to get some flowers, a backyard, maybe a dog."

Jess's brows flew up. "Like a pet?"

Um, was there another kind? "Yes. I love furry little creatures."

Jess burst into giggles. "I am so sorry." She laughed. "You must think I'm crazy, but up here we don't see many dogs. You know, the whole bear growly thing."

"Oh!" That made sense. Sort of. "No wonder it's so quiet."

Jess snorted, standing to open lids on pots over the stove. "Stick around here when one of these guys is angry. Trust me, it is anything but quiet."

"It's very nice up here though. So open and green," she murmured. The idea of a place outside the city rooted in her brain.

"Winter can be harsh," Jess said, picking up a glass of ice water and taking a sip. "But if you have a cuddly someone to keep you warm, then it isn't so bad." She winked.

"I bet." A nice big bear with lots of body heat to help keep her warm sounded really good.

"Jess, mom would like for you to help Mrs. Roberts go back to her cabin," Ky said from the other room.

"Darn it." Jess sighed. She turned off the heat on the pots and glanced at Nita. "The food is ready. Today's special is baked salmon and vegetables for lunch and beef stew for dinner. The salad is in the fridge."

Wow. Talk about multitasking. "You really didn't have to."

She raised a hand and stopped Nita. "I did. You do not want to be eating PB&J all day today and then tomorrow too. It's sweet that he tries, but it gets old real soon. I had to endure a week of it when I got sick once and mom and dad were traveling. Suffice it to say I am no longer a fan."

Nita was caught off guard by Jess's impromptu hug as she headed out the door.

"It's been lovely meeting you, Nita. We'll have to catch up before you go home."

"Absolutely. Thanks so much for the food." She waved goodbye. Jess made her feel so at home. As if she were part of the family. Other than Tally, Nita didn't have real close friends. It was nice to meet another woman who didn't appear to be a psychotic bitch. With Nita's luck, they always started out friendly enough and ended up blaming her for their bad decisions in life. It's why she didn't have many friends. It was why she only spoke to Tally about her life.

She closed the kitchen door and locked it. Then she headed for the sound of Kyer's voice. Gliding her hand over beautiful carved wooden eagles, bears and foxes, she marveled at the craftsmanship. Someone had taken a long time to create those decorative pieces.

A smile crept over her lips as she listened to his voice grow closer.

"No. We will not back down and let it go. Tell them if we catch one of them on our land there's not going to be calling the sheriff next time."

Something about a man being so commanding and aggressive shot a spark of lust down her spine. She was such a sick freak. God. All she needed to do was get on all fours now and ask the big bear to spank her. Or even better, lick her honey. She bit back a laugh. Hah!

You need therapy. And sex too!

She reached the massive office and stood there at first, watching him face the large wall of glass showing a beautiful view of the woods. His big shoulders tensed. Then he pressed a button on the cell phone.

"Selfish assholes!" he barked and turned to face her.

"Want to talk about it?"

Where the hell had that come from? She didn't like talking about her own problems and there she was genuinely interested in whatever was frustrating the sexy bear. She'd prefer to see him smiling again instead of frowning.

She couldn't stop herself from strolling right to him. It was as though her body had a mind of its own. She wanted near him. Closer. She stopped a foot away, watching his chest rise and fall with every breath.

"Your sister left," she said.

Still he said nothing. The way his gaze focused on her mouth, dropping to her breasts and then sliding down the rest of her body almost started a brush fire in her veins.

"The food is ready," she tried again, watching him lick his lips, his gaze stuck on her chest. If only he'd do something. Anything. She was so close to tearing at his clothes it wasn't funny. "Are you hungry?"

"Starved," he finally replied.

"Oh, well good. What are you in the mood for? There's two different options on the stove. One's a beef and the other a fish. I don't have a preference."

He closed the single step between them and grabbed her arms. "I'm not hungry for food."

Thank. You. God.

She swallowed hard at the dryness in her throat. "Whatever you're in the mood for, take it."

If he needed more than that then he wasn't as intuitive as she thought. She was pretty much offering herself to him for the taking. She held her breath and waited. And watched him. The deep frown lines lifted and his features changed into a sinful smile.

"Oh, I'm taking it. All of it."

She didn't get a chance to reply. He dropped his head and locked their lips together. The kiss—Dear God what a kiss —was better than any of the previous ones. This was full of hunger. Passion. Demand. It was as if the animal side of him had taken control.

She loved it. The way with which he slid his hand down her arms to the edge of her shirt. The warmth of his hands when he pulled the material up and above her head. Their kiss broke for all of a second before their lips were once again pressed together, tongues rubbing and breaths mingling. She gripped his shirt in her hands, the material soft yet annoying. There was too much between her hands and his body. She wanted it all out of the way.

She tugged on his shirt, until he got the hint and the thing came off. A sigh fell from her lips at the feel of his warm smooth skin. Blazing need pooled at her core. Her body vibrated with desire for Ky. This thirst for his touch, it was unlike anything she'd ever experienced before. Somehow, someway, he'd managed to reach deeper in a few hours than other men had in the span of months. She didn't know if it was his genuine interest in her and what she said, all she knew was the she wanted him more than she'd ever wanted anyone. It was new and almost scary to want him with every fiber of her being.

Bone-deep desire for the man sliding his hands up her back and removing her bra grew with each of her breaths. His abs contracted under her palms. She glided her hands up his chest, through the slight mat of hair and scored her nails down his pecs.

A loud hoarse groan sounded from him. He broke their kiss, eyes bright with a hunger she loved seeing in their depths.

Her bra came off and his gaze slowly trailed down to her tits.

"You are by far the most beautiful woman I've ever seen."

She couldn't say if it was the way he said the words, with so much honesty, but hearing him say it and watching his expression fill with lust broke her control.

"Touch me, please," she begged in a soft cry.

"I can do better than touching," he murmured. "I can lick, suck and fuck you for the rest of my life. Your body is an addiction I never want to give up."

He yanked on the button to her shorts, pulling them and her panties down her legs. He didn't give her a chance to enjoy the heated smile over his lips. He led her to a big brown sofa against the wall. The back of her legs hit the sofa and she fell on the cushion. She tugged on the fly of his jeans. The pants fell down his legs and that's when she realized he went commando. Hot damn!

"My..." she gasped.

Breaths rushed out of her lungs while she tried to take in the entire vision of his body. His very big body with those really mind-muddling muscles. He was way past sexy and into hot damn of body categories. With his slightly hairy chest, legs and arms, he made her fantasize while being wide-awake. Then there was his cock. Large, stiff and with beads of pre-cum dripping from the slit. Her throat went dry with every peek she took at his shaft. To make things more interesting, she'd swear the more she looked at it, the harder and bigger it got.

"Touch me, Nita," he whispered.

She raised a hand to touch him, stroking the hot hard length of him. She grasped him tight in her hand, moving her hand up and down his shaft. Once she got to the tip, she wet her thumb with the moisture dripping from his slit and rubbed it over the head of his cock.

She moved closer, ready to take him in her mouth, but he grabbed her face in his hands, forcing her to look up at him. He shook his head and dropped down to his knees, moving his hands to her thighs, pushing her legs wide open.

"Not yet, beautiful," he said in a low gruff whisper. "I need to taste you before I lose my control."

His features tightened with need. A large brown fuzz of fur had grown over his sideburns. She couldn't have liked the view more. He was losing control over her. Her. Not some other woman. Nita. A primitive need to lose her own control along with him pushed her to act. She slid her fingers into his hair, gripping and tugging him up to her.

A new clash of their lips and she was on fire. He cupped her breasts, thumbing her nipples roughly. The ache in her pussy grew by leaps and bounds. She wanted him to fill her with his cock. She needed to be his.

She tugged her face to the side, breaking their kiss and moaning. "Please."

Dear God if she didn't get him inside her soon she might explode. He slid his lips down her jaw. Biting. Kissing. Licking.

Wetness dripped from her pussy. She was soaked. He sucked a nipple into his mouth and fireworks went off behind her lids. "Yes! Keep doing that. I like your mouth on my tits."

The roughness of his beard combined with the painful bite from his teeth shot electric currents from her nipples to her clit. Intense arousal shook her to the core.

He squeezed her tits together, licking and sucking from one nipple to the other. The delightful torture only intensified her desperation.

"For the love of sanity, fuck me. Please…"

She sucked in breaths, trying to keep her brain in working order but the reality was she was so far gone nothing could help. Nothing but his body taking hers. Owning hers.

"Ky…I need more," she groaned.

He lifted his head from her breast, her nipple still in his mouth and let go with a resounding pop.

"Your skin tastes so fucking good. Like hot sex and whipped cream." He kissed the valley of her breasts and ran circles with his tongue down her belly. At the juncture of her thighs, he pushed her legs open and stared at her pussy. He inhaled and groaned. "Your pussy smells like the sweetest honey." He licked his lips. "Bears like honey. And I think I will love eating your pussy and tasting that sweetness glistening on your pretty pink lips."

With other men, her instinct would have been to suck her belly in and try not to notice the bump that she had. Not so with him. She was very aware of her body. She was a big girl and she'd accepted long ago she was not going to be any smaller. Heck, she'd embraced her curves and had come to love them. But that tiny niggling doubt tried to push its way forward to bring up the insecurity she'd fought so hard and won years back.

Ky caressed her inner thigh, heating her to the core with his penetrating stare. "You're beautiful, Nita. Every single inch of you makes my mouth water. Don't hide from me."

It was as though he'd looked inside her mind and knew that small niggling insecurity had tried to worm out of the hole she'd shoved it in. His words had brought back the security she had in her body. She was hot. She wasn't tiny, but she was hot. And she knew he wanted her. From the tight lines of his face. From the way he licked his lips and inhaled. More importantly, from the hard cock she'd touched earlier.

"I want you. I want to fuck you in every way possible," he said the words as a promise. "I want to slide so deep in you there will be nothing between us. I want my cock in your ass, fucking that dark hole too."

"Ky..." she called to him in a soft whimper. "Please..."

His head dropped between her legs. He treated her large thighs with such gentleness, spreading them wider and displaying her for his view. His breath caressed her pussy. He curled his arms around her thighs and she ended up with her legs over his big shoulders.

"How badly do you want me to lick your pussy, darling?" His words taunted her.

"I want it so bad. More than anything," she whimpered.

"Do you want me to flick my tongue on your clit or suck on it?"

"Suck it, lick it, and bite it. Do it all. I don't care, just do something before I die waiting to come."

She groaned, tilting her hips, trying to reach his lips. She needed that touch. His mouth on her twitching clit. Her muscles burned with need.

Right when she thought she couldn't possibly survive another second without his touch, his lips grazed her pussy in a kiss so light she moaned at the torture.

"You're so evil..."

He chuckled. The laughter caused his shoulders and her legs to shake with the movement.

"Baby." He kissed the hard nubbin of her desire. "You have no idea how good I can be."

She gripped his short hair in her fists. "I don't want to hear how good you are," she panted. "Show me."

He licked her pussy again. Harder. Rougher. He splayed his tongue flat and swiped it up from ass to clit in a blood boiling lick meant to reduce her brain cells to jelly.

"Oh. My. God!"

There was no stopping her whimpers any longer. Nor the wiggling of her hips as he rolled his tongue over her clit then down to her entrance, sucking at her sleek core, making slurping noises she was even more turned on by.

A loud rumble sounded from his chest as he fucked her pussy with his tongue. She pushed back into the sofa, her muscles almost locking from the quick rise to the edge.

The delicious torture didn't stop there. He slid a finger into her, hooking it and rubbing her insides at the same time he sucked on her clit.

She didn't get a single warning. The winding tension at her core snapped to the point she was shoved into the wild waves of pleasure. She screamed louder than she ever had. A call for Ky tore from her throat.

The orgasm pushed to the forefront, taking her breath away. An explosion of desire washed over her tense muscles, cooling her sizzling pores. Her legs shook on his shoulders. It was unlike any other experience. No man had ever made her body's need for him scorch her from the inside. There had never been an orgasm that left her spent. Her body ached as though she'd run miles and worked out like she hadn't in years.

"Christ!"

She blinked her vision back into focus and watched Ky slide his cheek on her thigh. Then he kissed her and repeated it with her other thigh.

She leaned forward, cupping his face in her hands and kissing him, enjoying the taste of her own body on his lips.

"Mmm."

With a gentle push, she got him to lay back on the carpet, their kiss unbroken. She met his gaze. His eyes had gone the color of the most clear-cut emeralds. Beautiful. It was the way he stared at her that made her breath catch in her chest. Like she was the sexiest woman in the world and he never wanted to look away. The heat of his gaze and the hardness of his arousal were like pulsing electrical currents through her veins. She didn't know how or why, but being there with him felt absolutely right. Any question of proceeding with a man she hardly knew were pushed out of her mind. There was a connection between them, deeper than even she wanted to analyze.

SIX

SHE STRADDLED HIM, stroking her slick pussy over his cock in a slow glide.

"Fuck!" he groaned.

He grabbed her tits and fondled her, tweaking her nipples with his calloused thumbs. She curved into his touch, moving her body forward.

"Oh, yes. Do that. I like when you tug on my nipples," she moaned, need burning tight in her chest.

He did it again. "Sweetheart, you need to let me in you or I will embarrass myself if you keep sliding yourself on my dick."

She lifted her hips and grabbed his slick cock with one hand to place it at the entrance of her sex. He pulsed in her hand, hard and hot. She met his gaze, a world of communication happened without either saying a word. Then, she pressed down. For every inch she slid down, her lungs burned hotter. She dug her nails into the mat of hair on his chest, using him for leverage.

"Oh, God..."

He slid his hands down from tweaking her nipples to hold her by the waist.

"I'm sorry, darling," he bit out through his clenched jaw.

"Why?" she asked with a gasp. The feeling of being stretched overpowered her senses.

"I can't do slow any longer," he growled. All of a sudden the world shifted. She was on her back with Ky pumping deep into her from above.

She gasped as he pressed his cock further and further, until she could swear there wasn't a single inch of space in her he couldn't reach.

He groaned, "Fuck, you feel so good."

Brushing his lips on the side of her neck, he pulled back. The quick thrust that followed tore a moan from her. She gripped his slick arms, digging her nails in an unforgiving bite. He licked her shoulder, grazing his teeth over her hot skin.

"Yes!" she encouraged. "More. Do me harder."

"Fuck, sweetheart. You're so tight I'm having a hard time controlling myself."

Control? What control? She'd given up on control a long time ago.

"I think," she panted. "The better words are...you're goddamned huge!"

He stopped inside her and laughed, the sound reverberating between them. "You're really good for my ego."

She wasn't exaggerating either. He really was the biggest she'd ever had. And that spoke volumes since— not that she was easy or anything —she'd been with her fair share of men. Bear man had it going on in size, depth and stroke.

He thrust and propelled back.

Deeper.

Harder.

Faster.

The sliding of his body over hers turned into a reminder of how delectable it was to have him filling her, taking her. Breaths puffed out of her lips in short quick bursts.

He lowered his head and kissed her, skating his tongue over her lips. In and out of her mouth in tandem with each plunge of his cock into her. Hunger expanded in her chest almost to near bursting. A new craving had taken over her body. She needed to come. Had to have him make her reach that peak she rarely got to go with a man.

Almost as if he'd read her mind, his drives turned harsher, animalistic. A rumble sounded from his chest. His bear was close to the surface and that only made him wilder. Lust raged inside her, blacking out everything but him. His body pressed her to the rug. He skimmed his hands up to her face to hold her head at the angle he wanted for his kisses.

A storm brewed in her blood. Then came that moment where her muscles tightened. She broke their kiss, searching for much needed air.

"Oh, Ky..." she choked.

He nibbled on her jaw and earlobe. "Come. Your body's ready and I want to feel your pussy tight on my cock."

She couldn't breathe or think or do more than feel the tension snap and a flood of pleasure assault her. A loud moan rushed up her throat and left her dry lips. Stars burst in the back of her lids. The world slowed to a crawl where only the sound of her heartbeats filled her ears.

His thrusts slowed. His body tensed above hers. Their gazes met. An inexplicable connection she'd felt there the moment he opened his eyes grew between them. He threw his head back and roared at the same time his cock pulsed inside her. Streams of cum filled her channel with his seed. He rolled them over, still inside her, until she lay on top of him again. They stayed that way for what felt like hours but was probably more like a few minutes, trying to catch their breaths.

"I have an idea," Ky said, his voice rough and deep.

"Hmmm?" She didn't have the energy to say actual words.

Heck, just thinking of moving away from her giant muscle man bed made her wince.

"Want to go to a bed?" He kissed her forehead, the brush of his lips on her sweaty skin felt wonderful.

He stroked his hands down her back to her ass and then back up again. It was a sensual embrace that stirred her desire for him anew.

"Mmmhmm."

He chuckled. "What about some food? I'm starving."

"Feed me, Sexy Bear."

He cupped her head, tugging it up to look into her eyes with a smile that melted any brain cells she had left. "I'll do more than feed you, beautiful. I'll take care of you."

Her heart flipped in her chest at the real concern she saw in his gaze. Maybe sex so quickly wouldn't mess up their budding relationship. Like she could keep her hands off him now. Sex with Ky had been the best decision she'd made aside from getting Mrs. Wilder to hook her up.

Being with the bear had been like winning the sexual lottery. Not only had he rocked her world with his tongue, but he had a cock to match. All her life she'd wanted a man that could give her attention, great sex and was not an asshole. It only took getting hooked up with a different species to get what she wanted. She already knew that she wanted more with her bear.

KY BROUGHT A tray of snacks to the table and chairs he'd set up by the creek behind his house. It was early still and he knew he'd have to go deal with some of his clan problems later. Much later. Right now he was focused on the curvy woman bending over in the water. Nita dipped into the water, flashing her ass as she did. The royal blue two piece bikini did nothing to hide the luscious body she had. Or her ass and what an ass that was.

She was more than he could have ever imagined she'd be as an adult. Sexy, funny but with a sensuality she probably didn't even know she possessed. Their years apart had been good to her. She wasn't the shy girl with body issues she used to be. He'd never understood it. Her curves seemed pretty damn perfect to him. Then again, he loved him a woman with some ass to grab and hips to grip. Not to mention her breasts.

He glanced down at his erection and shook his head. The semi-aroused state he'd been in since opening his eyes and finding Nita in his kitchen had not gone away. If his intentions weren't to keep her as his mate, he might have felt like a pervert.

She looked up and smiled. That smile of hers reached into his chest and warmed his heart. He waved her over to the table he'd set up with snacks for them. She'd always loved fruit. His sister had made a point of stocking his fridge with all of Nita's favorites. He had no idea how she'd found out, but he was grateful for Jess. He wore his black framed glasses now. She'd already seen them, but had gotten him to promise he'd wear them the next time they had sex. She'd said he looked really sexy wearing them.

"Hey, that looks awesome," she said, rushing over and picking up a towel.

"Are you cold?"

"A little. It's not as warm as it should be in order to be getting into that creek." She snuggled into the towel. He frowned when she bounced on her heels trying to warm herself up.

Instinctively, he wrapped his arms around her, rubbing up and down her sides to warm her up. She glanced up, her eyes filled with an openness he hadn't noticed before.

"Thank you," she said, her voice low and seductive. There was something else there, more than just need or lust. He couldn't define it, but he liked it.

Thump

The sound of something hitting the ground broke the moment. He glanced around and noticed a branch rolling off his wood shed.

She cleared her throat and sat down, grabbing a plate and piling it up with fruit. "This reminds me of the whole cabin in the woods from scary movies."

He chuckled and sat across from her, watching her take bites of watermelon and strawberry.

"It's really not that scary up here. In the dead of winter I put up some floodlights around the pathways for anyone that might get lost."

She shook her head and scrunched her nose. "I don't know if I could be walking around here unless there was some form of brightness to ease my fear of the dark."

"You're afraid of the dark?" He blinked, trying not to show the surprise he felt. That was something he'd never known about her.

She shrugged. He sensed her unease. She wrapped the towel tighter around her shoulders. Her gaze dropped down to her plate. "Yeah. It's something from when I was a kid."

The way she hesitated brought out his curiosity. That was an action that the younger Nita would have done. The woman he'd seen so far didn't have that insecurity so it worried him that whatever caused her fear was still present in her life. "What happened?"

A loose tendril of her hair dropped from her ponytail and floated over her shoulder. With the sunlight showcasing her beautiful caramel skin, he had no problem sitting there and staring at her for hours.

"Not much. Just kids. Kids can be mean." She sighed.

He knew that. He'd been picked on as a kid for being slim compared to the other kids in the clan. Even his father had picked on him. To add insult to injury, his need to wear glasses and braces made the comments hurtful and cruel. He'd never told anyone, though. Not even his wonderful mother and sister. He learned to tell himself that he wouldn't always be the little guy. That one day he'd grow up and be able to defend himself against bullies.

That day was his eighteenth birthday. It seemed puberty hit him overnight. Muscles had filled out his once puny arms. The braces had gone and women were noticing him in a new light. Even his father had stopped speaking to him like a weakling and started addressing him like the future clan leader.

"What does that have to do with you being afraid of the dark?"

She smiled but it didn't reach her eyes. "When I was twelve some girls invited me to a sleepover party. I thought they wanted to be friends." Shadows crossed her features. Pain. Sadness. "I never did anything with anyone other than Tally, my cousin. So this was something new." She cleared her throat and glanced up, away from him and to the distance. "Anyway, they asked me to get something in one of the closets and closed the door behind me, locking me in."

He knew she was reliving the nightmare with the way her breaths quickened and how fast she rushed the words out. She picked up a glass of iced tea and took a sip. Her hand shook bringing the glass back to the table.

He didn't want to say anything to sound like he was pitying her, but he knew all too well how difficult being mistreated by other children could feel.

"What happened then?"

She gave a dry laugh. "Not much. I pounded on the door, kicked, screamed and cried. I could hear them calling me all kinds of names because of my weight." She licked her lips, pursing them before going on. "Eventually one of the parents showed up to check on us, noticed I wasn't there and made the girls tell them where I was."

Jesus. His chest throbbed from the pressure of holding back the urge to roar. To stomp around and knock down a few trees. Knowing she'd been through something like that increased his urge to hold her and make things that much better for her.

"It's okay," she said, obviously reading his features. "I'm not fond of small spaces either but the dark is what gets me."

He'd light up that forest like a fucking Christmas tree if it made her feel better. His bear huffed inside. Neither liked the idea of Nita being afraid.

"What about you? Are you scared of anything?" She smiled, the dark shadows leaving her eyes.

"Does my own cooking count?"

She burst into laughter. The sound soothed his agitated bear.

"No. But I will admit that I'm not the best cook either. Don't feel too bad. I usually eat out." She picked up a piece of strawberry and took a tiny bite. The juice coated her lips. Animal instinct told him to lick it off her lips, but he fought it. They'd done a lot more than kiss for the past few hours. He could control himself. He would control himself. Even if it gave him blue balls.

"Tell me one of your biggest pet peeves," she said suddenly.

"Hmmm, I guess women who try to be something they're not. I don't want the perfect woman, I just want someone who is comfortable in her own skin. Someone who wants to genuinely be with me. No drama. No bullshit." He knew what he wanted. Her. "Your turn. Biggest pet peeve?"

She bit her lip in thought.

"Uh-oh. Are you one of those that have a laundry list of things you dislike?" he joked.

She laughed. "Now I might not tell you."

"Come on, I was kidding." He grinned. "You gotta admit you took long enough to worry me."

"You are so bad. So, pet peeve. I guess if I had to pick, my biggest pet peeve is liars. I try to be honest at all times about everything with people. Especially in a relationship. I hate it when men say one thing and then I find out they have five other women they're dating and a handful of baby mommas." She raised her brows. "Do you have any baby mamas you need to tell me about?"

He almost fell out his chair laughing. "No." He chortled. "No baby mamas here. I am keeping my need to have babies locked away until I get a mate."

"Good man. Waiting for marriage. I hope you're not expecting a ring after last night," she flirted, her gaze dropping down to his lips. "I mean, you'd need to show me more skills before I can decide on something so important."

"You need more skills? Will my genius math skills help?"

"Are you?" she asked, laughter sparkled in the depth of her eyes. "Are you a genius?"

"When I was a kid most others thought I was too smart for my own good." Smart and scrawny.

Her eyes widened and she blinked, her jaw hanging open. "Were you a geek?"

"You don't need to sound so surprised." He twisted his lips in a wry smile. "I'm not all brawn and no brains."

She swiped her tongue over her bottom lip, licking the juice from the strawberries. Talk about torture in the first degree.

"Oh, I know you're more than just brawn. It takes some serious smart to do some the stuff you did with your tongue." She winked.

Heat crowded his cheeks. She made him blush. That was a new one. He hadn't blushed in almost fifteen years. "That's it, I won't say anything else or you'll definitely peg me a geek."

She laughed, the sound sweet music to his ears. "It can't be that bad."

He folded his arms over his chest, enjoying the way she stared at him. She couldn't have denied she wanted him. It was clear for him to see and scent. "Yes it can."

"What's your favorite movie?"

"Star Trek. The original, not that remake crap they have."

Her mouth formed into a surprised O.

"I told you."

She waved her hand. "A lot of people like that. That doesn't make you a geek."

Wind tossed loose tendrils of her hair around her shoulders. He loved the sight of her skin shining from the sun and water. The bronze color glowed in the light.

"All right, suit yourself." He knew he was treading on dangerous ground. She might figure out who he was if he kept talking about his past. He might look different, but the things he'd enjoyed as a teen were the same he liked as an adult.

"Hmmm." She leaned forward and tapped the table. "What's your favorite TV show?"

"Doctor Who."

She frowned. "Who?"

"Yeah."

"What?"

"Doctor Who."

"I don't understand." She pouted her lips prettily. "Who's Doctor?"

He barked a laugh. She was a riot and didn't even realize it. "It's a TV show. The name of the show is Doctor Who. It is also the name of the main character. Sorry if I confused you."

"Oh," she said, still sounding puzzled. "Okay, I'll admit that one threw me off."

"I told you so."

"Whatever." She rolled her eyes. "It's not like you have boxes of mint condition comic books in your room and some plastic gloves to read them with."

He must've given himself away because she gasped.

Busted!

"You *do* have comic books." Her voice was filled with awe. "Are they in little plastic baggies?"

"No." He snorted as if that were some sort of crime. "I have them in a clear enclosure to display them without getting dusty. In my guest room."

Yeah, that made him sound so much less the geek.

She stood up and strolled around the table to his side only to sit on his lap, curling her hands around his neck. "You know what? I think you're sexy whether you read comic books, go to Comic-Con or watch reruns of the original Star Trek."

He held her by the waist, pressing her closer. "You don't think being a geek is stupid?"

She leaned forward and brushed her lips over his. "I think, Mr. Bear, you are the hottest geek I've ever met."

He'd never been told that before. Usually when women found out his entertainment preferences, and the fact that he analyzed everything, they tended to pull away. If they found out about his net worth or that of his clan then things changed. They'd get real close to him. He didn't need to dress in button-down shirts or wear a Rolex because he had money. He was a bear shifter. He'd happily spend his time fishing and cuddling with a woman. Not just any woman. Nita.

NITA DIDN'T UNDERSTAND the surprise on Ky's face. How could he think that because he enjoyed different things than she did, it made him somehow undesirable? Hell, the way he looked in those glasses, like a hot college professor, made her thoughts go straight to the gutter every few minutes. She was having a difficult time reminding her body to stay in control.

"Anybody home?" someone called out. It sounded like Liam.

"We're back here," she replied and stood. The last thing she wanted was to make a bad impression on his clan member.

There was a brief struggle and some giggles when Ky tried to keep her sitting on his lap. She stuck her tongue out at him and ran around the table to sit across from him.

"You do know I have to go home today." She watched him for a reaction.

"I'll come with you," he offered. "You don't need to make the drive home all alone."

She grinned. "No way Mr. Bear. It's been awesome but I have some work to do."

Her stomach twisted in fearful knots. Was she going too fast too soon with him? Maybe trusting her instinct that this was the right man wasn't what she should be doing.

"I can make it worth your while to stay." He waggled his brows.

"Hah!" She didn't need to say that he definitely could make her stay. All he had to do was say the word.

"What's so funny?" Liam asked walking out from the kitchen. He had a T-shirt that said Born to be Wild on it.

"I have to go home," she answered, wrapping the towel around her torso in a more discreet cover up.

"Already? I thought for sure the chief would find a way to keep you here." He winked.

Her cheeks heated with embarrassment. "Believe me, it wasn't for lack of trying. But I do have a job to do. And I kinda ran out of clean clothes."

Liam shrugged. He filled a glass with iced tea and took a gulp. "Clothes are overrated."

"My thoughts exactly," said Ky.

She choked on a giggle, trying to keep a straight face but failed miserably. "Figures you guys would think that."

She eyed Ky's naked torso, slowly lifting her vision up to meet his gaze. His smile told her he knew she was bullshitting. If she could figure out a way to keep him naked then she'd happily allow it.

"I'll go change." She stood to go to the small cabin but stopped a few feet away and turned back to Ky. "I might find myself taking some more time off. If I'm invited back, I'd happily return."

"Are you leaving already?" Liam asked.

"No. I'll be back in a few."

Liam waved as she walked away. By the time she reached the cabin her phone was buzzing with text messages from Tally, Mrs. Wilder and one from Ky. His was the only one she wanted to see.

No invitation needed. I want you here with me all the time.

She grinned like a fool and went to take a shower. She'd probably lose her job taking all that time off, but she hadn't taken vacation time in a few years. All those hours of unused time off were going to come in handy now. She knew what she'd do. Go home and get more time off, then visit Tally and Mrs. Wilder before heading back. So what if she looked sort of desperate? She liked being with Ky. It wasn't all about sex either. He was a genuinely nice guy. That meant more to her than anything.

SEVEN

NITA TOOK LONGER than she anticipated showering, dressing and packing her bag. By the time she returned to Ky's cabin, Jess was there but there was no sign of Ky.

"Hi," she said to Jess. "I'm heading out, don't want to wait until it's too dark before I go. Do you know where Ky went?"

Jess winced, her hands gripping some oven mitts before she finally threw them on a counter. "There's a problem he went to handle. I don't know when he'll be back."

That didn't sound good. Especially not the way Jess said it.

"I guess I'll go home then." Shit. She'd really wanted to see him. Maybe kiss him goodbye. Give him a hug. Ah, damn. She was much too attached to the big guy. Distance was probably a good thing. "He has my number and we'll talk when he isn't so busy." She strolled forward to give Jess a hug. "Thanks so much for feeding me while I've been here."

"Oh, you're very welcome." Jess sighed. She patted her on the back and marched to the front of the house where Nita's energy saver was parked. "I'm just happy you're back."

Nita stopped by the car door and turned to Jess. "Back?"

Jess's sparkling hazel eyes filled with happiness. "Yes! I'm so happy that Ky finally got you back."

Say what? "Got me back from where?"

"Oh," she gushed. "You know. You were his first love back in high school."

Oh. My. God.

It couldn't be real. She had to be kidding. Ky wouldn't have withheld that kind of information. Would he? "His first love?"

"Let me think." Jess's brow puckered. "You guys were like fourteen or fifteen I think. Anyway, he'd gone to live with one of our uncles at Silver Falls. He and my dad didn't get along. But that's another story. You went to the same school." Jess grinned. "I'm sure you've talked about it already, but I just think it's so awesome that you're here. And he's got the woman he always wanted."

Silver Falls. The word resounded in her head like a painful drum. Jess's words were drowned out by the painfully loud beat of her heart. He'd been her high school best friend?

Jess gave her another hug. "Drive safe and come back soon! I know Ky will be counting the minutes until you do."

"Right," she mumbled and slid behind the wheel of her car.

She got lost in her thoughts. Hours flew, one after another, and her mind turned to a complete mess of questions. Why hadn't he told her who he was? She felt like a fucking idiot for not putting two and two together. He didn't look so much like he had back in school that she'd assume he was the same person. The vile taste of acid rolled up the back of her throat. Bastard!

"How?" she asked herself.

Her phone rang repeatedly but she refused to look at it.

She was hurt. Angry. Frustrated. An emptiness took hold of her chest. He'd lied to her. It didn't matter that it was by omission. For every mile she drove, the sense of desolation and sadness grew.

She got home late that night, having spent hours stuck in traffic with nothing to do but think. Hectic sounds of the city surrounded her once she hit the main roads. None of that mattered.

After a quick shower, she lay on her sofa, trying to decide what to do. The days with him had been so nice. So...perfect. Why would he choose to not tell her about their past if he'd had feelings as Jess said.

Thump! Thump! Thump!

She jerked up on the sofa, her heart beating double time. Had the building fallen around her and she hadn't noticed?

"If you're in there open up, Nita!" Tally yelled, her knocks bouncing off the door. "I'm ten seconds from calling the police and filing a missing person's report."

Scurrying to open the door, she almost fell over her slippers. She cursed her tendency to trip over her own two feet and jerked the door open.

Tally shoved her way in without waiting for an invitation.

"Come in," she said sarcastically.

"What the hell, Nita?" Tally asked with shock. Then she gave her a once over and frowned. "What's wrong? What happened?"

"Nothing happened. I'm tired."

"Bullshit!"

Argh! She hated that Tally knew her so well she could tell when Nita was upset.

"Really, Tally. It's not a big deal. I'm unsure where this is going with Ky."

Tally marched for the kitchen, ignoring Nita's words as if she'd said come in instead.

"What are you doing?" Nita asked. She followed after Tally into her small but open kitchen.

"Tea. It's too late for coffee."

"I'm surprised Theron and Connor aren't here with you," Nita said of Tally's mates. Wherever Tally went, the men followed.

Tally sat down on the breakfast nook and motioned her to take a seat. "They don't need to be here with me. This is girl talk."

Nita raised a brow. "What did you do, leave them in the car?"

Tally sighed. "No. I'm an independent woman. I can get around without them. I did it for most of my life." She shrugged. "Plus, I warned them that if they even suggested coming along I'd probably stab them in their sleep with a fork."

"That sounds more like you."

"Forget about me," Tally stated. "What happened to you? Why do you look so...sad?"

Tally stood and got teacups and sugar, and then proceeded to unwrap something from a bag she'd carried in.

"Is that—?"

"Yes. Cake. I knew that if you weren't answering me you'd need this."

Okay, maybe she wasn't too upset that Tally had shown up. Besides, Tally was probably the only person she trusted enough to tell how she felt and discuss what happened.

"Tally, you didn't have to." She forked a piece of cake and shoved it in her mouth. "But I am glad you did."

Tally sat down again, her arms resting on the kitchen table. "Okay, so what happened that things went from you having a great time with Mr. Beautiful Eyes, to you being home moping?"

"I'm not moping," she grumbled. Disgusted with herself, she slammed the fork down on the plate. "He lied to me!"

Tally's scared wide-eyed stare almost made her laugh. "Lied how?"

She inhaled sharply, trying to rein in the anger over the bear's sly omissions. "He is the Ky I knew back in high school."

Tally's eyes got even wider. "Wait. The one you said was your best friend?"

"That one," she growled.

"You didn't notice this when you first saw him?" Tally sounded as confused as she felt. Welcome to the club, sister.

"I need some liquor. This tea shit ain't gonna cut it."

"Nita!" Tally burst into laughter.

"What? It's true!" She remembered her first view of Ky. Half-naked and passed out on his kitchen floor. "As for noticing, no. He's changed. A lot. He's all big and buff and..."

"And what?" Tally asked, leaning forward.

"And sexy as hell. He was a cute guy back in school, but he had braces and his hair was kind of long. He was shy so he was always hunched over a little. God!" she hissed. "I must have been really stupid to him. Not knowing he was the one guy I trusted back then."

"Oh, Nita. I'm sure he had a reason not to tell you."

"Yeah?" she snapped. "What? Because as far as I'm concerned he was my best friend. You'd think that after the friendship we had he would be acknowledging that right away. Besides," she huffed. "His sister said he'd been in love with me back then. More of a reason for him to tell me who he was."

"But honey, men are stupid."

"Yes, we know that. But he's smart. This is Ky Stone. He was in advanced classes. About to head off to an early college program. He's really fucking smart. So he can't use stupidity as an excuse when he's a genius. And," she groaned, shoulders dropping. "Tally he's so sexy. He did things..."

Tally blinked. "What things?"

A hot shiver ran down her spine. "Things no man had ever done with his tongue. I swear my legs melted to the floor the first time we had sex."

"Damn, girl!"

"Why would he do this?" she asked herself more than Tally. Ky had changed. Not just physically. He was hiding things from her. That's not something the younger version of him had ever done. They'd been honest with each other. There had been more than just friendship between them. A special bond had formed and now she wondered if what she felt was all an illusion. An illusion created by the new Ky Stone. A lie.

"I think you need to talk to him."

"If I see him, I won't be responsible for my actions." Already she visualized smacking him upside the head with her frying pan. That would teach the bear to mess with her. She didn't care that he was bigger and buffer than her. She had Latin genes on her side.

"Stop and think for second. He treated you so well while you were up there with him. You had a great time. You got to know each other," Tally said suggestively. "In every sense of the word."

"I also opened up to him. I told him things only you know."

"I'm sorry, prima." Tally placed a hand over Nita's on the table, squeezing her in an attempt at comfort. "We'll figure it out. If you need me to go up there and castrate him, say the word."

Tally had grown a lot more aggressive since her mating to the two wolf shifters. It helped Nita feel better to know her cousin had her back. Not that she wanted to truly hurt Ky. The more she thought about it, the more she worried she'd developed more than just feelings of attraction for him. She'd never felt so hurt or distraught over a man. It didn't matter that she'd only spent a handful of days with him. Ky was an anomaly. He'd slipped in through the cracks and gave her emotions a run for their money.

She hated to admit it, but she feared she fell in love with him. This was so not the way things were supposed to go.

KY TRIED AGAIN to reach Nita. Nothing. They'd had an amazing time together. He couldn't figure out what happened. His cell phone rang just as he was getting ready to leave his house.

"Liam?"

"I'm down by the river. There's a group of outsiders here."

"I'm coming," he growled.

He'd decide on Nita later. As it was, the fishing problem needed resolution.

He stripped out of his clothes and dashed out of the cabin. No more asking nicely. The bear grunted, ready to take control. As he ran, the shift took over. His bear roared the moment he was out. Anger over his missing woman and now the trespassers meant the bear wanted to knock some heads off.

He arrived at the river bend in time to catch David and Liam fighting with some brown bears. They didn't seem to be from the neighboring clan. He roared loud for all to hear.

The fight didn't stop but two of the bears left, scared. Then Ky noticed a large brown bear off to the side, watching him. The brown made a dash for Ky.

Ky waited for the other bear to reach him, he knew that scent. It was a neighbor from two clans down the mountain. He'd been in talks with them for use of the river once in a while, but nothing definite had been decided. It seemed they'd taken it upon themselves to go fishing at his river anyway.

The bear swung, digging his claws into Ky's fur. Ky's bear roared with rage. He bit and shoved at the other animal, doing some serious damage with his own claws. Black bears were the most dangerous out there. They shoved back and forth, Ky biting on the side of the brown bear's muzzle.

Roars and growls sounded all around. His attention was focused on the brown trying to best him. The brown huffed, tackling Ky and trying to take him down. Unfortunately for him, Ky wasn't Chief of his clan just for show. He tackled with his guards all the time for fighting practice. Ky slammed a giant claw on the brown's neck. The brown pulled back, almost falling on his back but he regained his balance. A loud pain-filled roar sounded from the brown. Ky bit down on his neck. The brown pushed away at the same moment Ky knocked him on the side with his claw.

The brown bled from the neck wound. The bastard didn't give in though.

"Get off of my land." Ky growled through their animal link. He slammed into the side of the brown and took him down.

The brown shoved back, finally knocking Ky on his ass.

They were both on their feet in seconds, Ky shoving and biting at the other bear's muzzle once again.

The brown tried using his claws to inflict pain in Ky's side, but the anger over the trespass and even worse, his frustration over his missing mate, kept him from dwelling on the pain.

Ky hit the bear on the shoulder where he'd bitten, to add to the pain he knew the intruder felt. The brown bit into Ky's arm. Fiery throbbing took hold of his limb. Ky didn't stop, he used the moment to his advantage and once again burrowed his canines into the brown. The metallic taste of the enemy's blood hit his tongue. It pushed the bear even more into a feral state of mind.

He shoved at the brown, knocking him down and pinning him to the ground. The enemy huffed, kicked at Ky's stomach and tried to get him off. Ky jabbed his claws into the bear's arms and pushed him further on his back. He bit the side of the brown's head, tearing at one of the bear's ears.

The brown shook, trying to get out of his hold but only managed to get a massive gash on the side of his face. Loud roaring sounded from all over.

"We'll go!" the brown finally whimpered.

"If you come back, I won't let you walk out of here alive," Ky promised, still holding the brown down. "Do you understand?"

"Yes," the other man mumbled between whimpers of pain.

Ky stood and roared loud. A warning to those standing there fighting his men. If they returned, there would be no getting out alive.

The group left. One limped away, the other helped carry the bear Ky had almost killed.

He, David and Liam stood there, watching the intruders go for a few minutes before finally shifting back into their human bodies. They had some gashes, and in Liam's case, a pretty ugly wound on his side, but overall they were fine.

They dove into the chilly river water to bathe the blood off their bodies.

EIGHT

BACK AT KY'S cabin, David asked the question Ky had been dreading. "So when is Nita coming back?"

Those words did what no amount of fighting had done. They opened up gashes in his heart. He couldn't get in touch with Nita. He didn't know what was wrong. All he knew was the she'd left and hadn't even said goodbye.

They sat in his backyard, drinking beer from a cooler. Liam had the grill going and on any other day Ky would've thought it was one of the best ways to spend some time relaxing. Not so that day.

"She's not," he replied.

"What?" Liam asked, stopping the beer midway to his mouth. He closed the grill top and marched for the picnic table. "Why not?"

"She's not answering my calls. I don't know what the hell is wrong," he growled.

Liam frowned, chugging down on his beer. "She didn't seem upset at all when we left."

"That's what's killing me," Ky said, rubbing a hand over the back of his wet neck. "The worst part is I don't have her address." He raised a hand when David opened his mouth. "She's unlisted, I checked everywhere. Why do you think it's been hard to find her all these years? It's not like I didn't try."

David slammed his bottle on the table. "I got it!" He smiled. "What? I do have a brain. I'm more than just good looks and charm, you know."

Liam laughed and returned to the grill. "What is it you think you got?"

David smiled at Ky. "How did you find her again?"

"I didn't. My sister called the Paranormal Dating Agency and somehow got her to come."

David raised his bottle as if he'd just cured all the world's problems. "I rest my case."

"You still haven't made any sense, cousin it." Liam took burgers off the grill and brought them to the picnic table.

"The dating people. They have her address."

The misery consuming Ky suddenly dissipated. "You're right!" He stood and turned to his house.

"Where are you going?" Liam asked. "Did I just cook all this food for you to leave it?"

"You sound like a wife," Ky joked, no longer so distressed. "David and his beard will help you get rid of it."

"Ha ha, real funny," David said, holding his beard out of the way to take a bite of his food.

"You're right," Liam agreed. "I'll make sure he eats more than the beard."

"Don't you have a woman to go get," David argued. "Quit it with my beard. The woman who falls for me will love it."

"You and I have to talk," Liam said, turning back to David. "That beard, bro. It's gotta go."

Ky headed for his cabin to dress and get in touch with the woman who ran the PDA. He knew that was the fastest way he could get Nita's address. But he also knew he'd have to plead his case in person. He doubted anyone would just hand off client information because he was in love. He would lay on the charm when it came to the owner of the service. One thing was for sure: he wasn't leaving her office without Nita's address.

No way in hell.

KY KNOCKED ON the door to Mrs. Wilder's apartment and tried not to stress. Jess had told him Mrs. Wilder was sort of brusque, but very good at her job. She then proceeded to hug him and wish him luck. When he'd called Mrs. Wilder from the road, she'd refused to speak to him over the phone and said he needed to come to her house if he wanted anything discussed.

The scent of fresh baked honey buns filled his nose. His stomach growled. So did the bear inside him. Shit. He'd forgotten to eat.

Mrs. Wilder's door swung open to a petite older woman with raised brows giving him the once over.

"My my my. You are every bit a bear, aren't you?" She whistled. "Check out those big arms. Just enough hair to make a woman want to rake her nails over them."

He wasn't sure what to do.

It wasn't that he hadn't been hit on by older women before, but this was uncomfortable. And a little scary.

"Thank you," he said, shifting from foot to foot like a schoolboy.

Mrs. Wilder continued eyeing his arms with renewed interest. "Well come inside. I don't have all day."

He snapped out of the weird younger man being eyed by a cougar moment and followed her inside the apartment.

"Go on and sit in the living room. I'll bring you a snack," she called out from the kitchen. "I know you big guys like to eat."

Did he ever. He sat down on one of the large sofas, taking up every bit of space and feeling like a giant. She finally showed up with a tray piled with honey buns. The twiddling of his thumbs stopped.

"Go on and grab one. They're not gonna bite you." She smiled. "But I just might."

He needed to get the information on Nita's address fast. Mrs. Wilder had that predatory smile that he knew all too well. He took a honey bun, placed it on a small plate and took a bite without making a mess. At least he hoped he hadn't made a mess of it all over his face.

"So, now that you're sitting and that bear of yours stopped growling for food, what can I do for you?" She filled a cup with tea and honey and placed it next to his plate.

"Nita. I want her address."

She didn't stop pouring her own tea. Instead she nodded and added sugar in complete silence. "And why should I break my client's trust and give you that information? If she wanted you to have it, she'd have given it to you herself."

He picked up a napkin and wiped his fingers. "She could be in trouble. Something had to have happened. When she left she said she'd be back and she's not answering her calls. She hasn't returned."

Mrs. Wilder frowned and picked up her cell phone. She pressed some buttons and then waited for a moment. It buzzed. She stared at the screen and put it down. "Nope. She's fine."

Fuck! That meant it was him. He'd had to have said or done something to upset her. Maybe she wanted him to outright tell her to stay versus sending her a text.

"Did you and Nita talk while she was there?" Mrs. Wilder asked, tucking a strand of hair behind her ear.

"Yes. Of course we talked. We did a lot of talking."

She leaned on one of the arms of her seat. "Did you at any point tell her who you were?"

Oh. Shit.

"No. I thought about it at first, but I liked that she didn't have the image of my scrawny insecure self from high school in mind."

She snorted and picked up her cup. "You silly boy. If she cared about you at all back then, don't you think she'd be happy to know you're the person she's been matched with?"

He didn't think of that. All he thought of was her seeing him again as the boy who stuttered and couldn't tell her how he felt.

"Has she changed from how she was back then?"

"Yes. She's different. More self-assured. Sexy. Still just as beautiful," he replied.

Mrs. Wilder pursed her lips. "And the time she spent with you, did you keep seeing her as the little girl you fell in love with or as the woman she is today?"

"No. She's still just as sweet as she was back then, but all grown up. The time we spent together only showed me new facets to the girl I knew.

It reinforced what I concluded when I was fourteen. That she's the one for me."

It hit him then. He'd fucked up. Big time. Instead of being honest with Nita from the beginning, telling her who he was and how he'd felt back in high school, he'd withheld the information and she'd found out about it.

Mrs. Wilder watched him like a hawk. "You know, I don't follow society's rules. I match people based on my gut and a little extra. I'll tell you this. I know you two are a good pair." She picked up a folded piece of paper from the coffee table. "Here. And for Christ's sakes, tell the woman how you feel."

He nodded and took the paper like she'd given him a sacred document. "I will."

"Word of advice: cut it with the lies even by omission. Women hate that."

"Yes, ma'am," he said, staring at Nita's address as if he would magically transport there.

Mrs. Wilder cleared her throat. "So what are you waiting for? Go get your girl!"

He jumped to his feet. Excitement bounced in his chest. "Thank you. Really."

She smiled and waved at him dismissively. "You can pay me back by sending more clients my way."

He laughed and marched for the door. "I will. I have two in mind that can use your help."

"Wonderful," she said as he ran down the hallway. "Good luck!"

Half an hour later he'd pounded on Nita's door multiple times. No one answered. He wouldn't leave until he spoke to her. His phone rang just as he vowed to sit by the door to Nita's apartment to wait for her.

"Hello?"

"Change of plans bear." It was Mrs. Wilder. "Your girl is headed to your house. I just heard Tally mention it to her mates. Get your ass in your car and catch up to her. She was very angry when she left," Mrs. Wilder said. "Try not to make her wait. Might add to her already agitated state and get you into even more trouble."

"I am on my way now." He moved toward the building entrance with the phone by his ear. "Do you know why she decided to go to my house?"

"Apparently Tally convinced her to talk to you and hear your side of the story. This is the one for you, bear. We both know it. Fix things with her and you'll be a happy man."

"I plan to. I might break some speeding laws to get there but I'll see her soon."

He ran out of the building and hopped in his jeep. He'd reach Nita and hopefully get her to listen to him.

NITA DROVE LIKE a bat out of hell. She finally slowed down once the visibility turned low in front of her due to the large amounts of rain.

"Stupid big sexy bastard," she growled. "Does he think he can just lie to me and get away with it?" She gripped the wheel. "Make me fall in love with him and not tell me who he was," she mumbled, pushing back the urge to cry. "He is so dead."

She'd finally given up waiting around trying to figure out what the hell possessed Ky to not tell her who he was. Instead, she was going to confront him head on. Only thing was the weather kept slowing her down. Stupid rain. Why did it have to come down in buckets now that she'd decided to go over there and see Ky face to face.

By the time she arrived, it was dark. She shoved the pepper spray in her pocket out of habit and searched for an umbrella. There was none. The lights in his cabin were on, but nobody came out. Growling internally at the lying bear, she hopped out of her car. Pellets of rain slid down her arms and head. She was soaked before she got a foot away from the car. The pretty dress she'd worn in order to tease the bear clung to her like a second skin. The thing had probably turned see-through. Hair plastered on her skull, she skidded through the mud and grass toward the cabin.

Knowing Ky was usually in the back, she ran for the kitchen entrance and found it locked. What the hell?

She knocked repeatedly. Went as far as yelling but nobody seemed to be around. Then she thought of the creek. It was possible he was there. In his bear body, he wouldn't care about the rain like a woman with frizzy curly hair would. Her hair was like a separate entity with a mind of its own. She didn't want to think about the hours it would take for her to dry it, then tame the 'fro into submission. That was what she'd gotten from her ancestors: gorgeous brown skin and a brillo pad for hair that took herculean strength to keep under control.

Squinting against the harsh drops of cool water, she turned toward the creek and slammed into a body.

She glanced up to meet a very angry face. The apology died in her mouth. She took a step back, but the guy grabbed her by the arm.

"Hey!" She tugged but the guy squeezed harder.

"You're his female. I scent him on you." The guy's voice sounded low and angry. "I'll show him to fuck with me."

She glanced down where he gripped her arm. His fingers were claws, digging painfully into her flesh. "What the hell are you doing? Let me go!"

"No. He shamed me in front of my guards. I won't let it go. I'll teach him a lesson with you and then kill him," the man growled.

A car approached from the distance. She couldn't see who it was, but either Ky was finally home, or someone was coming to visit.

She tugged on her arm again. "Let go you jerk. If he shamed you then you did something to deserve it you asshole!"

Instead the guy pulled her arm harder. She swore he'd torn it out of the socket for a second before he dragged her down the path by the baby cabin.

"You're coming with me," the guy yelled. "He beat me in front of my clansmen. I'll kill you and him."

What the hell? She glanced over her shoulder, watching another body appear in the distance. She slapped the brute but he didn't stop.

"Ky!" she screamed his name at the top of her lungs, hoping that it was him who'd just arrived.

The man jerked her harder down the path, pulling her toward the river's edge. She slipped on the mud, her feet covered in wet earth through her open sandals. Wearing the pretty shoes and dress had been the worse idea she'd had that day.

"Ky!" she hollered as loud as possible.

A massive roar sounded at her back. Then another. Closer. The guy hauling her stopped. He shoved her out of the way and she fell on the mud with a splat. Rain thundered and fell harder.

"I'll kill you," the guy yelled at Ky. "I'll do what my men didn't when they came to your cabin. I'll destroy you. Your river will be mine," he bellowed.

"I let you live last time. I won't make the same mistake twice," Ky said through the booming rain.

The moonlight allowed her to make out what was going on. A roar sounded from the stranger and he tore through his clothes with his shift into a big brown bear.

She crawled back and away from him. A glance to her left showed an even bigger black bear running toward them. Ky.

There was no hesitation. He growled and threw himself at the other bear. They tumbled midway down the hill and stood. She got up, rushed to them and watched from a safe distance.

Both men were covered in mud. She only knew Ky by size. He was bigger and louder with his roars. He slapped the other bear hard on the face. She winced at the sound of bone cracking.

The smaller bear bit Ky's arm and shook his head as if trying to tear a piece of him off. Fear exploded in her chest. She wanted to help Ky. But how? She didn't have a death wish. She was the human out of the three of them and would most likely die for getting in the way.

NINE

NITA TOED THE sandals off her feet. Creeping closer to the fighting bears from the side, she pulled out the pepper spray from her dress pocket. She couldn't stop staring at the fighting giants. The brown bear was in deep shit. His muzzle was in Ky's mouth. And Ky was biting down. More sounds of crunching could be heard coming from the two. They clawed at each other's arms. Huffing and growling, the two bears continued to battle.

The brown did something at that point. He raked a claw over Ky's muzzle and got him to let go. Ky grunted and roared again. The brown charged. They fell to the ground in a heap of arms and kicking legs. The brown bit the same spot on Ky's shoulder he'd done before.

Nita winced. She knew that had to hurt. The sounds of pain and anger from both worried her. She might be angry at Ky, but she didn't want him dead. Oh no, she wanted him very alive to make him grovel and pay for lying to her. Plus she loved sex with him. Hell, who was she kidding? She loved him.

Standing there watching the crazy fight only sealed the deal in her mind. Now he just needed to hurry up and kick the other bear's ass so she could give him a piece of her mind.

They were on their feet again. Shoving and tugging back and forth. With each movement, they got much closer. It wasn't safe for her, but she'd decided she had to help somehow. The brown careened forward, pushing Ky straight into a massive tree a handful of feet away from her. Ky fell on his back. Before he had a chance to stand, the brown turned toward Nita. He didn't charge, there was no need, it wasn't like she was trying to run from him. He stood in front of her, roared and lowered his giant head level with her face. She didn't think. His beady eyes stared angrily at her. She raised a hand and sprayed the pepper spray into his eyes. The bear reeled back and bellowed. He shook his head repeatedly, waving his paws around.

Ky tackled the bear from the side. He held him down on the muddy ground and bit down the brown's neck. The attack didn't stop. Even when the brown slowed down, his movements tired, Ky continued to bite and tear at the other bear's neck. He didn't stop until the other bear quit moving altogether. A cold chill ran down her spine along with a thread of fear. She watched Ky stand and turn to her. Still a bear and still looking mighty pissed.

There were cuts and gashes all over his fur. She couldn't tell how bad they were from the lack of light and the sheeting rain. He met her gaze and prowled toward her. Instinct told her to run, to get away from him. He had a dangerous look she'd never seen before. The beast controlled him.

She eyed the muddy hill. It was going to be impossible for her to get up there. She'd just keep sliding back down, making a fool of herself if she tried. Then he was there, in front of her. She glanced up and gasped. He lowered and opened his arms for her. She held on to his furry neck. There was no fear as he lifted her legs in his arms, careful not to dig his claws in her skin. Still very much in his bear body, he carried her in the direction of his cabin.

It was easy for him to use the tree limbs to climb back up the hill. When they reached the creek, she wiggled in his hold.

"Put me down!"

He did so, gently.

"You come back to your human body. I need to talk to you," she demanded.

She stepped away from him, waiting for the shift. In his human body, she saw his cuts with more clarity. He had bruises but nothing appeared to be life threatening.

"Nita!" he called when she turned away. "I'm sorry."

She whipped around to face him again, inhaling hard and ignoring the harsh raindrops stroking her body. "Why didn't you tell me?"

"I was stupid," he said, stepping closer.

"Don't give me that crap!" she threw back. It was hard enough to keep her eyes from straying down his body. Now he wanted to feed her some corny line. "We both know how intelligent you are. Why didn't you tell me we knew each other?"

His gaze dropped to the ground, his chest heaved from the shift and the fight. He looked so good wet.

"I didn't want you to judge me based on the awkward kid I used to be," he admitted.

Maybe he really was stupid. Her mind and body struggled for dominance. She wanted to tackle him and rub herself all over his naked body and at the same time slap some sense into him.

"Are you serious?" She turned away, blood boiling with frustration. "I can't do this."

She marched toward the car, trying to ignore the icky feeling of the mud sliding in between her toes. She'd only gone a few yards when he grabbed her arms and tugged her around to face him.

"What do you want from me?" His face was soaked. Water streamed down his body from the pouring rain.

"I want the truth!" She didn't know what possessed her to scream at him, but she already knew her feelings. There was no going back after this. If they had any chance at all they had to be honest with each other.

"The truth? Fine." He jerked her close into his arms. "The truth is I knew from the moment I saw you seventeen years ago that you were the only one for me." His gaze bore into her. The raw honesty in his eyes kept her unmoving. "At first it was an attraction, a pull, I couldn't understand. When we started spending more time together it was clear to me that we had a connection that went beyond the physical. Yes, I was attracted to you back then. Even with how shy you were. Despite my inability to say a full sentence to you without stuttering from nerves, I knew you were my one."

She swallowed at the dryness in her throat. Her stomach twisted in knots with every word that came out of his gorgeous mouth.

"How do you think I felt, the kid that everyone picked on because I was skinnier than anyone in the clan? I wore braces and probably the ugliest glasses in the world. I had minimal self-esteem. But when I was with you, I was on top of the world."

She blinked back the tears filling her eyes. She knew firsthand how hard school had been for a kid that was picked on. She'd lived it. Emotions overwhelmed her. Hope. Sadness. Pain. All of them swirled around in her chest filling her heart to near bursting. She heard the raw honesty in his words. Saw it in his eyes. They had more than most people ever dreamed of, a connection since the first time they met as kids. She struggled to swallow back the knot in her throat.

"Ky—" Her heart ached. Tears burned in her eyes. So much had been suffered by both already.

"Let me finish." He lowered his head a fraction. "Do you know it broke my heart when you moved away? You never even told me where you were going. You just left."

"I'm...I'm sorry." She loved him so much at that moment. He'd told how he felt and stood in front of her, still wanting to be with her. It was time to stop fighting it and find their happily ever after.

"No. I did not tell you who I was when I woke up in my kitchen floor with you leaning over me. At first I was in shock. Do you know how many times I dreamed of something like that? But when I realized you didn't recognize me I thought it was for the best. I'm not the insecure kid I used to be." He licked the raindrops that continued to fall off his lips. "Although you can reduce me to a hormonal teenage boy, I am a different person today."

She shook her head, ignoring her soaked state and the clothes clinging to her like second skin. "No. You're not. You're still the sweet, nice boy I fell in love with back then." His eyes went wide and she smiled. If he could open up about his feelings then she could too. "Yeah. I had a crush on the geeky boy that tutored me. That connection you speak of? I felt it too! And now..." She glanced down at his lips then back at his eyes. "Now I'm in love with the adult version of Ky Stone."

He stood there, staring at her. Saying nothing.

She cleared her throat. "I'm in love with you, Ky. I love you."

There was a heartbeat of silence. Then his lips crashed over hers. Passion flared brighter than the last time they'd been together. He held her lips captive, driving his tongue into her mouth with a new aggression she hadn't seen before. Need pooled at her core, scorching her brain cells and pushing all rational thought out the window.

He tore his mouth from hers to drop kisses all over her face, down her jaw and to her neck. She didn't notice when they fell to the ground in a tight embrace. Nor when her dress came off. What did burn into her brain was the feel of his lips on her skin at the same time rain drops continued to fall on them.

The heat of his mouth encasing her nipple, combined with the cool drops of water added to the raging fire in her blood. He sucked her hard nubs, grazing his teeth over them and tugging.

"Oh, Ky..."

He slid his hands down, tearing at her panties. "Yes, sweetheart. Say my name. I like hearing it out of your lips."

She moaned, spread her thighs open and gasped at the finger he slid inside her.

"Fuck! You're ready for me, aren't you?"

She bit her bottom lip and whimpered. "I need you. Ky...I—"

He was at her entrance, pressing the head of his cock into her wet sheath. "I love you, Nita." He drove forth. In a single smooth slide he filled her.

A gasp of pleasure tore from her throat. "Yes!"

He rumbled and pulled back. The heat from his body cocooned her in a warm embrace. Their lips met again. Another scorching kiss with their tongues rubbing over each other. His thrusts increased in speed and strength.

"I'm sorry." He sucked on the pulse at the base of her throat. The errant pulse that ran at a million miles per hour. "I can't slow down," he groaned. "I want you more than you know."

She clung to his shoulders, curling her legs around his hips. "I can imagine. I want you just as bad."

There were no more words after that, just his body moving in and out of hers in powerful thrusts. Tension curled into a ball at her core. Her pussy felt aflame. She gasped and moaned, unable to speak a coherent word. For every thrust, he sucked at her shoulder.

She became lost in the sensation of pleasure. The feeling of fulfillment from the one man she finally opened her heart to. He pulled out of her and flipped her on her stomach. The rain continued to fall on them, cooling their bodies.

She wiggled on all fours and glanced over her shoulder at him. "Fuck me, Ky."

He slapped a hand on her hip and guided his cock into her pussy with the other. Again, there was no soft and careful. He drove forward swiftly. One deep penetrating thrust that left her gasping for air. He gripped her hips and fucked her fast, hard. With a wild animal abandon she'd never experienced before. It was amazing and perfect.

There was no need for sweet words at this point. She knew he loved her. What she wanted now was for him to make the ache in her pussy ease. She needed for him to help that tightness in her muscles turn into a wave of pleasure coursing from her head to her toes.

"You've always been mine," he said, tapping her right ass cheek with his palm.

"God, yes."

His powerful drives increased in speed. Only the sound of the rain and the slapping of his body on hers sounded in the forest.

"Tell me you'll be mine forever, baby," he said, voice rough and deep.

There was no question or doubt in her mind that she wanted to be with him. He was the first and only man her heart had allowed inside.

"Yes. I'm yours," she moaned. "Forever."

He dropped on all fours, caging her.

"I'm going to take you every way possible," he breathed by her ear. "Your mouth. I love your mouth. I can't wait to see my cock down your throat."

She hitched a breath, feeling the burn of her blood on boil.

"Your pussy. Shit," he groaned. "I love fucking you deep and hard, feeling it close around my dick like a silky tongue." He angled his hips and she almost saw double.

"Oh, but your ass," he grunted, moving his hand from her waist and slipping it between their bodies. He slid a finger around her ass and pressed at her hole. The sensation was more than she could handle at that moment. Even though they weren't ready for it, she wanted him to do her there so bad she hurt from how tight her muscles were.

She moaned and pressed into his finger. It slid just a fraction into her asshole.

He licked her back and panted. "That's going to be the biggest treat. I can't wait to fuck your tight little hole and fill you with my cum back there."

She shoved her ass into each of his thrusts. He brought his hand back up to her waist and gripped her firmly. Harder than he'd done before.

"I'm marking you as mine," he said. "I want you as my mate."

"Do it. I'll always be yours. Only yours."

He fucked her in firm solid strokes. So harsh she swore he'd break her in half soon. His cock felt like heated steel inside her, branding her as his. He hit her at an angle. Her eyes rolled back. Christ he was fucking amazing. He pulled her body up, switching the depth of his penetration. She moaned at the new feeling of fullness.

He slipped the hand he had on her waist between her legs and flicked over her clit, rubbing on the nerve bundle back and forth. She gasped. The tightness in her body snapped.

"God, yes!" he roared. "Come on my dick and squeeze tight with your pussy."

She screamed his name. A rush of pleasure liquefied her bones. Her muscles shook and she'd have fallen on her face if he didn't have her tight in his grasp. Her pussy clutched at his driving cock. He moved his hand back to her waist, digging his claws into her flesh at the same time he bit her back. Her body continued to wade through the pouring of euphoria from her first orgasm and the one that followed when he bit her.

He growled, still biting her back and drove a final time into her. Deep. He filled her with his seed then. Her pussy milked him of his cum. It was by far the most erotic experience of her life.

Blinking her brain back to reality took a while. She was still gasping for breath minutes later when he pulled out of her.

He kissed her back and picked her up in his arms. She sighed and snuggled into him. They were wet, muddy and covered in leaves. If that wasn't wild sex she had no idea what was. Instead of heading for the cabin, he jumped into the creek with her in his arms.

She screeched when they came up for air.

"Are you insane?" She slapped his shoulder and curled her legs and arms around him like he was her only form of salvation.

He chuckled and kissed her. "We're dirty. This is the easiest way to get clean."

She raised her brows. "Did you forget I can't swim?"

A playful grin covered his lips. "Then I guess you'll have to hold on to me, won't you?"

She rolled her eyes, but tightened her hold on him just in case. "You know, you're lucky I'm so patient."

His flirty grin turned into a full blown smile. "I know. I love you. All sides of you."

"Flattery will get you—" She sighed. "Oh, alright. It works. Especially if you promise me some of the awesome stuff you do with your tongue."

He roared a laugh. "You really are great for my ego."

She cupped his face in her hands and stared him in the eyes. "Don't ever lie to me again. Even by omission. I won't stand for it. If you really love me then you won't do anything that hurts me." She was all seriousness as she spoke. "Tell me the truth all the time, no matter how bad you think it is and we'll always work through it."

"I'm sorry, Nita. I'll never lie to you again."

She harrumphed. "Good, because if you do, I've got Tally ready to bite your furry ass off. Trust me, she's vicious."

He slid the hair away from her face. "Your cousin can stand down. I don't need her to come bite me anywhere. I will allow you to do it whenever you want though."

"Now that has some good possibilities, Mr. Bear."

A MONTH LATER, Nita stared at the claw marks on her hip. The night he'd mated her in the rain he'd scratched her to mark her as his. The scratches had healed but now she had claw marks that would never go away. He entered the bedroom from his shower, rubbing a towel over his head to dry off.

"What are you doing?"

She slapped her hand on her hip. "Look!"

He grinned. "I see."

"You think this is funny? I have claw marks on my hip. And teeth marks on my back." She frowned. "I don't even want to know what Grandma Kate will say the next time we see her."

"When is that?" he asked, tossing the towel on the bed and marching to where she stood.

"Next week."

"You can tell her you're ready to hibernate for the winter with me," he joked and rubbed his erection on her back.

She turned around, curled her arms around his neck and smiled. "You're a pervert. I didn't realize how much of one you are. I like it."

"I aim to please," he said, squeezing her ass cheek.

She yawned and leaned into his hug. "I need a nap."

"You'll be needing lots of those soon, darling."

"Why?" She jerked her head up and stared into his smiling hazel eyes.

Oh.

Shit.

"Yeah, that," he said. He must have seen the realization of her state dawn on her face.

"This is all your fault." She tried to sound chastising but couldn't when all she felt was absolutely happy. "Sexy ass geeky bear. Get me pregnant and you find it funny. Now when will I ever go back to work?"

"Never. You don't have to work. But if you want something to do, you can be my sex slave."

"That one sounds like something we should discuss."

He pulled away from her arms with a laugh. "Wait here."

She stared at the claw marks on her hip again. Well, at least they weren't on her belly. With a growing pregnancy they'd end up looking like big foot prints.

He returned with two boxes in hand. "I come bearing gifts."

She laughed. "Hah! I get it. You silly bear."

He frowned then laughed as if just realizing what he'd said. He handed her the larger box first. "This is for you. A symbol of how much you mean to me."

She opened it carefully, wondering what he'd gotten her. Inside the box there was a pendant. The pendant was a bear wearing glasses. She flipped it over and read the inscription.

"A bear is only as smart as the woman who puts up with his growling."

She grinned. "I like that."

The smaller box came next. She was about to open it when he took it back. "I thought of this day since I was fourteen. I know it sounds stupid but it's true."

"Ky—"

He dropped down on one knee. "I love you, Nita. Will you spend the winters putting up with my growly ass and the summers mating with me in every way possible? Forever?" He cleared his throat. "Will you marry me?"

She nodded. "Yes. But I think I'd like the mating to take place year round. I don't know if I can live that long without it. I'm pretty addicted to that body of yours."

He slid the antique style ring over her finger and pulled her in for a kiss.

"I love you, geek bear."

"I love you, beautiful."

EPILOGUE

GERRI OPENED UP an email she'd gotten a few days back. She needed to stop hanging out with her nephew and baking or she'd never get her business off the ground.

Dr. Mrs. Wilder,

My name is Alyssa Moran. I'm a co-worker of Tally's. She mentioned your services and I've met her men. They're hot. Like panty-dropping sexy. Yeah, you guessed it. I want my own hot man. I don't expect you to match me up with two of them, lord knows one is a feat on its own. I'd love to meet a nice guy for once. Maybe a guy that likes a woman with some curves. I've always been afraid of using dating services because men are only looking for sex and people never look like they say. Attached is a full body photo of me that I took today. Please don't laugh at the three cats. They're my only company. If you can send a man my way that likes cats, I'd be eternally grateful.

Gerri glanced down at the open file on her desk, grinning. The leader of a tiger pride needed a mate. He'd been recommended by the bear. Apparently he lived in a neighboring area. The tiger needed a mate soon or he'd be challenged for his pride. She'd need to find him someone willing to take on a hissing tiger.

Time to get to work. She hit the reply button on the email and started typing.

Dear Ms. Moran,

I'd love for you to come visit me so we can chat some more about what you're looking for. Sometimes the right man can be more than what my clients can handle...

And sometimes, they can be exactly what they need.

THE END

HER PURRFECT *Match*

book 3

ONE

"Relax, Alyssa. Gerri really isn't as bad as you're thinking," Tally, her coworker, said to her.

Alyssa Moran added more sugar to her tepid coffee and winced. She didn't even like that much sugar, but her nerves were all over. Placing the spoon on the plate with a small clink, she moved her hands to her lap. Unable to sit still, she wiped the sweat off her palms on her suit pants.

"I'm not nervous." Liar! "Mrs. Wilder sounded like a lovely person over email." A very strange but nice person. She'd asked some stuff Lyss had never been asked before. Ever.

"I know." Tally chuckled. "Her methods are unconventional, but they work. Look at me."

Yeah. Look at her. Before Mrs. Wilder had matched Tally with her two men, Lyss had sworn Tally was a man-hater. Nothing good ever came out of her mouth when it came to men. Especially if her ex-husband's name was discussed. Then one day she showed up with a glow and a smile. Ever since Lyss had seen the change in Tally, she wondered if maybe she wouldn't have to live the life of a thirty-five year old cat lady with an addiction to National Geographic and buying sex toys.

Unlike what her mother liked to say, Lyss was no prude. She loved sex. She liked it a hell of a lot, but she didn't want to keep doing it with the wrong men. Getting into a relationship with a loser just because he could rock her world didn't make sense anymore. Her last live-in boyfriend had the bad luck syndrome. If he got fired he blamed his eternal bad luck. She got so tired of it, she'd finally snapped at him and yelled, "No you dumb fuck, if you don't go to work, you will get fired."

And that was the end of that relationship. At least from her end. The moocher had tried to prolong the agony by saying he had nowhere to go. Asking her to please give him another chance. That he'd go find a job and make her proud. Then he went and tried to get her ATM card so he could 'borrow' some money.

If she was the kind of person who believed in bad luck, she'd think she was destined to be alone. Lyss was too positive for that. She knew there was a man out there for her. At this point she would take him being human, shifter or dead. Fuck that shit.

"Sorry I'm late girls," a woman dressed in an impeccable peach suit said, walking toward them.

Mrs. Wilder. Lyss stared, open-mouthed as the older woman winked at the waiter passing by.

"Traffic was a bitch, but what can you do, right?" She stopped next to Tally who jumped to her feet and hugged Mrs. Wilder. "Lovely to see you, Tally."

"Now that I don't live in the same building I miss you more, Gerri."

Mrs. Wilder made a dismissive gesture. "Nah. You miss my cakes."

"That too." Tally sighed.

Mrs. Wilder turned to her, her gaze piercing and filled with interest. "You must be Alyssa."

She'd stood at the same time as Tally, so she offered Mrs. Wilder her hand. "Mrs. Wilder—"

"None of that. Gerri. Though Your Matchmaking Highness has a nice ring to it too. But no Mrs. Wilder. I'm still very young for that." She pulled Lyss's offered hand and gave her a hug.

That shocked her. She wasn't used to public displays of affection. Her mother would complain over Lyss's choice of perfume or body spray so she'd never given her hugs, kisses or kind words in general.

"It's nice to meet you, Gerri." She waited until everyone sat down again to follow suit. "Thanks so much for coming."

Tally grinned. "Okay, now that you have some company, I'm going home early. I'll see you tomorrow."

Tally came around the table and gave her a hug. "Don't worry, Gerri will take good care of you. If I know her well, I bet she's got someone in mind already."

"Thanks for sitting with me."

"Bye, darling." Gerri hugged Tally as well. "Tell my nephew to bring you by tomorrow. I'll make some of his favorite cake."

Tally hugged Gerri again. "I so love you. And your baking."

Once Tally had gone, Gerri ordered some tea and pulled out a notebook. "Let's talk."

Lyss swallowed hard. "What about?"

"Why what you want in a man, of course." Gerri placed her elbow on the table and cupped her chin with her hand, tapping a finger on her cheek. "I know you said you wanted a man that likes cats."

She nodded quickly. "He has to. Or at least not be allergic and not be bothered by them."

"A man who likes pussy," Gerri said as she wrote. "Got it."

Lyss blinked. Then she burst into giggles.

Gerri gave her a side smile. "You got that, huh?"

"Heck yeah. I definitely need a man who likes erm...that. You know, Tally had said you were unique, but wow. I'm so glad you decided to help me."

Gerri patted her on the hand. "I wouldn't turn down a friend of Tally's. Besides, your letter made me laugh and that's not something that happens often."

She didn't remember what she'd written to make Gerri laugh, but she was glad she had the matchmaker on her side.

"What else?"

"I'm really sick of trying to be the savior. Fuck that," she said then slapped a hand over her mouth. "Sorry!"

Gerri laughed. "Don't mind me, I have my moments with words that would make you blush."

"Right. So men. I'm a big girl. But it seems like most of them I attract want to live off me because, according to some people, I can't get anything better since I'm too big."

"Who said that nonsense?" Gerri asked, her brows dropping in a fierce scowl.

"My mother, my exes. Don't worry, I don't believe them at all." She didn't. She knew that there were men out there that liked a bigger girl. So what if she had a tummy that was soft and big hips and thighs? Maybe her ass was larger than most but all that didn't faze her. She believed in her heart there was a man out there who would like a woman like her. Why?

Because there were more women that were big than small. And she knew Tally was not the only one able to get herself a set of hot men that loved her curves.

"I'm glad you didn't listen to them. There is someone or in some cases a few someones for everyone. It's just a matter of finding each other." Gerri put her pen down and pinned Lyss with a serious stare. "You're obviously aware that I don't match women with just any man. They're paranormals. Mostly shifters."

She might be a hopeless romantic, but she wanted a man to love her like her father had her mother. Except, she wouldn't treat him like her mother had her father. Lyss wanted to feel that emotional connection with someone and know he cared about her just as much as she did for him. Her hopes that every relationship would progress into the love she wanted was why she'd lasted so long in them. And why she always ended up disappointed.

She sighed and stared at Gerri. "My mother says I'm a fool. That love doesn't exist. That I should give up on the idea."

"Don't you dare! Love exists. You just need the right man."

"I want love," she murmured softly. "I want to be wanted for once. Not just for the troubles I can fix for a man. I want to be wanted for who I am and what I can give back. I want to be loved."

Gerri nodded. "And we will get you love."

Lyss hadn't found a single man who'd made her believe he truly loved her. Sure they were good at telling her words they thought she wanted to hear, but the proof was in the pudding. Her exes were selfish and it would take a man proving with actions and not words that he cared.

"There's another thing," she said. "This one is really the main reason why I contacted you."

"Hit me," Gerri said.

She'd probably never get used to how Gerri looked and the stuff she said. It never matched. "I want kids."

"Kids?" Gerri looked at her, confused.

"My biological clock is gonna give me a concussion soon from hitting me so hard. I want babies. I need to find someone to be with long-term who wants children." She sighed. "I've wanted a family for so long it's kind of sad. The men in my past have always said yes and then turned out to be such losers I never saw them as father material."

"So you want a man who wants a family. Children."

She nodded. "I want a man who wants that as a priority. Marriage. Kids. The whole nine yards."

Gerri scrunched her nose in thought and then smiled. "I think I can help you there as well. So you are okay that my male clients are shifters? You know that's the kind of matchmaking business I run."

Her hands shook again. She couldn't stop the excitement dancing in her veins. Shifters were hot. Like nuclear-bomb-explosion-in-her-panties kind of hot. One who wanted babies as much as she did would be perfect.

"I know." Actually, she was more than happy to see if she could be a potential mate to one of those sexy men with their alpha personalities. She'd heard they liked to tear panties off. She had a damn big collection and was willing to give them all up if her man wanted to try that.

"Great, so you're okay with growls, hisses and roars during sex." Gerri made more notes.

She cleared her throat and glanced around, thinking of the people in their immediate area, but there were none close enough to hear them. "Do you think you can help me?"

Gerri sighed.

Shit. Maybe she couldn't.

"Of course I can. I have a person I'd love for you to meet. Here's the thing. He's not close enough where you can just meet up for dinner. He'll need you to go spend a few days where he lives to see if you are a match."

She'd never really traveled. Not because she didn't like it, but she really didn't have anywhere to go. And nobody to go with. An out of town date sounded out of the ordinary. What if they hit it off? What if they didn't? It was a game of chance. Her only hope was that if they did, they could figure out how to make it work without it being a strange long-distance relationship. That was not her idea of a happy future.

"I know going somewhere to meet a man can be a turn off," Gerri admitted. "Especially when you're unsure what you're getting into. I really think this could be good for you."

Hmm. Gerri had been right twice from what Tally said. Still, Lyss didn't know what would be considered casual clothes. She spent her life in either work suits or sweats. There was no middle ground with her.

"This is so stupid to say, but I don't know what I'd wear on a date where I'd be gone for more than a day or two."

Gerri blinked, confusion clear in her eyes. "What do you mean?"

"Are sweats considered to be the kind of stuff you wear on a trip to meet a possible match?"

Gerri inhaled sharply. "Oh, honey. Don't you ever shop?"

"Not if I can help it. I can never find stuff that looks good. I know I'm a big girl, but why do clothes that fit at my hips have to be huge at the waist?" she grumbled. "And I don't have the rack a woman my size should. I feel like I'm missing on top to even out the rest of my body."

Gerri shook her head in mock horror. "We must get you new outfits. Not because sweats aren't good attire, but do you really feel sexy in sweats or suits?"

Not really. In fact, she felt the least feminine in those things. "Okay. I'm game." She pushed a stray lock of brown hair behind her ear. "I would like to feel sexy."

"Then we're going to make you feel like the sexiest woman in the world. And I want you to remember that if the man I match you with turns out to be the right man for you, he will say it. Don't for a second think that he'd lie to you."

She nodded. "He'd be my right match if things work out."

"No, darling. He's your purrfect match."

Did she say purrfect? She must have heard wrong. "Can you tell me a little about this guy?"

Gerri shook her head and motioned for the check. "No. I don't want you to go into this with any preconceived ideas. I'd like for you to get to know him in his um...natural habitat."

That didn't sound so bad. She'd heard Tally's cousin had been matched with a bear-shifter. What if she got one of those? Did bears like cats? She didn't think so. She bet bears didn't really like much of anything. Maybe she'd get a wolf like Tally. Those guys were supposed to be wild in bed. She could use some wild in her life.

Gerri shooed her hand away when she attempted to make a grab for the check. She paid and stood. "Shall we go?"

"Any advice you can give me for this whole date thing?" She worried her bottom lip and grabbed her bag, ready to follow behind Gerri.

"Have an open mind. Speak your thoughts. Don't let anyone tell you what to do and for goodness sakes be you." Gerri slipped on dark sunglasses over her eyes. They left the restaurant and strolled down the busy street filled with shops. "If there is a time to show a man who you are and what you expect, it's at the beginning. Whatever you do or don't allow then is what will follow you through the rest of your relationship."

Where had Gerri been when Lyss had been with David the loser? She'd spent so many months allowing him to feed her excuses. She'd known he was lying and cheating, but she'd sucked up David's pathetic stories for a number of reasons. For one because she really didn't want to hear her mother's mouth about another man dumping her. How was it that her mom never believed Lyss was the one doing the dumping?

"Speaking my mind has never gotten me good results," she muttered.

Gerri stopped and glanced at her. She couldn't make out the other woman's expression through the large sunglasses, but her pursed lips spoke volumes.

"Listen to me very carefully, Alyssa. The moment you allow anyone to slide with lies, cheating and treating you poorly, that person will take your kindness for weakness and do it again and again."

She'd never really stopped to think about that. Not that she allowed her exes to really take advantage of her. She'd just given the relationship time. Even after she'd known it was going nowhere. "I do tend to stay in relationships even once I have come to the conclusion it's not going to work."

"If it's not working, cut it loose. Your time is valuable. You won't be young forever. Don't waste months or years of your life on someone who's not right when you could be looking for the one who is," Gerri said. She stopped at a well-known ladies clothing store and opened the door. "Now let's get you some feel sexy clothes."

Two hours later and what she swore was the fiftieth outfit, Lyss was no closer to being done shopping. She left the fitting room in a pair of tight capri pants and sexy low-cut sparkly top.

Gerri sat on a chair messing with her phone. She glanced up and beamed. "You look great!"

Lyss turned to stare at herself in the mirror. She didn't have sexy clothes in her closet. Her mother had taught her to be practical at all times. When she was growing up, she'd tried to hide behind her clothes. Not that she was shy, she just didn't want attention drawn to her body. As an adult, she learned to be herself. To like herself for who she was, but now she had no clue about style.

"Do you think it looks okay?"

Gerri stood and turned Lyss to face her. "Look at me, Alyssa. You're beautiful."

She smiled. "Nobody has ever called me that."

"Well you are. Are you looking to keep your hair curled like that or did we want to go check out a hairdresser and makeup artist as well?"

She cleared her throat and winced. "I don't wear makeup."

"Ever?"

She shook her head. "I wear chapstick. Does that count?"

Gerri's eyes widened. "No! We'll have to—Wait. Do you even like makeup?"

"No," she said and scrunched her nose. "I don't like feeling stuff on my face. I get itchy and on the few occasions I've been made up I forget and start rubbing my eyes and end up looking like a raccoon."

"That could be a problem."

She snorted. "Tell me about it. I once had to be in a wedding party and the makeup artist used this great stuff to give me that smoky eye effect. I rubbed one eye during the evening and I started getting strange looks. When I finally saw my face, my eye shadow and mascara had run together and I looked like I had a black eye!"

Gerri laughed. "Oh, you poor thing."

"The worst part was seeing my friend's wedding photos. I was a mess in all of them."

Gerri shook her head. "Let's stay away from makeup then. What about your hair?"

Her shoulders slumped. "I have frizzy hair. Nothing anyone does makes it better."

"There are products that can help tame the curls, Alyssa. Just because your hair is curly doesn't mean it has to look..."

"Like I got electrocuted?"

Gerri burst into giggles. "Something like that."

"If you can find me something to keep this hair from looking like dry straw I will be happy to try it. Taming my curls has been the bane of my existence. Cutting it wouldn't help. It'd just puff up and I'll end up looking like a giant Chia pet."

TWO

Lyss could have sworn she'd gone around that bend before. Shit. She might be slightly off path. Her stupid GPS had lost satellite signal ten miles back and now she had no idea where the hell she was. Though she'd always thought she could find her way to anywhere, clearly it was not the case.

Great sense of direction my ass.

Where the hell was she? And more importantly, why hadn't she thought to take the handwritten directions Gerri had given her instead of leaving them on her dining room table. Trying to remember didn't seem to work. She was obviously going around in circles.

Crack!

The sudden slump as her old Camry dropped into a pothole made her wince.

"Fucking hell!"

Things just got better and better. Her car swerved, screeching with the force of what must be a flat tire. She pressed down on the brake while trying to control the car before coming to a complete stop.

Slapping her hands on the wheel, she growled in frustration and hopped out of the car. This was just not her day. Her blow-dryer decided to die while she'd tried to dry her mass of super curly hair. It was humid. She now had the world's biggest Afro. To make it worse, she'd gotten a ticket trying to leave her apartment building. Apparently telling a cop that she was late for a date wasn't a good enough reason to speed. Following that up with growling wasn't advised either.

Bright sunlight blinded her. She glanced around but recognized nothing. There were no signs on the road and no businesses nearby. It was official. She was lost. Lost in the deep woods from the looks of things.

"Awesome. Just fucking awesome!"

She marched around the front of the car to the passenger side. The tire was torn and flat on the ground. She was stuck. She walked several yards away from the front of her car to see if she noticed anything up the road, but she saw nothing.

Could the day get any worse?

Loud noises coming from the forest caught her attention. She did a full circle, searching for whatever was out there. The sounds came again. A combination of branches breaking and moving. She peered into the woods and focused on the area she swore the noise came from.

Then she heard it. A loud roar. The angry bellow turned her blood to ice. Her heart jumped to her throat.

What. The. Hell. Was. That?

She blinked and almost missed it. A massive tiger leapt from between the trees, landing so close to her she gasped and took an instinctive step back.

Well over six feet in length and with canines that looked to be the size of her entire hand, the animal scared the daylights out of her.

"Nice kitty..."

What the heck was she supposed to do? The tiger roared again and took a step closer, his eyes flashed the golden amber color she normally found fascinating on TV. Right at that moment she found it scary as hell.

Didn't the nature shows say you were supposed to stand still when approached by a big cat? She bit her lip, watching the animal scrunch his face as he roared again.

Screw standing still.

Without taking her gaze off him, she took a step back and whirled around to face her car. Dammit it was far. Fuck it. It was either run or die. Or both. She didn't think twice and made a break for her car. She never ran, so she hoped those yards wouldn't take her down before she reached the vehicle.

Another roar sounded at her back. Oh, shit! She ran faster, but decided to test her fate, half turning to glance over her shoulder. Not a good idea. She tripped on something and went down, landing on her ass. The massive tiger was on her within a heartbeat.

She closed her eyes tight, praying to god that the big animal was a vegetarian but waiting for the first painful bite.

"Why did you run?" a loud male voice asked.

She jerked her eyes open and glanced past the tiger to a man standing just a few feet back. He was tall with blonde hair and golden brown eyes almost as yellow as the ones on the tiger. The tiger didn't bother moving away from her, caging her on the ground.

"What?" she asked, her gaze straying to the animal. It really was beautiful. Even with his big canines on display and the low roaring he continued to do.

"I said, why did you run?"

That had to be the stupidest question ever. "Big animal. Big teeth. Big fear."

The guy smiled, a row of perfectly white teeth. "You're not supposed to run or they chase. When you stand still you have more of a chance of not getting attacked."

"Right." She rolled her eyes. "Because being chased by a huge-ass tiger is normal for me." She tried, but failed to ignore that the tiger had lowered his big head closer to her. "My instinct to survive said run. I ran. What…um…what is he doing?"

The tiger took a long whiff and continued to lower his head to her.

The guy lifted a brow and watched the animal sniff the air around her. "One of two things."

She blinked at the big golden eyes coming closer and closer. "Yeah…um, is either of those getting ready to take a bite out of me?"

"It's possible."

"What!" she screeched.

The tiger stopped and licked his lips. Uh-oh. She was dinner.

The guy laughed. "Relax. It seems he likes you. He never likes strangers or human or other tigers."

Sounded like the tiger didn't like anybody. "Great…so could you tell him to move back a little? Enough where I don't have to feel like he's eyeing me for his next meal."

"You're funny." The guy laughed.

Sadly, she wasn't joking. "Yeah. I'm a riot."

The tiger stepped back enough for the guy to offer a hand so she could stand. But the moment their hands touched, the animal was right there, baring his teeth again. Only this time it was at his master.

She wiped her butt and hoped there were no stains on her new clothes. She'd been careful to dress appropriately with some nice but simple pants and one of the sexy tops Gerri had gotten her to buy. She now knew way too much about what colors combined with each other and why she shouldn't wear black. Apparently it made her look pale and washed out.

"Looks like you need to train him to know who the boss is." She grinned.

"Oh, he knows who the boss is," the guy said and took step away from her. "I'm Tynder."

"I'm Alyssa Moran." She wiped her hands on the sides of her pants. She glanced down and noticed dirt spots on her pants. This wouldn't do for a good first impression. Her date would think she liked to roll around in the dirt. "I had a flat tire and would really appreciate if you could tell me where the nearest town is and if you know anyone that I can have fix my car."

Tynder glanced at the car a few feet behind her. "Looks bad."

She winced. "Yeah. Tore the tire right up. I don't really know much about vehicles so point me in the direction of help and I'd gladly appreciate it."

The tiger decided to push at her side at that moment. She jumped back, still wary of the massive animal. He came closer and nudged her hand with his head. Did this beast want her to pet him?

She ran her hand over the top of his head, sliding her fingers deep into his fur. His fur was soft and warm. She did it again, this time scraping her nails on his flesh. The tiger purred.

"Could you stop that," Tynder mumbled, shuffling from foot to foot.

"Why? He's kinda cute when he's not showing his big teeth."

"It's weird to watch him being stroked." He coughed. "He definitely likes you."

She blinked, frowning in confusion. "Isn't that better than him wanting to tear me a new asshole?"

He cocked his head but said nothing. This guy was so weird.

"I'll take you to my pride and we'll help get your car fixed."

She nodded with a smile. "That would be so helpful!"

And her mother said there weren't any nice people in the world. Her car broke down and she wasn't being abducted or being offered to a god as a sacrifice. Things were starting to look up. Then again, her mother was such a sour apple she didn't associate with most people. It had taken Lyss a long time to get some friends.

For most of her youth her mother discouraged her from hanging out with other kids. Being a big girl didn't help. Her only form of contact with the outside world had been volunteering at the local animal adoption center. There, she'd hugged puppies and kittens. She'd fallen for the sweet helpless animals. It was there she realized she liked cats.

Though solitary, cats could be very loyal. She'd grown up to love cats and had adopted a few of her own the moment she'd moved out. Her cats were the only thing she had. Without a man or children, her hissy kitties took up her time. They gave her the attention she hadn't gotten from her mother or her previous relationships.

Tynder smiled and pointed to the woods. "I'm happy to help."

She decided that she would trust Tynder. Not because he had a trusting type of face or personality, but because that tiger of his seemed to have switched sides and was not moving away from her. Instant protector.

They walked down a path in the woods, slowly coming up on a jeep. Tynder eyed the tiger that glanced up at her. She wasn't sure what to do, but all of a sudden her protector took off in a sprint. There went her savior.

"Don't worry, you'll see him soon enough."

She slid into the passenger side, wondering what her date would think of her being so late. At this rate, she wouldn't get there until tomorrow.

They rode down a hill to a town. In less than ten minutes, she was at a mechanic's shop. She glanced around, but the tiger wasn't there. There was a woman by the entrance who stared at her as she neared.

Tynder stood next to Lyss and introduced her. "Kat this is Alyssa."

Kat sniffed, her brows rose and her gaze snapped to Tynder. "Her?"

"I don't make the rules," he said. "I follow them."

"But–"

"No buts, Katherine. Call Stripes to come out here and look at her car."

"But–"

"Now!"

Kat huffed and threw Lyss a glare before marching off.

She'd tried to keep track of the conversation but it seemed there was something she missed at some point.

"Come," he said. "I'll take you to meet Gray."

"And who is that?"

"Our pride leader."

The way he said the other guy's name made her a little wary.

Looking around, she noticed that the town was not so large. All the houses or cabins had the same look and feel. As if one person had designed them all.

They walked down a few streets until they went up a deserted road. Further in the woods, she finally saw it. A massive cabin sat in the middle of nowhere with no other structures surrounding it. It was as if it had just sprung up between the large trees.

Tynder pushed the front door open and waited for her to enter. She glanced around, her vision taking in the wooden furniture, the open space and the massive windows that brought the outdoors inside.

"Who are you?"

She squeaked for the second time that day, slapping a hand to her chest to stop her heart from popping out and then searching for the owner of the deep rumbling voice.

She'd been so taken with the surroundings, she hadn't seen him standing in a corner, within the shadows. It was hard to make the guy out, but he was big. Like really big. And she wasn't a small girl, so that made him huge. Her hand flew to her hair and she patted it to try and tame it.

"I'm Alyssa Moran. I was on my way to Green Edge when my car broke down."

He stepped out of the shadows and her breath caught in her throat. He was gorgeous. He wasn't even pretty boy gorgeous. He had a rugged look that made her girl parts sigh. With piercing golden eyes, that looked eerily familiar, he kept her captivated. The square jaw and that hint of beard made her thoughts scatter in her head. Her past experience with men left her ill-prepared for this hunk of man meat. She blinked repeatedly in case she'd imagined him. What a joke. She'd never imagined anyone that sinfully delicious before.

"What are you doing here?"

Dear god, that voice. She might just beg him to keep talking. He had a deep sexy rumble that most men just couldn't achieve. In fact, his whole demeanor said rough and tough. His plain white T-shirt clung to his body like a second skin, showing off the muscles of his arms and abs. She swallowed hard. Then there were the jeans. The button was still undone. Holy crap. It was as if she'd walked in on him getting dressed.

She threw Tynder a side glare. If he'd brought her earlier, she might have gotten to see Gray with fewer clothes on. Now all she could do was imagine what he looked like under those jeans. Would he take his clothes off if she begged?

THREE

GRAYSON GREEN BIT back a curse. He didn't know who she was or why she was in his territory, but he wanted her. His tiger wanted her. And she definitely wanted him by the scent drifting off her.

She glanced over his body with her beautiful cinnamon-brown eyes, her gaze sliding down in a trail of heat. His cock hardened at her perusal of his body. When he'd first seen her standing in the middle of the road, instinct to mate had taken over. He'd had a hell of a time pulling the tiger back enough that he wouldn't tear through her clothes. Her fear had helped keep the animal in check.

"What are you doing here?" he asked again.

If she kept staring at him with such open need he'd have to ask questions later and take her to bed now. Gray couldn't help doing his own gazing of her luscious body. He'd always liked women with curves he could hold on to. Alyssa had more than enough. Her long, dark hair hung in a long ponytail of curls down her back. Her outfit, though clearly not meant to tempt, did exactly that. A yellow sparkly tank top displayed a large amount of her golden brown skin. The plunging neckline gave more than a hint of her breasts, while the cropped jeans clung to her wide hips showing off the curves he wanted.

It was nearing mating season and the tiger inside him was roaring with need. Alyssa appeared to have shown up as if sent from the gods. Now all he needed to do was figure out what she wanted in his pride.

He opened his mouth to speak, only to be interrupted by one of his guards and best friend, Stripes.

"I need to speak with you, Gray." Stripes rushed forward, stopping only to throw a smile at Alyssa. She frowned and turned to Tynder.

His guard had brought her to his home. Exactly as he knew Gray wanted.

"Not now, Stripes. I'm busy." He continued to stare at his future mate. She shifted from foot to foot. Her discomfort was obvious and he didn't like it.

"That's why I need to talk to you."

"Excuse me," Alyssa broke in. "Could someone just tell me how to get to Green Edge? I sort of have a meeting with someone and I'm really late."

"Gray—" Stripes started but stopped when he raised a hand.

Gray glanced her way. "Who are you meeting there?"

She shoved a hand into her pocket and pulled out her cell phone. She pressed a few buttons and glanced up to meet his gaze. "A Mr. Green?"

"She's here for you," Stripes whispered so she wouldn't hear.

"What?" Gray hissed. It wasn't that he didn't want her; he just didn't understand why Stripes went looking for a woman for him.

Gray watched as the largest of his guards shuffled from foot to foot, nervous. "I signed you up on a matchmaking site," he mumbled quietly under his breath. "You need cubs."

Tynder broke into laughter but quickly stopped and cleared his throat when Gray glared his way.

"Do you think we should go?" she whispered to Tynder. "The big, sexy one is pretty pissed for some reason."

This was one of those times Gray thanked his ability to hear even the furthest of sounds due to his sensitive shifter hearing.

Tynder choked on his laughter again. "I don't think we should move right now."

Gray glanced at Stripes again. "Explain. Now."

"You've got to mate. You need someone by mating season, which is only a few days away. I spoke to one of our neighboring bear clans. He mentioned using the Paranormal Dating Agency and being matched with the love of his life."

"I don't believe in love," he argued in a low voice so his guest wouldn't hear him.

"But you believe in keeping your pride!" Stripes snapped quietly. "So you either mate and get some cubs born as soon as possible or fight to keep the pride for another few months until the next person wants to challenge. How long will you go on that way?"

Gray glared at Stripes. From the corner of his eye, he watched Tynder motion for Alyssa to take a seat so she wouldn't have to stand any longer.

"But how did you know she was the one?" he asked confused.

Stripes shrugged his massive shoulders like a little kid. "I didn't. But this Mrs. Wilder woman has a great reputation so far. I had a feeling she'd find the right one for you." Stripes motioned over his shoulder with his head. "And she did."

"This is crazy. Does she even know what she's getting into?"

"Yes...sort of..." Stripes trailed off. "Mrs. Wilder said she'd know she was going on a date with a shifter."

"I'm not looking for a date with her. I don't even want to mate her, but...she's mine."

"Fine. Good. Hell, great. But you sort of have to convince her of that. She's not here to be turned into your personal sex toy for the mating season. She's here to meet you and get to know you to see if you are a match."

"She's mine."

Stripes scrubbed a hand over the back of his head. "Do you have any idea how hard it is to date a human? Oh, you don't. Let me fill you in. They are moody and can decide you're being a dick just because you want sex all the time. So tread carefully." Stripes threw a glance over his shoulder at Alyssa then gave Gray a pleading look. "Don't mess up your chances by letting your lust and desire to mate push you. Not to mention the need to get her to have cubs as soon as possible and that never goes over well with any woman."

"I can handle it."

Stripes shook his head. "No, you can't. You're likely to get straight to the point and piss her off. 'Have my cubs' is not the first thing a woman wants to hear."

A loud rumble sounded in the back of Gray's throat. His tiger didn't like the idea of waiting to mate Alyssa, but he'd do things the right way. Whatever the fuck that meant. So if he had to talk to her before stripping her body of those clothes and getting up close and personal with every delicious curve, then he'd do it.

"Fine. I'll play this your way."

"Try to stay within the area," Stripes said, meeting his gaze. "The word has spread that you have a female here for you. It's only a matter of time before someone tries to stop you from mating."

"Just let them try." He glanced at Alyssa. The need to take her grew with every smile she threw his way. "Now take Tynder and get out."

"I really think one of us should stay–"

"Now!" he hissed under his breath. They'd done a good job of keeping their argument low enough his new guest hadn't known they were debating over her. "I don't need help talking."

"Yes, you do. You hate people."

"That's true, but I like her. I like her a lot." And he really wanted her naked. As soon as possible.

"Gray, let us help."

He lifted his lips in a half-grin. "You already have. You've found my mate. Now let me claim her."

Stripes sighed. He turned his back on Stripes and walked down to the other side of the room where Tynder and Alyssa sat. "Let's go. We'll be summoned to fix shit later, just watch."

Tynder and Stripes said their goodbyes to Alyssa. She watched both men leave and then turned to him, pinning Gray with her soulful brown eyes.

"Something got your tail in a twist? You sounded pretty angry before."

He stopped mid-stride to her. "Did you say I have my tail in a twist?"

She nodded, her big eyes full of laughter. Her lips curved up in a beautiful smile as she glanced down at his crotch. "I would have said panties, but you don't look like you have anything under those jeans."

He didn't. He realized then she was joking and he didn't know how to react. Nobody joked with him. His serious and reserved attitude pushed most of his pride away. Not to mention he liked his solitary life. Other than making sure nobody bothered his people, he liked peace and being on his own.

"Are you hungry? Thirsty?" he asked, now wishing he'd let Stripes and Tynder stick around. He hadn't spent much time alone with females unless it was to have an easy night of sex. And when that happened few words were exchanged.

Women in the pride knew the deal when it came to sex. The need to continue their pride and set up for future leaders was important. Males and females were not as discerning with emotional attachments like humans were. When a female went into heat, she'd look for a single male. Emotions were kept to a minimum. Tigers were sexual creatures. They liked sex a lot. Even more when the need to mate and breed took hold.

She shook her head and swiped her tongue over her lower lip, causing his gaze to zoom to her mouth and linger there. "I'm fine. So want to tell me what it was you and your friend there were all hush-hush about?"

He cleared his throat. Now he really felt all kinds of weird chatting with her. Women didn't question him. He wasn't sure how to handle her questions without saying something to piss her off.

Air. He needed to get her outside. The open space would help clear his mind and at the same time allow him to figure out how to talk to a human female. What did one say to a woman other than 'take your clothes off'?

"Let's take a walk. You came all this way and you'll want to see the area."

He grabbed her hand to guide her to the door. A jolt of electricity shot down his spine. He met her wide gaze and inhaled hard. She was definitely the one. Even if there had been a doubt before, there was none now. Touching her had spread a warmth through him that his chilled heart had never felt before.

"Am I...am I very far from Green Edge?" she asked as they exited his home through a side entrance.

He couldn't stand living in a space too enclosed, so his cabin had lots of large windows and doors bringing the outside in.

"You are in Green Edge," he said, holding her hand hostage. She'd tried to pull out of his grasp, but he found he quite liked how she felt near him.

She stopped and frowned. "Then maybe you can tell me where I can find Mr. Green. I bet he'll be pissed I'm late for our date."

"That's doubtful," he murmured.

She shook her head, her long ponytail of curls bouncing around her back. "No. Mrs. Wilder said he didn't like people making him wait." She sighed. "I bet I just messed up the first possible date I've had in months. Figures."

He watched her shoulders droop. The idea of her being upset wasn't one that sat well with him. His tiger already wanted to push out of the skin and have her petting him again. The normally antisocial animal was ready to get on his back so she could rub his belly.

"I'm Grayson Green."

She stopped again and swept her gaze from his face down to his bare feet and back up. "You? Why would you sign up for a dating service? You don't look like you'd need anyone to hook you up."

He grinned. She said the words with such disbelief it was hard to stop the chuckle past his lips. "I don't, under normal circumstances."

"Great." She jerked her hand out of his grasp and slapped them on her hips. "So what, do you need like a fake girlfriend or something?" Her eyes blazed with anger. "I didn't come here to play games, Mr. Green. You don't sound like you even want a date."

Frickin' hell. He'd been alone with her for about five minutes and he'd already managed to offend her. Stripes was right. He didn't know how to talk to women. Hell, he didn't know how to talk to most people unless he was giving them orders.

"You don't understand." He tried to pacify her by grasping her hand again and holding it up to his bare chest. "I'm looking for more. For someone who will be right for me."

Her brows rose slowly with interest. She was so warm and her skin was so smooth. He wanted to touch a lot more of her. "More? Like a serious relationship, Mr. Green?"

Mating was as serious as it got so yes. "Stop calling me Mr. Green. It's Gray."

"Fine, Gray. Are you looking for a serious relationship?"

"There is only one mate. That is what I need."

She reeled back as if he'd hit her. "You need?"

Crap he'd fucked up again. "I mean that's the only kind I want at this time."

She stared at him quietly for a moment and then turned to glance at the open forest around them. "Why go through Mrs. Wilder, though? I mean. You're hot. You must know that. I bet you don't have a single problem picking up women." She snorted. "Or stopping them from throwing themselves at you."

Her candor was quite refreshing. She'd called him hot. And he liked it. "Why did you go to Mrs. Wilder?" He followed next to her as they made their way deeper into the woods.

With each step further from the restrictions of his pride or the expectations of mating, he loosened up more. He wasn't worried. He could protect her and himself if need be.

"Apparently I have a bad habit of staying in a relationship that isn't working. Mrs. Wilder said she'd find one that would work for me."

"What exactly do you want in this relationship?"

They were deep out in the forest now, but he knew his way back with his eyes closed.

She glanced at him quickly before turning her face away. "The truth?"

Was there anything else? "Yes."

"I want a family. I want love. I want to get married one day. I would like to have children. You know. The stuff most women dream of. I am sick of my own mother calling me an old, cat lady."

He grinned. "You're not old."

"Hah! But I *am* a cat lady. And for your information, I feel quite old at this point."

"Cats are great. I'm glad you like them. Don't give age too much thought." He liked knowing she wouldn't have problems with his feline. "Old is just a state of mind."

"Says the hot young one." She laughed.

There she went again. He could tell she wasn't thinking about actively flirting with him. There was no sly smiles or overt sexual pouts. That was new. "You're beautiful. Don't put yourself down."

FOUR

Lyss didn't know what to say. This really gorgeous man she'd never dreamed would need a date was holding her hand and calling her beautiful. Most of her exes weren't bad looking, but hunk-man gave them a kick in the balls on the sexiness Richter scale.

"Hang on a second." She glanced around between the trees, searching for a camera crew. "Am I being Punk'd? Because that'd be some real cruel shit but I wouldn't put it past my mother."

"What?" Gray asked.

"Look. It's not every day I get a man that looks like you telling me he is looking for a long-term relationship and thinks I'm beautiful. So yes, I'm questioning it. To be completely honest, I'm wondering if you're high, being real or joking."

His lips lifted in a grin. Lord almighty what a smile. His eyes shone with laughter. The previously golden color had sparks of blue in them. They were truly mesmerizing. Why would a man this handsome and clearly in touch with his sexiness go to a dating agency? The women in that town were either blind or stupid.

She had the urge to fidget and glance down at her clothes. Did she look okay? Thank God Gerri had taken her shopping. She doubted he'd be saying she was beautiful if he saw her in a pair of too big sweats, bed head and surrounded by cats. Christ. The image alone scared the shit out of her.

"First, I am not high. There is no drug out there that could do a thing for me. Second, I don't think you understand. You *are* beautiful and I *am* looking for a long-term relationship," he said. "But I'll tell you something. If anyone thinks calling you beautiful is a good way to joke then they don't see what I see."

She cleared her throat at the quick change of his tone. He'd gone from sexy and flirty to deadpan and serious. "And what's that?"

"A woman who doesn't need the trappings of war paint and too tight outfits to display how beautiful she is. Inside and out."

Oh, wow.

"Um, war paint?"

He frowned. "You women call it makeup."

A slow smile crept over her lips and a giddy sensation of excitement buzzed in her veins.

He moved forward, crowding her with the heat of his large body. Oh boy. She didn't move for fear she'd blink and he'd disappear. He slid his hands up her arms, grasping her by the shoulders and tugged her close. So close there wasn't an inch of space between their bodies.

She licked her dry lips again. Heck, her entire throat had turned to sandpaper.

"You keep doing that and I won't be held accountable for my actions," he murmured, his voice low and deep.

"Doing what?" she asked, staring at the fuzz of facial hair she wanted to rake her nails over. She'd never been one to like men with beards but that short hint of one on Gray was making her insane.

"Licking your lips." He slowly lowered his head toward hers. "It's like an invitation for me to kiss you."

Was it? She'd never had that response before. Maybe now was a good time to find out what kind of chemistry they had. It was one thing for her to think he was hot, but quite another for him to make her panties wet. Okay, wetter. The man was a sight with that tattooed body and short blonde hair begging for her to grip.

"Do it," she said boldly, not believing for a second he'd follow through. "Kiss me."

Much to her surprise, he did. He dropped his head until his lips brushed softly over hers. Once. Twice. And then she lost patience and gripped the front of his T-shirt, yanking him closer to mesh their lips in a passionate kiss.

His tongue slid into her mouth and dominated. With each swipe over hers, he heightened the passion flaring in her blood. He glided his hands up to cup her face at first. Then he slid them around the back of her head and tugged the ribbon holding her hair up to let the long, thick strands tumble free.

She moaned into the kiss. Christ he was so good with that tongue, rubbing and grazing it back and forth over hers. Her nipples puckered tight under her top. They ached with an intensity she'd never felt before. All her muscles locked into place. It was like none of the kisses she'd ever been given had been real. Nothing compared to Gray's lips pressing over hers. To his tongue fondling hers. To his hands gripping her hair. And to, oh dear God, the hard bar of his cock rubbing on her belly. Lust pooled at her core and heated her from the inside like a forest fire.

Need grew in her for the man doing with a single kiss what others could not do with months of sex. She moaned. He grunted and moved his hands down her neck to cup her breasts over her shirt. Hot shudders raced down her spine to her clit. A new throbbing took hold of her pussy. She wanted this big, sexy guy naked. Now.

He fondled her breasts, massaging and tweaking her nipples. With every squeeze her pussy fluttered. Her panties had gone past damp to soaked.

She pulled away from him, just enough to catch her breath and look into his bright golden eyes. The need and lust she saw there made her shiver.

"I want you," he said, his voice firm, low and rough.

Those had to be the best words any man had ever said to her. Not because she'd never been told she was wanted before, she had, but because he said it in such a way she knew it was true. He said it as if it was killing him to not be inside her and by God that made the words all the more special.

"I—"

She didn't get a chance to say anything. Her words died in her throat. His gaze jerked up from her face and his features turned feral, animalistic and angry. The warmth inside her died a sudden death and was replaced with icy fear.

He turned around, pushing her behind him until she was pressed between him and a tree.

Loud roaring sounded all around her. She tried to peek over Gray but it was hard since he was so damn big. She was, however, able to listen to the conversation without any problems.

"Leave." Gray's voice was loud and harsh.

She finally got around his arm enough to see two tall men standing several yards away.

"We've come to speak with you," one guy said. He glanced down and caught sight of her. He frowned, his face twisting in anger. "You've got no mate. A pride leader needs cubs to ensure his line."

She didn't really understand what all that meant, but Gray clearly did. His muscles tensed, almost shaking.

"My mate is not of your concern, Lucas. Why are you and Eli really here?"

Great! Now she knew the guys' names. The bigger, staring daggers at her, was Lucas and the shorter, not as evil-looking, was Eli.

"There's been talk." Eli glanced at Lucas, shifting from foot to foot. "Some are saying you won't be leader for long."

"We need to know what you will do about the mate problem," Lucas said, his gaze never wavering from Lyss. "Or do you plan to fight to keep your place."

"Again, not your business. You are overstepping and you both know what happens when anyone questions me." He didn't yell the words, but the effect was instant. The two men took hasty steps back and eyed each other. "You have thirty seconds to go before I decide you've come here to fight me yourselves."

Eli was first to rush back, tugging a hesitant Lucas with him.

"We'll go," said Lucas. "But this doesn't change anything. Others will come. You can't be leader without a mate."

Lyss swallowed at the fear clogging her throat. She gripped Gray's T-shirt so hard in her fists her knuckles had gone white. They stood there a few minutes until she felt his muscles loosen.

"Let's go back," he said and turned to face her. His eyes were filled with anger. "I don't think you should be out here right now in case they decide to come back."

She frowned. This pride of his sounded like some nasty neighbors. "They'd do something to you?"

He shook his head. "Not me, but they'd try to get to you. They've seen you."

She allowed him to hold her hand on their way back to his cabin. This time, the walk was silent and filled with unease. She finally spoke when they reached the kitchen.

"Is that my overnight bag?" she asked, glancing at what looked like her luggage.

"Yes, Stripes or Tynder brought it up for your comfort."

She raised her brows and glanced at him. "But I'm supposed to stay at some guest cabin."

"No. I want you here."

Okay. Except she wasn't used to being in any man's home on a first date. It was a little strange. What if she woke up in the middle of the night and decided to climb into his bed and get her freak on? Would he object? "Um..."

"You can have your own room," he said softly, his gaze dropping down to her lips. Butterflies and all kinds of fluttering sensations took hold of her chest. "If that's what you wish."

Wish? Wish! She wished she could get him out of his clothes ASAP but that wasn't happening, now was it?

"Thank you."

He picked up her bag and led her up to the second floor. She should have paid more attention to the surroundings, but his slap-worthy ass was all she could focus on. The entire way to the guest room all she did was debate on biting or wanting to dig her nails into his cheeks. She had problems.

The room he showed her was a nice clean one with the bare necessities. She stopped in the middle of the room and glanced around. "I guess you don't get many guests, do you?"

He put her bag on a chair and turned to face her. "No. I like my space."

"So who were those guys? And what did they mean that you need a mate?" She had been dying to ask but her stupid hormones had almost made her forget on the way up to the guest room.

He leaned back on the open entry. "We're tigers, we need to mate."

She blinked. "You're a what?"

He frowned. "A tiger. Didn't you know?"

"No!" she said, growing confused. "Mrs. Wilder never said what you were. I assumed—"

His brows rose with interest. "You assumed?"

"Um..." Shit. She'd been so stupid. Mrs. Wilder didn't tell her what kind of shifter because she didn't want her to have any preconceived notions. Lyss knew better than to assume anything, but she'd seen Tally with her two wolves and she'd sort of thought she'd get a wolf too. "I thought you'd be a wolf."

"Like hell!"

She winced. "I'm sorry. I shouldn't have assumed. It's just that a coworker of mine used the PDA and got a pair of wolves. I wasn't sure what I'd get but I kind of expected a wolf for some reason."

His brows darted down in a fierce scowl. "I see. I'll leave you to unpack."

She held her breath as he turned on his heel and left her room. Fuck. She'd done a great job of insulting the tiger. Well, Gerri had given her a cat alright. A big ass cat. And just like her cats at home, this one didn't like being compared to a puppy.

She marched to her overnight case and opened it. The first thing she noticed was her bag of sex toys. She couldn't have known if they'd have any chemistry and she wasn't going to leave home without them. Now all she wanted was for him to use some of her favorites on her.

Fuck. Guilt crept up her throat. She had to apologize. He'd looked so surprised and then disappointed over her words. It made her feel awful to have hurt his feelings somehow.

She left the bedroom and listened for the sound of footsteps. His cabin was well built. The wood was strong and blended with the colors of autumn from the outside. A few doors down from her room she stopped. She must have reached his bedroom. He'd left the door ajar and she heard his footsteps inside.

Inhaling some courage she wasn't sure she possessed, she pushed the door open. "I'm sorry, Gray, I—"

Oh. Dear. God.

FIVE

Lyss blinked. Then blinked again. He was naked. Like so naked there wasn't even shoes on him to detract from the powerful muscles and amazing tattoos covering his back and arms. She'd been right. He had an ass she definitely wanted to bite and slap.

He turned to face her slowly. If possible, his front was even better to look at. She didn't even attempt not glancing at his cock. Her brain short-circuited when she did. Her gaze shot up to meet his with a gasp. He was big. He was hard. He was ready.

"I'm...I'm sorry for barging in." She cleared her throat. "I...just...how did you get naked so fast?" she blurted out.

His lips lifted into another of those panty-melting smiles. "We tend to be naked a lot."

Oh. Her gaze strayed down to his cock again. She curled fingers into her palms, squeezing them into fists. "I'll—I'll go—"

"Don't," he broke in and slowly prowled toward her. "Don't go."

Shit. What to do? She really should get out of his room and leave him to whatever he'd been doing. Her dirty mind turned vivid with images of him stroking himself. Nope. Not the thing to be imagining right now.

He inhaled and groaned. "I don't know if you understand, but I've been hard from the moment I laid eyes on you."

Jesus. Maybe she could stay a few minutes. Or hours.

He came closer, his lightly tanned skin covered in tattoos called her attention. The blue and black lines of his ink captivated her.

"Do you want to know what I was about to do in here?" He taunted her with his soft words.

She shook her head jerkily. No. She didn't want to know, she wanted to watch him do it.

He stopped just a hairsbreadth away and lifted a hand to cup her cheek, sliding his thumb over her bottom lip. "I was going to imagine those full lips of yours wrapped around my dick."

This was better than anything her mind could have conjured up. Way better and hotter. He grabbed her fingers with his other hand and brought them down to his abs, placing her hand flat. Air pounded in and out of her lungs as she slipped her fingers down his navel to his straining erection.

His eyes held her captive, the gold and blue bright with arousal. "I can't stop thinking of you naked," he breathed.

She reached his long thick shaft and gulped. "Just naked?"

He glanced at her lips, his chest rising and falling with every hard breath. "Naked. On my bed. Spread open for me to feast on." He licked his lips. "I can already taste how sweet your pretty pussy will be. I know you're wet. I want to lick your pussy and drive my tongue and cock into your cunt. Deep. So deep you'll never want me out of your body."

Holy hell. If the words were anything to go by, she'd done the right thing staying there.

She watched his facial lines tighten. The knowledge that he was so close to losing his control sparked an evil need to push him inside her. Curling her hand over his hot length, she grazed her nails from his balls up to the head of his cock. Then she slid a thumb over the slit, spreading the bead of moisture at the tip.

"Put the words in action, Tiger-man."

He moved faster than she expected. One second they were standing there and the next his lips were on hers, kissing her like the zombie-apocalypse had started. He tugged at her clothes, ripping and tearing. Not that she had half a mind to give a fuck. So what if the clothes were new. She'd spent hours in shopping hell to buy outfits with the hopes he'd like them. Tearing them off her sure qualified as liking in her book.

She lifted her arms for her top to come off and shimmied out of her pants when he yanked them down. The usual insecurity of being naked with a new man tried to push forth. God. This wasn't just any new man. This guy was the epitome of tall dark and make-my-eyes-water sexy. She had long ago learned to live with the body she had. She might not be the sexiest dresser or the best at wearing stuff to entice men, but she was fine with being a big girl. A really big girl.

Except now. Right now all she wanted to do was glance down at her body and see what he saw. Did he see the rolls and the too small breasts for her size? Was he turned off by the fact her thighs might be bigger than most women? She hoped he liked ass because she had quite a big one back there. With a deep breath, she met his gaze and all those questions were sent to hell. His look stopped any feelings of discomfort with being so curvy dead on their tracks.

He'd pulled her pants and shoes off her feet and glanced up. The lust she saw there filled her with a new sense of excitement. He definitely wanted her. She gasped and groaned as he slid his finger up her legs when he stood. Each glide of his digits on her flesh felt like ribbons of fire stroking her.

She opened her mouth but he shook his head. His gaze swept her from head to feet and back up, stopping at her lips. "I was right. You're beautiful."

It was her at that point who lost control. She curled her arms around his neck and pulled his head down, pressing her mouth to his. He caressed his tongue over hers, decadently rubbing her and fanning the flames lighting her core. There was a new tug and her bra came off. The hiss of a tear and her panties were gone. And she loved it.

He picked her up as if she weighed nothing but a feather which only made her want him even more. In a few steps they were on the bed. The plush comforter warmed her back while he sat back on his heels and glanced at her naked body.

"Gray…"

"Shh, darling." He pushed her legs open and stroked her pussy with a finger, sliding it up and down her slick lips. "I told you you'd be wet."

She could hardly hear past the sound of her heavy breathing. Gripping clumps of the comforter in her fists, she waited for him to make a move.

"That's such a gorgeous sight." His voice was low and deep. He pushed her thighs wider and got on his belly.

Oh this was going much better than she expected.

He inhaled and groaned. "I can scent how much you want me."

"I do," she murmured. "I want you."

His eyes flashed that golden color she loved. "I want to fuck you." He pressed his finger over her clit in lazy circles that pushed her breathing into the heart attack zone. "I want my cock coated in your pussy juices." He lowered his head, his gaze still locked on hers and swiped his tongue over her folds. "Mmm. I knew you'd be sweet."

Lord Jesus. She groaned, her eyes wanting to shut and her body begging for more. "Oh, please."

"I like the sound of you asking me to do more." He did another lick from her ass to her clit again and then rained small bites on her inner thigh. "Do you know how hard it is not to slide my cock into your slick hot pussy and fill you with my cum?"

No. She didn't but she wanted that just as badly as he did. "Don't hold back," she panted. "Do it."

Another slide of his tongue over her clit and she saw stars. She moaned and pressed her pussy closer to his mouth.

"My dick hurts from how much I want you. I want to watch my cock slide into your pussy and come out wet with your scent." He flicked his tongue over her clit and slid his finger into her channel, slowly fucking her with it.

"Oh! Oh, God," she groaned.

Hot and cold sensations rushed her body. Her mind focused solely on the lips and tongue sucking her clit and the fingers invading her body and pushing her to orgasm.

Her legs pressed against his head but he curled his arms around her large thighs and urged her to lay them over his muscled shoulders. Another suck and lick and her pussy squeezed around his fingers.

"Fuck!" he grunted, his lips barely above her mound. "You're hot and wet. So fucking sexy."

Her muscles shook from how hard it was to hang on. She couldn't think, breathe or do much more than lay there and feel. And it felt fucking amazing. He added a third finger gliding into her pussy and something pressed into her asshole. She inhaled and let it out slowly, allowing her body to relax so his finger could get in her.

"That's it, beautiful," he breathed from between her legs. "Let me fuck your pussy and ass with my fingers because soon it'll be my dick in your pussy. Soon, gorgeous, it will be my cock in your tight ass."

Her body bucked at the dual penetration of his fingers in her pussy and ass. "Gray!"

Tension swirled into a ball of explosives in her belly. Her chest felt compressed and she couldn't get enough air into her lungs.

She let go of the comforter and gripped his blonde hair in her fists, wiggling and rocking her hips over his lips. The fire inside grew in intensity. She was so close. The promise of an orgasm threw her into single-minded focus. She had to come.

He sucked her clit harder, plunging his fingers in and out of her in a faster speed with each lick. She moaned loud, not caring about being quiet. Fuck who heard her.

His head lifted and she glanced at him from lowered lids, her chest heaving while she struggled for breaths.

"Come for me, beautiful." He nibbled her clit, his fingers driving in and out faster than she could catch a breath. He splayed his tongue flat on her pussy, pressing on her clit and then sucking it between his lips.

"Oh," she gasped. "Oh my—"

The world shattered then and there. She screamed, her body unravelling and letting go so fast she could do nothing but let it happen. A massive wave of pleasure rushed her. Her bones liquefied and her ability to breathe stopped. Shockwaves of bliss spread through her body, down to the smallest cell.

She blinked her eyes open and glanced down. Her legs shook and her belly still quivered. Gray was on all fours, licking his lips.

"I love how sweet your pussy tastes, but now I want to feel it stroking my dick as I slide into you."

Her desire shot right back up. She was dying for him to take her, to slide into her body and give her a new taste of the amazing release she'd just had. She widened her legs, pulling her knees up to allow him more access to her body.

"I like that," he said, his lips lifting into a sinful grin. "You do have a pretty pussy. It's so pink and wet." He glanced up and met her gaze. "Ready to be fucked."

Oh, yeah. She was ready, willing and desperate.

She reached for him but he shook his head. "Not yet."

Instead he lowered and kissed her belly, licking his way up to the valley of her breasts. Then he sucked one of her nipples between his lips, the heat of his mouth enveloping her breast.

"Oh, my God!" Her mind turned to baby food.

His powerful legs rubbed the inside of her thighs. Her breath caught in her chest. His lips were driving her wild. His nips and sucks on her nipple were like electric currents between her breast and clit. She'd never known such exquisite torture.

He released her nipple and continued his licking journey up to her lips. The head of his cock pressed at her slick entrance. Steely hard and silky smooth, he slipped easily between her drenched folds.

She gasped, her gaze locked on his. He clenched his jaw, the vein on the side of his cheek popped to show the hard time he was having taking it slow. He pressed forward, his cock sliding into her in a drawn-out slide.

"Fuck, Alyssa. You really are tight."

He said that like it was a bad thing. It wasn't her fault he was big and her previous men had been…well, smaller.

She gripped his slick shoulders, digging her nails into his sweaty flesh and pushed a breath out. "You're taking too long."

Curling her legs around his hips, she used the balls of her feet to press at his ass and push him forward faster. The movement worked, but she hadn't expected the burning of his cock stretching her pussy walls and filling her until she felt invaded by him.

"Christ!" he rumbled and blinked his golden eyes down at her. "Your body is soft, tight. Perfect for me to fuck."

"Do it, Gray. Do me hard."

"I want to fill you with my scent, sweet Alyssa," he breathed. "I want to come deep inside you. To mark you as mine."

She might not understand his words but she knew one thing, she wanted whatever he wanted to give her. "Do whatever you want. Just do it already."

"Do you want me to come inside you?"

"Yes. Fuck me and fill me with your cum." Where were these words coming from? She liked dirty talking as much as the next person but that right there was unlike her.

A feral smile split his lips. "I'll do just that. I'll fuck your sweet cunt so hard you'll never forget how good we are together."

She raised her head and met his lips with hers. The kiss was not soft or sweet. It was a rough mating of mouths with groaning, moaning and biting. He pulled back, almost sliding out of her and then pushed forward. She whimpered. His drives didn't slow or stop. Neither did the kiss. Their tongues tangled at the same time his cock drove deep and retreated. In. Out. Harder. Faster. Blazing arousal pumped her blood straight to her head.

Sex had never been this untamed. She'd had sex for enough years of her life that she considered herself well prepared for anything. Not this time. But his rough fucking only opened something wild inside her too. A new need to let go filled her. She scored her nails down his sides. When she reached his ass, she squeezed and dug them into his meaty flesh.

"Yes," she moaned. "Fuck me hard."

Loud grunts and hard breathing filled the room along with the sounds of skin-slapping. She'd couldn't think of a time where she'd ever been so turned on by it. She pushed on her side, pressing an elbow into the mattress and turned them so he could be on the bed and she on top.

He broke their kiss, grabbed her by the waist and pushed her to a sitting position.

"Feel like riding, do you?"

They were still connected. He was fully embedded deep inside her. She couldn't believe how fucking sexy it was to look down at him while sitting on his cock.

She licked her lips and rocked. The new position hit somewhere sensitive in her pussy. She groaned, dropped her arms to his chest and rocked. Again, her body got the flutters of an impending orgasm so fast it left her breathless.

"Ah, baby," Gray groaned. "You need to keep moving or you'll find yourself flat on your back again. And next time I won't stop until your pussy's dripping with my cum."

"Gray," she moaned. "You feel good inside me."

She leaned down and licked his lips. Where was this sudden urge to be bold coming from? She didn't know but right then she didn't give a shit. She liked watching desire tighten his features.

"I think you feel better sucking my cock with your pussy." His hands slid up to her tits and he squeezed them, thumbing her nipples back and forth. "That's it baby," he said, his voice rough with need. "Ride me. Slide on my dick. Enfold my cock with your silkiness."

Christ. She'd only been on him for all of a minute and his words pushed her closer to orgasm faster than any of her vibrators.

She rolled her hips, gasping and whimpering at how good it felt to have him hot and stiff stroking her insides.

"Ride me harder," he breathed, tugging her head down to kiss her.

He sucked on her bottom lip, nibbling and swiping his tongue in and out of her mouth in a dirty and sensual mating ritual.

He curled a hand around her neck, grasping her long hair and pulling her closer to him, while he slid his other hand between her legs and played with her clit.

He continued biting and sucking her lips and jaw. Her stomach flipped with the intense look of desire he gave her.

"Your pussy rocking on my dick feels fucking amazing." He gripped her hair tighter, lifting his head to spread kisses up to her ear. "But your ass, that tight little hole driving me crazy, is just waiting for me to fuck it." He licked her lobe and a shudder raced down her spine.

"God, yes!"

"I'm going to drive deep in your ass," he said, his breaths heavy. He fondled her clit, flicking his thumb on her hard little nub. "I can't wait. First I'm going to lick all around that little asshole." He groaned and swiped his tongue on her cheek. "Then, I'll flick my tongue over your entrance like I'm doing now with my finger."

Her movements grew shaky with the tension growing inside her. "Please..."

"Please what? Please shove my cock so far up your ass you won't be able to do anything but take it? Please fill your tight little ass with my cum until it comes sliding out of your hole? Or please rub harder on your clit?" he said, pressing a kiss to her dry lips. "Which is it?"

"Make me come. I can't—"

"You can," he urged, moving the hand on her hair to her waist and lifting his hips off the bed to meet her downward slides with an upward thrust. "You're going to come for me, beautiful. My dick can't wait to feel your pussy walls quivering when you do."

She gasped, locking her gaze with his. A silent communication happened then. Air fought its way in and out of her lungs in a rush. She was so close. Digging her nails into his abs, she increased the speed of her rocking. At the same time, he flicked harder on her clit. Then everything ceased and a blast of color flashed before her eyes. Her body tensed and then let go. Tension unraveled in a rush. Pleasure filled her, seeping down to the bone.

A scream tore from her throat, leaving her gasping for air.

He moved his hands a little lower, down to her hips, his fingers biting deep into her flesh. Gray lifted and dropped her, prolonging the orgasm she experienced. He threw his head back, the veins on his neck popping with exertion.

A loud roar sounded from him and then he was driving his cock so far into her she was left speechless. His body vibrated under her. He pulsed inside her, filling her with his cum.

"That's it," he muttered, rocking into her. "You're so fucking sexy, Alyssa. Your pussy keeps sucking my cock."

She could still feel her insides quivering from her orgasm. She shivered as the last of his cum filled her. She inhaled and let it out in a quick breath. "Wow."

"Next time I'll make it even better." He pulled her head down for a quick kiss. Heat emanated from him in waves.

She sighed, and leaned down to lay on him, snuggling into the curve of his neck. "You do that and I'll end up dead."

"You won't die from great sex."

"We don't know that. I've never had sex this good," she admitted. Why lie when it would only make her look ridiculous.

She listened to his heart beating harsh against her ear. They were both sticky and sweaty. She could think of nothing better to do but lay there.

"There are things we need to discuss," he said after a moment of silence.

Great. The morning after talk and it wasn't even the morning after.

"Like?" She tried to keep her voice light, but she hadn't come this far to have sex and leave. The whole point of the PDA was to match her up with the right man. Sexually, Gray was perfect for her. In every other aspect? She had no frickin' clue.

They'd spent all of a few hours together before she let her hormones do their own version of Girls Gone Wild. They hadn't used protection and she didn't care. In fact, she sort of wished something bigger would develop between them. Trust her body to decide that the first man she meets who has some potential is now to be the father of her future offspring. If only he knew where her thoughts had gone he'd jump off that bed so quickly she'd never see it happen.

"We didn't use anything to stop conception," he said.

Ahhh. The baby conversation. "I want to tell you not to worry, but the truth is I am not on birth control and I haven't been with anyone in a while so there's been no reason to use any." She lifted her head and met his gaze. "This took me by surprise."

He pressed her head back on his chest and caressed her hair. "Me too. I've never reacted so quickly to any female."

She shouldn't be happy he said that, but she was. He wanted her and he'd lost control over her. Her. Alyssa Moran, dowdy law office assistant with too many curves to count. The feminine side of her squealed and high-fived itself. The rational side of her tried to tell her this was just the beginning. To not get her hopes up.

Too late.

"What do we do?"

SIX

Gray listened to Alyssa's question unsure what to say. He didn't want to scare her by saying 'I hope you're pregnant so I can kick the nonsense about losing my pride in the ass'. "We'll wait. It could be nothing."

She sighed, her body losing some of the tension she'd gotten when he said they had to talk.

"Are you ever going to tell me what those guys were talking about? You needing a mate and your pride and all that?"

Great. That was exactly what he didn't want to talk about. "What do you want to know?"

Sliding his fingers through her hair, he was able to keep the tiger calm. He had to open up to her or things between them would never work. Opening up to anyone was not something he was familiar with. It was something he never did.

"Tell me what that means. The things they said."

He sighed and thought back to his father. He'd warned him that his reluctance to find a mate and bear cubs would be his downfall. The previous pride leader of Green Edge had been old and wise. Too bad Gray had decided to ignore his suggestions and continue things the way he wanted.

"My tiger pride has a hierarchy. I am the pride leader," he said, reminding himself that he never allowed anyone to bully him into making any decision. He was his own man and he'd be damned if he mated anyone just to keep his pride. He'd fight for it, but he wouldn't do that to Alyssa. He wanted her for purely selfish reasons. He wanted her for himself.

"So you're the leader, then you're fine, right?" There was a hint of worry in her voice.

He hugged her closer, enjoying her naked curves laying on him. The breeze drifting through the windows helped cool their heated bodies. "More or less. They're pressuring me to mate."

She was quiet for a moment. "What do you mean mate? I haven't gotten all the terminology down of your kind. Doesn't that mean like marriage?"

He pressed a kiss to the top of her head and caught himself. When had he ever done that before? Never. But already he acted as though she were his mate. As though there was nothing between them but time to develop the relationship.

"Yes. Something like that. If I don't produce cubs soon, I will be seen as weak and unable to lead the pride. Some of the females offered to bear my cubs, but I don't like being pressured into anything."

She jerked in his arms, her head rising quickly and her wide gaze meeting his with open shock. "They offered to just have your babies? Just like that? No commitment expected?"

She sat up, grabbing the sheet dangling from the foot of the bed and wrapping her naked body with it. He disliked the lack of view of her curves and disliked even more that she'd moved away. He didn't think, just acted. Grabbing hold of the sheet, he tugged her back on the bed next to him. He unraveled the material until she was once again flush against him with the sheet covering both of them.

"So?" She leaned her head on his arm and stared expectantly at him. "They just offered to have your babies no questions asked?"

He sighed. "That's the way of the pride. Many leaders have cubs with as many females as they want. It ensures that they'll have multiple future leaders."

Her lips pressed into a tight line. "I've never heard of women doing that."

"Like I said, it's the way of prides. Only I didn't want to be forced into mating or having cubs to keep being leader. I was born to lead. I'll fight to keep my place."

She gasped, her eyes filled with horror. "Would it really go to that? Fighting?"

He nodded, not willing to lie to her. "Yes. It will. It's only a matter of time."

Her tense muscles and the fear drifting from her body told him it was time to change the subject. "What about you? Why did you choose to use a Paranormal Dating Agency to find someone?"

"Well, I've dated every jerk known to man and I figured 'why not date every jerk known to the paranormal too'?" She laughed. "Not really. I'd heard great things about Mrs. Wilder. She's a very hands on type of matchmaker and she does great from what Tally, my coworker, said."

"You've been in other relationships before. What happened?" He felt her loosen up. He knew she'd soon be asleep, but he still wanted to hear more about her life. Plus, he loved listening to her speak. She had a huskiness to her tone that made his cock jerk.

She yawned and ran her nails up and down his chest. It was an innocent move but the intimacy of it hit him hard in the gut. This felt right. She felt right.

"I tend to give too many chances. Even when I know I shouldn't. I have a hard time breaking it off with men. I guess they take my kindness for weakness and decide to cling to me however long they can."

He picked up a long curl and stared at the multiple shades of brown in her hair. "So what do you want now?"

She yawned again, her hand stopping to lay on his chest. "Love. I want to be loved."

He didn't ask any further questions and lay there, listening to her sleep. She wanted love. He didn't believe in it. How could they ever make it work?

For much of his life, his parents had been cold people, dedicated to the pride. His father had instilled in him the need to protect and care for the pride. His family had stopped living when his younger brother had been killed. The death had sparked a divide in the pride. Someone had known the leader would pass his rule to one of his children and they'd tried to get rid of them. No attempts had been made on Gray, but his brother didn't have the same luck. The younger tiger had been cocky and believed he could do whatever he wanted without consequences. Then one day he was found dead.

Gray, already a loner at the time, grew even more antisocial. The females in the pride had tried getting his attention, but he'd focused on the overall care of business and command.

Once his father had gone, Gray had fought others for the prime leader position. Just because he was his father's son didn't mean it was automatic in his world. But he'd destroyed his opponents and now had to try and figure out how to keep his pride.

Frustration reared its ugly head. He hated being put in a position to fight for what he'd already obtained. The pride was his.

GRAY STOOD IN his kitchen in a pair of boxers, fixing dinner for Alyssa. She'd wake up soon and he knew she'd be starved. Hell, he was. Someone knocked at the back door before it swung open.

Stripes walked in. He glanced around and then headed straight for the refrigerator. "I see you're still alive."

Gray shook his head. His guard was as much a talker as he was. "I am."

"Did you talk to her about mating? Giving you some cubs and maybe getting some of these assholes off our backs?" Stripes asked, holding a can of soda in his hand and popping it open with the flick of a finger.

He shook his head, closed the lids on the food he'd prepared and moved around to make some coffee. "No. I won't put that kind of pressure on her. She didn't come here for that."

Stripes groaned, sat down at the dining table and glared at him. "Why do you think I signed you up for the whole matchmaking site? It's not for your good looks and personality."

Gray's lips quirked. Stripes was a hard-ass, but he knew firsthand that his best guard would not put a human in the line of fire, especially not Gray's mate. "I think Alyssa would disagree with you. I have amazing skills. She just screamed it to the world about an hour ago."

Stripes held the can by his lips and shook his head. "Thanks. I really needed that. It's not enough my sister is ready to drop her pants like you're a sexpert or something. Now I have to hear about your success with someone you met only a few hours ago?"

Hearing Stripes say it like that didn't sit well with him. He had met Alyssa about six hours back, but there was something there. She was his mate. They had a connection. "She's not just someone. She's mine."

Stripes sighed. "Yeah, okay. I get it. So what will we do?"

His mind had gone distant, thinking about Alyssa naked in his bed. "About?"

"Lucas, Eli and others trying to push you out."

There was not much to do. He could wait it out and prepare for an attack, or he could do what was usually done and find himself someone to bear him some cubs. Ideally his mate. Rage heated his blood to boiling. "We'll wait. If they want to fight, they'll get a fight."

Stripes stood, dropped the empty soda can in the recycling bin and stopped at the kitchen door. He turned to glance at Gray. "I'm glad my signing you up for the PDA got your mate."

Gray folded his arms over his chest. "I'm glad too. I don't like the idea of her being around here but I don't want her far either." He clenched his teeth, biting back the urge to roar. "Keeping her near is the best way to protect her. Eli and Lucas got a good look at her. They know."

Stripes frowned. "Do you need someone on hand to help guard her?"

Gray thought about it but decided against it. She was his. His responsibility. If she needed guarding then he'd watch over her. What kind of mate would he be to push her off on someone else? Her. The most precious person in his life.

"We're fine."

Stripes nodded and walked out the door. Gray managed to stand there for a few minutes, wondering how to explain to Alyssa that he didn't want her to ever leave his side without sounding like a maniac.

Soft footsteps sounded coming down the stairs. He knew she'd woken. He waited for her to enter the kitchen. When she did, she took his breath away. She'd put on one of his T-shirts in lieu of her clothes. The shirt landed mid-thigh, showing off her flesh. Her nipples were clearly delineated through the soft cotton material. He couldn't have picked a better outfit for her himself. There was just one thing he needed to know.

"What do you have on under the shirt?"

She smiled, a sexy little grin that did all kinds of things to his heart. "Nothing."

SEVEN

Lyss grinned, slowly making her way to Gray. Clad only in a pair of boxers, she'd forgotten what she was going to say when she first saw him. Dear lord please make the boxers disappear didn't sound right.

"I have a proposition for you," she said, coming closer to him.

He leaned on the kitchen island, his gaze dropping to her chest. She was sure her hard nipples were visible through the thin fabric. Instead of going to her room and putting on her own clothes, she'd decided to go against her instinct for once in her life and seduce the sexy tiger.

What he'd said earlier, about needing a woman and some kids, she'd thought about it for a while and decided she could help him. Though she tended to be too nice with guys and allowed them to overstay their welcome, she'd come to the conclusion that Gray needed help. And she'd give it.

Already he treated her so differently than most of the men she'd been with. He listened. Not just nodding and faking it, he actively spoke and asked her about herself. He'd fucked her brain-dead. That alone was enough to drop her to her knees and beg him to let her stay as his sex slave for life.

Looking at Gray, her stomach flipped flopped and her heart clenched with all kinds of new and strange emotions. Nothing she'd ever experienced before.

He frowned, his gaze sweeping down to where the shirt ended and then back to her face. "What kind of proposition?"

"So you know how you said you need some babies?" She'd always wanted kids. In fact, her urge to procreate was the reason she'd gone to Mrs. Wilder in the first place. She'd gotten tired of the losers and wanted to find her own long-term happiness.

"Yes..." His voice sounded hesitant.

She stopped a foot away from him, lifted a hand to his naked chest and ran a nail down to his belly button. Christ almighty the man was hot. He sucked his breath in and her pussy throbbed anew. "I can help you out with that."

"You want to have my cubs?"

Yes, please. She wanted his cubs, bears, puppies, whatever he wanted to give her. With the way he was staring at her and licking his lips she'd probably settle for as little as a kiss, but she really did want to help him out. Why? She just did. Maybe she was stupid like her mother said and allowed herself to get into situations where men took advantage of her, but her entire life she'd always believed in giving people the benefit of the doubt. Right now she felt Gray needed someone to be there for him. She knew she could be that someone. At the same time, she could get her own wishes fulfilled.

"Why?"

She blinked, not expecting the question. "Um, you need someone to do it? We have great chemistry and I've been wanting children for a while now."

He turned away from her, suddenly giving her his back and she felt a stab of rejection at his movement. He turned around to face her so quickly she was caught off guard. "You'd do that for me?"

She grinned. He sounded so skeptical. Like he couldn't believe it. "Yes. But you have to understand I'm getting something I want out of this too."

"We'll need to take you home, get your stuff. Move you here full time." He started throwing out a to-do list so long she wondered what the hell happened. One second he was quiet and thoughtful and the next he was moving around the island to the kitchen table. He picked up his cell phone and started to dial a number.

"Um, Gray?"

"You'll live here with me obviously." He continued talking and texting and then glanced up at her. "My bed is large."

Okay. She figured that by his stating he wanted someone long-term and going to the PDA that he was also looking for love. Her only hope was that the chemistry and connection they experienced would grow into something more meaningful in time. Already she wanted to be close to him. It was not just sex either.

There was something about him that tugged at her heart. She wasn't sure if it was the fact he seemed so lonely or the amount of responsibility he had to carry all on his own. Whatever it was, she wanted to help him carry the burden.

"Gray, I have a job," she said, hoping he'd slow down the flying texts she saw him sending. She was pretty sure they were all about what they'd just decided.

She knew this was getting deep for her real fast. Being a romantic at heart, she wanted Gray to be her one. Her heart told her he was. That she'd finally found the love she'd been searching for, but she wasn't stupid. Things had to develop with time and communication. She'd been open and honest with what she wanted with him from the first. He's used few words, but she'd gotten the gist. He had to be searching for a person to love too, or why else would Mrs. Wilder have sent her to him. She knew what Lyss wanted.

He stopped and stared at her as if she'd grown another head. "You don't plan to continue that, do you?"

Excuse me? "Uh, yeah. That's how I pay my bills. Not that I live paycheck to paycheck or anything. I'm really good at saving money." She grinned. "And I suck at shopping for myself so I never do it."

"But you'd have to travel to your office. Anything can happen to you on your way there or back."

She shook her head. "You're growing a little paranoid there, Kitty man. Don't get your tail in a twist. I'm sure stuff is not as bad as you think."

He marched to her, his eyes somber and dark. A grim expression covered his features. "You don't understand. Tigers can be vicious."

She nodded. "I'm sure."

"No. You really don't understand. When my father first announced he was going to move on from being pride leader of Elder Prime, things went into chaos. Some of the younger, stronger pride members decided they'd take us out and take over."

"What?" she gasped, her hand flying to her chest. Her heart pounded hard with fear for him. Who cared that she'd met him a handful of hours back? She'd already become attached to keeping him alive.

"My brother was the first target," he said, his voice dropping to a low, hushed tone.

She couldn't stop herself from throwing her arms around him and giving him a hug. The desolation in his eyes dug deep into her heart and plowed holes there.

"Tell me what happened."

He dropped his head on her shoulder and inhaled sharply. "I don't think—"

She pulled back and stared into his eyes. "Don't think. Just talk to me. If we're going to do this, I need to know you. Your life. Your family. I need you to open up."

He drew her toward the dining table and sat on a chair, pulling her on his lap. This was the first time a man had done that. What would normally be seen as a sexy move was somehow intimate this time. She sat on his lap with his arms tight around her waist.

"Dustin was fast with his mouth. He'd gotten one of the women in the pride pregnant and told everyone he'd sealed his place in line as pride leader."

She gulped, her stomach churned knowing the worst part of the story was coming. "What happened?"

He probably didn't realize how he tightened his hands around her waist, pulling her closer. "We found Sandra dead in their cabin and Dustin down by the river."

"Oh my God!" He'd lost a sibling. From the sounds of it his only one. She didn't think. She threw her arms around his shoulders and pressed her face to his neck. "I'm sorry. That's terrible."

He pulled her back and stared into her eyes, his gaze filled with pain. "I don't want anything to happen to you."

She had always believed there was someone out there for her. While she might not have thought that love at first sight existed, she knew there was a connection between her and Gray. Was it love at first sight? If she turned wistful like she did after a bottle of wine when she was home on a Friday night, she'd start to believe they were soul mates. As it was, she firmly believed whatever they had could be really special.

Should they have a baby without using the word love, though? Some people had kids with less commitment and managed it. At least they had chemistry. One of the things Mrs. Wilder had been very specific about was how careful and considerate the shifters were about their women. That was another plus.

"Relax, Gray," she said soothingly.

He kissed her shoulder and rubbed his cheek on her arm. "I can't when the idea of anything happening to you makes my animal agitated. I don't like it."

All in all, having a baby with a hot, dedicated and protecting man didn't sound like a bad idea to her. Her big worry was wondering if he'd ever develop feelings of love for her. She could lie to the world but not herself. She was already imagining Gray telling her he loved her which was probably insane since a day ago she didn't even know him. But who was she to argue with her heart?

'You never pick who you love' her dad used to tell her when she was a little girl. It's why he tolerated her mother for so many years and Lyss never understood it. Her dad had dedicated himself hand and foot to her mother. What did he get in return? Complaints and accusations of being slow to do her bidding. When her mother left her father, it killed him. He'd died of a broken heart.

Lyss knew there were good men out there like her dad. That's why she'd kept hoping that she'd find a good guy to be with. Something told her Gray was that guy. So he was a bit on the quiet side. He liked life as a solitary creature from what she saw and she noticed he didn't make idle conversation. Even with all that, her heart still told her he was the one for her.

"Nothing will happen." She said the words with conviction. No, she couldn't see the future, but she'd never been threatened in her life. She and Gray would just have to keep their plans to themselves. "We'll just keep our plan between us and that way nobody will get the urge to slice me into bits."

He frowned but nodded. "You're right. That's probably the best thing to do."

She glanced toward the food and then back at him. "Think we can eat?"

He jumped to his feet and almost dropped her. "I'm sorry. I'll get that."

"Don't rush on my account," she said, then thought better of it when her stomach growled. "On second thought, yeah, rush. I'm starving."

Gray laughed. It was music to her ears. He'd gotten upset and worried and they'd only spoken of her giving him cubs. They hadn't actually done anything yet. No, not really. They'd done quite a lot on his bed. Still, she didn't want him to get all super protective to the point he felt she needed him to watch her twenty-four seven.

After dinner, she decided to get dressed in case anyone showed up since he told her his two friends had a tendency of coming and going.

"They're my guards," he explained.

"Are they your friends?"

"Yes."

"Okay, so I was right," she said, sticking her tongue out at him as she slipped into a pair of sweats.

"I have to make a few calls."

She shooed him out of the bedroom. "Go, I can wander around and entertain myself."

After aimlessly roaming the inside of the cabin, while Gray sat in his office making calls, she'd gotten the lay of the land. She now knew there were five bedrooms, a ton of windows, which sort of creeped her out now that it was nighttime, and too much silence. She'd become accustomed to listening to her neighbors yelling on either side of her house. Plus, living on a busy street, she heard cars coming and going at all hours.

Her tour of the cabin ended in what she thought was a family room. The giant TV reminded her of the programs she had not watched all week. Flicking through the channels, she found one of her favorites. She settled in to watch and almost didn't hear when Gray entered the room.

He sat down next to her, picked up her feet and laid them on his lap.

"You watch reality TV?" He sounded surprised.

"Hey, Deadliest Catch is epic. I still miss Captain Phil and have high hopes the Cornelia Marie will make a comeback. Although, Captain Sig is my all-time fave."

"Who?"

"Never mind." She laughed. There was no point in discussing a show he had no idea about. "Obviously you don't watch this. So what do you watch on TV?"

He shrugged. "The news."

Ugh. "Are you one of those that all you ever watch is news related stuff?"

He chuckled and started rubbing her feet. Hmm that was actually really nice.

"Yeah, I will watch movies too, though."

She groaned. Boy he was good with massages. "What kind of movies?"

"Military blow things up kind of stuff."

"Oh?" she asked, surprised. "Military?"

He nodded. "I was military for a few years so it is great to figure out what they do wrong in a movie that would never be done in real life."

"Sorry," she groaned. "I don't watch military stuff. I do love anything with nature."

He pressed on the arch of her feet and she leaned back on the sofa, enjoying every second of his kneading her skin. Men didn't give her soft touches. She'd given an ex a rub down once when he'd complained of neck pains. Once she'd found out the reason he was getting neck pains was due to peeping on her neighbor through her bathroom window, the massages were dead.

"What about your family?" he asked. "How do they feel about you searching for a mate via the PDA?"

Her leg muscles tensed at the mention of her family. Her mother didn't know. Heck, she'd love to keep her mother unaware for say twenty years before she told her. Especially if they went through with the whole having babies idea. If Gray changed his mind at any point, she didn't want to hear about how she'd let another man get away.

"My mother doesn't know. She feels very strongly that I push men away." Lyss still didn't understand how telling her exes she wouldn't tolerate cheating and lying was pushing them away.

She glanced up from where he massaged her feet, to his face.

"Do you think she will mind when she finds out? We are agreeing to possible offspring here."

"Since she's not the one having the babies and I don't live in her house and haven't for a long time, I don't really care what she thinks."

So maybe that came out a little harsh, but she was tired of listening to other people try to run her life. Her mother didn't have a man. Didn't want a man. And somehow knew better than Lyss on what she should be doing to keep a man. All her advice revolved around Lyss sucking up the stupid shit men did and letting it slide. Not happening.

EIGHT

Gray left Alyssa alone for the first time in three days. He didn't like it. The tiger inside pressed at his skin, searching for a shift, in agitation.

"She's fine. Try and focus on what we're doing," Stripes said.

"She's alone."

"Tynder is with her. She's far from alone. If she can ever get him to shut up then we might owe her big time."

"She's great, isn't she?" he said with a smile.

"She's fantastic. I'm not sure what she did to make you so receptive lately."

He frowned. "What do you mean?"

Stripes chuckled. "You have never done more than grunt a word or two. You don't hold long conversations and you don't like people. But for the past few days you've been talking, interacting and communicating more than you have in the past ten years."

He didn't realize he'd changed so much since Alyssa's arrival. He didn't know what to think. Her company brought out a new side of him. He enjoyed talking to her. She was funny and smart.

Her addiction for reality TV still puzzled him, but he laughed whenever she watched something and yelled at the TV like the characters on the show could hear her.

"Do you see anything?" Stripes asked, his gaze focused on the ground.

They'd been searching for anything to show that intruders had come near his home. "No, nothing."

"This doesn't mean they won't come back."

Stripes was right. Eli and Lucas had made it known they wanted him out of the way. One or both wanted the pride and the only way to get it was to get rid of Gray.

"She needs to go home," he said, once again thinking of Alyssa.

Stripes whistled low. "How are you going to handle her being gone?"

He wasn't. "I'm going with her."

Stripes laughed. "I had a feeling that would be your answer. You've got it bad. If I didn't know better I'd say you're in love."

His chest compressed. Love? Nonsense. He'd recognized his mate and needed to protect her. Wanting to spend his time with her did not mean he was in love. Her smile flashed through his mind. He loved when she smiled. It made him happy to know there was joy in her life.

That still didn't mean he was in love. Grayson Green did not do love. Gray knew that since he'd been a kid. It had been drilled into him first by his family and then by the military. Love was an emotion that could destroy a person.

"I don't do love." He said the words more to himself than Stripes. He didn't need love. He had Alyssa. "Emotions can be messy."

Stripes sighed. "That's true. But love won't hurt you. I think you loving Alyssa would only make you happier. You should think about it.

"We can't help who we fall in love with, Gray." Stripes slapped him on the shoulder. "Sometimes we fall and don't even know it."

Not Gray. He was pride leader. He was stronger. Tougher. Love made a person weak. It messed with areas of the heart Gray never looked at.

"I don't."

"Just remember that falling in love doesn't make you less of a man," Stripes said. "It makes you whole."

"DAVID?" ALYSSA ASKED, confused. "What are you doing here?"

They'd gone into her house to pick up some of her stuff. After requesting last minute vacation time, she had gotten Gray to take her to her house. She'd inquired about her car, but apparently it needed a lot more work than just a tire replacement. They'd been inside the house for all of thirty seconds when her ex came out of her bedroom.

David stared at Gray with a shocked expression. Gray, on the other hand, pushed her behind him, his stance pure dominance.

"I need somewhere to stay, Lyssie."

She winced. Had he always sounded so whiny? She stared at him through new eyes, wondering what the hell had been wrong with her to allow this man to do whatever he did and not send him packing. "I'm sorry, David. You can't stay in my house. We broke up over a year ago."

David looked so confused she almost felt pity for him. Almost. But David had cheated on her repeatedly and blamed his 'inability to feel adequate with women' for his inability to keep his dick in his pants.

"Do you want me to wait until your guest leaves?" David asked, trying to see more of her without Gray in the way.

He just didn't learn. Looking at David now, after being with Gray, she noticed two things. The first was that David was an immature, pathetic excuse for a man. One who gave women terrible sex, no orgasms and wasn't faithful. The second was that Gray might not talk to her as much as David had, but at least she knew whatever came out of Gray's lips was real. He didn't sugarcoat. He didn't try to buy her with words. He was rough, tough, and had a great cock. That was more than enough for her.

She grabbed Gray's shirt and continued to peek at David around his side. "David, you need to go."

"But—"

Gray, who had been quiet for the past few minutes suddenly spoke up. "You need to go. Now," he said, his voice a mere growl.

David paled, took a step back but did not run out the door like she'd expected. Not a good time for him to decide and grow a pair. Considering he'd been such a dick during her entire relationship with him, she wondered why he was pushing things now.

"David, you really should go. We've been done for a long time now. I still don't understand what you're doing here."

"Okay, I know we ended things awkwardly—"

She shook her head and laughed drily. "I found you with your dick in my neighbor. Not sure awkward is the right word, but okay."

"That was an accident."

She laughed. The nerve of the man to give her such a sad excuse. "Wow. You need to watch it. Falling and landing on a woman's pussy will definitely get you into trouble. Some women won't be receptive to a stranger's penis up in their business."

David flinched but gave her a pleading look. "I just need to lay low for a while."

She snorted. "What did you do, sleep with your boss's wife or something?"

He scrunched his face in a grimace. "I didn't really think he'd find out."

Holy shit. What a fucking idiot! Thank God she'd finally decided to give David the boot before he'd brought that kind of bullshit into her life. "I'm sorry for your stupidity, David. But you should go before Gray decides to take a bite out of your ass."

David ran backward to the back door, tripping on his own feet and landing on his ass. "He's one of those shifters?"

"The really dangerous kind." She nodded, smiling at David's fear. Who knew she was such a sadist? "He's really possessive too. Doesn't like anyone near me."

Gray glanced over his shoulder at her. "If he isn't gone in the next thirty seconds, I will not hold the tiger back."

The smile fell from her lips. "David, go. I'm trying to help you stay alive. Get out!"

David ran out of the house with the duffle bag he had set by the door in his hands. She raced to the open entrance to shut the door. When she turned around, she lost the air in her lungs. "Why do you have that look on your face?"

He clenched and unclenched his hands at his sides, standing stiffly. "Why did you wait so long to send him away?"

She blinked. "I'm sorry, can you repeat that?"

"If you didn't want him," he growled. "Why did it take you so long to tell him to get out?"

"Hey!" she snapped. "I didn't invite him here!"

"He had a key. Clearly you gave it to him," he threw back, his eyes starting to glow bright gold.

"Yes, I did. But we broke up and I got my key back. That means he must have made a spare without telling me. I don't know why, but I didn't give him permission to." What the hell? When did David showing up out of nowhere become her fault?

"You didn't seem bothered that he was here. In fact, you appeared amused."

He was jealous. She inhaled and let it out slowly. She didn't have much experience with men being jealous. Okay, she didn't have any experience with anyone being jealous. It was new. Refreshing. It was awesome!

"I wasn't expecting him. You need to relax there, tiger. We came to see about getting my clothes. David is not important. I don't want him."

"I disagree. I know what I saw." He said the words in a low animalistic growl.

Anger flooded her veins. Being sexy and the leader of his pride didn't mean she was going to let him insinuate bullshit. She stomped up to him and poked him in the chest. "You asshole! I might not be in your pride where women throw themselves at you and decide they'll sacrifice their ovaries to bear your children for nothing, but I'm not brainless."

She had principles. And she had never been unfaithful in a relationship, which she had a feeling was what he suggested with his short clipped words and that frown she wanted to smack off his too sexy face.

"They don't sacrifice themselves." His lips quirked in what looked like an attempt at a smile.

She rolled her eyes. "My bad. They just throw themselves at you and beg for the chance to be your baby mama. Your pride is weird. Most women value a relationship and want to have children with a single man. Do you ever have multiple men get told they're the father of a single child? I bet there's a list of visits to the Maury show with you guys," she snapped.

"I don't understand what you're talking about."

She sighed. Ah, well. It was only fun if he understood. She better not mention how full her DVR was of Jerry Springer and The Real Housewives or he might start to wonder about her.

His brows shot down in a furious glare again. "What about you, Alyssa?"

She took a step back, not liking the way he said her name. There was too much brightness in his eyes. His gaze roamed her face and focused on her mouth. No way. He wasn't just going to insult her and then switch shit up so they'd have sex. She wasn't *that* easy. Okay, she was, but not this time.

"What about me?" Still, she couldn't stop the giddiness at knowing he wanted her again. Gray was a very sexual man with magical hands and a tongue she could worship even in her sleep.

She continued moving until her back hit the door. He'd marched forward, closing the distance on her. She bit her lip and waited.

"What is it you want from me?" He raised a hand to cup her breast over her shirt and she whimpered.

Panting as if she'd run a marathon, she glanced up and met his gaze. "Me? I just want you for your cock and tongue."

He curled his lip in a small grin. "Sex? You just want me for sex?"

He squeezed her tit in his grasp, rolling her hardened nipple between thumb and forefinger. Sex was good, but she wanted so much more from him. Too much. It's why she'd focused on sex because if she started to tell him how her stomach did flip flops when he kissed her or how her legs shook when he looked at her a certain way, she'd be telling him too much.

"I," she moaned. "I want you for sex, yes. But also for whatever else you want to give me."

Love. I want your love. She refused to voice her thoughts. Love would come with time. If he was open to it, she assumed he was seeing as he'd signed up to find his perfect match.

He pressed his body closer and she loved it. Every time he was this close she felt his body heat drain her tension away and fill her with a new expectation.

"What about your ex?"

She frowned. Her mind had already started to focus on the need to get naked so it took her a few seconds before the words clicked. She shoved at his chest and moved out of his hold. Stomping away from him, she yelled over her shoulder, "I told you I don't want him. I told you I didn't invite him. You either believe me the first time I say things, or get the fuck out and forget this—"

She had reached the sofa when he grabbed her arm and turned her to face him.

"Don't run from me," he said before tugging her into his arms and slamming his lips over hers. The kiss was bold, filled with an angry spark she didn't normally experience. Was this what people called make up sex? Technically they hadn't made up. Holy shit! She was about to have angry sex. That sounded even better than make up sex.

Gray's tongue pushed past her lips and stroked her with command. He showed her with his mouth and tongue he was in charge. That she was his. And she wasn't going to fight it. He tore at her clothes. The sounds of material ripping filled the air. She gasped when he deepened the kiss. He nibbled and sucked on her lips then plunged his tongue back into her mouth.

His hands weren't soft or careful. He yanked the torn clothes off her. Instead of being outraged or scared, she got more turned on the wilder he got. Men didn't do that with her. They didn't lose control. They didn't have angry sex with Lyss. This was surreal.

Her own hands weren't idle. She tugged on his shirt, sliding her hands under the Tee and feeling the smooth, warm muscles beneath. His abs contracted and a six pack formed under her fingertips. She grazed her nails down to the waistband of his jeans. His already erect cock pushed at the zipper, wanting out.

She undid his jeans and pushed them down, filling her hand with his velvety hot flesh. Christ he was hard. Hard and big. Both great since he knew how to do amazing things with his cock.

Pulling away from his kiss was difficult, but she really wanted something else in her mouth. She glanced at his bright eyes and licked her lips, panting.

"I want you to fuck me," she said bluntly.

"I'm happy to oblige," he breathed, his gaze dropping back to her lips. "Right now."

She shook her head. "I have something else in mind first."

The need to feel him in her overwhelmed. Some might think she felt a primitive urge to be taken. All she knew was that the thought of him inside her set her hormones to an explosive blaze. She tugged on his shirt.

He peeled it off to reveal the skin she'd been touching earlier. He kicked his boots off and the jeans along with them. Then he stood in front of her fully naked with his erection calling her attention.

Liquid fire shot from her belly down to her cunt. Wetness from her pussy slid down her legs. She grabbed his dick and jerked him ever so slowly. Her gaze glided up his body in a drawn-out caress, until she reached his eyes.

She smiled. He was tense. Need held his muscles stiff. She stroked down his shaft, cupping his balls and massaging them in her hand.

"Do you want me to suck your cock, Gray?"

He groaned when she put some pressure at the base and squeezed. "Fuck, yes!"

She glanced at the sofa to her left and grabbed a throw pillow, dropping it in front of her feet. Then she lowered down to her knees and continued fondling him. "Tell me what you want me to do. Be specific."

He moaned and cursed. "I want my dick in your mouth, surrounded by your pretty lips."

With every word he spoke, it felt as if he grew harder in her grasp. Her pussy was soaked, ready to be fucked.

She didn't run from him. She and David had been done for over a year. Maybe talking to him for a while had confused Gray, but she was shocked to find David in her home. Who in their right mind would go to their ex's house and try to get her to let him stay?

She raked her nails over his length in a gentle massage. Cupping his balls and fondling them with one hand, she curled her other hand over the base of his cock. A quick glance up and she caught him breathing hard, his jaw clenched tight, his eyes glowing bright gold.

Without looking away, she ran her tongue over him, twirling it in circles at the head and sliding him into her mouth.

"Ah, fuck that feels good," he moaned.

She sucked her cheeks in tight and used her saliva to lubricate his dick. Christ the man really was big. Big and hard. She jerked him with one hand and took more of him into her mouth.

"That's it. Suck me deeper into your hot mouth."

She jerked him harder, pulling back and pressing forward to glide his cock further down her throat.

"Fuck, yes, sweetheart. My dick looks so good going in and out of your luscious lips," he groaned. "Look at that," he said. "Every time you pull back I'm soaked with your spit. Suck it harder."

NINE

SHE DID. SHE took him as far as she could and continued to jerk him. Saliva dripped down the sides of his cock and her chin. She bobbed her head, sucking, licking and pulling back. Then she did it again and moaned. Her pussy was wet and she wanted to get fucked.

"That's a good girl." He gripped her curls in his fist and thrust faster into her mouth. "I like the view from up here. You sucking my dick and your tits bouncing as you do."

Lord the man had a mouth on him. She slipped a hand between her legs and moaned around his cock. Her pussy ached. She fingered her hard clit. A gentle tap and she had to stop. Her body shivered from how ready she was.

"This feels fucking amazing," he said, pulling her face away from his erection. "But now I want to fuck."

She licked her lips and stood. "Follow me, Tiger-man."

The first door to the right was her bedroom. She turned her lights on dim and went straight to her toy drawer. She got some lube and a vibrator. Things were about to get a whole lot dirtier. Stopping by the bed, she motioned him to her with the crook of her finger. God, he was so fucking hot. The way he looked her up and down like he wanted to eat her sent fire straight to her pussy.

He marched up to her and curled an arm around her waist, sliding it down to her ass and squeezing. "Is this for me?"

She grinned and pushed the vibe and lube into his free hand. "Let's have some fun."

He threw the lube and vibe on the bed and kissed her. Raw. Hungry. Desperate. The kiss was what she'd expect from a man on the verge of losing his control. His tongue swept into her mouth and dominated. With each lick and suck he showed her, she belonged to him. It was an overwhelming erotic sensation.

Her insides felt aflame. Any second now she'd implode. It didn't happen, though. Instead, he pulled back and met her gaze. "Are you sure?"

She nodded, crawled on the bed and got on all fours. Men never gave her wild sex. Until Gray she'd never even had a decent orgasm. Now she wanted everything and anything he wanted to try. She threw a glance over her shoulder and smiled.

"Fuck me, Gray."

A feral grin split his lips. He got to the edge of the bed, curled his arms around her thighs and pulled her back. She gasped, her upper body dropping down to the blanket. There was no time to react. He pulled her ass cheeks apart and licked up and down the hole.

Holy mother of all things naughty. Gray licked between her cheeks and down to her pussy. He rode up her slick curve and back down. Again and again.

"Oh, God," she moaned.

He flicked his tongued around her ass. The sensation was one that turned her nipples rock hard. She gasped for air, whimpering at the delectable feelings of being consumed. Gray thrust his tongue into her pussy and fucked her with it.

She groaned, gripping her sheet, grateful he held her up. Her legs shook. She could barely keep herself on her knees.

"Look at your pretty little asshole," Gray whispered. "Can I fuck it?"

She gulped. "*Yesss.*"

"That's what I like to hear."

Cool lube slid down the crack of her ass, traveling south until he stopped it and worked his fingers into her dark hole.

"Fuck! You're squeezing my fingers hard. I want you to do that to my dick when I'm inside you," he said, pushing a second finger in and out of her ass.

She relaxed her body, pushing out at the invasive fingers and moaning. He stretched her ass muscles and thrust deep into her. The bite of pain and pleasure combined was new and incredibly erotic.

"Gray..."

"That's it, baby. Take my fingers deep."

She slid down on the bed and Gray stopped. He flipped her over on to her back. She lay at the edge, with Gray standing by her feet, working her ass with one hand. He grabbed the vibrator with his free hand and turned it on.

She choked on a moan when the cool rod slipped into her pussy while he continued to finger fuck her ass. Her gaze met his and her hands moved to tweak at her nipples. Adding a new kind of pain to the mix shot her pleasure level out of orbit.

"Oh, you like that. I know you do," he said, his voice low and rough. She nodded and groaned. "You'll like it more when I'm fucking you," he promised with the hint of a growl. "I'm going to shove my dick inside you and come deep in your ass."

The vibe wasn't on one of the higher speeds, so all it did was torture her with a low buzz in her pussy.

Gray spread her legs wider, pushing her knees to her chest. "That's my girl. Open wide for me."

She held her legs close to her chest and watched. Her gaze focused on him and the way he greased his cock with the lube, stroking up and down and turning it shiny with the liquid.

Her breath caught when he hit the next speed on the vibe and pressed the head of his cock at the entrance to her ass. She bit her lip and whimpered at the burning sensation. He inched his way in so slowly she almost went cross-eyed from the painful pleasure.

"Gray," she gasped. Not that she could say anymore. Her mind wasn't working. She didn't even know words were possible at this point.

"Hang. On." He bit the words out through clenched teeth, pushing and pulling back in slow seesaw movements, until he was balls deep in her ass.

The speed on the vibrator increased again. He pulled back almost leaving her body before pushing deep. The feeling of fullness was one she might never get used to. The vibrator wasn't small. She wondered how it felt for him to feel it buzzing inside her.

There wasn't a chance to ask. His thrusts increased in speed as did the vibe. He kept her legs in place by holding her feet and pushing them to her chest. That allowed her to tug at her nipple with one hand and finger her clit with the other.

She moaned, her muscles tightened and a ball of fire expanded at her core.

"Ahh, that's it. Squeeze my dick with your tight ass," he grunted and cursed.

"I need..." she breathed. Her legs shook profusely. His drives into her propelled the vibe deeper.

He pushed her finger away from her clit and tapped at the nerve bundle. The small hit sent her soaring.

"Gray!" she screamed.

The world stopped moving while a wave of absolute bliss rushed through her body. She was faintly aware of Gray's body tensing and his cock pulsing in her ass as he came. He roared through his release and came for what felt like a long time in short jerky spurts.

He released her legs and pulled the toy out of her slowly. She gasped for breath, her body shaking like a giant lump of jelly. Gray went to her bathroom and returned with a wet washcloth to clean her. When he left a second time, she crawled up the bed, dropped her head on a pillow and tried to wait until her brain and body returned to working order.

A few moments later, he returned and joined her on the bed. He curled his body around her, pulling her close and holding her around the waist. Her back ended up plastered to his front with his semi-hard cock nestled between her ass cheeks.

She'd never had sex like this. So wild. So dirty. So fucking amazing. Gray was a man unlike any she'd ever been with. He took her pleasure seriously. She loved that. Loved how good he was about learning her body and bringing her to the heights of ecstasy.

Gray was an all-around alpha male. Strong. Dedicated. Passionate. She didn't think he even realized that he automatically put her needs before his own. David never had. None of her exes had. In order for her to get some kind of hot sex she had to give it to herself. Now there was Gray. The big, bad, sexy tiger she loved.

WAKING UP IN Gray's bed had its perks. He appeared to never grow tired of her or her body. After so many days, he still woke her up in a most delectable way. He'd roam his hands down her body, sliding them between her legs and dipping into her slick folds.

"I never tire of how wet you get."

She grinned, her eyes still closed. "I am sure we can figure out how to keep that going."

She tried to snuggle closer into him, but he flipped over on top of her. She blinked sleepy eyes open and stared into his bright gaze. "You're much too awake for this ungodly hour. What is it, like ten?"

A smile broke over his lips. It turned his face from sexy serious to holy wet panties gorgeous. "I have somewhere I want to take you."

This was interesting. He'd been sort of paranoid for the past few days and now he seemed calm. She liked seeing him like this. "As long as there isn't any running we can go wherever you want."

He laughed, dropped his head and kissed her soundly. "Why no running?"

She blew a raspberry. "I don't run. Ever."

His eyes widened. "Never?"

"Nope. So you might as well get used to the idea."

He stood, helped her off the bed and led her to the big bathroom attached to his master suite. "I don't think I could ever not run."

"Well, you have a massive tiger inside you. I don't." She slapped his ass and giggled when he stared at her over his shoulder. "Sorry. It was calling my name."

"You're so cute." He laughed.

That was a first too. She wondered what got into him. It didn't matter because she really liked him like this. She was glad she'd taken time off her job to spend with Gray. Maybe that had been a step too far, but she wasn't a quitter. Being with him the past few days had been better than any time she'd spent with any man in the past.

She didn't even care that he got growly and silent at times when she wanted to talk. Or often left to run the tiger out in the woods. He wasn't a regular man and she could understand his need for space. What she really loved was that he didn't make her feel uncomfortable that she was in his space. Instead, he tried to make her feel welcome.

While flipping through the channels, she'd found he'd started to DVR her favorite shows. Without her asking him to. He'd gotten Tynder to go to town a few times and pick up her favorite cookies and cakes. All to please her.

He'd yet to use love words, but she knew it was soon. She wasn't in a rush. She knew how she felt though. Clammy hands, her increased heartbeat and the overwhelming happiness at being near him were all signs she was more emotionally invested than she cared to think about. The night he'd kissed her softly in the moonlight and told her she was the one he wanted forever had burned in her brain as one of the most romantic memories ever.

She was in love. Who cared that it was soon or with a man she was still getting to know. 'You don't control your feelings or who you fall in love with' her father had said. He'd been right.

"Alright, take me wherever you want." She sighed. "But feed me first."

He helped her into the shower, under the warm spray of multiple shower heads. "Have I starved you so far?"

Nope. One thing she couldn't argue with was how good he was at making sure she was always comfortable. She really loved that about Gray. For a man who didn't like people, he sure didn't seem to mind being around her.

"No. But be warned, if you ever change and I start to go hungry, you'll be in deep trouble. I might run away and then what will you do?" She curled her arms around his neck and kissed his wet chest.

"I'll just have to cuff you to my bed and make sure you never go anywhere."

She laughed at the irony of his words. "I can undo cuffs, Tiger-man. Now what?"

He frowned, the water sluicing down his face to make his body slippery. "You can undo handcuffs?"

She nodded. "Yeah. I know it's weird, but I learned to pick locks when I was a kid. My dad was a master locksmith. He taught me how."

Gray blinked. "Any lock?"

She grinned at his stunned expression. Most people didn't see her as a lock picker. She was much too law abiding. "Any lock. My dad was the best."

"I guess I'll use zip ties then," he said.

She burst into laughter and shook her head. "You're bad."

"And you." He slid his hands down to cup her ass. "Are taking too long and distracting me when I have somewhere I want to take you."

TEN

IT WAS A garden by the river. She couldn't take her gaze off it. The patch of grass he'd chosen was surrounded by wild flowers and a stream that veered off the river. Her breath caught at the beauty of the spot. She figured she had the world's stupidest grin on her face and she couldn't make it go away.

"I like to come here when I'm stressed or need to be alone," he said softly.

She squeezed his hand in hers. He was sharing his favorite spot. This was big in the way of communication. She flung her arms around his waist and smiled. "You got some brownie points. This place is gorgeous."

His laughter warmed her heart. "I never know what's going to come out of your mouth."

She winked at him and pouted. "How about we go back to the cabin and..."

He hugged her tight. "And?"

"Get some food, I'm starving."

He dropped a kiss on the top of head and sighed. "You see what I mean?"

"I have no idea what you're talking about. Now let's go eat." She tugged him back to the cabin. "Next time we'll bring a picnic and I can watch you laze around in your tiger body."

The image of pancakes and coffee made her jerk at his hand harder. "Come on you big lazy tiger. Move your ass."

She pulled him all the way to the cabin. When they neared the back door she rushed inside ready to scavenge for food. Gray was a few steps behind her.

"Hurry up!" She removed a pin from her hair. The damn things just wouldn't hold back the crazy mass of curls. She still had it in her hand when all hell broke loose.

Gray entered the kitchen and the smile he'd had since she'd woken up that morning dropped from his face. She opened her mouth to ask what was wrong but was left speechless. He broke out of his skin and clothes in a change so fast she would have missed it had she blinked. In a heartbeat, she had a massive tiger in front of her. He roared loud. So loud her heart felt like it stopped in her chest.

Buzz

Something broke through the air and hit Gray. He reared back, standing on his hind legs to cover her. Another zip and something else hit him.

She glanced around but saw no one. Then, when Gray roared again, a third buzz sounded. Everything happened so fast. Within the space of thirty seconds, she'd been left standing there, watching Gray roar and slam to the floor.

She dropped down to her knees, wondering what the hell she could do. The two guys she'd seen before, Eli and Lucas, appeared after a second. Lucas had a dart gun pointed at Gray and Eli had a real gun pointed at her.

"Don't try anything and we won't have to kill you... right now."

She swallowed back the vile that hit her throat. Poor Gray. She needed to help him. She nodded and curled her shoulders into her chest to appear weak and scared.

"Let's take them to the other room and chain him up," Lucas said.

"What about her?" Eli asked.

Lucas threw her a hate filled glare. "She's human. She couldn't break through anything. Pathetic weaklings."

She ignored his evil words and instead slipped her hairpin into the back pocket of her capri pants.

"I have handcuffs." Eli grinned. "I've been carrying them around to see if I can get my mate interested in trying but she keeps laughing in my face."

"That's because you're a fucking idiot," Lucas growled. "Bring one of the kitchen chairs to the living room and cuff her to it. I'll get the chain for Gray."

"Then what?" Eli asked.

"I don't fucking know. Is not like we started out with a plan."

Eli winced. "If we kill Gray, you can challenge for prime leader."

Lucas nodded. "I know, but there are others stronger than me that will want to take over."

Eli motioned for her to walk ahead of him while he pointed the gun with one hand and carried a chair with the other. In the living room, he put the chair by the fireplace.

"Sit!"

She sat down and kept her arms behind her, hoping he wouldn't make it harder for her and put them over the chair. Eli was too preoccupied watching Lucas drag a massive passed out Gray into the living room to pay her much attention. He cuffed her hand to one of the wooden bars on the chair.

"Fucking hell," Lucas groaned. "Why did I shoot him when he was shifted? I tried to hit him the moment he entered but he was too fast."

Gray must have realized right away they were in the cabin and shifted before Lucas shot the first dart.

Eli turned to glance at her. "You stay right there, little human. Don't make me kill you right now."

"Get the chain," Lucas ordered.

Lucas continued to struggle to drag the giant tiger into the living room while Eli was gone.

"Why are you doing this?" The question slipped out before she had a chance to stop it.

Lucas huffed and stopped, dropping the tiger's head on the floor with a loud thump. "Why?"

She nodded and stared at him, her free hand reaching into her back pocket to make sure she hadn't lost the pin. Awesome, it was still there.

"This is the only way we can have a shot at prime leader. With Gray out of the way things will be easier."

She frowned and bit back the urge to call him a coward.

"I know what you're thinking," he said. "Why kill Gray? Because he's a danger. He's too strong to be stopped." He pointed at the tiger. "Look at him. He's only dozing on a dosage of a tranquilizer that should have killed him. Is he dead? No." He kicked the tiger with enough force that she had to clench her teeth to stop from saying something that would get her into more trouble.

"You said there are others that can challenge for prime leader once Gray is out of the way."

Lucas bent down and grabbed clumps of the tiger's fur and pulled him again. He dragged Gray until he reached her side. Then he let go of the tiger and leaned on another chair.

"There are others. We might have to get rid of them until I'm the most likely to win in a challenge for prime leader."

What a fucking loser. There were obviously pathetic excuses for men in the shifter world too.

Eli returned, dragging a massive chain. They twined it around the tiger along with a thinner chain to keep him bound in case he tried to shift. The chain appeared to be really tight around his neck and middle.

Lucas turned to Eli. "I'm going to go get something to try and get rid of him. Those darts knocked him out but he's still alive. I need something stronger."

Eli nodded. "I'll watch him."

Lucas rushed toward the kitchen, leaving her alone with Eli.

Eli sat on the sofa and started channel surfing. "There's never anything to watch."

"Have you tried watching reality shows?" she mumbled, reaching into her pocket to pull the pin out.

"What are those?" Eli said, flicking through the TV stations.

"Oh, they're great. If you check out the DVR I have some you might like recorded on there." Having dealt with the idiots she'd had relationships with, she knew not to underestimate a man and make him feel stupid. "Try Jerry," she suggested.

A few seconds later an episode of multiple strippers fighting for one man came on the screen and Eli was absorbed in the women dancing on the pole to show why they were better than the other girl.

"Thanks. For a human you're not so bad," Eli said, glancing at her and away from the TV for a second. "We still have to kill you, you understand."

She gave him a humorless smile. "Of course."

Gray huffed and shook against the chain. She had to hurry or he'd wake fully and make it harder for her to open his locks.

Eli was once again engrossed in the show and she was just gotten her cuff off without making a sound. She was lucky Eli's back was turned mostly away from her. It allowed her to check on him every few seconds while she leaned down and tried to open Gray's lock.

She watched Eli and jiggled the pin into the first lock holding the chain around Gray. The chain rattled. She held her breath and glanced up. Eli shifted positions in his seat but leaned forward to continue watching the women showing their boobs. She hurried to the second lock and was glad it was of the same type as the first. Easy peasy.

Lock number two was undone. Now to do the last one. Thankfully, they hadn't used anything too difficult. Once she was done unlocking them, she removed the locks and put them under the cushion of the chair next to hers.

The dart gun was on the sofa next to Eli and she couldn't reach it without getting caught. She sat up on her seat. Gray needed to wake up soon or they'd be out of time.

She removed her shoe and rubbed the big tiger with her foot. "Wake up, Gray."

"He can't hear ya," Eli said. "He's out like a light. Those were some powerful tranqs."

She swallowed hard and shoved the tiger harder with her foot, making the chain rattle.

His tail moved. Thank God! She wiggled her foot between the chains and pushed him again.

"I'm back!" Lucas yelled from the kitchen entrance.

She couldn't wait any longer. Lucas put something down on the kitchen table and started walking toward them.

She prayed Gray would wake up with what she was about to do because if not they were both dead. Her heart hammered so hard she thought she might pass out and throw up.

With a hard wiggle, she made her chair fall sideways, on top of the tiger. She kicked him hard on his side and whispered by his ear, "Wake up! I need you."

"Hey!" Eli yelled, coming toward her after she fell. "I told you, you won't be getting out of those cuffs."

Lucas rushed forward. He picked both her and the chair up. "Do that again, and I'll shoot you myself. I have no problems killing you. Do you understand?"

That's what did it. A loud roar broke through the living room. Chains rattled and the massive tiger next to her jumped to his feet. It was like he'd never been out. He didn't waste any time. He grabbed the closest one, Lucas, and bit into his leg.

"Ahhhh!" Lucas screamed and pushed the giant tiger off him to no avail.

"Hang on, Lucas," Eli yelled and tried to head for the sofa where the dart gun was located. It was her turn to do something. Instinct drove her actions. She grabbed a poker from the fireplace on the other side of her chair and hit Eli over the back of his head before he got a chance to reach the dart gun.

He turned around with a growl, his eyes glowing gold.

Fuck. Shit. Fuck.

He was going to shift. She couldn't even think about what the hell was going on with Gray and Lucas when this one looked ready to kill her.

She hit him with the poker again. He started bleeding profusely. Another hit and she got him in the neck. He tried to shift. His muscles contorted but she hit him again. And again. Blood sprayed over her. The neck area appeared to be his most vulnerable. She went for it again and again. Not thinking, just doing. Her stomach revolted at the sight of so much blood. Especially since a lot of it was on her.

Gray and Lucas were fighting behind her. She could hear the sound of roars and furniture breaking. Her arms ached and she wanted to drop the poker but as long as Eli kept moving, she kept slamming it down on him.

She hit him one final time and he stopped moving. There was a massive gaping wound on his neck from when the poker stuck through the flesh and pulled back. She didn't stare at it for long but turned to Gray and Lucas.

Gray had Lucas on the floor. He was digging into his chest with his paws. There was blood everywhere. On the tiger. It was clear Lucas was dead but the tiger didn't stop chewing on his arm or pawing at his neck and chest.

She winced and reigned in the urge to vomit. "Gray?"

The tiger stopped. He dropped the arm he'd been chewing on and moved closer to her. She dropped down on a sofa chair and watched him.

His golden eyes were those of a predator. Yet she wasn't afraid. Gray was in there. She only hoped he knew how to control the animal. That he knew it was her sitting there in front of him.

She held out a shaking hand, palm up and open. The tiger sniffed at her hand and pushed his massive head into it. She slid her fingers into the thick furry coat and sighed. What the hell had she gotten herself into? Love.

The tiger glanced at her and sat down by her feet. He leaned forward, putting his head on her lap. She stroked his blood splattered fur and hoped that love was worth this amount of strange.

Gray shifted to his human body a few minutes later. He didn't speak and neither did she. He called his guards to come clean up his house. A short time later the cabin was surrounded, but only Tynder and Stripes came inside.

"We're not really shocked they showed up to attack you, Gray," Stripes said, dragging what was left of Lucas through the kitchen exit.

"There had been a rumor about getting rid of you, but they had mentioned waiting for Alyssa to be gone," Tynder added.

Great. She'd been the only reason they hadn't tried to kill Gray sooner.

"It doesn't matter. Anyone else who wants to challenge is welcome to do so. But in order to get the pride they'll have to follow our rules."

Tynder nodded. "The elders have spoken and said that unless the challenge is openly stated in front of them, your death does not mean your family loses the pride leader position. It will just go to the next one of your appointment."

Stripes returned at that moment. "Yes. They're saying from now on you'll have to make a list of backups in case something happens to you and that list will be sealed and guarded. No one can get to it. It would only be opened if something happened to you. If for whatever reason the seal is broken and you're alive, they'd request a new list from you."

Gray nodded.

Lyss swallowed hard, feeling cold and shaky all of a sudden. "Do you all mind not talking about Gray dying right now?"

"Sorry," Tynder and Stripes apologized.

"Let's get you cleaned up, darling." He carried her up to the shower while the lower level was scrubbed. Then he took her to bed once they'd showered. There was no need for words. He made love to her like a man starved. A man who needed her. She needed him as well. She'd come to the conclusion she needed him a lot more than she'd realized. She loved him.

ELEVEN

ALYSSA RUSHED TO open the door after the third knock. Gray had installed a security system so she could see who was nearby while watching TV. He wasn't home but she recognized the woman on the screen and rushed to open the door.

"Hi." She smiled at the young woman. "You're Katherine from the auto shop, right? Or is it Kat? Got my car fixed?"

Katherine nodded. "Either is fine. I came to bring you your keys."

Lyss took them from her and opened the door wider. "Thank you. Would you like to come in?"

Katherine glanced at the inside and shook her head. "No. I should go." She turned on her heel and stopped. Then she glanced at Lyss again. "I admit, I'm surprised."

"At what?" she asked, feeling out of the loop.

"I was always under the impression human women wanted love out of a relationship. But from what I've heard, you're perfect for Gray because you don't."

She frowned. "Excuse me?"

Katherine shrugged. "I guess I had my facts wrong. Good luck with Gray. He's a great leader."

Lyss watched Katherine leave with concern. She was still standing by the door when Tynder arrived. He was supposed to go grab some of her belonging from her house. Gray didn't like the idea of her going back and finding David there again.

"Ready to go?"

"Yes." She slipped out of the house and into his truck quietly. Her thoughts were a jumbled mess. Why would Katherine say that? She'd never told anyone she didn't want love. In fact, she'd specifically told Gray that she did.

She waited until they were almost at her house before she finally said something. "Tynder, may I ask you a question?"

He glanced at her quickly before looking back at the road. "Of course, Alyssa. Whatever you need I will help."

She smiled. He'd become a good friend the past few weeks. "Why did Katherine say that I didn't want love and was therefore okay for Gray?"

Tynder squeezed the steering wheel and gave her an apologetic smile. "She doesn't know what she's talking about."

She knew he was lying. How? She had no clue, but she knew. "Tell me. Please."

"Everyone knows Gray doesn't believe in love. Hell, he didn't even sign himself up for the PDA, Stripes did."

"What?" She froze in place. "You mean he didn't really want to be matched with anyone?"

Tynder sighed. "No, he didn't. But you both worked it out where he could have what he needed and you don't have crazy expectations of love."

She didn't? So what the hell was the point of everything they'd agreed to? Why was she living with Gray and allowing her cats to fall in love with him as much as she had? There was only one person who could tell her what the hell had been on the request for Gray's match. Mrs. Wilder.

"Forget going to my house," she said, her throat closing up on her. "We need to make a quick stop somewhere else."

SOMETHING WAS WRONG. He didn't know what, but he had a feeling it was Alyssa.

"What's up?" Stripes asked from the passenger side.

"I need to go to Alyssa."

Stripes pulled out his phone. "Where are you?" He'd called Tynder.

A few moments later, he hung up. "They went to Gerri Wilder's place."

"Did he say if Alyssa's okay?" His gut twisted in knots. Something was definitely wrong. He sensed her distress even from this far apart.

"She's not. She's very upset and he says he can't tell us because he's been threatened to be neutered if he does."

He floored it, breaking speed limits and not giving a fuck. He had to get to her and find out what was wrong.

When he arrived at Gerri Wilder's apartment, an older woman with a serious frown opened the door. "Let me guess, you're the kitty?"

Kitty? He'd been called a lot of things in his time but kitty was certainly not one of them. "I'm Grayson Green. Are you Mrs. Wilder?"

"Gerri, please. And yes, I am." She glanced up and down his body before moving to stare openly at Stripes. "Oh, you're a fine one."

"Excuse me, Gerri, but I'm looking for Alyssa."

She nodded. "I know that. But she's pissed at you right now."

He frowned. "Can you tell me why?"

He hadn't said or done anything for Alyssa to be angry. They'd been getting along great. He'd never wanted to be around anyone like he did her. She was refreshing and fun. She didn't try to tell him what to do or suggest he change anything about himself. She just let him be.

"Did you or did you not sign up for my services?" Gerri snapped, her eyes glowing gold.

"No, he didn't." Stripes grabbed Gerri's hand and smiled. "I did on his behalf."

Gerri moved close in front of Stripes and yanked her hand out of his grasp. Stripes turned to Gray and shrugged. Clearly the older woman wasn't in the mood for Stripes to try and smooth things over.

Gray opened his mouth to say something when suddenly Gerri slapped the side of Stripes' head. "Do either of you pussies understand what a matchmaking site is for?"

She'd called them pussies. Gray had a hard enough time wrapping his mind around that and the fact she'd smacked Stripes upside his head without adding whatever was going on with Alyssa.

"It" —she breathed out slowly— "is to find love. The right person to be with."

He nodded, feeling almost as if he didn't, he'd be in even bigger trouble with the older woman.

"So why, did Alyssa come here and say you were not looking for love?" Gerri folded her arms over her chest and raised a brow high. "Explain that one to me hairball."

He bit back the urge to tell her to quit calling him names. "I don't do love. Everyone in my pride knows that."

Gerri narrowed her eyes. "Well it would have been nice if it was put on your application. Now I have a woman who's in love with you and is distressed because she thinks you don't love her back and never will." Gerri's gaze traveled back and forth between him and Stripes. "I swear to God, I need to hire an assistant before I lose my mind and bite someone's head off when shit like this happens."

"She's wrong," he said.

Gerri stopped and stared at him. "Oh?"

"She's wrong. It's not what she thinks." He nodded. "I know it looks bad, but let me talk to her."

"I don't know, she's really angry right now." She gave him a once-over again. "I'd promised her love, marriage and children."

He nodded. "Let me talk to her. I can fix it."

She gazed deep into his eyes and smiled. "Come on in." She pushed her front door open and let them in. "I'm going to need to keep a bottle of Vodka handy for these kind of visits."

Gray walked into the large apartment and immediately saw Alyssa standing by a window. She turned to look at him with so much sadness, his heart shattered.

"Why didn't you tell me you didn't do love?" she asked. "I told you from the beginning what I wanted."

He cleared his throat, ignored his two guards and the old woman and marched to Alyssa's side.

"I wanted you from the moment I saw you," he admitted.

"Want is not love." She turned to glance out the window again. "You let me believe we could have something. That in time you might grow to love me."

"Alyssa."

"No! I opened myself up to you from the moment you held my hand and walked me around the woods. I nurtured my feelings and let them grow to the point I couldn't control how much I felt for you." She turned back to him, eyes filled with tears. "How much I loved you."

He swallowed hard. The tiger in him hurt seeing her so upset. "I'm sorry."

She shook her head. "I refuse to be some woman you have sex with. I deserve more. I deserve to be loved."

"You're right."

"I'm glad you feel that way. I've decided our agreement will not work. You can just ship my stuff and I'll send someone to get my car."

His lungs tightened. A dull throbbing took hold of his chest at the thought of her not being with him anymore. She was his and nothing was going to change that. "I'm sorry. Our agreement can't be broken."

She wiped at the tears racing down her cheeks. "Why not?"

He had to do it. He had to tell her or lose her. "Two things. The first is, I can't live without you."

She gasped. "How can you say that? You know how hard this is right now. Why not let me go?"

He closed the distance between them. "I can't let you go." He took a deep breath and finally said the words living inside his heart. "Because I love you."

"You don't do love."

He held her by her arms and turned her to face him. The tears in her eyes were like daggers to his heart. "I may not do love, but it doesn't mean I control my emotions." He lifted a hand and cupped her jaw. "From the first time I saw you, I decided to label my feelings as lust and need." Her bottom lip trembled punching new agony through his body. "The truth was that what I felt was deeper, stronger, better than anything I'd ever felt for anyone in my life."

He couldn't take it. He pulled her into his arms and hugged her. "I'm so sorry, my love. I do love you. Please don't cry, it hurts to see you this way."

"I'm not crying. I never cry." She sniffled and sobbed.

"Right, okay. What can I do to help you stop 'not' crying?" he asked, the human side and the tiger both beyond agitated. "I was scared to acknowledge my feelings as love."

She inhaled sharply. A fresh wave of tears dropped down her cheeks. "You don't want to love me."

"It's not that I don't want to love you. I'm not used to feeling so many things for one person." He sighed, wishing he had the right words to explain himself. Always the loner and quiet, he'd never had to explain his feelings like he did at that moment.

"You don't choose who you love," she murmured.

He pulled back and met her gaze. There was so much pain there. Sadness. "I was afraid to admit how I felt."

She sniffled and frowned. "Why?"

"I didn't want to be at the mercy of my feelings. You could hurt me and that wasn't something I was used to."

She shook her head and glanced down at his chest. "I'd never hurt you. I love you."

"I love you too, Alyssa. Please give me a chance to prove it to you. Come home with me. I won't hold back anymore."

Alyssa had never been so torn in her life. She could give Gray a chance at proving he really did love her, or she could move on. She had promised herself she wouldn't let men take her for a fool anymore, but her heart broke at the thought of not being with Gray. He'd been the first man to accept her exactly as she was. Curvy, silly, and obsessed with her cats. Sex with Gray had opened a new door to a passion she'd never experienced before. He truly wanted her as she was.

"Okay," she blurted before she changed her mind. "I'll give you another chance on one condition."

"Anything!"

"Needing your space is fine, but pushing me away is not. Emotional distance creates pain and I won't tolerate it. If you mean what you're saying you will open up to me."

He nodded and enveloped her in a tight hug again. She sighed, no longer as upset as when she'd first walked in.

"So what's the second thing?" Gerri asked, intruding in the moment. "I gotta say, I've been dying to hear the second part to that speech." She smiled at Alyssa. "I told you I'd find you the right man. Sometimes I need to pull them by the tail, but I found him."

Alyssa smiled and gazed up at him. "What is the second thing?"

"You're carrying my cubs."

She gasped, pushed away from him and felt her belly. "I'm pregnant?"

He nodded, a slight frown marring his brow. "You're not angry are you?"

She might be a little scared, but—wait. "Did you say cubs? As in plural?"

Gerri laughed. "Congratulations. This will be the most interesting five months of your life."

Five months? She rubbed a hand on her temple. "This is a little much to take in."

He helped her sit down and hugged her to his side. "I'll do whatever you need. I promise."

"Can you tell me what you meant when you said cubs?" She hoped he didn't mean there were literal cubs growing in her womb. That would be too weird even for her.

"Babies. Sorry. Not actual tigers."

She breathed a shaky sigh of relief. "Okay. *That* I can handle. Now how many are we talking about?"

She'd never held more than one baby. Thinking of multiples started to make her lightheaded.

"Three."

Three! Holy shit that was two more babies than she was sure she could handle at a time. She glanced at Gray and couldn't hold back the love she felt for him. He looked scared as if she'd be upset because she was carrying multiples.

"I guess we better get to work on that nursery," she said and threw her arms around his neck.

"God, I love you."

She grinned, inhaling the scent she now recognized as uniquely him. "I love you too."

EPILOGUE

"I swear, Geraldine, I don't understand these boys."

Gerri dropped some sugar into her tea and winced. "If you call me Geraldine one more time I will start telling random people on the street your real age."

Her friend Margaret laughed. "Sorry, Gerri. You know it's all in love."

"Yeah, yeah. So how is your boy and his beta? Did they find a mate yet?"

Margaret growled and slammed her teacup on the saucer. "No. Those little mutts. I swear I can't believe I birthed one of them. How is it that they can't find a woman who wants two very hot and wonderful men? Granted, they are pigheaded, but they're great!"

"So what's the problem?" Gerri asked, interested.

"Seems they are just not finding the 'right' woman to complete their triad." Margaret sighed. "How did your nephew do it?"

Gerri grinned. "I helped."

Margaret lifted her brows in interest. "Really?"

"Oh, yes. Now they're one of the strongest triads in the north."

Margaret tapped her chin. "I have an idea."

Gerri nodded. "I like ideas."

"It could get us in trouble."

Gerri laughed. "Even better."

THE END

CURVES 'EM Right

book 4

ONE

DANIELLA FLORES GLANCED around the library she worked at and sighed. She pushed her glasses above her head and scrubbed her eyes. Another boring day in the life of a librarian. Stacks of romance books sat on her desk. As an avid reader, she tended to get lost in the love between the pages of a good book. Hell, might as well. Not like her love life was seeing any mileage.

Her cell phone buzzed and she immediately snatched it up, hoping that something interesting was going on with somebody she knew. The last thing she wanted was to sit there and field calls for her brother, Marcos.

Sure enough. A glance at her screen told her it was her brother texting.

Call me.

Wow. A man of so many words. Not.

She left her assistant watching the empty library and walked outside. The main street in Red Valley was unusually quiet for the middle of the day.

She dialed her brother and slowly strolled down to the bakery next to the library. Already the scent of fresh baked cookies and scones made her mouth water. At least it wasn't Tom again. She hated the multiple calls with the school teacher who had recently proposed in a very unusual way.

"Hey, Marcos. What's going on?" She stared at the display of baked goods, at the same time her stomach rumbled.

She should go eat that salad she left in the office fridge instead of drooling over a piece of cake.

"Dani, you at work?"

"Duh." She waved at her friend Aurelis, the baker, through the glass window.

"How old are you, twelve?" Marcos admonished.

"No. I know very well how old I am." As if her upcoming birthday wasn't enough to remind her she was over thirty, her co-workers were good at constantly asking her when she would find a man and settle down. It was like all three of them had decided she was in desperate need of a man because they all had one.

"Listen, you know I'm going out of town for a few weeks. It's the annual fishing trip with some of the guys from college."

Ah, yes. The lovely three weeks when she got to have two jobs. Her own and sitting for her brother's dogs. "Yeah, yeah. I know you want me to take care of the hounds from hell."

"If you'd stop feeding them all day long, they wouldn't attack you for a treat every few seconds," he said, sounding impatient.

"Hey! So I'm a little soft around the big mutts. I can't help it. They're cute."

Well, cute in a dogs-almost-as-big-as-her kind of way.

"Stop overfeeding the dogs, Dani. Anyway, if you need anything, Blake and Kane are only a short walk away."

Oh, boy. Blake and Kane. When she thought of them, her heart did that stupid flip-flopping in her chest that she'd swear meant she was going to have a heart attack. Blake and Kane. Shifters. Hot. Badasses. And so out of her league she'd given up on them noticing her since she was sixteen. They were around her brother's age, which made them only about five years older than her, but boy were they sexy.

Since they'd been friends with Marcos for the longest time, she'd been around the pair most of her life. They'd never seen her as more than Marcos's little sister. Even though she'd tried. Much to her embarrassment. Remembering the episode where she'd put on her mother's heels and had tried to walk around the guys, only to fall flat on her ass, made her cringe. She knew better now. She stayed away from all that sexy if she could help it.

"I'll be fine."

In fact, the last time she'd seen them was a few years back and they lived pretty close to her brother.

"Okay, then. Call them if you need anything."

"Stop worrying. I love you, now go have fun! See you in a few weeks." She hung up the phone, pushed the door to the bakery wide open and inhaled. "Oh, Aurelis. How can you do this to me?"

She moaned and grabbed the piece of cake her friend put on the counter for her. "You're evil," she grumbled as she took a bite. Another moan escaped her when the cake touched her tongue. "Really evil."

Aurelis laughed, added some cookies, fruit and a scone to the plate, and carried it to a table where drinks were already waiting for them. "I knew you'd come over here. Frankly, I prefer to just get everything ready rather than hear you complain over how long it took me to get you a piece of cake."

She sipped on her latte and sighed. Instead of cake, what she should be eating was the salad at work waiting for her. But she'd never been that much into salad unless it was accompanied by a piece of chicken or fish. A lonely salad didn't feel like lunch. It was more like torture. "I'm supposed to be eating healthier."

Aurelis grinned. "How's that working for ya?"

They both knew the answer to that. Dani had a lot of curves. She wasn't little anywhere and for the most part she was okay with that. It was when her co-workers roped her into their healthy eating challenges that she became a female version of hulk. She was not very nice if she was hungry. "I've lost some self-respect. Does that count as weight loss?"

Aurelis choked on a giggle. "Why would you say that? What did you do?"

"Come on. I have to hide what I eat from the weight obsessed women at work or I won't hear the end of it. Doesn't help that one of them is my boss."

"Yeah. That part sucks." Aurelis picked up a grape and popped it into her mouth. "This isn't technically unhealthy. We have fruit."

"Which I will gladly eat along with my scone, thank you very much." She drank her coffee and sat back with a sigh.

Her boss and co-workers weren't exactly mean. Dani would never sit there and let anyone talk shit about her weight to her. But they were stuck on the fact that she needed to lose some weight and be healthier.

"Do you tell them how many miles you walk and how you measure your food?" Aurelis asked.

"No. If I did, all it would do is open other doors for them to try and 'help me'."

It was true. Her weight wasn't really a problem for Dani. After going through mass dieting as a teen, she realized her body tended to be on the big girl side and she was okay with that. So why did it bother her co-workers so much? It wasn't like she sat down doing nothing all day. She walked, she ate healthy and she only ate cake a few times a month.

"You should just tell them you're fine the way you are. Suggest they worry about their own problems instead of your body."

She was close to doing just that, but she didn't want the backlash that would follow. Especially from her boss. The woman had gotten it into her head that Dani couldn't possibly know what healthy eating was because she was big. Or that she needed to be told to exercise when Dani walked to and from work every day, which was a few miles each trip. So she had a sweet tooth, big friggin' deal.

"I might have to quit this job if they don't stop it," she said and bit into a strawberry. She scrunched her nose at the way the flavor of the fruit didn't go with her coffee. "They are going to drive me to murder."

Aurelis raised a brow. "Wow. That bad, huh? I told you. Just tell them to mind their own business."

She chewed the fruit slowly. "They weren't this bad before. I don't know what's gotten into them."

"The fact they're getting married and think the only thing standing between you and your dream man is your extra pounds."

Dani snorted, "Too bad. Whatever man decides to love me is going to have a lot to love because I'm not going to kill myself to lose weight just to please a guy. I'm a big girl. I have curves."

"That we do," Aurelis agreed.

"I have flub and big thighs and a pudgy belly and if a man loves me then he won't care."

"Also true."

"And any man who likes me will like my body as is. I'm not expecting to meet a man and immediately look for ways to change him. So he has to do the same with me."

"Here, here!" Aurelis raised her coffee cup in salute. "You said it, chica!"

Dani giggled and broke off a piece of her scone. "I'm telling you. I'm sick of all the expectations some people have. This is me. Like it or don't but I won't change for anybody."

"And that's as it should be," said a third person.

The women glanced over to the bakery entrance and saw an older woman walking in.

"Hi, Mrs. Wilder." Aurelis waved her over. "Come sit with us."

"I think I will," Mrs. Wilder said, strolling over to their table. She was an older woman with a commanding presence and impeccable attire. Her powder-blue dress appeared to have been made for her. Though clearly older, she'd aged gracefully. With bright eyes and a wide smile, Dani could tell that she was definitely comfortable with herself.

"What are you doing here? You and I both know your cake can kick mine in the ass." Aurelis smiled.

"Child, please. We both know cake is like beauty. Different preferences for different people." Mrs. Wilder eyed Dani with interest. "You must be Daniella."

She smiled wide. How the woman knew her, she couldn't know but her best guess was that Aurelis had mentioned her lunchtime visits. "I am.

Let me start off by saying that whatever you've heard is probably true but was either done under the influence of too much or not enough liquor."

Mrs. Wilder broke into laughter. "I like her."

"Uh-oh," Aurelis said. "That's never a good sign."

"That's not true." Dani winked at her friend. "What if Mrs. Wilder has a super-hot son she wants to hook me up with? She'll change her mind listening to you."

Mrs. Wilder raised a brow. "Please, call me Gerri."

"And she probably can hook you up with a sexy guy, but I don't think she has a son. Do you, Gerri?" Aurelis asked.

"I don't. Sadly, my husband and I never had children. As far as finding you a man..." Her gaze roamed over Dani's face, searching for something. "I can help you find a mate if that's what you would like."

Dani shook her head and laughed. "I was kidding."

Aurelis' eyes widened. "No, she can help you. She has a matchmaking business. The Paranormal Dating Agency. They're shifters. Hot shifters."

"Really? But—"

"Wait. What about Tom?" Aurelis asked.

Gerri frowned. "You are seeing someone?"

Dani groaned. "Only in his mind. We've gone to some local events in a group and somehow he's now under the impression we'd make a great match." She frowned. "I disagree."

Aurelis grinned. "He's very persistent."

Dani pursed her lips. "I keep rejecting him and he keeps coming back for more. I think he's a masochist. Gerri, I don't know—"

Gerri raised a hand to stop her mid-speech. "I do think I have what you need."

The door dinged and Aurelis stood. "I have to go take care of this delivery but you sit here and talk. I'll be back soon." She patted Gerri on the shoulder. "I'll send someone over to bring you tea."

Gerri nodded and turned to face Dani fully. "Are you looking for a match?"

Was she? She'd given up on being the cream in a Kane and Blake's cookie sandwich years ago. But most men were afraid of her brother and didn't usually survive past "the talk" he had with them. The hurt-my-sister-and-I'll-hurt-you talk.

She'd had boyfriends, but after a while she lost interest. The men she dated were boring. It was one thing for her to live with her head in romance books and quite another to make her own romance happen. Reality was she dated boring accountants and teachers, and the combination was lacking more than a little in every area. So much so that she ended up breaking things off after a few months. No man held her interest long enough for her to fall in love. Or even fall in lust.

"I might be harder for you to match than your usual clients," she started. "I am a librarian. I love romance novels. My expectations of what a relationship should be about are probably way out there."

Gerri nodded. "Tell me what it is you want." She pulled out a notepad from her handbag and started jotting stuff down.

"Um. I guess I'd like to find that connection with someone that's real. No fake shit." She thought back to her last relationship and winced. "I'm tired of men thinking they're doing me a favor by being with me. I want a man who will be dying to be with me. Not just some lame sex with a guy who thinks he has to 'settle' for the big girl." She stared Gerri in the eyes. "If I'm matched with any man who acts like I should be glad he's even looking at me, I won't be responsible for what happens."

"No need for that. The men requiring my services love curves. They appreciate and want a woman for who she is. Generally, my clients prefer someone who loves the body she has. Ideally with lots to hold on to."

Dani blinked. "And these are shifters, like Aurelis said?"

Gerri nodded slowly. "All of them."

Wow. She sighed. "That's good then."

"May I ask, are you averse to multiples?"

Say what? "I'm sorry what do you mean? Multiple what? Dates?"

"Multiple men. I'm not sure if you are aware, but some shifter packs have what's called a Triad. That means two leaders need a female to complete their Alpha set and lead the pack. Together. They mate together and they sleep together. Almost all the time."

She raised her brows in surprise. "You mean like a ménage but forever?"

"Yeah. Happily ménage ever after."

"Well, shit. Count me in. I don't care if you can get me one, two, or a whole pack of men who want me. As long as they genuinely want to be with me and are not just doing it out of some duty to help out the fat girl."

"My clients are not that kind. They're aggressive. Possessive. Jealous. They love their women because of their curves, not despite them. And they will show it."

"They sound like what I need."

Gerri stopped writing and cocked her head to the side. "You know. I really like you. You're very open-minded."

No. She was sort of desperate from the sounds of the stuff coming out of her mouth. The likelihood there'd be two men out there who'd want her for a partner was not something she fully grasped. And while she was more than okay with her body and her curves, the reality was there were a lot of men out there who were not. She wasn't blind or stupid, she knew that.

"All right. I think I have a good idea of what you need, Daniella." Gerri shut the notebook and slipped it into her bag. She glanced at Daniella's hair. Uh-oh. "Do you normally wear shades of purple in your hair?"

Dani smiled. "Not really. I recently went wild and decided I wanted to get some purple in there. My boss wasn't amused but since I've been at the library for years, she didn't cause a stir. I normally wear my hair in a bun so you can barely see the purple."

"I think it's beautiful. It's good to see a different kind of librarian," Gerri said.

She frowned. "You mean because of the hair? Or the fact I'm not wearing a buttoned-up blouse with dress pants?"

"That dress is very pretty," Gerri pointed out. "It makes you look very youthful."

She snorted a giggle. "Nah. I just don't like wearing buttoned-up anything. I feel like it's choking me. Though my boss has tried. But she's used to me doing my own thing. Don't get me wrong, I wear some covered up stuff some days and then when I feel all girly I put on pretty dresses."

"See. That's another thing I like. You're not afraid to break rules and go your own way."

She sighed. "Well that's more due to my older brother. He's always been very overprotective and somehow that's pushed me to want to be a little rebellious." She laughed. "Not much since I am still a librarian, but enough to get me to wear a low cut dress once in a while and put purple in my hair."

"That's enough to let your personality shine through."

She glanced down at her watch and groaned. "I need to go back to work." She pulled out a piece of paper and pen and wrote down her information, handed it to Gerri and stood. "It was really nice to meet you, Gerri," she said, shaking Gerri's hand. "I don't expect miracles, so if you can't find anyone for me I'll understand."

Gerri's lips lifted in a wide grin. "Have some faith. I know of a few men who'd love to meet someone as spunky as you."

She cleared her throat, ribbons of heat crowding her cheeks. "Thanks. I'll wait for you to call with further information."

"You bet. I'll get in touch with you later," Gerri promised.

She went back to her office feeling excited. Maybe Gerri wouldn't find her the perfect man, but she was sure any shifter she got matched with would be a lot more interesting than the men she'd dated her entire life.

TWO

KANE SWUNG THE axe into the piece of wood, splitting it in half without much effort.

"Hello, darling," his mother called out from his kitchen entrance. He knew she loved to visit since she considered him to be a loner. Though his Omega, Blake, lived next door, they wouldn't share a home until they had a mate to bring them together.

"Hello, mother," he said, swinging his axe again on the final piece of wood. He wiped his brow with the back of his hand and turned to glance at her.

"Come inside. I'll make you some lunch and we can talk," she said, her smile wide with enthusiasm.

That couldn't possibly be good. His mother had been trying to push him and Blake to accept one of the women in the pack as a mate, but she knew the rules. Their animals had to be in agreement that whoever the female they ended up with was right. And right didn't just mean appeal sexually. She had to appeal to the human and animal sides. She'd have to bring a link to make the Triad strong and the Alpha set unique.

He slammed the axe down once more and left it wedged in the center of the tree trunk. The day had started to chill. With summer almost on its way out, he and Blake would need to move soon and get a mate. The problem was, no female in the pack caught their attention.

He entered the kitchen and his mother stood by the island while Blake sat at the dining table.

"I'm so glad you're both here," his mother said.

Yeah. Definitely not good. "What's going on, Mother?"

She stopped fixing sandwiches and turned to him, a frown marring her features. "You know, if I didn't know better, I'd say you're already skeptical of my visit."

Blake snorted and leaned back in his seat. His Omega and pack co-leader knew him so well. "That's because he is, Margaret."

She sniffed and continued preparing lunch. "I had an idea."

"I'll be right back", he called out as he walked past. He washed his hands and took off his sweaty T-shirt, tossing it in a basket in the laundry room next to the kitchen. Before his mother got a chance to talk about whatever she wanted, he rushed to his room for a quick shower. No way was he going to sit and eat lunch when he was so sweaty.

After showering, he threw on a pair of jeans and a clean shirt, and hurried back before she started calling out to him.

"So what did you want to tell me?" he asked back in the kitchen.

"I was about to tell you my idea before you rushed out of here."

"Mother, your ideas always mean one of us has to settle for a woman we don't want. A woman who won't complete us." He sighed and sat down at the table. "A woman who's not right for us."

She rolled her eyes and pursed her lips. "If you weren't so damn hardheaded, you'd have found a mate by now. But all you want to do is sit in the backyard building furniture. And you..." she said, pointing a chef knife at Blake. "All you ever look at are the pack accounts like they're suddenly going to disappear overnight."

Kane grinned. The look of confusion in Blake's eyes was funny. His Omega couldn't live without being emotionally linked to the pack or physically connected to his laptop and cell phone. Blake was a businessman with his own accounting firm and enough work to make anyone wince. On top of that, he had pack accounts and pack emotions to handle. It wasn't easy being the Omega.

"Margaret, people in the pack stressing creates issues. I help them reduce stress. Money creates stress. I handle their money and ensure their life savings are well taken care of."

"Yeah, yeah. We all know that." She rolled her eyes, dismissing him. "Anyway, I invited someone to come over and join us for lunch." She grinned and neatly placed the sandwiches on a large tray. "She'll be here shorty and she's going to help."

"Mother—"

She pinned him with a serious stare. "I don't want to hear anything. You've tried your way, now you're trying mine."

Blake raised his brows in question. Kane knew what Blake wondered. What was his mother up to now?

"What is it we're trying?" he asked, rolling his shoulders and lifting his arms over his head.

His mother smiled. It was the same smile she gave him when he was a kid and it was the night before his birthday. He'd tried to get her to tell him what he was getting as a gift. She'd never told and she'd shocked him every single time. "You're going to talk to my friend, Gerri and she's going to find you two a mate."

"Uh-oh," Blake groaned. He finally put his phone away and paid attention to Kane and Margaret.

"Mother, I've told you we can find our own mate."

"You know what? You two are the most pigheaded men I have ever met!" she yelled. "I can't believe I birthed you, Kane Reed!"

Dammit. She was going the emotional route. "Mom—"

"No. Don't 'Mom' me. It would serve you right to find a mate and then for her to be a difficult woman that will give you both gray hairs!"

Wow. That was just mean. "No need to get all hysterical, Mother."

She inhaled and let it out while glaring at him. "You're right. There's no need."

The doorbell rang and she wiped her hands with a paper towel. "I'll get that. That's Gerri." She smirked. "Let's see how well you do with her."

The minute she stepped out of the kitchen, Blake turned to him. "So is this for real? Your mother is going to ask the PDA lady to find us a mate?"

Kane opened his eyes wide. "PDA? You know Gerri?"

"Paranormal Dating Agency. Who doesn't know Gerri? She's Connor and Theron's aunt from the Wildwoods Pack further to the south and she's the one who matched them with each other."

Right. He knew them. Like the Red Valley Pack, Wildwoods were formed of a Triad Alpha set leading the pack. The Alpha, Omega and their female. Maybe this wasn't such a bad idea.

"I don't think she can get that lucky twice in a row," Kane said.

Blake snorted. "Are you kidding me? This is Gerri Wilder. She can find the perfect match for a ketchup bottle."

Kane grinned. "What's that, an order of fries?"

Blake laughed and slapped a hand on the table, making the sandwich tray jump. He then eyed the sandwiches. "Think she'll get mad if I grab one?"

He leaned back in his seat. "Well, depends. How much do you value your hand?"

"Ouch. Never mind. So what if Gerri can find us a mate?"

Kane shook his head, sliding his fingers through his hair. "I doubt it."

Blake smirked in such a way Kane knew he was up to something. "Care to make it interesting?"

"All the time," he returned without missing a beat.

"I say she'll find us the perfect mate. And if she does, that means you will have to stop building shit for a while and get to know whoever we get."

He curled his lip in mock horror. "Are you out of your mind? I build stuff for a living."

Blake narrowed his eyes. "You're the Alpha of Red Valley. You can do whatever the hell you want. I am your Omega, your financial analyst, accountant and best friend! I would know."

"Fine," he growled. "I'll do it. But let it be known that I think this isn't even remotely likely to happen." He picked up an apple from a bowl of fruit in the center of the table and took a bite, chewed and swallowed. "What do I get if she doesn't find us a mate?"

Blake shrugged in his perfectly pressed shirt. "I don't know. What do you want?"

He thought about it for a moment. "We'll go to another town and search for a woman. No more putting me off on that."

Blake sighed. "Fine. We'll search elsewhere. Although that alone can give us problems with some of the pack women. Not to mention the men."

"I'm the Alpha. I don't care what anyone thinks. If they have a problem they can come to me. By the way, did Marcos call you?" He remembered his good friend's request for them to keep an eye on his baby sister.

"Yeah. Check on Dani and all that." Blake frowned. "I feel like we haven't seen her in years."

"That's because we haven't. She went off to college. Came back and has been living in a library ever since."

"She lives in a library?" Blake asked, looking confused.

"Not literally. She works there." He remembered Daniella. She'd always been shy as a kid. And he also remembered she liked both him and Blake. More than a she should have, considering how young she was. Back then he'd been hell-bent on ignoring her and any attraction he felt for her. She'd been a minor and even worse, his friend's little sister. Not that it took away from how much he'd wanted her or how his wolf had gone crazy pushing him to mate her. That had been massively scary.

"She was such a nice girl. So quiet. Reserved. Never a bad word out of her lips," Blake mused. "I think she had a thing for us."

Kane nodded. "Yeah. And if we want to keep our friendship with Marcos we'll ignore that thing and focus on finding our third."

The sound of voices approaching from the living room had them cutting their conversation short. Both men stood and waited for Margaret and her friend to show up. The women walked in a second later.

"Boys, I want you to meet my friend Gerri Wilder," his mother said with enthusiasm. "Gerri this is Kane, my son," she said, pointing to him. "And that handsome boy with those big brown eyes is Blake."

Kane choked on a chuckle and grinned at his mother's friend. "Nice to meet you Mrs. Wilder."

Gerri Wilder glanced at his face for a moment. The ring of gold around her eyes was bright with her animal. She did the same with Blake and nodded. "I can help you both."

He wanted to roll his eyes. "Really? Just like that?"

This lady definitely couldn't find them a mate when they had looked at every possible female in Red Valley and the adjoining areas and hadn't been able to find one themselves.

"Mrs. Wilder," Blake began.

"Call me Gerri."

"Gerri. We've looked at every female in Red Valley. There's no one here. I'm not sure you really can help us."

"You see what I mean?" Margaret barged in, her eyes narrowed.

"Yes. You were right. They are pigheaded," Gerri said. "I'll still find them someone if you want..."

"Oh, please!" Margaret hugged Gerri. "They need our help. Sit down and eat. We can tell them whatever you feel they need to know."

Gerri stared at Kane for a quiet moment before smiling. "You don't think I can find you someone?"

He grinned, not hiding his thoughts. "No. I apologize. It's not that I don't think you're good at matching people with their right mate, but we're in need of a third to join our Triad. Not only that, but if the female we mate doesn't take to shifting, we could have serious problems with the pack. Things are a lot more complicated than finding a pretty face to sleep with."

Gerri raised her brows high. "She must be pretty?"

Ah, fuck. What the hell had he gotten into? "Not necessarily pretty, but definitely hot. Physical attraction would be necessary."

"What do you consider hot?" she asked. "A woman with no physical flaws, a slim figure and so on?"

He frowned. Was she crazy? "Slim? No. Not that I haven't been with a smaller woman, but we prefer a woman with curves," he said, holding his hands out and making an hourglass shape. "Big curves."

Gerri grinned. "And you agree?" she asked Blake.

He nodded. "Curves are sexy. They make a woman real. We want someone who is happy being in her own skin. That likes her body and can find herself being sexually appealing to us."

"Okay. So no shy virgins here, huh?" asked Gerri.

Blake choked on his drink and slapped a hand over his mouth, obviously trying hard not to spit it all over. He visibly swallowed and coughed repeatedly before answering her. "She can be shy if that's her, but we'd like someone who is willing to try things. She's going to have two men for Christ's sake. That means she should at least be open-minded."

"Right. The wolves want a freak." Gerri laughed. "Wow. If half my clients were this specific I'd never get anyone hooked up."

Kane's mother grinned and patted Gerri on her arm. "You and I both know your nephew and his Omega are loving their new mate."

"True." Gerri gave Kane a shrewd gaze. "What about love? I don't want to hear crap about not needing love because no woman will want to even consider a lifetime relationship without the possibility of love."

He dropped his shoulders and sighed. "If love happens, it happens. I am not opposed to it. I don't think Blake is either." He waited for Blake to agree. Once he saw his Omega nod he went on. "But a woman willing to take on two mates, a difficult pack and the change can be a lot to ask for."

"Not to mention she has to be curvy, a freak in bed and probably a great cook, huh?" Gerri asked.

Blake laughed. "It could really help us out if she was."

"I never promised miracles. I promised a mate."

That sounded ominous. "Right. So can you help?"

Gerri's lips tilted upward in a slow smile. "Here's what I want you to do..."

THREE

DANI PUSHED THE mask higher on her face and winced. A masquerade ball blind date. This was what she'd allowed herself to be talked into. All to meet a man that might be the one for her. When Gerri mentioned her annual ball would be the place she'd meet her date, she hadn't given it much thought. But now that she wore the zipped up tight red corset with leather accents and a short black bustle skirt that showed off her thigh highs, she wondered if she'd lost her mind. Probably. Okay, not probably, definitely.

Lord help her when she had to go to the bathroom. She'd have to ask someone for help. Why did she let her neighbor and good friend make the damn thing so tight she felt like her boobs were going to pop out at any second and flash the party a big hello? She'd wanted to feel sexy. And she had, until she reached the front door of the massive mansion in the woods.

The place was huge with expensive cars lined up along a circular driveway. She pulled the short red cape around her shoulders, trying to take the attention away from her breasts. It was useless. She'd thought a sexy red riding hood outfit would be great for a masked ball, but now she felt all sorts of uncomfortable.

Gerri was easy to find. She stood at the center of the grand ballroom dressed as a Greek goddess. Her long toga and gold arm bands looked amazing on her.

She rushed over to Dani's side and hugged her. "Daniella, so nice to see you."

"How did you know it was me?" Stupid costume did a bad job of hiding her identity. She'd gone with her contacts for the night, hoping they would help her look sexier than having black rimmed glasses over a face mask.

Gerri grinned. She was the only person without a mask. "I can scent you. Which defeats the purpose of the mask. Come with me."

She tugged her to a side door and into a private parlor. Dani glanced around the sumptuously decorated room. It looked like something straight out of a romance novel. A massive four poster bed with big satin pillows and sheer drapes sat in the middle of the room. Gerri sauntered over to a locked case and used a key to open it. She brought out a box of pills and a spray bottle and turned to face Dani. She opened the box and took out a small pill, passing it to Dani.

"Put that on your tongue," she said. "It will dissolve before you know it."

Dani did as she was told. The little pill was tasteless and in the blink of an eye had dissolved.

Next, Gerri put down the box and pointed the spray bottle at her. "Come here, child. Let's make this interesting."

Her words worried Dani a little. What was the woman up to? She moved closer and stood in front of her thinking Gerri would spray her with a perfume or something of the kind. She did spray her, but there was no discernible smell to the spray.

Gerri did a full circle, spraying her from head to toe until she swore she was covered in whatever the mist was. Then she went as far as sniffing her neck and back.

"Open your hands." She sprayed her hands and feet. Heck, she even told her to lift the skirt so she could get at her lower body.

Once Gerri sniffed a few more times and seemed satisfied with whatever she'd done, she smiled and put the bottle back in the case.

"I don't smell anything, Gerri," she said, smelling her hands and arms.

"That's the idea." Gerri smiled. "The thing is, I need you to have an open mind tonight."

Uh-oh. Why did that sound like she should be worried?

"I do have an open mind. I'm here in this playmate red riding hood costume, aren't I?"

Gerri chuckled and sat on an antique chair by the bed. "You are, but there's something I need you to do for me."

"What?"

"Follow your instinct tonight. You might find yourself in a position to choose something new over what you are used to. I want you to listen to your heart."

She nodded. She wasn't really used to anything. Her disappointment in men came from their inability to accept her as she was. Some of them thought she was the kind who felt so insecure about her body that she had to be okay with any man offering sex. That she wasn't worthy of a real relationship based on a man thinking she was hot. Fuck that.

She knew she was hot. Maybe not in the way society deemed women to be hot, but she was. Her body had curves. She had big hips and a small waist. Men had not gotten the message that Dani wasn't desperate to hear pretty words. She wanted real words. She wanted to see the passion and lust in a man's eyes. She wanted to be taken up against a door and have her clothes torn off her. She did not want to hear about him needing a few beers before the word sex popped up. That was not romantic.

"Now, I'm going to have someone usher you to the open indoor garden on the right side of the house. Hang out there and your date will meet up with you."

She nodded and gulped. Gerri had mentioned she'd find her a man that would want her as she was and not try to change her into something else. Someone that looked like what he thought his dream girl should be.

They strolled out of the room together and a man showed up to guide her away. She waved at Gerri and left the older woman smiling in the middle of the room. That smile sort of creeped her out a little. Aurelis had told her that Gerri was a great matchmaker that could decide to hook her up with someone she might not be expecting. At that moment, all she expected was a decent man.

Her escort led her down a long hallway bypassing people in costume to a set of French doors. She went through and gasped. There was a giant private indoor garden the size of her house on that side. Large glass doors had been opened to allow guests in and out of the garden. At the moment, it was empty and she was the only one there. She walked around, fascinated with the multitude of plants and flowers. Then she saw it. A giant swing in the center of the room, facing the outdoors and the forest. The swing was a giant two person seat, covered in white and pink frilly lace cushions. The ropes it hung from on the ceiling were twined with sheer fabric. The seat looked inviting and comfortable, not to mention incredibly romantic.

"Beautiful, isn't it?" a voice said.

She glanced around the room, her gaze searching through the pockets of darkness to find a figure leaning against a pillar by a door.

"It's very beautiful," she said softly. Shit. When the hell had her voice turned so low and husky? "If you're looking to be alone, I can go."

He left the wall and prowled to her. The light filtering from outside allowed her to make out his costume. She didn't know what he was. Her best guess was a pirate. His pants were torn as was his shirt. His chest was exposed for her view. The closer he came, the more nervous she got.

"I'm here to meet you," he said.

She frowned, paying more attention to his voice. She knew that voice. "Kane?"

His lips lifted in a sinful smile that made her belly heat with desire. "That's me. And you're my Little Red, I guess?"

She wanted to laugh but she couldn't. This was Kane. Her brother's best friend. How could he not realize it was her? Kane had never looked at her with all that open hunger before. He eyed her up and down as if she was a meal and he was starving.

"I am," she said, her voice still a mere whisper.

If Kane was here, that meant...

"She looks just as good from behind as she does from the front," another voice said.

She glanced over her shoulder. Sure enough it was Blake in a costume identical to the one Kane had on. She knew she'd worn a face mask, but how did they not recognize her? Of course. They'd never really seen her like this. Without her glasses, and the last time she'd seen the two of them was years ago when she was in college. Back then she'd hidden behind big long dresses and sweats. It was only a few years ago that she'd changed her whole way of dressing to blend with her personality.

"You're Blake," she breathed as the two men crowded around her.

Kane removed his face mask and sniffed. His brows dropped down in a frown. "I can't scent you."

Blake touched her arm and goose bumps broke over her skin. She glanced at him and watched him inhale. "I can't either."

"You're not supposed to scent me," she said, her voice growing huskier. "You're supposed to follow your instinct." She fed them the same line Gerri had given her.

It was like her biggest fantasy come true. Blake and Kane. Both men she'd wanted years ago paying attention to her. She wanted to say something but feared the more she spoke, the easier it would be for them to realize it was her. She didn't want the fantasy to end. If she could get a night with them, she would give up Aurelis's cakes for a year. Okay, a month, but that was huge for her.

"Take the mask off," Kane said, reaching for her hand.

She shook her head, feeling brave under the mask. These men were her brother's friends. They would run out of that garden faster than a speeding bullet if they knew it was her. For years she'd known that being Marcos's sister had made her the one person they wouldn't touch. So she'd stayed away from them. Not like she needed the temptation anyway. But now here they were. Both showing interest in her and she had done nothing but stand there and say a handful of words. Maybe she wouldn't find her one true love tonight, but she was sure going along with whatever these two had in mind for her.

"I'd feel better with it on," she whispered, keeping her voice soft. It wasn't hard when her chest felt tight from lack of oxygen. Sweat gathered in her palms. She swiped them on the short skirt, gripping the material in her fists.

Kane drew closer his face mere inches from hers, and inhaled. "Nothing. It's so strange. I can't scent you but something tells me you're the right one."

Excitement flooded her veins in a quick dizzying high. She bit her lip in order to not say anything incriminating and glanced at Blake.

His eyes were bright with the power of his animal. "I feel the same."

"Did she tell you about us? That we're a pair?" Kane asked, pulling her long hair from inside her cape and gliding his fingers through her tresses.

She swallowed back a moan and stopped herself from leaning into his touch. Jesus. She wanted so badly to say something to them to the effect of "get naked and show me what you got", but didn't think that would go over well.

"She did."

Kane grabbed her hand and placed it flat on his chest. The shifting muscles under his shirt made her palm tingle. "Is this what you want?"

Lord, yes! Definitely times a billion to the power of the hell yes. She glanced up from where her hand lay on his chest and met his gaze. His eyes had also gone bright with his animal. It was so fucking sexy to know they both wanted her. There was no holding back because she was Marcos's sister. These were two incredibly sexual men filled with lust. It was pure animal attraction. She loved it.

She lifted her lips in a grin and stared at his mouth. "I might need something to drink."

Blake pulled away from her. "I'll get you some champagne."

"So? Is this what you want?" Kane asked again, his big body looming so close she wanted to rub herself on him with every breath she took.

She turned to face him fully, sliding the hand on his chest up to his shoulder. Christ! He had a mountain man's body. Big and buff with enough muscles to make her beg to let her climb him. She licked her lips and he sucked in a breath.

"I don't know. I've never been with two men." She was certainly not opposed to it, especially when it came to Kane and Blake, but she had no idea what the hell being with both entailed other than probably better sex than she'd ever had.

He curled a hand around her neck and pulled her close. "Too late, Little Red. These wolves want you."

She smiled at his aggression. This was what she wanted from a man. To show her that she was desirable as she was. "I might need convincing."

There was no time to pat herself on the back over her little quip. All she could do was inhale and watch his head descend to press their lips together. Passion blazed and an electric shudder raced down her spine at the first brush of his lips over hers. He plunged his tongue into her mouth and owned her. Rubbing his mouth over hers like some sinful mating ritual, he pushed her to submit to his touch. To the invisible control he had with a single kiss.

She dug her nails into his shoulders. Her body pressed tight to his. He slid his big hands down her back, until he reached her ass and squeezed her cheeks. The kiss deepened. God that felt good. His hands on her, his lips on her, felt fucking amazing. He nibbled and sucked on her tongue. Her nipples pebbled tight, aching with the need to be touched under the restraining material of her corset. Lord, she'd never wanted to be naked like she did at that moment.

Heat poured over her in waves, seeping through her pores and warming her to the marrow. Her heartbeats thudded in her ears. No kiss had ever done this to her. It made her lose herself completely in the moment.

She pulled away from him, gasping for a breath. "You" —she cleared her throat, her entire body aching with suppressed tension— "made your point."

It was pure luck that he'd decided not to tear the mask off her face and be done with her mystery. He curled his hand around her jaw. "You're tempting the beast, Little Red."

She blinked. The fire in his eyes made her pussy throb. This was the first time a man or any men had looked at her like she was sex on heels. It was really frickin' awesome.

She wanted to squeal and throw herself at him. Maybe order him down on his knees and tell him to do her then and there, but what would that say about her? She choked back a snort. That she was damn horny and hadn't had sex in a while is what he'd think. Which was the truth. She'd been so disappointed and angered with the past men in her life she'd pretty much lived an almost celibate life, except for her awesome battery operated friends in her private drawer.

"How do you know I'm not a mistake?" she asked.

She was realistic. The minute Blake and Kane realized who she was under the mask and costume, they'd treat her like she had the plague again. All because of that stupid friendship code. And the fact that Marcos was so overprotective.

His gaze roamed over her again, like a slow seductive caress. Her temperature spiked from that single sizzling glance. "You're no mistake. I can tell. Even though I can't catch your scent, my animal is pushing me to take you."

His rough and rugged voice opened a new door to her need. Men didn't talk to her like that. Ever.

"What will you do if I'm not what you truly want?"

A slight lift of his lips was the only hint of his smile. She stared at the scruffy jaw and shaggy haircut that made him look like a real life pirate. Perhaps it was that she had denied herself for too long from seeing Kane and Blake. When they'd both been what she'd desired secretly for so many years, but being this close to him made her question his real motives. She knew she wasn't mate material. Not for them. They needed a third like them. A shifter. Everyone knew that's how the Triads worked.

He lowered his head and she knew he wanted to kiss her again. Lord how she wanted that. More than she wanted to take off her damp panties.

"I'll put it to you this way," he breathed, his lips floating over hers. "I want to fuck your pretty lips. I want to slide up between your sexy thighs and feel your pussy wet and hot around my cock. And then, I want to come inside you. Again and again." He rested his lips by her ear. "I have been thinking of every way I can get this outfit off you for the past ten minutes." He sucked her earlobe between his teeth and tugged.

FOUR

A HEADY THRILL rushed her. She bit her lip and moaned, pressing closer to him. "Is my costume not nice enough?"

"Oh, yeah. It's sexy as fuck. From the heels to the garters up to that top showing off your tits, it's all one tempting little package." He kissed his way to her lips. Her pulse skipped a beat. She might die just from his hand on her ass, squeezing her cheek. "The skirt hides your delectable ass. The top is hard to move and keeping me from touching your nipples."

She swallowed the sand clogging her throat. "You can get it off…"

What the hell was she doing? She'd just given him permission to strip her at a party. Blake would return at any moment and the idea of him finding her and Kane together only pushed her anticipation. Would he join in? She knew they'd share a mate at some point, but did they share women regularly? That was something she wasn't aware of and by god she wanted to find out firsthand.

Kane glanced down at the zipper on the front of her corset with another of those mind-fucking grins. "You're right."

The zipper hissed as he pulled it down, opening the tight corset at the front and leaving her bare on top. The material fell to the floor with a thump.

"This is a beautiful sight," he said, his words so rough she could barely make them out. He cupped her breasts, lifting the heavy weight in his warm palms and thumbing her aching nipples. She groaned, her heartbeat increasing with the fondling he did. "Do you like me touching you, Little Red?"

She pushed closer into him, arching her back and pressing her chest into his hands. "God, yes!"

He brought his head down closer to her chest and sucked one of her nipples into the warm cavern of his mouth. Her body had a mind of its own at that point. She raised her hands up to his hair and clutched at the strands. Her belly quaked. Multiple shudders ran down her spine straight to her pussy.

She'd become so enthralled in his lips sucking her nipples, she'd forgotten anyone could walk in on them at any time. The sound of footsteps and laughter came from outside the garden. She tried to force her body to cooperate, but instead she gripped Kane's hair harder and moaned. "So good..."

He lifted her in his arms and moved a few steps back before setting her down on the swing she'd seen when she'd first walked into the room. She leaned back into the cushion, her skirt hiked up to reveal her itty bitty panties and thigh highs.

"Christ. Is that a garter?"

She met his gaze with a grin. His reaction empowered her. The way he groaned the words out and pushed her legs open spoke volumes. The lust so evident in him was something she'd never seen in any man.

"Like it?"

"Little Red, I fucking love it."

She leaned back in the cushioned swing, watching him as she raised her hands to her chest to tweak her own nipples. This was a new experience. But the look on his face was priceless. She reveled in these new sexy woman feelings.

Kane dropped down to kneel in front of her. He pushed her legs wider.

"This has to go," he said, slicing through the panties with his claws. The soft sound of material tearing filled the quiet garden for a nanosecond. He peeled the see-through panties off her and growled. "That's fucking, beautiful."

She licked her lips, squeezing her breasts a little harder than before. Her pussy creamed as she watched his features tighten and his eyes glow brighter. For once she didn't worry about how soft her belly looked or how thick her legs were. Instead, she focused on embracing the sensuality he brought out in her.

"My tongue is going to lap every little drop from your pussy," he groaned softly, pressing his lips to her leg. "I want your wetness on me. I want to lick my lips and taste you over and over again."

She had a hard time keeping her knees from shaking. Her blood sizzled with arousal. His words were like a magical movie playing in her mind. He swiped his tongue on her thigh.

She inhaled sharply and gulped. "How do I taste?"

"I can't scent you, but from how beautiful your pretty pink folds are, I know you're fucking delicious. I want to spend the rest of the night with my face in your pussy, feasting on you."

His licks and kisses moved to the center of her need. Her muscles tensed. She waited with baited breath for him to do something, anything. Men didn't really give Dani oral. Not usually. They complained her thighs were too wide and she tended to squeeze their heads when she got excited. A man who willingly wanted to do that without her having to push his head down was a miracle. This was something that turned her on beyond belief.

"Kane..." she groaned.

He curled his arms around her large thighs and held her in place, draping her legs over his shoulders. Her heels pressed at his back and he didn't seem to mind.

"You in this little outfit will be forever burned in the back of my brain."

Good gracious he knew just what to say.

"Why?"

"Heels, garters and thigh highs have to be some of the sexiest things to see a woman with your body in."

She pushed back the urge to groan. "Because I'm big?"

"You're not big. You're beautiful. Lush. You have a body made for fucking."

She blinked back the visions of him doing just that. "I've never heard that."

"It's true." He placed butterfly kisses on one thigh then the other. "All I can think about right now is keeping your legs wide open and watching my cock slide deep into your wetness. I want to fuck you. Everywhere."

"Looks like you two are having fun without me," came Blake's voice from the doorway. He clicked the door lock behind him and placed glasses filled with champagne on a table by the entrance.

She moaned, not caring that he'd caught them in the middle of Kane kissing his way to her pussy.

"You look divine laying there," Blake said, prowling closer.

Kane didn't stop. He brushed his lips over her clit in a sweep so light she gasped, and then waited for him to do it again.

She pinched her nipples harder, wiggling her hips lower to meet Kane's mouth.

"Patience," Kane murmured between her thighs.

"I can't," she gasped, shutting her eyes and pressing her head back into the cushion of the swing.

"You can," Blake said. "Here, let me help you, beautiful."

Blake sat next to her on the big swing. He shifted to his side and picked her hands up and placed them on his chest. She watched his beautiful dark eyes glow with his animal. He brought his lips down over hers, sucking the air out of her lungs. Crawling her hands over his chest, she gripped the material of his shirt and tugged him closer at the same time Kane licked her folds.

Blake swept his tongue into her mouth. Probing. Taking. She moaned into the kiss and shuddered when Kane flicked his tongue in circles over her clit.

She ignored the tiny voice in her head telling her she shouldn't do this. These were her brother's friends but she wanted a relationship. Things like this never happened to Dani so she'd take it and enjoy it. She'd enjoy every second of Kane's mouth on her pussy, sucking and licking like she was a tasty piece of fruit. She'd enjoy Blake's mouth pressing over hers, his fingers molding her breasts and pulling at her nipples.

Daniella knew this wouldn't last. It was too good. Too perfect to have these two sexual creatures lapping at her body as though she were a gift from the gods.

She dug her nails into Blake's chest. Though toned and muscular, Blake had a less bulky frame than big mountain man Kane. Blake's skin felt hot under his torn shirt. He grunted into the kiss, his thumbs pressing at her aching nipples. He moved away from her lips, leaving her to fight her lungs for some air.

Passion flooded her veins with both men caressing her body. Blake encased one of her nipples in his mouth. He grazed his teeth over the swollen mound and sucked hard. Electricity sparked through her, making her shudder.

She threw her head back, slid one hand into his short hair and held him tight to her chest. Christ that felt good. His mouth on her breast, licking and biting, reduced her ability to think and form a coherent sentence. She gripped Kane's longer shaggy hair with her other hand and rocked her hips on his lips.

It was surreal. The fantasy she'd always had but never thought would come true. Both men wanting, licking, and sucking on her body to bring her to the heights of pleasure. Kane drove his tongue into her channel, fucking her with it and growling to create a vibration that drove her wild.

"Yes! God, yes!" she screamed.

Her pussy grasped at Kane's driving tongue. He didn't stop. He licked her, pushing the tension curling in her stomach to form into a tight ball ready to explode at any moment. Her brain tried to take in the actions of both men heating her blood to boiling.

Kane brushed his tongue up from her ass to her clit in slow wide licks. She groaned with each swipe of his tongue on her slick flesh. He sucked her throbbing clit between his teeth.

"Oh, my god! More, more, more..."

Both men bit her in tandem. She was glad she was sitting on the swing since her muscles felt heavy and weak. Kane growled on her pussy, nibbling her clit hard. Blake did the same on her breast, her nipple tight between his teeth. The vibrations rocking her body blew the tension at her core into millions of pieces. She choked on a scream, her body slowly loosening as a tidal wave of pleasure swept her under.

She sucked breaths into her deprived lungs, mini rockets shooting from her core outward to her heavy limbs.

Kane continued to kiss her inner thighs, working his way down to her knees. Blake pulled back, pushing some of the sweaty strands of hair away from her face. Her body started to cool after the massive inferno that consumed it moments before. She sat up slowly, fixing her skirt and watching Kane stand.

Blake took hold of her mask and tugged. "You won't need this anymore," he murmured, peeling the black half mask off her face.

She screeched and tried to hide her face only to hear both men gasp. Fuck.

"Daniella?" Kane asked, standing before her with a scowl fierce enough to scare small children.

She looked around for her corset. No way in hell was she having a talk with them while half naked. She struggled to zip the corset up, knowing that the damn thing needed to be loosened at the back so it could close at the front. Right at that moment her brain didn't want to think about that. All she wanted was to not be naked while she discussed with her brother's friends why she'd just let them give her oral sex and why she hadn't said a thing about who she was.

She growled and pressed the open corset over her naked breasts, holding it up with shaky hands. Hell. Of all the times for them to realize who she was, this was not the one she'd envisioned when they'd started earlier.

"Hi." She pressed the material over her body, using it almost like a safety shield.

They stared at each other. "What are you doing here?"

"Being set up on a date."

"You? She set us up with you?" Kane growled.

His tone made her frown. Hadn't they just been all over her like they couldn't get enough of her just thirty seconds ago? What happened to that?

"Well what the hell is wrong with me? I thought you just told me I was perfect." Jerk. Figures that he'd say the right words just to get her naked. Or mostly naked.

"You are perfect," Blake said. "You're also Marcos's sister."

She shrugged. "So?"

This whole thing of her being Marcos's little sister annoyed the shit out of her. Weren't these grown men?

"Your brother once told us that we needed to keep our hands off you," Kane said, walking to one of the open doors leading to the back and leaning on the frame. "We've been careful to not damage our friendship with him."

That rat bastard! "You mean to tell me that you two could want me and will not touch me because of Marcos?"

She clenched her jaw so hard she swore her teeth would break at any moment.

Kane and Blake glanced back and forth at each other before both frowning at her and answering at the same time, "Yes."

Tired of fighting to keep the open corset from revealing her body, she snagged a folded throw off a chair and threw it over her shoulder, allowing the corset to slide off without showing her breasts. She folded the corset and held it in front of her along with the sides of the blanket like a shield. With measured steps, she marched to the door Blake had locked when he'd brought them champagne.

"What are you doing," Blake asked, his voice filled with concern.

She stopped, turned and cleared her throat. "I'm getting out of here. You two have no clue what you want. It's obvious that Mrs. Wilder made a mistake in bringing us together."

Dammit, she'd been so close to getting both men naked. The injustice.

"Don't go!" Blake ran a hand through his short cropped hair. He appeared torn and she couldn't understand it. It shouldn't be this hard to make a decision about wanting her. They either did or didn't.

They weren't bound to Marcos for any reason other than friendship, so why couldn't they be with her if that's what made them happy?

"What exactly do you want?" she asked.

Blake pinned her with his slowly dimming golden gaze. "When it comes to you it's not about what we want. It's about what we promised. And we promised Marcos that we would stay away from you."

Fucking hell! "This is starting to sound like a broken record covered in total bullshit to be honest," she said, her hand hovering over the knob.

FIVE

KANE INHALED SHARPLY. "Your brother is our friend," he said, his voice so rough she swore he'd shift at any second. "We made a vow to keep our hands to ourselves. You're much too important to your brother for us to damage our friendship with him or your expectations of the future."

What expectations? Jesus H. Christ they made it sound like she was ready to marry them. All she wanted was some hot sex from the two of them. Why was it so hard for them to comprehend that?

She glared from one man to the other, frustration and anger growing by leaps and bounds inside her chest. She felt like she was sixteen once again and being rejected over some stupid brotherly friend code.

Swallowing back the hurt, she unlocked the door, turned the knob and walked out of the room, ignoring both men calling out to her.

Bypassing one of the hallways she'd been escorted through, she opened up a set of French doors and rushed out into the night.

Bright moonlight lit her path as she tried not to fall in her heels on her way to the front of the house.

What a mistake it was to have come and done this. Mrs. Wilder wasn't to blame, though. She couldn't have known that there was a history between Dani and the shifters. Once Dani saw them in their costumes, she should have expected that there was never going to be a chance with Blake and Kane. Her hope had grown with the desire they'd openly shown her. But that hadn't been enough for them to take a chance and ignore whatever they'd promised Marcos.

A pair of strong hands grabbed her by her sides, jerking her to a stop as she rounded the corner of the house to turn for the driveway. Her heels sank in the grass, making it almost impossible to stand upright.

"Dani," Blake said, turning her to face him. "You can't go. You don't understand what's going on."

She rolled her eyes and gripped the blanket harder, holding back the urge to yell at him. "Please, Blake. I don't need explanations. This is the second time you've both made it clear that there is no chance for me with you. There won't be a third time."

She tried to tug her arms out of his hold, but he was strong. Kane was nowhere in sight. She wondered if Blake was the one sent to talk to her because he was the peacemaker of their pack. The one who calmed ruffled feathers and reduced anger levels.

"No matter how much we don't want to want you...we still do."

How could she even begin to explain to him what his words did to her? She'd finally heard the words that she'd dreamt of come out of his mouth. Maybe she should be checked for hallucinations. Her stomach twisted in all kinds of knots and a flare of pleasure bloomed over what he said. They really wanted her. Probably not as badly as she wanted to tear at their clothes and hump them, but it was something! Unfortunately, if they worked this hard at fighting it, then maybe she needed to let it go.

She didn't think they'd understand how much she'd wanted both of them for so many years.

"I can't do this. It is clear that your friendship means more to you guys then a night with me."

Her mind played instant erotic images of her with both men. What a night that would be. It was unreal that with a mask on she'd almost gotten into the fantasy she'd been waiting for, but the minute it'd come off, reality had hit her in the face like a ton of bricks.

"You don't understand," Blake growled. He shifted from foot to foot and scrubbed a hand over the back of his neck. Then he growled again.

She raised her brows in curiosity. Blake had never lost his temper or shown any signs of frustration. This was new, even for him.

"It wouldn't just be a night. We're looking for a mate. We need someone to help us create the bond necessary for our Alpha Triad."

She shook her head, shoulders slumping, and glanced away. "I can't help you. I know how this works. You need a shifter and I'm certainly not one."

Reality was, she'd give anything to be part of their Triad. But she had her feet firmly planted on this planet. These were powerful strong beings. She was a human. To create the Triad that they needed, they had to find a female that would be able to shift. A woman who was strong and could give them Alpha babies. She couldn't give them anything other than herself.

The truth was, she should focus on finding a human man who could rock her world. Her first use of the PDA and things had already gone wrong. Obviously, paranormal dating wasn't for her.

"Look, Blake, this is more than what I signed up for."

"I understand, but now that we've been so close to you without knowing it was you, it changed things. Our guards were always up when you were around because of your brother. We realize that we might have to rethink staying away."

She gave a dry laugh and shook her head. "You'll have to keep rethinking it. I'm not just some object you can decide all of a sudden you want. I'm a woman who has feelings. I have a lot to offer the right man. The last thing I want is to hear that I'm not what you really want, but you'll rethink being with me because your dick is thinking for you. That's not how I work."

She jerked away from his hold and moved toward the front of the house. It wasn't going to be easy but she'd get past this.

It had been so simple to let herself get caught up in the fantasy that both men wanted to be with her. The reality was that they needed a mate but she wasn't the one for them.

BLAKE STARED IN the distance watching their future mate walk away and didn't know why he allowed it. Pain drifted off her pores, pushing his wolf to the surface with a growl he had to bite back. It was clear that he had upset her. Not that he'd meant to, but he refused to lie to her. They needed a third and they had vowed to Marcos that they would not touch his sister.

They didn't plan on following Marcos's request any longer. For years they had, they'd been depriving themselves of Daniella and making their Triad whole.

When Blake and Kane had become friends with the humans, Marcos had made it clear that his sister was off limits. At first they'd thought it was because he didn't understand shifters, but the truth was that he'd understood them more than they realized. Both Blake and Kane had been respectful of his concern for Daniella and had tried to abide by the rules of their friendship. They'd stayed away from her.

Their interest had been piqued at their first meeting when she had been nothing but a teenager. But tonight, seeing her without knowing who she was, sent them over the edge. Licking her. Touching her. It all brought out feelings and mating desires no other female had. It was more than they were used to and they didn't know how to proceed. On one hand, they had their friendship to think about, but on the other hand, he knew they would not find another to fill the gap in their Alpha Triad. She was their one. The only one for them.

"So what do we do?" Kane's voice floated from behind him as he stopped by Blake's side.

Blake turned to face his friend. They'd never had this kind of thing happen before. "I don't know," he murmured, for once completely confused and unsure of how to fix things. Though Kane was the Alpha leader and the one that everyone looked up to, Blake was the problem solver. Blake knew when pack members where upset. He spent most of his time calming frustrations, soothing anger and ensuring the pack thrived in peace.

"I want her." Those words from Kane's mouth sealed the deal.

Blake wanted her too. But it wasn't that simple. If they mated with someone like Daniella, who was a human, they were subjecting themselves to having to explain to their people that they were still just as strong with a human being that they would be with a third shifter. She might not take to the change. She might be a human forever. How would their pack handle that?

"If we take her, we will have to deal with Marcos, the pack, and proving to her that she's the one for us." He'd seen the heat in her eyes for them. On that account they were fine. It wouldn't be hard to get her to accept them sexually.

"That shouldn't be a problem," Kane said, his voice dripping with his Alpha authority. He slapped Blake on the shoulder and grinned. "Piece of cake."

"Do you even know women? They are the most complicated creatures on the planet. Just a single word can take your relationship from being happy to being so miserable that your balls crawl up your ass."

Kane laughed and shook his head. "I don't see Dani as being that type of woman."

Blake snorted. He definitely didn't know women. "I think that in order for us to get Daniella to want to be with us, we will have to work really hard and get her mind onboard for the long term."

"Looked to me like she was ready to let us both get a lot closer with her tonight."

"Yes, she was. But one night does not make a lifetime and we want her forever." Blake didn't want to have a sexy and deliciously curvy woman to sleep with for a single night. He wanted her as a partner. In order for that to work, he needed to make sure she knew how special she was to them.

"What do you have in mind?" Kane asked, folding his arms over his chest. They ambled to the area they'd left Kane's truck at and continued to discuss Daniella.

"You and I are a team," Blake said, reiterating what they both knew. "We have been since we were born. We know that we are both going to be sharing this woman for the rest of our lives. But in order to make it work we have to be on point to get her to see that long-term with us is not just a possibility. It's a reality that we can make happen."

They slipped into Kane's truck. He put the key in the ignition, twisted it and the engine roared to life. Kane turned to glance his way. "I already know that. So what do you suggest?"

"First, I want to go make sure she got home okay. I think she was agitated and it is still bothering me to think she's upset over us. You know I can't let it go."

Kane nodded and gunned the engine. The truck sped forward through the night as they left the party. They'd only lasted all of a handful of hours in the mansion. It had been enough time to realize they'd been ignoring the one woman that could make them whole.

"I think we need to makes her days just a little bit better. Show her that two of us caring for her isn't all bad. We have to bring her out of the idea that this is only going to be about sex."

"It's not?" Kane asked, raising his brows.

"No. It is not. It's about commitment, remember?"

"Wait, so no sex?" The alarm in Kane's voice made him chuckle.

"Of course there will be sex. In fact, I think we should go give her a preview of how good things can be."

Kane turned to glance at him, a slow smile curving over his lips. "That's got to be one of the best ideas you've ever had."

"Remember. We'll want to show her the relationship between three can be just as great, if not better, than two."

Kane nodded. "I think you should visit her at the library and show her the wonders of...books."

Books. Right. Blake choked on his laughter, already knowing what Kane had in mind. "Fine. I'll do it."

"I think I'll take the second round and possibly invite her to come over to my place for dinner and a movie."

"That's great." Blake nodded. This was shaping up better than he expected.

"What about doing something together? Or do we want to be one on one for a while so she doesn't get overwhelmed?"

Blake thought about it. Kane made a right turn at the street leading to Dani's house. Luckily, Marcos had messaged them her address when he'd left so they'd know where to go to check up on her. "Let's go with the flow. See how she reacts to both of us showing up at her place first."

Kane nodded.

"You will have to talk to Marcos."

Kane gripped the wheel and sighed. "Marcos is going to be hard. He's been very clear about keeping his sister away from our type of life. I don't know what it is about it that he doesn't agree with, but we'll need for him to know we are serious about Daniella."

Blake thought back to the conversations they'd had with Marcos and remembered that one of the things his friend had always been adamant about was that his sister was not a toy. That she deserved to be loved in a serious relationship. Marcos always discussed his anger over the men Dani dated and how they treated her. He also knew that shifters were highly sexual and therefore were fine with multiple partners. It was clear that he wanted to make sure his friends wouldn't use her for sex. If only things were so simple. He wondered what to do to ensure that Daniela would understand how special she was to him and Kane.

There was so little he knew about her. He bet Kane knew very little too. Keeping a distance from her all these years didn't seem to have helped lessen the desire for the curvy temptress. Now things were going to be a lot different.

He had no doubt sex with Daniella would be good after having watched her come earlier. Just the idea had his cock hardening in his pants. Fuck. He wanted to slide inside her and feel her pussy rippling against his dick with every contraction from her orgasm.

Kane cleared his throat and smiled at him. "We really need to work hard at making her comfortable between us."

They had a bond. One nobody could deny. With that bond came the need to unite with a female who would increase their Alpha strength by linking them together as a Triad. It wasn't just sex. It was so much more. A bone-deep connection between the three that would flow the moment they mated with her. They'd be like a single entity. Stronger than anything and at the same time a lot more emotionally bonded than any other couple.

"What will we do if Marcos decides this will be the end of our friendship?" Blake asked. He hated to think about it, but it could happen. Marcos had been a no-nonsense type of man. If he'd been a shifter, he'd definitely be an Alpha. His need to protect Dani had always pushed Blake and Kane away from her.

"I really don't want to think about that," Kane grumbled. "We've been so close for so long it would be completely devastating to see our friendship destroyed. But I'm not giving up Daniella. She is our missing piece. I want her. And I won't settle for anyone else."

Kane had never been a pushy Alpha. He led by quiet example and, unless things turned violent, he let his people do as they wished. Always ready to embrace ideas, he'd been the perfect partner through the years. He'd been open to Blake's suggestions in the past. For him to say those words, it was clear that his wolf was ready to mate. Blake's wolf agreed. They both wanted Daniella. To mate. To take. To keep.

SIX

DANIELLA FLOORED THE gas pedal while growling at her inability to stop thinking about what the men had done to her in the garden. Jesus Christ! How could they have been so good at touching and kissing her? Never mind the licking, the sucking and oh goddess of wet panties, the biting.

She swore every pleasure point in her body had been rediscovered. Every caress and kiss had brought her to new heights of ecstasy. And they hadn't even moved to the good parts. Thinking about it made her squirm in her seat.

Stupid hot shifters. Blake and Kane had moved to a whole new level of evil by turning her on the way they had, only to push her away with their words. Why did they have to have this whole friendship pact, anyway? All it meant was that now she'd have a very lonely night with a vibrator. From what she'd experienced with Blake and Kane, her battery operated boyfriend would never be as good as one or both of those guys.

When she got to her house, she threw the corset on a sofa and rushed to her bedroom to remove the annoying costume.

She strolled past a full-length mirror and stopped to stare at herself. Holy shit. She looked like she'd been rolling around with two men. Her hair was a long, tangled mess. Her lips were still swollen and she had red blotches on her neck from where Blake had rubbed his five o'clock shadow on her. A shiver raced down her spine at the memory.

She took off the skirt and kicked the heels to the side. They hit her dresser and bounced on the carpet. Her hands hovered over the garter and thigh highs, ready to remove them when her doorbell rang.

Slipping on a short robe, she went to open the door while wondering if it was her neighbor coming to find out how the party had gone. She'd mentioned to Dani she'd stop by if she returned early enough to chat about the masquerade.

After a peek through her window, she almost ran back to her bedroom. Her heart pounded hard in her chest. They were out there. Both of them. What the heck was she supposed to do? The thought of them coming to her home hadn't crossed her mind once since she'd left. Her begging them to finish what they'd started certainly had, but that was another story. She should probably not stand there like an idiot and decide what to do very fast.

"Dani," Blake said from the other side of her door. "We know you're standing behind the door. Let us in."

Ah, hell! These guys were going to be the death of her. At the very least, the reason she'd have to go to therapy soon.

She squeaked and jumped away from the door. "Go away," she ordered. "You were very clear with what you said earlier. I'm not into games. What I'd wanted from you two isn't going to happen."

There was a moment of silence before Kane replied. "We are not here to play games, beautiful. We want to talk to you."

Shit. He'd gone and called her beautiful. Not that she hadn't been called that before, but never by them. It somehow felt special to hear it from Kane. She bit her lip and shifted from foot to foot wondering what to do. Finally, after much debate, she opened the door. Struggling to keep her nerves under control, she moved away, allowing both men to enter her home.

First, Kane walked in. His big sexy body took up most of her living room. Then Blake entered. Their gazes roamed over her body in a swift and heated caress. Her nerves jumped like there was a trampoline competition going on in her stomach. She swore that the room size diminished by at least half.

She stared from one to the other watching as Blake shut her door, closing them both inside with her. She prayed her legs kept her upright because all of a sudden her muscles felt weak.

"What do you want?" she asked again, her stomach flipping and flopping like she'd just been on the world's craziest roller coaster.

Kane moved forward at the same time Blake came around her side. She tried to keep calm as both men's intense gazes closed in on her, but her heartbeat accelerated quickly.

"We came to make sure that you arrived home okay," Kane said, his voice a mere growl. "We were worried about you." He took another step toward her. "To be honest, we just couldn't let you go."

She retreated until her back hit the wall. "Well too bad. I don't want you anymore."

They looked at each other, then turned and grinned at her.

"You lie, Little One," Blake said, grasping her hand and kissing the tips of her fingers. "Let us show you how good we can be together."

She had to wake up. This had to be a dream. There was no way they'd said what they had and now wanted to get her naked. And they appeared really ready to get her naked quickly.

"I—"

"Shh," Kane groaned, looming over her and cupping her neck with his giant hand. "Don't fight it, Dani." He gripped the neck of her robe with his other hand and pulled her to him.

She gasped as her body came flush to his. God, he was hard all over. And big, so very big and warm. The heat from their bodies enveloped her to the point that she got goose bumps all over. Once she'd taken two steps toward Kane, Blake pressed at her body from behind. Talk about being between a rock and hard place.

"You're so beautiful," Blake murmured, pushing her hair over her shoulder and brushing his lips over the curve of her neck. "I want to see you naked."

Oxygen froze in her lungs. She tried to make sense of what was going on but it was hard. The fact that they were both touching her at the same time seemed to have short-circuited her thinking abilities.

Kane tugged on the tie at her waist, opening her robe, and stared down at her body. Only the nylons and garter remained on her but those bits of material did nothing to hide her body.

"You are gorgeous," he breathed as if he'd run a marathon, his voice rough and rusty. He lowered his head and brushed his lips over hers. The kiss was soft, sweet, and delicate. None of the things Kane had ever shown to be. It was like seeing a new side to him. The big shifter could be more than what met the eye.

Blake pulled on the robe until it swooshed down to the floor, pooling at her feet. He slid his hand down her spine slowly, lighting fires along the way, until he reached her ass and squeezed at her bare cheeks.

"This is what I like," Blake groaned. "This is what we need. Your body is lush. Sexy," he mumbled, kissing up to the back of her ear.

She could do nothing but push her ass back into his erection. At the same time, Kane moved forward, rubbing his arousal over her belly. She'd never been so turned on in her life.

Blake moved a hand around her waist, cupping her mound and sliding his fingers between her slick lips. "Christ," he groaned. "You're fucking wet. I can't wait to lick your pussy."

She loved how he said it. So raw. So sexy. Like he was ready to fall to his knees for a taste of her.

Kane continued to kiss her slowly. He pulled his lips away from hers and pinned her with his heated stare. "Tell us you want this." He cupped her breasts and squeezed. Her nipples ached and pleasure shot down to her clit in an electrifying charge. "Tell us you need us as much as we need you."

She nodded, unable to say anything else. The words died in her throat along with her ability to speak.

This was it. Years of fantasizing had come to a reality she still couldn't believe. This was what she'd always wanted.

She moaned at Blake's slight strokes on her clit. He thrust at her ass, letting her feel how hard he was. The two men she had almost daily fantasies about for years wanted her body. Her big boobs, big ass, and big thighs. Thank God!

She had always been honest with herself. She knew she was a big girl. She had curves and rolls and she was more than okay with that. To her co-workers' dismay, she actually liked her body. She felt at ease with her shape. A lot of people didn't understand how much she loved herself and her figure. She'd learned that while others lived in a world of desperate need to change themselves or those around them, she happened to want to stay as she was. Curvy, big or whatever they wanted to call her, she was Dani no matter her shape or size. Anyone who loved her would love her how she came.

"God, beautiful," Kane groaned. "I can't wait to slide deep inside you."

Kane brought his lips down to her chest, pulling a nipple into the wet suction of his mouth. She moaned, arching her back to press the aching bud deeper into his face. Fucking hell that felt good.

He twirled his tongue around her nipple at the same time he tweaked at her other one with his thumb and forefinger.

"Oh, God, yes!"

Blake pressed at the center of her need. Her clit throbbed as if ready to burst into flames. "That's it. Rub your ass on my cock. Soon, you'll be rubbing it on my face."

She jumped as bone-deep shudders racked her core. "Please," she moaned. "I— God."

She kept herself upright by some miracle force of nature. Digging her nails into Kane's gigantic shoulders, she'd been able to use him to cling to.

Kane released her nipple after a final bite which sent moisture dripping down her thighs. He led her to a reclining chair and motioned for her to sit. She did.

"Spread your legs for me," Blake said, showing her his sinful grin.

"Let me see how wet you are," Kane stood in front of her. "Show us."

She leaned back on the chair, her back rubbing against the leather and warming it with her body heat. Then she splayed her legs open, placing them over the armrests and giving them a front row view of her wetness.

"Fuck her pussy with your tongue," Kane told Blake. "I want to see her lips wrapped around my cock."

How in the hell had she gotten into this? Oh, who cared? This was Blake and Kane. Both of them licking their lips and gazing at her as if she was a feast and they were starving. It was surreal and amazing at the same time.

Blake dropped to his knees in front of her seat, immediately lowering his head between her legs. He curled his arms around her large thighs and kissed his way to her pussy. Once again, she could have been self-conscious over being a big girl in a non-flattering position. But it was hard to care about that when all she could think about was reaching the highest orgasmic peak. Right now. There was no place for insecurity, not that she had any. She knew she might not be what society considered sexy, but screw it, she definitely felt sexy.

She turned to face Kane. He'd stripped out of his clothes while she'd watched Blake ratchet up the tension in her body. Kane naked was a work of art. Big, with large muscles and no body fat, he had a body any woman would worship day or night. She swept her gaze down his beautiful torso to his erection. He was hard and wet. Beads of moisture dripped from the head of his cock which he used to jerk himself and lubricate his length.

Her gaze ran back up to his face.

"Suck my dick," Kane ordered, his voice pure churned gravel. "I want to feel you sucking me off."

She licked her lips, lifted her hand to push his away and wrapped it around his cock. "Come closer. I want you sliding down my throat."

He groaned and pushed closer, his cock level with her lips. Need shook her to the core. She'd never wanted something as badly as these two men taking her. Owning her. She opened her lips wide, sliding his smooth length into her, furiously flicking her tongue side to side the further he went.

"Ah, Daniella. That mouth of yours is magic," Kane groaned.

She loved how he said it. So low and sexy with a hint of desperation. Almost like he couldn't get enough and would stoop to begging soon. He slid his fingers into her hair, pulling the long strands away from her face.

She slowly pumped his shaft and bobbed back and forth, leaving a wet trail of saliva coating him.

Her mind switched gears from his moans of encouragement to focus on Blake's tongue swiping up and down her pussy. He took a long lick and then drove his finger into her, rumbling against her clit.

She couldn't hold it. Her body gave and the tension insider her unraveled at light speed. She pulled Kane out of her mouth and groaned as she continued to jerk him with her hand. Her pussy grasped at Blake's fingers, but a second later he was gone. They changed positions on her.

Kane pulled her ass up off the seat and drove into her in one swift drive.

"Oh, Dear God!"

He groaned. "Fucking hell, that feels amazing."

Blake came around, lowering his head to suck on her tits. Kane fucked her hard, raw, without stopping. His grunts and groans made her wetter and hotter than anything else. Then there was Blake, licking and biting on her nipples. Her sanity flew out the window with how good it felt to have Kane inside her. He plunged into her in quick hard drives. Each one deeper, harder than the last.

Her mind muddled and her breaths turned into short rasps. She clawed at the chair, trying to reach for the cliff her body pushed her toward.

"Fuck, Little Red. You're wet and tight. So slick and hot," Kane snarled. "Watching my dick come out drenched in your wetness is so goddamned sexy."

Blake bit down on one nipple then moved to the other. He slid a hand down between her legs, to tap at her exposed clit.

"Ah, yes," Kane muttered. "Squeeze my dick, baby."

"Kane. God, Kane. Fuck me harder. Please...just a little longer," she moaned.

"Anything you want, beautiful," he said, plunging into her, leaving her breathless.

Her pelvic muscles contracted. Blake tapped her clit again, biting her nipple harder and she flew. Her back arched, her pussy clasped around Kane's cock and she screamed. Blake pulled back, jerked himself over her breasts, and spurted his cum over her chest. Kane thrust deep, his dick pulsing inside her, filling her with his seed.

"You look so sexy, with his cum on your chest and mine seeping out of your pussy," Kane said.

"Let's take you to bed and continue this there." Blake grinned.

She was still catching her breath. All she could do was nod and hope they helped her there. Her legs weren't working yet. None of her muscles were.

Blake lifted her into his arms and grinned. "Come on, curvy goddess. It's my turn to fuck you next."

SEVEN

THE NEXT MORNING she woke up alone in her bed with no one in her home. She wasn't sure if she should be worried that they'd gone without saying a word or if she should be hurt. Neither man had made an effort to stay for the morning after. Wow. She couldn't believe that Blake and Kane would do that. It wasn't like them. Not after all the things they had done the night before and then they left without a word. It was pretty disappointing.

She got out of bed with a heavy sigh. Her muscles ached. A reminder of the sex filled night they'd had.

Not that she was upset over the pain. She loved every single sore muscle. A slow smile crept over her lips. The guys really knew what they were doing when it came to making a woman feel like the center of attention and special. Too bad it had only been one night. But now it was time to go back to reality and back to her day job.

A nice, long, warm shower helped her rethink her love life. Tom wanted something deeper with her but she'd pushed him away because she only saw him as a friend. Ideally, her record-breaking night of sex with Blake and Kane would have been a wonderful way to start a new relationship. She knew that neither man wanted to test the waters and possibly put their friendship with Marcos on the line. So she brushed it off as a one-night stand.

It was sad that she would probably lose her only chance with both men because of their unbending will to break any of the friendship rules with her brother.

After checking on her brother's dogs, and maneuvering it so that the biggest one didn't pin her to the floor and lick her for a good five minutes, she headed in to work.

WHEN SHE ARRIVED at the library her co-workers had gathered around her desk, watching her with interest.

"What's going on?" she asked.

"Nothing," her boss replied, her voice holding a hint of anger. "Seems like you have an admirer."

She walked into her office. There sat a gigantic mixed flower arrangement in a crystal vase so large it took up her entire desk. The flowers had been chosen in her favorite colors of pink and purple.

She dashed forward to grab the card on the bouquet hoping against hope. Realistically, she expected that they were from the only man that ever sent her flowers, which was her brother.

Her fingers shook as she tore open the envelope to glance at the tiny card inside.

This is only the beginning. The note said.

It was signed from Kane and Blake

Her heart did a quick flip and butterflies took flight in her chest. A new wave of excitement flooded her system.

They hadn't forgotten her. More than that, it sounded like they didn't want things to end with just one night. From the note, she was sure that they were ready for more. Maybe they were not so worried about the friendship with Marcos getting in the way.

"Who's it from?" her nosy boss asked, her voice pure acid.

She cleared her throat, shoved the card in her pocket and smiled. "My brother."

Privacy was important to her. She cherished her personal life and didn't need anyone poking around trying to figure out what she did during her free time or who she was dating. As it was, Tom had shown up a few times to offer to take her to lunch and they were already under the impression that he was her boyfriend. Denying it only made her look like she had something to hide, so she didn't.

Her boss and co-workers had enough to say about her weight without her telling them that she might be seeing two men at the same time. All hell would break loose. It was difficult to work with judgmental people. Not that she cared about their opinions in the least. But she had to work with them and it could make her job, something she loved to do, very difficult.

Everyone moved away from her desk as if nothing had happened. She knew that things were going to be different even if it was only for a little while. Now it was only a matter of time to see how they could make things work in relationship of three. At least until her two wolves found their third.

Her phone rang and a glance at the screen showed her brother's face.

"Hi, Marcos. How are you?"

"I'm great. How are the pups?" he asked, his voice coming in and out as if going through a massive static storm. Reception was bad so she knew that he was likely out of range and calling the moment he'd gotten a couple of bars.

"They're good." She sighed. "I checked on them this morning and I went over there yesterday afternoon like I told you I would." He loved to question everything. He'd been gone for all of a handful of days and she knew he was thinking she hadn't been minding the dogs.

"You could have stayed over at my place if you'd wanted to." His words sounded like an accusation. Yep. He really thought she didn't know how to care for his pups. Something she did every single year.

"No, I'm okay." She ground her teeth until her jaw ached. "I prefer to stay in my own place and your puppies like to run around a lot." Puppies. Hah. More like evil dogs from hell. She'd been tackled to the ground yet again. Usually, she had better luck keeping them at bay. This time, they'd made it their mission to get her on the ground and keep her there like a chew toy.

"They have a doggie door, you know?" he said in that you-don't-know-what-you're-doing tone of voice that made her want to scream. "They come and go as they please. All you have to do is feed them and make sure that they're okay." There was a short pause and then he added, "If it's too much for you I can ask someone else to do it."

"Marcos, shut up! I know what I have to do. You don't have to remind me. You act like I'm a little kid," she snapped.

"What's your problem? I never said you were a little kid. I just wanted to make sure that you can handle the dogs."

Right. The dogs. He's so worried about the dogs but he was the reason Blake and Kane had never gotten more than ten feet near her. She narrowed her eyes and glared at her computer screen, her anger rising by the second. "You know you can be a real jerk. It's a wonder why I care so much about you."

"Maybe because we only have each other," he said, as if that explained everything in the world. "Have you seen Blake and Kane? I asked them to keep an eye on you while I was gone."

Oh she'd seen them all right. She'd seen a whole lot more than what he probably expected her to. It was funny how for so many years she'd wanted so badly to be between both men and now that she had been, she wanted nothing more than to be there again. Every single minute of the day felt like a hardship, thinking of them being so far away, but having to work cataloguing books.

"Yes, they came by."

There was a heartbeat of silence before Marcos spoke. The static got louder on the line. "They just came by?"

What the heck was she supposed to say? *They came by and did amazing things to my body that no man has ever done before.* "Yes, they came by and checked on me. Then they left. What do you want to hear? I didn't invite them to stay the night if that's what you're worried about."

Marcos swore. "I hope you were nice to them. They're only doing what I asked."

She choked back a snort, took off her glasses and started cleaning them of dust. She highly doubted any of what they had done had been her brother's request. "I was very nice. You can ask them yourself."

She didn't think for a second that they would admit to Marcos what had happened the night before between the three. A night like that was best left to be relived in the most sacred places for fond memories of the past.

"They should be coming by again often to check on you."

Hallelujah! That is exactly what she wanted to happen. Maybe not in the same way her brother did, but as long as Blake and Kane came back over again and again to show her how much they wanted her, in every way possible, she couldn't care less how long it lasted.

"Look, don't worry. I'm pretty sure that everything will be fine. Besides, I've known them all my life too, you know."

"All right, all right. If you have any problems or questions about anything, whether it's with the dogs or any issues at the house, just let them know and they'll take care of it for you until I get home. I've got to go, but hopefully in the next few days I'll be able to find reception again and I'll give you another call."

And if life cared even a little bit about her, he would not find reception. She wanted to go get her freak on with two furry guys again without his knowledge.

"Have fun, Marcos," she said, cheerfully. "Forget about me and the dogs." Please, Lord let him forget her. "We'll still be here when you come home."

She hung up the call feeling like she was in a better position now. Ready to engage in a sexual relationship with them. Was that wrong? Should she feel maybe a little bad about doing her brother's friends? Nah. You only live once and all that crap.

The phone buzzed again with a new text message.

I'm hoping that you had a good time at the party last night. When you have a moment, please give me a call or come by and see me. There are some things I need to discuss with you. I'm not sure if you're aware but the men I set you up with need a person to complete their Alpha Triad. I need to give you information for your future.

How sweet. Gerri actually thought that Danielle had a chance at becoming Blake and Kane's mate.

She sent a short reply back telling Gerri she was aware and knew exactly what needed to happen. In fact she was more than aware. It would be hard to let go of the men but she would do it because it was what was right for them.

Her boss and co-workers decided to go out for lunch to celebrate one of their birthdays. Daniella was too wrapped up in her previous night and decided to stay behind. Her body still hummed with electric charges from her time at the mercy of Kane and Blake. Besides, lunchtime at the library meant absolute quiet and she could think more about their next encounter. Okay, she could fantasize.

There were two single older gentlemen in the library. Her usual newspaper readers, sitting at the front, by the entrance. She fixed her glasses over the bridge of her nose and combed a hand through her hair. She'd just left it loose and could only have it that way while her bitchy boss was gone. Her phone buzzed again.

It was Blake. She almost hyperventilated when she saw his name pop up on her screen. She'd logged his and Kane's numbers in from the message Marcos had emailed her in his desperate need to ensure she had backup for his pups. Crap. What if they'd changed their mind and decided they were skipping any time with her and going to find their mate? Screw it, she'd blackmail them if she had to. They were not going to give her fantasies and leave her wanting more. No way in hell. She opened the text message and grinned when she read it.

You're the sexiest librarian ever. Are you wearing a skirt?

She pushed her glasses above her head and glanced around the massive library in hopes of seeing him. She giggled quietly, feeling completely naughty reading his text.

I sure am.

She was so bad. It took a moment before another message came through.

Lift your skirt up. Her eyes stayed stuck on the screen and the second part popped up. *Nobody can see under your desk. I want you to touch yourself.*

Was he there? She did another sweep of the room with her gaze but there was no one out of the ordinary that she could see.

Should she do it?

Well…It wasn't like there were any cameras. Plus, there was that whole you only live once deal she'd decided on. Of course, getting kicked out of the library for indecent exposure wasn't her idea of fun. There were still people coming and going. Her heart pounded double-time in her chest. Her co-workers could catch her at any moment.

The thrill of doing something she wasn't supposed to had her giddy with excitement.

She lifted her short blue skirt up to her hips, bunching it there. Then she slowly stroked over her panties and bit back a moan. Oh, that felt good. So bad and good at the same time. Her nipples ached. She wanted so badly to reach up and squeeze her tits.

Her phone buzzed with a new message.

Push the panties to the side and feel yourself. Slide your fingers over your pussy lips and rub a little circle over your clit. Show me you like it.

Oh, mother of all things naughty she was in trouble. Her body heated instantly. There wasn't much she could do but follow his instructions.

Was it a bad idea? Absolutely, but this was a fantasy. One of the many she wanted to make real.

She did what he asked her to. Stroking her pussy, feeling the wetness from her center drip to drench her panties. Her nipples rubbed against the normally soft cotton of her bra. Right at that moment it felt rough and painful. A new sensation to heighten her desire. Nerves and need turned her muscles tense.

Blake sent another text. She bit her lip, swallowing back the whimpers riding her throat.

I love the look on your face when you're touching yourself. Are you thinking of us? Wishing it was one of us touching you?

Lord, yes! She lifted a trembling hand from gripping her desk and replied a simple yes. Her other hand was busy between her legs.

Another buzz from Blake.

Tap at your clit for me. I bet it'll feel so good.

She read the message and slapped two fingers on her clit under her desk. She jerked in her seat, still holding on to her desk with her other hand. The light tap set her body on fire. A soft gasp escaped her throat.

At that point, all she could do was stare, ensuring no one watched.

Another message.

Keep doing that beautiful. Your face is flushed and you look gorgeous. I can't wait to fuck your pussy. I bet you're so wet. Wet and ready to be fucked hard, aren't you?

One of the old men stood to go and she stopped, the air pumping hard in and out of her lungs. What the hell was she doing? This was the kind of stuff that would get someone fired.

She didn't care. She couldn't care. Her mind was too far gone. All she could think about was that Blake was in the library watching her. And that thought alone drove her crazy. It pushed her to do something she'd never done before, like what she was doing at that moment.

She sucked in harsh breaths, trying to stop herself from moaning and groaning as she dipped two digits into her pussy and it squeezed around them. She wasn't wet. She was soaked.

A new message came through.

One more person gone. Don't worry beautiful very soon.

Very soon what? If she didn't come soon, she might scream. She stopped touching herself when she noticed the second older man stand. Holy crap! He was coming her way. She tried to appear composed as the man neared her desk.

"I'm going to the bakery, miss. Would you like me to get you something?" he asked. He was a regular, always coming to read the paper.

Shaking her head slightly, she smiled. "Thank you, but no. I'm fine."

"All right. I'll be back in a little while." He grinned, his face wrinkling as he did. He tipped his hat and turned around, heading for the door.

She wasn't a hundred percent sure there was no one else around. People sometimes sat down between the aisles to read books or browse a particular section. She didn't get a chance to think about that too long before a new message came in from Blake.

Wild animal section. Now.

EIGHT

SHE WASN'T SURE what was there. Hot shudders shot down her spine. Her palms tingled with sweat and exhilaration.

She jumped to her feet and made her way to the back of the library where the section devoted to books on wild animals and their habitats had been created. It was several corridors away from the main section but had been popular from the very beginning.

When she neared the last corner her heart pounded hard in her ears to the tune of a thousand drums. What she'd find there, she didn't know. One thing was for sure, she needed to keep the game going. Blake and Kane had uncovered something new, something different inside her. They'd given her hope that there were men who could want a woman just as she was with the body she had. That they could go crazy for her and that there was no need for her to change and turn into a different woman altogether.

At her final turn a hand shot out and grabbed her. She squeaked for a second or two. Then his lips crashed over hers, and at the same time, he pushed her against the wall, pressing his hard body over hers.

She moaned. Her need to have him inside her renewed and burned with an intensity she hadn't ever felt before. His hands were all over, pulling her skirt up, taking her panties aside, and dipping into her wet heat. He groaned.

He spread his fingers between her pussy lips, rubbing up and down her cleft and then fucking her so slowly she almost passed out from lack of oxygen. He swept his tongue into her mouth, gliding it over hers in bold, sensual strokes. She didn't know what to do other than grip his hair and wiggle her hips on his hand. Dear God, if this was a dream she did not want to wake up.

Blake fingered her pussy like a fucking pro, sliding deep into her. He went in and pulled out repeatedly, until she was squirming. She clung to him, clawing at his shirt and gasping for breath.

She needed him inside her or she'd die. Her body worked on auto pilot. She released her material-tearing hold of his shirt and moved her hands down to his jeans, unzipping and immediately stroking him. With one hand back up on his shoulder, she held on. Then she pulled his hard cock out.

He groaned deeper, the sound animalistic and fucking sexy as hell. She curled a leg around his waist, rubbing herself on him like a cat in heat. Their lips never parted as he slid into her in a single, quick, harsh thrust.

All she could think of was how amazingly perfect he felt. When he withdrew and pushed back in, her whole world turned upside down. Colors and thoughts jumbled in her mind. There wasn't a way to keep anything straight. All she could do was breathe and hold on. Her back slammed hard against the concrete wall. Luckily for her, this wall was by the door and there were no book files near it. Or they'd have been in deep shit with how hard her back was hitting that wall. He thrust in and out of her quickly, repeatedly and with an aggression that made even more moisture drip from her slit.

He grunted, his lips still stuck on hers. He delved his tongue into her mouth, rubbing it on hers. Her body fevered to a boil. Her skin felt tight and her nipples swelled to hard, aching little points. What she'd give for him to bite them while he fucked her.

She tore her lips away from his, gasping for air, looking for a way to make her lungs work just a little harder. The pleasure mounted inside her into a ball of tension she knew would soon explode.

He thrust in and she bit back a moan. Another drive and she scored her nails on his neck, leaving long, red lines on his pale skin. She met his gaze. The gold in his eyes only increased her pleasure.

"You're so fucking hot," he whispered, his voice a growl. "I've never fucked in a library, but with a sexy librarian like you, I couldn't help myself."

He grabbed her legs lifting her completely off the floor, urging her to curl them around his waist. He held her up by her cheeks and squeezed her large ass.

"Please..." she breathed on a soft moan, trying to keep herself from saying anything in case anyone heard them.

"Fuck, baby. You're so slick and hot." He pounded her even harder.

"Oh!"

"That's it, little librarian. Take my cock," he bit through gritted teeth. "Take all of it. God, your hot little pussy feels fucking perfect sucking and squeezing my dick."

Oh, Dear God. She was going to die before she came. It wasn't fair. "Blake," she mumbled. "Please!"

"Please what, beautiful?" he asked, his lips twisting into a flirty grin. "Please keep fucking you here? Where anyone can catch us? Or please make your hot little cunt milk my cock of my cum?"

She let out a breathy groan. "Please help me come. I can't take this much longer."

"I can. Your pussy feels so good. So wet. So fucking perfect I can't wait for you to come around my dick."

He squeezed her ass cheeks, tilting her hips so that he could reach even deeper.

"Come little librarian." He lowered his head to brush his lips over hers. "Wet my dick with your pussy. You know you want to come."

He placed kisses over the curve of her neck and jaw, grazing his lips over her like a gentle caress.

"Come," he whispered in her ear. "Let go."

Her body listened to his words as if he were some sort of magician. Just as he'd told her to, she felt the tension start to unravel inside her.

She gasped, rubbing her cheek on his much scruffier one and groaned. So close. She was so close and still too far.

Then he did something he hadn't done.

He plunged into her at an angle. Her body broke. The tension inside her shattered into a million pieces. She fought for air, clutching and gripping at his hair. He kissed her hard, drinking in the scream that left her lips without her consent.

And then he tensed. His thrusts slowed until he held stiff inside her while he came, filling her with his seed. There wasn't time for her to catch her bearings. She was still trying to get her legs to function when he put her back down on her feet.

"Baby, someone's coming. You need to go back to your desk." He held her steady, giving her legs a chance to work while he fixed both of their clothing.

For a second, he rained kisses over her face. She leaned into him, holding him in a hug and not wanting the moment to end. He caressed his hands up her back to her front to cup her breasts and rub his thumbs over her nipples. Even covered, she moaned from how sensitive they were to the touch.

"And you are supposed to be the innocent librarian with glasses and dresses." He chuckled and pressed a kiss to her forehead. "God, you're so fucking hot. Definitely not innocent."

She swallowed hard and licked her lips, testing her feet and taking a step away from him. "I've never said I was an innocent anything."

He shook his head and helped her back to her desk. She'd just sat down when her boss and co-workers decided to make their entrance. So she jumped back to her feet to stand next to him.

He made a final grab for her ass before walking away while thanking her for her help. He didn't say anything else to anyone and instead chose that moment to glance at her a final time, wink and leave.

Her boss stared behind him and then turned back to her, an ugly frown covering her features. "Let's have a meeting on the upcoming book drive and then you can take your lunch hour, Daniella."

Christ. She wouldn't be able to change out of the soaked panties yet. If she didn't know any better, she'd swear she'd dreamt up what he'd just done to her. Much to her discomfort, she had the evidence between her legs to show that Blake was the dirty Omega. She couldn't wait to do it all over again with him, Kane or possibly both.

The rest of her day went by in a blur. It was hard for her to get any work done after that. It was a good thing that nobody seemed to notice her lack of concentration. Those that did probably thought that she was thinking about Aurelis and her baked goods. Kane and Blake had officially taken over as being much better than anything baked.

That night, she got a message on her cell phone from Kane asking to see her the following day. He said he wanted to spend some time with her and he hoped she was open to dinner and a movie at his place.

There was no hesitation to her response. How could she say anything but yes when what she needed was to spend time with him? She wondered if this would last long enough for her to get both men out of her system. She didn't think so.

With every moment that she spent with them and every thought that filled her mind about them, she fell just a little bit more into an abyss of emotions for both. It would take a lot more than hot sex to get them past the hurdle of their Alpha Triad third. For now, she could dream, because one day she would have to say good-bye. And when that day came they would have to go and look for the real woman who could complete their Triad.

She was about to go to bed when she got a phone call from Tom.

"How are you?" he asked, his voice a lot more chipper than she felt at the moment.

"I'm fine," she said indecisively. She had never wanted to hurt Tom's feelings. He needed to know once again that there was no future for them other than friendship. His last voice message to her had worried her and she knew she'd have to repeat the same words to him.

"I would have called you earlier but I was at a teacher conference out of town and it was difficult," he apologized.

"Tom, don't worry about it. It's not a big deal." She sighed, staring at the ceiling in her bedroom. She'd commissioned someone to paint stars to help her relax and fall asleep. She wasn't anywhere near relaxed.

"Have you given any thought to my proposal?" he asked with enthusiasm. Shit. He really didn't get the picture even though she'd declined before.

Her stomach twisted in knots. She hated this part.

"I'm sorry, Tom. I told you already I can only be your friend. There's too much going on in my life right now and I don't see us going any further than friendship," she said gently, hoping not to hurt his feelings.

There was a quiet moment and then he replied, "You should think about it. We get along so well and I know that in time you would come to care for me."

"I already care for you. But you have to understand that I don't love you. I need to love whoever I marry. It would not be fair for me or you for us to get engaged when I don't have those feelings." She blinked up at the fake stars, wishing they could help her get through this conversation. "I've told you time and again, I love you as a friend. You are a really nice man and a wonderful teacher." She swallowed hard, fidgeting with one of her frizzy curls. She hadn't bothered straightening her hair that morning and now the curls had grown a life of their own. "But the chemistry needed for us to have the relationship I want in my future is not there." She bit her lip and winced. "I really hope that you find the right woman for you because you are an amazing man."

"Dani, I know that in time things could change." He sounded so hopeful it pained her to disagree with him. If she felt even a little bit of the sexual attraction she had for Kane and Blake, she would have considered it a long time ago. She didn't. What she felt was friendship and a little bit of pity for Tom.

"Things won't change. I'm really sorry, Tom. I am here as your friend for however long you want me, but anything else is out of the question."

She felt like an absolute jerk turning away such a wonderful guy. But she refused to accept less than what she wanted. And she wanted chemistry. She wanted love. She wanted much more than being with a man because they were good friends. Tom was a nice guy. However, she was done with settling for anything. He did not make her crazy with lust like Blake and Kane did.

"Maybe if we went out a couple of times," he insisted.

"No," she refused emphatically. "Going out on any kind of date is not going to make me change my mind. We are not compatible in that sense. And while I know you don't understand you've got to accept my words."

"I just don't think you're giving this a chance. We are so good together."

Good together? What in the world was he talking about? She sighed, rubbing a hand over her temple.

"Tom we are not good. We are friends. From a distance at that. You've never even hugged me. How could you know that a relationship that involves sex would be any good for us?"

"Sex is overrated," he said quickly.

Overrated her ass. Not the kind of sex Kane and Blake had given her. This was starting to piss her off. "Look, Tom, sex might be overrated for you but I want someone to rock my world. I want a man to want me. I want to be licked all over. And I really, *really* want to scream his name at the heat of my passion. Do you understand?"

Silence reigned over the line.

"If you can't give me that, there's nothing else for us to talk about."

Tom sighed loudly through the phone line. "I thought you were different."

"I don't know what you expected from me. I'm just a woman. A woman with needs and wants."

Right then her wants and needs were much more important than accepting a friendship-based marriage that would be dull and in which she would end up sexually frustrated and buying sex toys by the bulk.

"I'm sorry I bothered you with my proposal." He sounded upset now. There was a high pitch and quiver to his voice. If she didn't know better she'd swear he was crying.

"Tom, don't do this. You're my friend and I care about you. I would never want to hurt you, but you need to understand you and I would never work out."

Her words fell on deaf ears.

"Goodnight, Daniella."

"Goodnight, Tom."

With a heavy heart she set her phone down. She hadn't meant to upset Tom or to be mean to him. But she just could not lie to herself or him. For so many years, she'd lived in bursts of relationships. Where she'd give in to other's suggestions and end up unhappy.

Then she'd find herself with a man who wanted her to change who she was to fit what he wanted. And that was just not going to happen anymore. She needed a man who wanted her as she was. With her quirks. With her purple hair and with her love for books. She needed a man that would want her body like no other woman existed in the world. But more than that, she wanted to feel cherished and loved because of who she was.

NINE

THE FOLLOWING MORNING Kane came by her office looking absolutely delicious. With his scruffy hair and days old beard she wanted to do nothing but whimper at the sight of him. Her boss rushed out of her office when he came to the desk.

"Can I help you?" Marla asked with a flirtatious smile.

"I'm here for Daniella." He smiled.

The moment the words came out of his mouth, her boss turned around with wide eyes and stared at her, the look she gave her was a combination of confusion and disbelief.

"Marla, Kane is a family friend," she said, trying to pacify her boss and at the same time keep the privacy of their relationship to herself.

Marla's brows rose with interest. She made it seem like Daniella couldn't have someone like Kane as a friend. After a heartbeat, Marla excused herself and turned around, flipping her long red hair over her shoulder. She headed back to the office. Probably to tell the others all about the unusual visit Dani had at the front.

"Hi." She smiled at Kane. She went around the front desk and stopped next to him. Her first instinct was to throw herself in his arms and give him a kiss on his sexy smirk, but she held back. It took every ounce of willpower, but she did it.

"Hello, little librarian," he said, in that deep voice that made her toes curl in her comfortable walking shoes. "You're a contradiction."

She frowned, wondering why he'd said that. "I don't think I am."

He turned away from the prying eyes at their back and took a few steps to the library entrance. He offered her a hand, but she knew if she took it, there would be hell to pay later with the amount of questioning she'd be subjected to. She shook her head and started walking. She really needed a better job, but she loved the library. She loved books. Hell, she even loved the old people that came and sat there day in and day out to read the newspaper for free.

"Why would you say that?" she asked.

"Because you are. You wear your beautiful long hair with purple streaks. Your outfits can be daring on some days but not on other days. You're a little angel with long skirts, comfortable shoes and glasses to hide your eyes behind. It never ceases to amaze me how many sides you have."

She wasn't sure if he was complimenting or insulting her so she asked. "Is that supposed to be a compliment?"

"Yes, it's a compliment. I know that you are never going to be boring because there's that wild sexy side of you. But there's also the quiet super intelligent librarian that can be so fucking hot," he said, his eyes going liquid gold.

Thank God he whispered the words or she might have died on the spot. For him to say her being a librarian was fucking hot was not something she heard every day. Okay, not something she heard ever.

"Kane, you are out of your mind. How is being a librarian sexy?"

He grinned, bringing his head down to just inches away from her, his eyes bright with the wild animal inside him. "Well, you being a librarian is sexy. Maybe not anyone else. Nobody does it the way you do. With your soft brown eyes looking deep into my soul. Those sexy lips asking me for a kiss. Not to mention those delectable curves hidden under all those clothes. You and I both know that you have a body made for loving and I want to taste you all over, sweep my tongue over your body like a blanket. Then I want to lick right between your legs. I want to see your wet pink folds. I want to see your body shake. I want to hear your moans and groans."

She blinked, her pussy aching from how turned on she was. "Kane...stop."

"I want to hear you beg for more. I want to make you scream my name. Grip my hair. Then I want to fuck you until there are no words that can come out of your mouth. Until all you can do is hold on to the bed while I pound deep into you." He lowered to bring his head even closer to her ear. "Then I want to come in your hot little pussy."

She stood there, unable to say a word. All she could do was listen intently as he went on and on about the things he wanted to do to her. Holy fuck! Was it wrong that she wanted him then and there? She really hoped not because the reality was that her mind was focused on the two men driving her crazy.

The front door opened and a group of kids brushed past them, breaking the spell. She'd almost melted to the floor and might have needed CPR if they hadn't been interrupted.

"Will you come to dinner tonight at my place?" he asked, lifting her hand to his lips and brushing a light kiss on her wrist.

Like there was any doubt. She should say no if she knew what was good for her. But she wouldn't. It was hard to resist wanting them even though she knew she shouldn't. She wanted Blake and Kane more than her next breath. All those years of waiting were nothing compared to being with them. "I'll come but I need you to understand that I know very well where I stand."

His brows curved downward. "What do you mean?"

"What I mean is that you and Blake need a third and you need one soon. I know this can't last. I am not a shifter and there's no guarantee that I ever will be. So yes I will take what time I can with you guys tonight but that doesn't change what you must do to keep your pack. I could not live with myself if you guys lost your people because of me."

He shook his head. "We will never lose our people. They are faithful to us. I'm sure you are just confused. We can choose whoever we want for a mate and you need to understand that."

"What I know is you need someone strong and a shifter is the best."

He coughed and rubbed a hand over the back of his neck. "Will you come, yes or no?"

"Yes. I said I would. But don't think for a second that I will forget this conversation. We both know where we stand."

He took a step toward her. She held her breath hoping that he wouldn't do what she could see in his eyes he wanted to do. He wanted to kiss her right then and there and as much as she wanted him to, it would only give her co-workers a way to get into her personal life.

He stopped before he touched her, curling his hands into fists and bringing them to his side. "You'll learn soon that you are not just some woman, you are more. You are special and we want to cherish you. Let us."

Christ, the way he said those words she wanted to get down on her knees and thank the Lord, but instead she just nodded. "I'll see you tonight thank you for the invite."

"Don't thank me yet. Wait until it's over. You might regret those words."

KANE LET HIS frustrations loose on a piece of wood. How could he convince the only woman that he and his wolf wanted to take a chance on them? He'd told Blake what she'd said. They had been hopeful that with time she would change her mind. It was clear that he needed to take drastic measures.

He put another piece of wood on the trunk, his mind drifting back a few nights to when they'd been at her home. She had been so sexy. Willing to allow both men to do as they pleased with her. It would have been so natural for the three of them to be together. And though they had shared women previously this was the first time they'd shared a future mate.

A gust of wind blew his hair over his face. The breeze cooled some of the frustration riding him.

How could he do it? How could he convince her that she was the right one for them?

His chest ached at the thought that she might not want to be with them for the long run. He no longer cared that she could or could not shift, that she might not take the change. All he wanted was more time. Time with Daniella.

In his years as Alpha, he learned that he had to work really hard to get what he wanted and not allow anyone to get in his way. But what was he to do if the one getting in his way was the one he wanted?

His mother had always told him one of his qualities as a leader was being able to think about obstacles and figure out strategic moves to get what he wanted. Whether it was with his pack or life in general, he knew everything was about strategy.

So what if she did not shift? He no longer cared about that. It had taken spending time with her, without knowing it was her, for them to realize she was who they had been missing. The woman they had been missing. His pack members were not stupid. They wouldn't question him unless they felt her being in the Triad would somehow mess with the pack.

Besides, he'd fight every single one of them for her. It was obvious to him and the animal within there was just her.

He needed to figure out how to make her see it.

His phone buzzed.

Marcos. He could pick up the phone and lie to his friend but he refused to do that. So he rejected the call until he was ready to admit to his friend how much he and Blake wanted Dani. Until he was ready to tell him how bleak the future seemed without her. It would take Marcos time to understand that they weren't trying to use Dani for sex. That they truly wanted a long lasting relationship with her.

He thought back to her beautiful brown eyes and long dark hair. Just the thought of touching her, watching her smile and say something silly, made him grin. She was so cute when she was confused. Back when she'd been a teen, they'd stayed away from her. Ignoring the pull of their animals to her had been hard, but friendship had been more important.

Now all he could think about was taking her. Mating her. Keeping her and cherishing every moment with her. No. Marcos wouldn't understand that at all.

He swung the axe again, the new piece of wood splitting in half and falling to either side of the tree trunk he'd been working on. He stood up straight, rubbing the back of his hand over his forehead and wiping his brow. He needed a shower. The pile of wood would be great to keep Dani warm once winter came. Fall was fast approaching and he intended to make sure her every comfort was taken care of.

"Are you working yourself to death?" his mother asked at his back.

He slammed the axe down, locking it in the center of the trunk and turned to face her. This was going to be hard. She'd been right all along.

"Hello, Mom. What brings you over?" He already knew, though. Her cat that ate the canary smile told him all he needed to know.

"So how was your date?"

Fucking incredible. "It was good."

Her grin widened. "That's all? Care to tell me anything about your woman?"

He shook his head, moving past her to head to the laundry room next to the kitchen. "What do you want to know?"

"What's she like?"

"I'm sure your friend Mrs. Wilder has given you a heads up already."

She laughed. "She only confirmed what I knew."

"And that was?"

"That you were too blind to see what was in front of your face. That all these years, ignoring Daniella had been the stupidest thing you and Blake have ever done."

He slipped out of his dirty jeans and sweaty T-shirt. "It's not stupid. We value our friendship with Marcos. We've been staying away from her at his request."

He entered the kitchen and caught her rolling her eyes.

"So what changed now? It's not like you've done anything different? Why did you finally decide to say to hell with what Marcos told you both and take matters into your own hands when it comes to Dani?"

They wanted her. Plain and simple. "It's not that we don't care about Marcos's request any longer, but now we're more concerned with her wants. She wants us."

She nodded and threw a long strand of blonde hair behind her ear. "How do you propose to keep her and the friendship?"

That was harder than accepting Dani wanting them. They might lose their friend. She was human. They might lose their pack. And getting Dani to understand she was the one meant to fulfill the role of Alpha Triad mate was going to be an even bigger challenge since she kept ignoring them whenever it was brought up.

"I don't know. I hope he can understand."

She sighed and tapped his sweaty arm. "I'm sorry, son. I know your friendship with Marcos means the world to you."

They'd been friends since they were teens. Marcos had always been overly protective of Daniella. She was a bigger girl and some of the kids had made fun which in turn had made Marcos do anything to shield her from the bullies. But even his overprotectiveness hadn't stopped Dani from developing into a smart-mouthed sexy curvy temptress.

Through the years, he'd learned to shut his wolf up when it wanted to get near Dani. Marcos had always had his back. Just like Blake. When his father and his Omega had passed in a plane crash, Marcos was the first person to offer support. He had stood up next to him, offering to take on anyone who wanted to fight for the Alpha position. Fortunately, at the time, it hadn't been necessary. But he'd learned that Marcos would never allow anyone to be with his sister if he thought she was being used. So he'd need to speak to Blake about being honest with their friend. He wanted Marcos's blessing.

Daniella had been a forbidden fruit for far too long. Now, all he could think about was touching her. Watching her push her sexy little glasses up the bridge of her nose and pout in surprise when she was caught off guard.

He'd stood outside the library for a while, watching her read something on her computer screen. She'd smiled, frowned and cocked her head as if that would help her understand whatever was confusing her. But it was the fact that she'd been so unaware of her sex appeal that he loved.

He'd watched her the night of the ball. She'd walked in with that sexy itty bitty costume and floored him. He hadn't known that it was her, but his first instinct was to take her. And when he'd realized he couldn't scent her, he still knew that she was special to him. That they shouldn't waste any time and take her as their own.

"What are you going to do about Dani?" his mother asked, breaking into his thoughts.

"We're going to do whatever we can to keep her. She's coming over tonight so we can spend some time together."

She nodded. "It's a good thing you can cook or I'd worry about you. You are such a good man, Kane. I know you are bossy, but you have that in your genes, from your father, of course."

She always told him that whenever she felt he needed a pep talk. Right now, he didn't. What he needed was a way to get Dani naked later. And then he wanted her agreement to join in their Alpha Triad.

"I need her to willingly agree to be with us."

"Damn. That's going to be tougher than sex, son."

He filled a cup with cold water and frowned. "Why? Why is that harder than sex? You'd think it would be the opposite."

She shook her head with a small smile. "Not at all. Women fantasize all the time about two hot men wanting them. You and Blake are probably a dream come true. But reality? That's scary. A relationship with two men? Most women don't think that can work. Especially human females. We know the score. Other shifters know what's needed to make a Triad work. Sex is fun. It's easy. All you need is chemistry and you're good. A relationship takes work. Effort. Commitment."

"I'm committed to making sure this works with Dani."

"That's because you already know deep down she's the one for you. In the human world, a person doesn't know that quickly. They don't have an animal giving them guidance and an extra sensory perception. All they have is their gut instinct. She'd have to follow her gut. Make sure that all your promises to her are things she wants as well."

"Thanks, mom." He bent down and kissed her cheek.

She smiled and sighed. "I wish there was more I could do to help you, but I know this is all about you and Blake. Make it special, Kane. Make her feel like she's the only one for you because that's exactly how it is."

He nodded. It was time to make Dani realize how special she was.

That evening, he went with his gut and decided to surprise her with something out of the ordinary. He'd done a lot of work lighting up the trees that led to a cool cliff overlooking the valley. There, he'd set up a picnic and even went as far as laying out cushions and blankets for their time together. He wanted to make sure she understood this was for her. That it was all about making her feel special.

TEN

DANI SHIVERED IN her pretty red flats. The black and red polka-dot dress had been a bargain find and she loved wearing it because it made her feel pretty and feminine. She'd even curled her hair for Kane. Not just curled with a hot iron, but spent hours straightening the frizzy hair and then curling it to make big bouncy curls. If he knew the times she'd burned herself with that thing, he'd think she was nuts for sure.

She left her car near his cabin and made it to the front door without tripping over her own two feet. Whenever she was nervous, she tended to get really clumsy. Marcos loved making fun of that but she would just smack him upside the head and call him a jerk.

She knocked softly, knowing he'd probably heard her arrive with his super shifter hearing anyway.

Not a minute later, Kane opened the door and she forgot how to breathe. He'd dressed up. For her. It was like something out of a movie. He'd put on a nice perfectly pressed black dress shirt and slacks. Gone were his well-worn and sometimes torn jeans that hugged his ass better than should be legal. His usual T-shirts were gone and the dress shirt sleeves were rolled up showing impressive forearms.

"Hi," she said, almost swallowing her tongue.

He smiled, pulled her into his arms and pressed his lips over hers in a scorching kiss. Then he pulled back, his smile full of heat. "You look beautiful."

Well, okay then. She wished she could bottle both him and Blake and keep them forever. How were they still single when both men wanted a mate more than anything in the world?

"Thanks."

He grabbed her hand, enveloping it with his much bigger, warmer one. "Come on, I have a surprise for you."

She didn't get a chance to look around the inside of his house. He tugged her through a giant living room, with only the bare necessities, and then through a giant kitchen, fit to feed an army, to the back door.

When they got to the yard, he lifted her hand to his lips and grinned. "Are you ready?"

She was worried about asking for what, so she nodded instead. He flipped a switch near the door and a row of trees lit up with white lanterns.

She gasped, turning to face him and smiled. "Wow. This is impressive."

He laughed and hugged her to his side. "There's more."

More than pretty lights? She really wasn't sure why he had gone to the trouble. Not that she'd complain, but all this romance made it hard to keep her feelings from trying to make something out of a dinner date.

With every step they took, she became more and more enthralled in the amount of work he'd put in to decorating these trees. It was a good few hundred yards before they reached the cliff overlooking the valley.

There, he'd set up various lanterns, a giant blanket with their meal and another one with cushions to sit or lay on.

"Oh, my God!" she shrieked, rushing over to look at the beautiful view from the ground. She could see the valley, and the moon and stars from that spot. Not to mention there was a giant tree right next to the blankets which he'd hung more lanterns from. The entire thing looked like something out of a fairy tale.

"Do you like it?" he asked, his wicked smile filled with pride. He knew she loved it.

"What do you think?" She ran back and threw her arms around him, pulling his head down for a kiss. "This is really an amazing way to start a date, Kane."

He kissed her long and hard, twisting his tongue over hers and lighting a new fire at her core. Her body throbbed with need. There was no urgency to his kiss. It was like he was only teasing her into seeing how good he was.

After making her so turned on she was ready to rip out of her clothes and ask him to take her then and there, he pulled away and shook his head. "Not yet, Little Red."

She groaned and pouted. "Are you still going to keep calling me that? It's not like you don't know who I am now."

He lifted a hand to caress her cheek, moving slowly to cup her neck, and then grabbing a fistful of hair to pull her head back.

She gulped, loving this unexpected aggression in him.

"You're my Little Red," he breathed, his lips hovering just above hers. "I keep visualizing you in that tiny outfit." His gaze locked on her lips before sweeping over her face. "I keep remembering your legs spread open with your wet pussy on display."

She whimpered. She remembered it too. Better than he knew. "Kane that was—"

"You. The you that you try to hide. You're a sensual woman, Daniella. I loved having my tongue inside you. I loved having my cock inside you. But more than that, I loved seeing that side of you."

"Why?"

"It's who you really are. Don't hide behind your glasses," he said, pulling away the glasses and shoving them in his shirt pocket. "Don't hide the beauty we both know lies beneath your clothes."

No man had ever spoken of her body in that way. No man had ever made her feel as if she was absolutely perfect as she was. Kane and Blake did that. It was why she was having a hard time keeping her feelings at bay. They were catering to the insecure woman inside her. The one who hated to hear men tell her she needed to drop the pounds or cover her body because she had too many curves.

"Come," he said, pulling her down on the blanket with all the cushions. He opened containers of salad, grilled chicken, fruit, cheese, cookies and cakes. He filled her plate with food and handed it over with a napkin and a fork.

She stared at the food in awe. "Did you cook this?"

He nodded, reaching for a bottle of wine and two crystal wine glasses. "Yes."

That was it. Just yes. No boasting about how hard he'd worked making a meal for her or even telling her she was lucky he'd cooked at all instead of getting takeout or having her eating burgers. Kane was a man that treated her better than any other had that had already gotten into her pants yet.

"You did a great job. I had no idea you knew how to cook." She ate slowly, enjoying the selection of items on her plate.

He shrugged and handed her a glass of wine before sipping his own. "My mom was home cooking many hours of the day when I was young, and I told her I wanted to help her do it."

She raised her brows. "With your father being an Alpha, didn't that cause problems?"

He shook his head and licked his lips. She forgot all about the food on her plate. "My dad was an Alpha, but he was also part of the Alpha Triad with his Omega and my mom. His Omega helped center him, and kept him from making decisions that would hurt my mother or our family. Not to mention our pack."

She thought about what he said for a moment. "Is that how it will be with you, Blake and your mate?"

The smile dropped from his lips. "Yes. Our mate will have both sides of our personalities. Once mated, a link forms between the three of us. It's why not just any woman will do."

She blinked. Wow. That sounded harder than finding true love. People found that all the time. Then they divorced it a few years later. "How do you know if you've found the right woman?" She stopped eating, put the plate to the side and took a sip of her wine.

He leaned forward, his open collar pressed against his chest and showed off a hint of the muscles hidden beneath. That body. He was going to drive her crazy soon from wanting to see him with the shirt off.

"We'll know we've found the right woman..." he said, curling his hands around her waist and setting her on his lap like she weighed no more than a feather. "When both of us and our animals feel a connection to her."

She wiggled on his lap, feeling the hardness of his erection pressing against her ass and turning her throat dry even as she drank wine. "You mean to tell me both of you and your inner beasts have to want the woman?"

"Not just want her." He pushed the hair blowing across her face over her shoulder. "We have to feel some kind of deep meaningful connection. More than sexual chemistry."

She met his gaze, losing herself in the pool of gold in his eyes. "I don't understand."

"It's a feeling. Like you've finally come home."

She sighed. Her heartbeat tripped in her chest.

He leaned in to her. "The thing is, Little Red. I'm already home."

Oxygen punched in and out of her lungs. Desire thickened her blood to the consistency of molasses. Lord, how could she survive the rest of this meal without doing something stupid like asking him to eat her instead? She didn't get a chance to ponder that question too much. Once their lips met, everything else flew out of her mind.

He kissed her softly. Tentatively. Almost as if giving her a chance to back away. She put the wine glass down, not caring if the thing spilled over. She grabbed the collar of his shirt and turned over to straddle him, placing her legs on either side of him and rocking over his cock. Her pussy ached with need and desperation.

She rubbed her palms over his chest. He was hard. She wanted so badly to touch the warm flesh hidden by the soft material. She tugged at the buttons, jerking until the shirt flew open. The moment her fingers touched his skin, she knew what he'd meant about feeling like being home. Both he and Kane had given her that feeling of perfect connection. Not just with the way they touched her body and made her go up in flames, but from the looks, the touches and the words that somehow hit a deep cord inside her.

He splayed his hands on her thighs, pushing her dress up and over her head causing them to break their kiss for it to come off. She allowed him to remove it, not even a little worried over him seeing her naked any longer. He kissed his way down her chest, tugging away the bra straps and freeing her breasts.

Then, just when she thought it couldn't get any better, he sucked a nipple into his mouth and she saw stars. She moaned, arched her back and pushed her chest forward. He cupped her ass with his other hand, squeezing, and then tearing at her panties. There wasn't time to think too hard. His mouth moved from nipple to nipple. Licking. Sucking. Biting. Her world had narrowed down to feeling.

She gripped his hair in her hands, sliding her fingers through his soft locks and then digging her nails into his skull. Her body moved over his involuntarily. She couldn't stop rocking over his pants, wanting him inside.

Each pull and tug he did on her nipples with his teeth sent fresh charges of heat down to her clit. Pulling away from him was hard, but she wanted him inside her. She crawled back, until she was able to help him pull down his pants and take off his shirt. Once he was naked, then she was happy. She pushed him to lay flat on the blanket with a cushion under his head.

"Come here," he said, his order low and rough.

She grinned, shaking her head. "No way. I get to touch you now."

He raised a brow, his eyes bright with his animal. "Touch me then, Little Red. I want your hands and lips all over me."

He didn't have to tell her twice. She moved up to his face, hovering above him and kissed his jaw. He had a few days old beard that tickled her lips. She found the damn beard so sexy. Just like his animal side. It reminded her how wild Kane was. How he had two sides that were opposites but could still make her insane with desire for him.

She licked her way down to his nipples and bit down on one of his tiny buds.

"Fuck, Dani!" He jerked under her, lifting his hips to rub his erection on her wet sheath.

He moved his hands up to her hair, holding the strands away from her face.

Flicking her tongue in circles over his skin, she tortured him a little longer. "Like that?" she asked, wanting to hear his thoughts.

"Baby, I fucking love it. Your mouth is pure magic. I've told you that before."

He had. The night of the masquerade. He'd told her that when she'd sucked his dick.

She continued licking her way down to his navel. His abs contracted under her kisses. She bit down on his belly button and heard him suck in a breath before going lower.

Finally, she reached his hard length. She wasted no time and licked from base to crown, enveloping the head of his cock with her lips.

"Ah, Little Red. Suck my dick, baby."

She let her saliva dribble down the sides of his cock and jerked him off as she sucked him deeper into her mouth. His moans and groans were music to her ears. Not to mention the way he gripped her hair, urging her head down to take him further, was sexy as hell. She sucked her cheeks in, ignoring the pinch of pain starting to take hold of her jaw in favor of bobbing her head up and down over him.

"That's it. Take me deeper. God, you have a tight little mouth. Do that thing with your tongue again," he groaned.

She swooshed her tongue from side to side, sweeping it on the underside and then up to the head of his cock. She jerked him in her grasp. He felt harder. Like her touch made him even more aroused.

"Watching you do that is so fucking sexy. My dick sliding into your mouth and coming out wet with your saliva is so hot."

She agreed. Taking him deep into her mouth and pulling back to see his cock coated with her saliva was more of a turn on than she could have imagined.

"Come on, Little Red. Spread your legs and take my cock into your wet pussy," he said, pulling her head away from his shaft. "It's time for me to get inside you. Balls deep."

Frickin' hell the man was a talking sex freak and she loved it. She crawled back over him, placing a leg on either side of him and holding him with one hand while she lowered her body to his. She placed the head of his cock at her entrance and slapped her hands on his chest, using him for leverage.

He held her by the waist and pulled her down, lifting to slide into her in one smooth glide.

She gasped, digging her nails into his chest. Her body shook. Her pussy muscles stretched to accommodate him. The combination of pain and pleasure overwhelmed her senses.

"Ah, baby. I was right. You're still just as tight as the first time."

She didn't know what to say, so she licked her lips and wiggled her hips. He took that as a sign to move and lifted her up and brought her back down in a swift drop. His dick grazed her inner muscles until she was left tingling from the sensations he brought out in her.

"Do you like me fucking you, Daniella?"

She whimpered and rocked her hips in a slow wave over him. The movement kept him deep in her body but he pressed at different areas inside her. New nerve endings flared to life with ardent need.

"Tell me," he ordered, lifting his hands to her chest and pinching her nipples.

"God, yes!" The pain and pleasure drove her to near madness.

He squeezed her breasts, pulling at her aching points repeatedly. Her muscles felt tight and sore. Her pussy felt on fire.

She continued rocking on him faster and faster. When she felt the tightening inside, she grabbed one of his hands and brought it down between her legs. She met his gaze and moaned, "Play with my clit. Make me come."

He rubbed his thumb over her hard little pleasure center. She shut her eyes, unable to fight the pull to let herself go. Her body moved on auto pilot.

"Come, Little Red. Let go," he murmured.

She pinched her own nipples, adding more pressure to the one building inside. "Oh, my..."

He pressed her clit harder. She rocked faster. Faster. And then it all stopped.

"Fuck, baby! Your pussy is squeezing tight!"

The tension unraveled so fast she shook as wave after wave of pleasure washed over her. Sights and sounds came alive. Breaths pounded in her ears and her heart tried to thump out of her chest.

She might have screamed, but she didn't know for sure. She felt as if she'd been swimming underwater and everything sounded far away. Kane howled loud, his hands gripping her waist tight. He pressed her down until their pelvises kissed and he was deep inside her, his cock pulsating, filling her with his cum.

It took her long moments to catch her breath and remember where she was and what they were doing. Kane pulled her down to lay on his chest. He was still inside her and she didn't want him out.

"Will you be our mate?"

ELEVEN

HIS QUESTION CAUGHT her off guard. She raised her head, her breaths still coming out ragged and then she frowned. "Why me?"

She lifted off him, not wanting to discuss something so important with so little clothing on. He must have seen the indecision on her face because he didn't try to stop her. Instead, he passed her the dress she'd had on earlier and started putting his pants back on. Once they were both clothed, he pulled her back down to sit next to him, both facing the view of the valley below. He refilled her wine glass and handed it to her.

Her nerves were all over the place. As much as she loved the idea of being theirs, the reality of her being a human and them needing a shifter wasn't lost on her.

"You're the one," he said softly. "The only one for us."

She took a sip of her wine and stared down at the tiny bright lights below. She loved living in the area. The town was small and everyone knew everyone. One of the things she appreciated was how nobody judged the shifters surrounding them. On the contrary. Because of Kane and Blake, there was a team of his men that kept watch over the town to ensure crime stayed low. Shifters in their valley were adored like chocolate in a room full of PMSing women. Still, she knew that the power Kane and Blake wielded meant both men needed someone like them, a strong shifter.

"You need a shifter. I heard Marcos say it once."

He took a deep breath and let it out slowly. "Normally, we've had shifters to create the Alpha Triad. But there have been other packs who've incorporated human females and they are strong, if not stronger, than having a shifter female."

She bit her bottom lip and gave him a side-glance. His facial features were tense and she knew he was worried about what she thought. She didn't know how she knew, but she did.

"What about your friendship with Marcos?" She held her breath and waited to hear his next words. Her brother had been the reason Kane and Blake had kept her at a distance for years. How would they react when Marcos was back in town?

"He'll need to understand. We want to make you happy."

She glanced down at her wine glass. "I need more, Kane. More time with you both. This is not an easy decision that I can make lightly. We'll be forever linked and I know how shifter mating works. There's no divorce. So whatever happens, I'll need to learn to deal with it." She lifted her gaze and glanced at him. "I want to make the best decision not just for me but for all of us."

He nodded, not pushing the issue. "You're right. We'll spend more time together. We'll do other things and hopefully that will show you that we're serious about mating with you."

Christ. Mating with her! It was like the world had gone upside down. Everyone always said be careful what you asked for. She'd asked for both men for so long and now that they were ready, willing and able, she was not sure it was the right thing to do. Not for lack of sexual chemistry, but for fear that she wasn't the right one for them.

THE NEXT FEW days, she saw them individually again. Blake took her to a movie and Kane took her for a hike. Sadly for Kane, he discovered during their hike that she hadn't gone hiking in years and was in serious bad shape. They ended up having to stop every few minutes for her to rest. Whoever invited hiking in hills and mountain trails needed to be shot in the balls!

The three were on a group date a week later when they discussed the topic of the pack and their acceptance.

"What happens if your pack doesn't like that I'm human?" She sat on the bed, between both men.

Kane placed a kiss on her shoulder while Blake drew circles on her palm with his finger.

"They have to accept you. Kane is Alpha. Nobody goes up against him. They know I have his back," Blake said.

That didn't really answer the question. "Could others get angry? Fight?"

She hated the idea of bringing them problems. Marcos had always spoken of the respect the pack had for both men. The last thing she wanted was to bring tension into their lives.

"There's always a possibility that someone will want to fight when there is a change. Shifters, especially wolves, tend to like to be leaders. Only the strongest can do it. Kane is a formidable Alpha. He's stronger than anyone in the pack."

"That's physically," Kane said. "With Blake by my side I'm even more. If we add you, the three of us would be unbeatable. Not to mention we'd have an even deeper link between me and Blake. You'd center us. Give us the ability to lead with a human and soul-reaching connection."

She leaned back against the pillows, her mind a whirlwind of emotions. Spending time with them had reinforced the feelings she'd developed long ago. This wasn't just lust. There was a big amount of that, but once you took that away, she was left wanting to spend time with both men anyway. She wanted to do simple things like have them watch their stupid sports while she read romance novels in bed. It was still amazing to her that they didn't fight over time with her or over who got to do what with her. They were so connected that they encouraged the other to do whatever made him happy. The result ended up being that they divided their time evenly with her.

If one came over to the library to meet her for lunch, the other one would spend time with her at dinner. Maybe the three would share meals or her bed, but it was never about spending more time with one over the other. She'd been confused at first, thinking it was just not possible for it to work, but it had. It had and now she didn't want it to stop. Now she wanted it to continue just like this. For them to be with her and make love to her and make her feel like she was the most precious person in their lives.

Marcos would return from his trip in a few days. How would his opinion impact the friendship of almost twenty years with the shifters? And more importantly, how would he react to knowing his sister had mated the two? That is, if she accepted their proposal.

She leaned into Kane, loving that he immediately pulled her into a hug.

"What's wrong?" he asked. "I can tell something's bothering you."

She glanced up at him with a sad smile. "I love Marcos. He's always been there for me. I don't want to hurt his feelings."

Blake sighed and lifted her hand to his lips, kissing her softly at the center of her palm. "We know. We don't want to damage our friendship with him either."

"What do we do?" she asked.

She didn't get a response. Her cell phone rang. A glance at the screen and she cringed. It was Tom. Again. She'd tried to politely decline his continued invitations, stating she was now seeing someone new. Other times, she'd plain ignored his calls. He was never rude or mean, just pushy. And that pushiness was starting to get on her last nerve.

She sent the call to voicemail and hoped he would stop calling. The past few weeks, he'd acted like none of the times she'd rejected his proposals had ever happened. He'd continued to invite her for dinners and outings. At first she thought he meant to continue their friendship, which she was more than happy to do, but then she'd heard from one of her co-workers that he'd come by on her day off and had told them that she was seeing him. That was an outright lie and she'd called him on it. He'd denied ever saying it, but she didn't trust him anymore. The friendship they'd shared was tainted with his inability to accept her refusal.

"Is everything okay?" Blake asked, his shrewd gaze on her face.

"Yes. Everything's good."

She'd have to tell Tom a little more forcefully that he needed to cut his crap and let it go. She'd gone to some outings with him as a friend but had never promised him anything. The day he'd proposed she'd been so shocked she hadn't known what to say. Who the hell proposed to someone without knowing them? Without kissing them? Hell, without even touching them? Tom did.

She wasn't going to think about him and his need to have a non-existent relationship with her. She needed to decide what to do about Kane and Blake.

"Suppose we mated and I don't change, what happens then?"

The tension-filled silence didn't reassure her much. She glanced at Kane for this one.

He slipped a hand into her hair and caressed her scalp. "Nothing happens. Our link would still form whether you shift or not. The pack would accept you."

For some reason, she didn't think that was all. He was holding back. Probably to keep her from worrying. Too bad since she was already worried about what that meant for them.

"And if they don't?"

"We'll make them accept you."

She frowned, looking deep into his bright golden eyes. "Can you do that?"

His jaw tightened. "I'm Alpha. I can do anything."

She really needed to remember to try and piss him off just to see what makeup sex would be like with him, angry and growly. She bet it'd be amazing.

The time to make a decision was now. They weren't going to wait on her forever and she wanted to get on with living. This hush-hush relationship was starting to stress her. She loved them both. There. It was crazy but true. For someone to be able to love two men was something she'd never thought possible but when they came to you as a team it was hard not to. Blake and Kane were like a single man divided in two. Kane the Alpha protector and Blake the emotional rock. Both created the perfect man and she could have them or she could let them go and allow some other woman to be their mate.

Screw it! She wasn't giving them up for anyone. "I'll do it."

Kane cupped her cheek and forced her chin up. "You want to be our third?"

She smiled at the surprise in his voice. Then she glanced over at Blake who appeared not surprised at all. "Yes. I do. I've come to realize that you only live once and this is how I want to do it. With you both by my side."

Kane pulled her face into his for kiss and then Blake did the same. It all felt so natural. To be kissed by both men.

"Are you sure?" Blake asked, worry filled the depth of his eyes.

"Yes. If Marcos doesn't like it I'll have to kick his ass into changing his mind." She laughed. "How does this work?"

Kane stared deep into her eyes and answered, "We take you at the same time and then I get to give you the mate bite on the back of your shoulder as I am Alpha. Blake will bite you at the same time on your opposite shoulder from the front."

Ouch. That was a lot of biting. "So when do we do this?" She glanced back and forth between the two and shivered at the lust in their gazes.

"Now," Kane declared. "We make you ours now."

Worked for her. More hot sex was something she'd never decline.

She watched them hop off the bed to get rid of their boxers, both sporting an impressive erection. She shrugged out of her panties and tank top, ready to play. "Looks like you boys were holding out on me."

Kane grinned, opening the top drawer of her dresser, pulling out a bottle of lube, and throwing it on the edge of the bed. The men moved to the front of the bed, both standing there, showing her what would soon belong to her.

"We're always hard for you, Little Red. Always for you. And only you," Kane said.

Yeah. She loved hearing those words. More than that, she loved seeing the truth behind his words on their bodies. She crawled to the edge of the bed, hopped off and grabbed Blake by the shoulders, pulling him to her. Their lips meshed in a tongue tangling kiss. He cupped her face, holding her head at an angle to dip deeper into her mouth.

Kane moved in from behind, pushing between her and the bed. He kissed his way down her bare back. She moaned into the kiss. Kane's hands swept down to her butt. He kissed his way to her cheeks, taking small bites of her curvy hips and groaning every few seconds. A sharp smack sounded as his hand made contact with her ass. She jerked from the pain and delightful pleasure of the tap.

"Your ass is fucking gorgeous," Kane groaned, licking down her crack, circling her hole and moving to her pussy. "*Mmmm.*"

She gasped at the multitude of sensations assaulting her. Heat, cold, pleasure, and an instant tightening in her gut.

Blake cupped her breasts, squeezing her tits and pinching her nipples between thumb and forefingers. Moisture fell down her legs from her wet folds. She rocked her hips, pushing back into Kane's face. He drove his tongue into her, thrusting and retreating. Licking and sucking on her sensitive flesh and sending her temperature soaring.

Blake devoured her with his lips. His tongue worked her mouth with the same erotic moves that Kane used on her pussy. Thrust. Retreat. Suck. Lick.

Dear God, she was going to melt into a puddle of nerve endings soon.

Kane spread her cheeks open and licked from clit to ass. Then back again. He lapped at her like a starving man. Desperate for more. He pressed a finger around her hole and she relaxed into his touch. He pushed in, slowly working his finger in and out of her ass. She moaned, gripping his hair with one hand behind her while using the other to keep Blake making love to her mouth.

Blake pulled back. His golden gaze was pure hunger. "I want to fuck you."

She nodded. "I want that too."

He kissed her lips, her jaw and the curve of her neck. "We're going to stuff you with cock."

She swallowed hard, unable to stop the whimper that left her lips. Her belly quaked from the internal shudders racking her body. Kane sucked on her clit and growled. The sound sent waves of vibrations shooting up her body. She felt her legs weaken but Blake was there, holding her up. She loved the look of adoration on his face. The past few weeks had shown her what a sweet pair of men they were. Though complete opposites, they somehow managed to blend perfectly together.

She reached down and grabbed hold of Blake's cock, stroking him and fondling his balls while her body tensed and readied to come.

"Oh, God! Oh, oh, oh!"

Blake licked around her earlobe, thrusting his cock into her hand and helping her jerk him off. "That's it, our curvy goddess. Come for us."

She blinked fast, trying to keep the world in focus but her world turned fuzzy. "Blake..."

"Do it, Dani. Come so we can fuck you every way possible. I want my dick in your pussy. And Kane will fill your ass with his cock."

The words, combined with Kane's sucking on her clit, sent her over the edge. Thunder and lightning exploded inside her. Then came the calm after the storm. A massive tidal wave of pleasure glided over her body like a second skin.

She wasn't coherent enough to notice much but soon Blake was sitting on the bed and she was straddling him. She lowered over Blake, taking his cock into her pussy in a slow sensual slide. She loved the way he stretched her. Her body went hot and cold at the same time. Once she was fully seated with Blake pulsing deep inside her, she leaned forward and kissed him.

Blake spread her ass cheeks while something cool crawled down her crack. It was lube.

Kane worked his fingers into her asshole slowly, scissoring them in and out of her. "Relax, Little Red," he whispered, licking the back of her shoulder. He continued to stretch her until he fit three fingers snugly in there. "Baby, you're so tight. So fucking tight."

Blake continued kissing her and rocking her ever so slowly over him so that he rubbed against her inner walls. She groaned at how good it felt.

Kane pushed the head of his dick into her asshole. She tensed for a second and slowly relaxed, thrusting her butt at the new invasion.

"That's it, beautiful. Relax and take me," he said in a low growl.

Blake leaned back and took her with him, the move lifting her butt higher in the air and allowing Kane a better position to penetrate her. He continued to slowly enter and retreat in tiny little moves, each time going further inside her while her body adjusted to him. After a few more times of the slow, torturous drives, he plunged deep into her ass.

She tore her lips from Blake's and moaned. Both men were big. And having them both in her at the same time was better than anything she could have ever imagined. Her muscles burned from exertion. She clutched at Blake's shoulders and rocked back and forth, at first taking the lead and loving the dual sensation of both men going in and out of her.

"Oh, m-my..." she choked out.

Kane curled an arm around her waist and thrust hard into her. "My turn to fuck you, princess."

Blake took a page from his book and lifted his hips, driving in and out of her in tandem with Kane's movements. When one went in, the other pulled out. She whimpered. Her heartbeats thundered hard in her chest, robbing her of the ability to breathe. Sweat coated their bodies and the slick slide of skin-on-skin was an erotic dance she'd never grow tired of.

Both men pounded her pussy and ass hard. Her muscles locked in tension. Kane licked at the back of her shoulder and Blake did the same to her left front side.

"I'm going to bite you when you come," Kane breathed by her ear. "I'm going to love feeling your ass squeezing me of my cum while I dig my canines into your back and make you mine."

She struggled to catch her breath. Kane slipped his other hand between her slick pussy folds and pressed on her clit. Her nubbin ached with the need to come. "Oh, Kane. Yes, do that."

Her brain faltered. Oxygen froze in her lungs and when he tapped at the throbbing little bundle of nerves, her core cracked. She screamed, the intensity of her orgasm more than she could handle. Kane and Blake struck then. Kane bit the back of her shoulder, embedding his canines into her flesh and driving his cock harshly into her ass. Blake bit down on her front left shoulder and plunged deep into her pussy.

The biting and harder thrusts sent her into a second climax. She trembled in their arms, her body no longer under her control. Her pussy grasped at Blake's driving cock, squeezing hard. Her ass clasped around Kane's dick.

They groaned, their teeth still deep in her flesh and then both men stopped their thrusting to jerk into her, filling her body with their cum.

She was still riding the high from her orgasmic explosion for long minutes later. She tried to regain focus on what was going on when she felt the warm washcloths Kane and Blake used to clean her up. They bundled her in the bed shortly thereafter with a man on either side. She leaned into Kane while pulling Blake closer from behind.

"You're ours now, Dani. Nothing can change that."

TWELVE

DANIELLA GLARED AT Tom. He'd followed her to the front of Marcos's house and had started questioning her like she owed him something.

"What are you doing here, Tom?"

He glanced back and forth between her and Marcos's home. Both Kane and Blake would be there shortly. They were readying to talk to Marcos later.

"Why aren't you answering my calls?" he demanded. Gone was the nice gentle guy she'd come to know. In his place stood an angry man with bloodshot eyes and a disheveled appearance.

"Tom, there's nothing between us." She grit her teeth. "Don't you understand?"

He folded his arms in front of him. A sure sign of defiance. "I asked you to marry me."

"You don't even know me!"

"What's going on here?" Kane asked from behind them. He and Blake focused on Tom, their gazes locked on him like a predator would their prey.

"Tom was leaving." Despite it all, she didn't want to see him hurt. Tom had been a friend.

Tom shook his head. The idiot. "I'm not going anywhere until she tells me why she's hanging out with you two when I proposed to her."

Kane and Blake turned to her, their expressions so shocked had she not been so pissed she would have found it comical.

"You were engaged?" Kane yelled.

She growled under her breath. "No! I was never engaged to Tom. He proposed and I said no!"

"Who's engaged?" Marcos asked, arriving at the worst possible time.

"Daniella. I proposed to her," Tom supplied again, bypassing the fact she'd said she wouldn't marry him.

She bit her lip to keep from screaming. "I'm not engaged to anybody!" she screeched.

Marcos moved in on Tom. "She says she's not engaged."

Two men and two women walked up Marcos's driveway, standing far enough to be seen but not close enough to be spoken to.

"Shit!" Blake growled. "It's the enforcers."

"What are you all doing here?" Marcos asked, glancing around and then down to the people on his driveway. "Anyone want to tell me what's going on?"

"I'll tell you," Tom jumped in. "Your sister refused to marry me. Me. A decent man. Instead, she chose to go rolling around, sleeping with these two."

"What?" Marcos's brows drew down in a scowl. "What's he talking about?"

"She was supposed to marry me!" Tom yelled. "I had it all worked out."

Oh, God. Shit had officially hit the fan.

"Shut the hell up for a moment," Marcos snapped at Tom and turned to face Kane and Blake. "What does he mean she's been sleeping with you two?"

The people down the driveway had crept up and closed the distance, surrounding them in a circle.

She blinked, wondering what the heck those guys wanted. "What are they doing here?"

Blake glared at one of the men, motioning for them to go. "They wanted to see if you are good enough for the pack. They probably want to test you."

"What the hell?" Marcos asked, curling his hands into fists. "Are you sleeping with my sister?"

Kane moved forward. "We asked Daniella to be our mate."

"You what?" Marcos hollered.

Dani winced at the anger in his voice. "Marcos, it's not that big a deal."

"Shut up!" he screamed at her, the panic in his voice rising with each word. "Do you have any clue what you've gotten yourself into?"

"Of course, I do! I'm a grown woman."

He shook his head as if she didn't know what she was talking about. "She can't be your mate." He gave her a worried glance. "Dani, I know you want to find love. You're a wonderful person, but this shifter lifestyle is rough. It's dangerous. It's not for a human."

"I'm sorry you feel that way," Blake said soothingly, trying to pacify Marcos's agitation. "But she's already accepted and we've already taken her as ours."

"You— you what?" Marcos's eyes widened. He swung at Kane, connecting with his jaw. The move was so unexpected that if she'd blinked she would have missed it. The sound of the hit was like a bullet being shot. A flurry of movement took place.

One of the men watching them jumped in, his body shifting into that of his wolf. He went for her brother. Oh, hell no!

She moved on instinct. The frustration Tom had fired up inside her escalated to a fever pitch. She growled and something new and strong moved under her skin. The sound of snarls, bones popping and a weird scream sounded so close to her she felt her stomach tighten. Her vision turned sharper. For a second it was as if life had slowed down while she tried to reach the shifter going for her brother. Her body ached and she swore she was going to fall flat on her face. But then she was moving faster. And things felt different. The air tasted crispier. She shoved at the wolf charging at her brother and she landed on the ground.

The wolf growled, turning his body to face Marcos again. It took her a moment to realize she was down on all fours now. Her instinct to fight the animal was calmed for a second when she glanced up at Marcos, Kane and Blake.

"What the fuck did you to her?" Marcos asked, his eyes wide with fear. "Oh, God, Dani. I'll get you some help."

She couldn't figure out what the heck he was yelling about. Until she glanced down, that is. Furry brown paws had replaced her hands. She snarled. She'd changed. Dear God! She'd been able to take to the shift and had fur on her ass. There was no time to think about it now. Her focus returned to the shifter trying to get closer to Marcos.

"Liam!" Kane growled. "Stand down."

But Liam didn't stand down. He made another move for Marcos and she jumped the wolf. He tried to shake her off, but she dug her claws deep into his side.

Everyone yelled at the same time, but all she focused on was the jerk wanting to hurt her brother. She bit down on his ear, not sure why the taste of his blood didn't disgust her or why she felt so much aggression.

"Stop, Dani. I need you to let Liam go."

She heard Blake say the words clearly inside her head. As if he'd whispered them by her ear.

"No way. He's just going to go for Marcos again."

"He won't. I promise. He's one of our enforcers and he was only trying to protect Kane when Marcos hit him." They continued their telepathic conversation while she bit down on the other wolf. There was a need to fight inside her. To show the other wolf that she was not going to allow him to hurt her family.

"Screw him. Doesn't he know friends fight?" She continued to claw at the bigger wolf's side.

He shook her off, finally getting her off him. She landed on her ass and got back up, ready to run for the animal again. He bared his teeth, waiting for her attack.

"Stand down, Dani. You've proven to them that you're more than able to help us defend our pack."

Defend the pack? What was he talking about? She'd been defending her brother. The wolf lowered his head, slowly creeping away from her.

"There. I've sent him away. Come back to us."

She glanced up to where Marcos stood with a trench coat in hand, the front door thrown open behind him.

"I don't know how to change back."

"It's easy, darling. Just tell the wolf you're in charge and visualize your human body," Kane said out loud.

She did that. Bones popped and fur receded. She glanced at her hands and she was back in her curvy body. A very naked curvy body. Kane helped her put on the trench coat so quickly she didn't get a chance to feel embarrassed over being seen naked by so many people.

She glanced around and noticed the other people had gone, along with the wolf she'd been fighting. Tom lay on the ground, his eyes closed.

"What happened to him?" she asked, clearing her dry throat.

Marcos glared at Tom's body. "He passed out when he saw you change." He walked over to her slowly, his gaze studying her face with concern. "Are you okay?"

She could more than see his fear for her, she scented it. The amount of concern he had for her was dizzying. She smiled and threw her arms around his neck, hoping to soothe some of his anxiety. "I'm great, Marcos."

"You're sure?" His voice trembled with unease.

"Yes." She moved back to stand between her men. "I'm happy."

Marcos glared at both men and then sighed, his shoulders drooping. "If that's the case then I'm happy for you. I just don't want you to get hurt."

Kane spoke up, "We would never allow anyone to hurt her."

"Good. Because if she ever tells me either of you did something to her, I will come hunt you both down."

She grinned. Marcos would never stop being overprotective.

"Fair enough," Blake said. "Are you okay with this, now?"

Marcos eyed Tom. "At least you two don't faint at the sight of someone shifting." He grinned and winked at her. "Keep my sister happy and I'll be okay with you for the foreseeable future."

"Can we go inside now?" she asked. "I'd like to put some clothes on."

"But why?" Blake laughed. "You look so delicious naked."

"Woah!" Marcos yelled, shoving Blake out of the way and heading inside the house. "Not what I want to hear. Ever."

Life as a human or a shifter was never easy. Not when surrounded by Alpha males. She smiled and loved the new connection she felt between her, Blake, and Kane. It was amazing to have such a depth of emotion going through them.

THAT EVENING, THEY made a call together.

"Hello?"

"Hi, Gerri."

"Daniella!" Gerri said with excitement. "How have you enjoyed mated life?"

Boy, news traveled fast. "Great. It's wonderful." She leaned into Blake's side and rested her feet over Kane's. "We just wanted to thank you for your help."

"We?"

"Yes," Blake and Kane said.

"Ahh. The hardheaded wolves. You know, Kane, your mother owes me dinner."

He frowned. "She does?"

She laughed, the tinkling sound clear across the line. "Yes. She bet me I couldn't get the three of you to mate without you both realizing it was Dani."

"Well you did an amazing job of keeping her scent a secret the first day," Blake said.

"I know. And no, I won't tell you how. But I am very happy you three have found happiness. You are happy, aren't you Daniella?"

Dani glanced from one man to the other and grinned. "I'm very happy."

They hung up the call and she casually decided to let her feelings out in the open. "I love you, big sexy, Omega," she said, pulling Blake's face to hers and meshing their lips in a quick kiss. Then she tugged Kane over and kissed him. "I love you, big, sexy Alpha."

"I love you too," they both said at the same time.

She sighed and eyed the remote control Kane had in hand. "So...wanna shut the TV off and get freaky?"

The TV went off before she got a chance to finish the question.

EPILOGUE

GERRI WILDER STARED at her list of accomplished matches. Maybe she could host a party and find out what each one was up to. It would sure be nice to know how Nita and her bear were doing. Or even Alyssa and her tiger. Besides, she'd put out a call for an assistant. That would be a great way to finally get herself organized.

Hopefully the person she hired would be able to fulfill her needs. She had a large number of applications to go through and not enough time to do it.

She rifled through the applications and came upon two that caught her eye. She glanced back and forth between two. A slow grin spread over her lips. Perfect.

THE END

ABOUT THE AUTHOR

New York Times and USA Today Bestselling Author Milly Taiden (AKA April Angel) loves to write sexy stories. How sexy? So sexy they will surely make your ereader sizzle. Usually paranormal or contemporary, her stories are a great quick way to satisfy your craving for fun heroines with curves and sexy alphas with fur.

Milly lives in New York City with her hubby, their boy child and their little dog "Needy Speedy". She's aware she's bossy, is addicted to shoe shopping, chocolate (but who isn't, right?) and Dunkin' Donuts coffee.

She loves to meet new readers!

Like my books? Want to stay on top of all things Milly? Sign up for my newsletter at http://mad.ly/signups/87477/join.

Find out more about Milly Taiden here:

Email: millytaiden@gmail.com
Website: http://www.millytaiden.com
Facebook: http://www.facebook.com/millytaidenpage
Twitter: https://www.twitter.com/millytaiden

If you liked this story, you might also enjoy by Milly Taiden:

Sassy Mates Series
Scent of a Mate *Sassy Mates Book One*
A Mate's Bite *Sassy Mates Book Two*
Unexpectedly Mated *Sassy Mates Book Three*
A Sassy Wedding *Short 3.7*
The Mate Challenge *Sassy Mates Book Four*
Sassy in Diapers *Short 4.3 (coming soon)*

Federal Paranormal Unit
Wolf Protector *Federal Paranormal Unit Book One*
Dangerous Protector *Federal Paranormal Unit Book Two*

Black Meadow Pack
Sharp Change *Black Meadows Pack Book One*
Caged Heat *Black Meadows Pack Book Two*

Paranormal Dating Agency
Twice the Growl *Book One*
Geek Bearing Gifts *Book Two*
The Purrfect Match *Book Three*
Curves 'Em Right *Book Four*
Tall, Dark and Panther *Book Five (coming soon)*

Other Works
Wolf Fever *Alpha Project Book One*
Fate's Wish
Wynter's Captive
Sinfully Naughty Vol. 1
Club Duo Boxed Set
Don't Drink and Hex
Hex Gone Wild
Hex and Kisses
Hex You Up *(coming soon)*
Hex with an Ex *(coming soon)*
Alpha Owned
Bitten by Night
Seduced by Days
Mated by Night
Taken by Night *(coming soon)*

Match Made in Hell *(coming soon)*

If you enjoyed the book, please consider leaving a review, even if it's only a line or two; it would make all the difference and would be very much appreciated.
Thank you!

Made in the USA
Coppell, TX
27 March 2021